John Yates Beall

Memoir of John Yates Beall

His Life, Trial, Correspondence, Diary

John Yates Beall

Memoir of John Yates Beall
His Life, Trial, Correspondence, Diary

ISBN/EAN: 9783337048280

Printed in Europe, USA, Canada, Australia, Japan

Cover: Foto ©Raphael Reischuk / pixelio.de

More available books at **www.hansebooks.com**

MEMOIR

OF

JOHN YATES BEALL:

HIS LIFE; TRIAL; CORRESPONDENCE;

DIARY;

AND PRIVATE MANUSCRIPT FOUND AMONG HIS PAPERS,

INCLUDING HIS OWN ACCOUNT OF

THE RAID ON LAKE ERIE.

MONTREAL:

PRINTED BY JOHN LOVELL, ST. NICHOLAS STREET.

1865.

TO THE PUBLIC.

In a letter written by the subject of this Memoir to the authorities of the Confederate States, he expressed the hope that if they could not protect his life they would at least vindicate his memory. About the same time the author addressed a letter to a mutual friend, in which he stated that if every effort to save his life should fail, he (the author) would place all the facts fairly and fully before the world, so that they might judge impartially between the condemned man, and his executioners. The author has felt himself bound, therefore, by a promise to give to the public such facts of the case as have been withheld from them, and he has, at the same time, availed himself of the opportunity to give to history, as far as lay in his power, the whole career of John Yates Beall during the progress of the late war.

Finding, moreover, among his papers, a Diary kept by himself, embracing a period of two years or more, the author has published it, first, on account of its interest as a running commentary on the events of the war, as they transpired; and secondly, as reflecting his general views, political sentiments, and religious convictions. In regard to this Diary, however, it should be remembered that it was written hurriedly, and apparently almost as rapidly as thought itself, without any revision or correction by its author, and was evidently never intended for any eye but his own. In it he, as it were, holds the mirror up to his own bosom. Hence its style is familiar, even colloquial, and will be recognized by his friends as a much better specimen of his *conversatio* · ′ ι ι literary ability. It will be seen by his letters written in prison, that, when writing for other eyes than his own, his style was distinguished by a simplicity, perspicuity, and nervous concentration rarely excelled.

In regard to this correspondence the author would state that there was one letter written to General Dix of which no copy was furnished Mr. Beall's friends, and another to a member of General Dix's staff, of which no copy could be obtained by him in time for insertion herein. With these exceptions, and except directions in connection with his will, every letter written during his imprisonment of which the author has any definite knowledge, has been inserted.

The reader of this volume, therefore, will have material sufficient to enable him to form a proper estimate of the character, principles, and motives of John Yates Beall. " The protest of right against deeds persists forever,"—in this eternal protest Beall's death may be regarded as a most eloquent, and emphatic appeal to the whole world; its sublimity has excited in the world a profound interest, and they are entitled to all the facts and incidents which can be furnished in regard to him. Impelled by this conviction, the author has kept nothing back which could shed light upon his character—" his virtues not extenuated wherein he was worthy, nor his offences enforced for which he suffered death." Posterity, which will need no other evidence than that of his enemies to believe him to have been, like Sidney, " a man of most extraordinary courage—a steady man even to obstinacy," will be enabled, through the testimony of his friends, to recognize other points of resemblance, in the integrity of his motives, the incorruptibility of his principles, and the injustice and illegality of his condemnation.

July 25th, 1865.

CONTENTS.

———

JOHN YATES BEALL.

CHAPTER I.

His birth—descent from Sir William Howard, or "Belted Will"—Education at the University of Virginia—Participates in the Revolution—A private under Stonewall Jackson—Is wounded under Turner Ashby—Escapes through the Federal lines to Canada.

THE Valley of Virginia, before its invasion by a Federal army, was one of the most beautiful regions on the continent, or perhaps in the world. From the romantic union of the waters of the Potomac and Shenandoah at Harper's Ferry, on the north and east, to Fisher's Gap, the top of the Blue Ridge, on the south and west, the traveller or tourist passes through a stretch of country which, in times of tranquillity, teems with the richest productions of our temperate latitudes. Jefferson, the extreme northern and eastern county of the Valley of the Shenandoah, has been named the "Garden Spot" of Virginia. For magnificence of scenery, fertility of soil, wealth, cultivation, and refinement of its inhabitants, no rural district of the United States excelled it. Harper's Ferry stood in relation to the Valley as the pass of Morgarten to Switzerland, or that of Thermopylæ to Greece,— it was the door or gate, while Jefferson was the threshold, through and over which an entrance was effected from the east.

It was in the heart of this beautiful country that John Yates Beall was born on the first day of January, 1835. *Walnut Grove*, the farm of his father, George Beall, large in extent, fruitful in soil, and most highly improved by cul-

B

tivation, took the premium at one of the State agricultural
fairs of Virginia, as the " model farm " in her limits. This
was not surprising, looking at the character of George Beall,
and the natural advantages of his farm.   Few men excelled
him in energy, industry, and systematic attention to business.
He was the son of Hezekiah Beall, and either his father or
grandfather is set down by Kercheval, in his " History of
the Valley of Virginia," as one of the earliest settlers. The
family is believed to be the same as that of Georgetown,
District of Columbia, after one of whom that town was
named.

Upon the father's side, John Y. Beall was in some way
related to the McGruders, which is the English or American
corruption of McGregor, the patronymic of the celebrated
Rob Roy.   Jean McGregor, the granddaughter of Rob Roy,
married one Alexander McGregor, doubtless a kinsman, who,
upon her death, early in this century, removed to America,
and from whom are descended the McGruders of Maryland
and Virginia.

But if upon the father's side John Y. Beall had in his
veins the blood of the McGregors, upon his mother's he was
descended in the direct line from " Belted Will," whose

> " Bilboa blade, by Marchmen felt,
>   Hung in a broad and studded belt."

Francis Yates, who was the first of his name who settled in
Cumberland, England, was descended from an honorable
family in Shropshire.   He became Rector of Moresby,
near Whitehaven, and Incumbent of St. James's in that
town.   He married Elizabeth, daughter of —— Wilson,
Esq., and niece of Right Rev. Thomas Wilson, Bishop
of Sodor and Man, a prelate of piety and distinction in
the reign of Queen Anne.   They had one son, also Francis,
Rector of Gargreve in Yorkshire, England.   He married
Anne, eldest daughter of William Orfeur, Esq., of Highclove,

by Jane, daughter of Michard Lamplugh of Ribton, and representative of Sir Christopher Lowther of Whitehaven. William Orfeur of Highclove, was descended in the direct line, and but four generations removed from Sir William Howard, called by the Borderers " Belted Will," the hero of the " Lay of the Last Minstrel." Francis Yates, and Anne his wife, had one daughter Jane, who married John Matthews of Wizton Hall, and three sons, the eldest of whom, Charles, became an American merchant, and, amassing a considerable fortune, settled in Virginia; Lowther, the second son, entered the Church, in which profession he attained considerable distinction, being a Doctor of Divinity, Master of St. Catherine's Hall, Cambridge, Vice-Chancellor of that University, a King's Preacher, Canon of Norwich Cathedral, and Rector of ——— in the county of Cork, to which living he was presented by his cousin Grace, Countess of Middlesex.

John Orfeur, the third son, married Mary, daughter of Henry Aglionby* of Nunnery, by Anne, daughter of Sir Christopher Musgrave of Edvilwell. They had two daughters and three sons, the second of whom, John Yates, the grandfather of John Yates Beall, was adopted by his uncle Charles Yates, and at the age of thirteen was sent out to Virginia, and eventually succeeded to the large landed estates of his uncle in this state.

John Yates was a man of strongly marked character, and left his impress on the community in which he resided. He had a strong, clearly-cut English face, which, in early life, must have been very handsome. The tightly compressed

---

* The Aglionbys of Nunnery, in the county of Cumberland, are a very ancient family, being descended from Walter D'Aguillon, (whose name was in process of time corrupted into Aglionby), who came to England with William the Conqueror from Normandy. The following account of them is found in Reference Book of Heraldry: "Aglionby, originally of Aglionby, county of Cumberland, seated there shortly after the Conquest, subsequently of Carlisle and Nunnery, now represented in the female line by Henry Aglionby Aglionby of Newbiggin Hall, M.P. for Cockermouth; and by his cousins, the daughters and co-heirs of the late Major Francis Aglionby of Nunnery. Arg. two bars, and in chief three martlets, Sa.— Crest a demi-eagle, displ. or.

intercourse out of the lecture-room, where he enjoyed that consideration and respect, to which a studious, retiring gentleman was entitled, and which at this institution he ever commanded. Within the narrow circle of his intimate friends he was much beloved, and recognised as a character as generous and fearless as he was modest, reticent, and retiring.

During his last session at the university he took the classes of junior law, and political economy. In both of these he was profoundly interested, and was persuaded by his friends to take such distinctions upon one or both as the college course allows : these were the only diplomas he ever received or stood for.

His father, George Beall, belonged to the " *Virginia School* " of politics—the States-Right-Democratic party ; his grand-father, John Yates, on the other hand, retained all his English conservatism, and was a warm adherent of the Federal or Whig party. It has been stated that, on one occasion, he refused to aid in the election of his son-in-law, George Beall, to the Virginia Legislature on the ground of their difference in political opinions. This was characteristic of the inflexible devotion of John Yates to *principle*. This preference of English conservatism over Anglo-American radicalism, his neighbours called " *prejudice*." He had left England an orphan boy, but thirteen years old ; he had been nurtured in the school of her chivalry, which taught that an insult unresented became a stain ; and, ere he had been in Virginia long, he was forced to the field of honour, where he received a painful but not a dangerous wound. This was before his removal to Jefferson County to reside. To the end of his life, John Yates was an Englishman in spirit ; he was never denationalized upon the one hand, nor naturalized upon the other. It was not strange, therefore, that at an advanced age, his end, as it were, in hailing distance, he should desire to return to the " old country " to die. He did so, and took with him a fair-haired, blue-eyed grandson, and namesake of fifteen or sixteen years—John Yates Beall. Through his last illness, and up to his death at the Nunnery, young Beall watched by the bed-side of his grandfather, and then returned to the United States. His recollections of this visit were always of the most agreeable character, and, up to the time of his capture, he kept up a correspondence with his cousins across the water.

John Beall had thus inherited, and cherished by association, a strong love of order, peace, and stable government; the teaching of his father, on the other hand, indoctrinated him into the Virginia School; and the ardour of his devotion to States rights, as understood by Jefferson, embodied in the famous Kentucky Resolutions of 1799, or taught by Madison and set forth in the still more celebrated Virginia Resolutions of 1798–1799, was not likely to be cooled under the shades of Monticello, and beneath the dome of the University of Virginia. The position of Beall, therefore, during the excitement antecedent to the commencement of actual hostilities between the sections, was both natural and logical. Loving order, he would have remained in the Union; devoted to honour he could not submit to the degradation of assisting in the subjugation of the Cotton States, because, in the exercise of their undoubted right, they had decided to sever the connection between themselves and the other States of the Federal Union; yet to this terrible alternative was Virginia driven by the tyrannical faction, then, for the first time, installed into the administration of the Government, and destined, in the end, to break down every guarantee of the Constitution, violate the most sacred principles of public liberty, and finally, to bring upon the country infinitely greater evils than disunion could ever have entailed. Virginia, who had taught her sisters of the Union that the right of secession not only existed, but was sanctioned by the spirit of the Constitution, and sustained by principles of international law older and more universal than that instrument itself,

could not be expected to unteach these doctrines at the point
of the bayonet, or to aid in any such unholy design ; and
John Beall, nurtured, reared, and educated under the teachings of the Virginia School, saw in the contest in which he
offered up his life, a high and sacred political principle worthy
of the sacrifice.　From beneath the paternal roof to the dome
of the university, and thence into the open sky of his own
native and revered State herself, the " steps of his faith " led
to no other conclusion than this—if wrong, it was Virginia's
error, not his ; it was a heresy which had been sanctioned in
turn by the popular vote of every State in the Union except
Massachussetts ; and, with the knowledge of this fact, the text
of the Declaration of Independence, the language of the Constitution, and the plain principles of international law before
them, the world and posterity must judge between Virginia
and her enemies.

Having finished his collegiate career in June, 1855, John
Beall returned to his father's house in Jefferson. He had chosen
law as a profession, rather in deference to his father's desire,
than in accordance with his own inclination.　He never
obtained a license to practice, nor is it certain that he ever
valued his legal attainments in any other light than (in the
language of Sir William Blackstone) as " the proper accomplishment of every gentleman and scholar—an essential part
of liberal and polite education."

It was about the 15th August, 1855, that, in company
with his oldest sister, he started for Dubuque, Iowa.　His
oldest brother had been for some years a resident of that
State, and was extensively engaged in business there.　This
was the early harvest, the " flush time " of North-Western
land speculation.　The empire of unsold public lands, donated
chiefly by Virginia, to the Federal Government, as a trust-
fund for revenue for its support, to diminish taxation, had
been converted, under the influence of unbridled democracy
and unrestrained demagoguism, into a corruption-fund for

controlling the politics, and securing the balance of power in
the administration of the country.   The pauper of yesterday
borrowed a few dollars, invested in a town-lot, and to-day
awakes, like Abou Hassan in the Arabian Nights, to find
himself a millionaire!   Railroad companies, schools, colleges,
churches, eleemosynary institutions—all have land given them
to *speculate* upon, and all speculate :—paper money, the
child (or parent ?) of speculation, floods the country ; the
path from "the rags to the purple, the hovel to the palace, is
paved with *shinplasters :*"—" *Wild cat*" *banks* spring up ;
Nature is dethroned to the extent that preachers, lawyers,
merchants, corporations, everybody is saying, "*here* there
shall be a town, or there a water-power," where Nature hath
said, "*there*, there shall not."

It was in this financial harvest that John Beall had determined to dip his scythe ; and had started, as above stated, for
Iowa to reside for years at least, if not permanently.   He
and his sister, however, had got no further than New York
city when a dispatch overtook them informing them of the
dangerous illness of their father.   They returned only to see
him die.   George Beall died on the 21st of August, 1855.
The impression made on John's mind by this event was per-
manent, and the effect upon his future career decided.   He
loved his father dearly, and, seven years after, thus feelingly
speaks of his death :

" Yesterday was the anniversary of father's death.   Seven
years have only shown our loss ; they have not blotted out
his memory !   The loss of a father is one of the greatest
that a family is called on to endure.   It seems impossible to
estimate it !   In our family, his strong hand would have
ruled the children, and made all of us more subject—he
would have restrained, and restraint was needed."

The lesson of his father's death was not lost upon young
Beall.   His mind upon religious subjects had oscillated between absolute faith and absolute scepticism.   The author

had sat with him beneath the sound, healthy, but not severely analytical lectures of the best teacher perhaps in America— Dr. McGuffey. Beall, at this period, evidently vacillated between a cynical dislike, almost amounting to contempt, for those plain, strong, mediocre minds who deemed it equal sacrilege to give or demand " a reason for the faith that was in them," on the one hand ; and a horror and dread of those who took refuge in Deism or absolute scepticism, upon the other. Upon the subject of religion he was unhappy ; his father's death resolved the riddle for him. His father was not a church-communicant, but his mother and sister were among the most devoutly pious of Christians. John had watched by the death-bed of both father and grandfather, and there was about each scene undoubtedly something of the moral sublimity of a strictly honest man's death. This lesson it was which aided in sustaining the son and grandson, when in a solitary cell, he revealed both his temptation and his triumph over it:

" I saw father and grandfather die, and they both took great comfort from the thought that no one could say that they had, of malice aforethought, injured them."

At the death of her husband, the family of Mrs. Beall consisted of herself and seven children, four daughters and three sons. The eldest son, Hezekiah, was, as I have stated, residing in or near Dubuque, Iowa. A widowed mother, four fatherless sisters, all younger than himself but one, and a younger brother scarcely in his teens—all appealed to John for protection and guardianship. The plan of his life was changed at the call of duty ; his dream of action and a wide scope for financial acumen and energy, the golden harvest in the West were all at once abandoned, and he took charge of his father's farm, as agent of, and manager for the executrix, &c., his mother. It is to this act of self-sacrifice on his own part that he alludes with satisfaction in his prison diary, published with his trial. " I never left my mother and sisters

voluntarily," &c.   He never left them until his country called
him to the field of battle in her defence.   Yet this sentence,
upon his trial, was used by the Judge Advocate to prove that
John Beall was a *conscript !*   The imperative force of patriotic
duty, stronger than the call of a thousand conscript officers,
could not project itself into the Judge Advocate's mind!
This was to have been expected from a member of a community who, according to one of their own countrymen,* reject
truth itself unless it can be shown to " pay *ten per cent!*"

But the death of George Beall was destined under God to
produce a change upon his son's convictions greater than it
necessitated in his business career ; and more important, in
the proportion that things spiritual and eternal outweigh
things material and temporal.   His religious convictions,
widened and deepened by his grief, wrought out a channel in
his nature, and ever after controlled the current of his life.
He united himself to the Episcopal church in Charlestown,
the county seat of Jefferson, and very soon ranked as a most
active and energetic member in its administration.   He
represented the parish afterwards as a lay-delegate to the
diocesan convention held at Charlottesville, Virginia..... The
beautiful village church which he attended in Charlestown,
the county-seat of Jefferson, formed no exception to the
destruction, spoliation, and desecration which, during the progress of the war, the Federal soldiery universally visited
upon the temples of the Episcopal church.   Being converted
into a barracks, the walls soon became the receptacle of
obscene texts, and pictures, while the platform on which the
pulpit was erected served, with the excavation beneath it, for
a " sink ;" the grave-yard attached, like the more imposing
Presbyterian cemetery not far distant, was used as a common
for the horses and cattle of the garrison.   In order that the
latter may not be suspected of *sectarianism* in their anger
against God, and his " dwelling-houses" (as the common

---

* Wendell Phillips.

law and our ancestry styled churches), it may be stated that they used the *Baptist* chapel, in the same village, for a *stable*.

About the time of John Brown's "Raid" upon Harper's Ferry and the contiguous farms of Jefferson, when that fanatic had been arrested in his career, and was undergoing trial in the Circuit Court of Jefferson, numerous military organizations sprang up in Virginia to resist the further aggression of New England *Conservatism*. Among these was organized a company in Jefferson, under the command of Capt. Lawson Botts (a nephew of Hon. John Minor Botts of Virginia), who subsequently fought under Jackson from the first Manassas to the second and more fearful struggle on the same plains, where he received a mortal wound, having in the meantime risen to the rank of Colonel in command of the 2nd Va. Regt. The "*Botts Greys*," as they were at first called, in the organization of the Volunteer force of Virginia previous to the breaking out of the war, were named Company "G," in the 2nd Va. Regt.; afterwards when these volunteers were turned over to the Confederate States, the 2nd Virginia, with four other regiments, all from the section of Virginia west of the Blue Ridge, composed the 1st Brigade of the army of Northern Virginia; that Brigade which a warrior, not unknown to fame, as he stood in his stirrups with the late glory of Falling Waters and first Manassas on his sword, and the promise of Kernstown, Richmond, Cross-Keys, Port Republic, Cedar Run, Second Manassas, Harper's Ferry, Antietam, Fredericksburg, and Chancellorsville in his eyes—declared to have been the "*first at Harper's Ferry—first at Manassas—first in the Division, and first in the heart of its commander!*" And surely priority in the heart of Jackson was something worthy of inscription on the banner of the immortal Stonewall Brigade!

It was as a private in this corps that John Beall commenced his military career. It was to the enrollment of such privates as John Beall,—each a hero in himself,—each an individual patriot,—each fired with enthusiasm in the cause to whose espousal honour, duty, patriotism, every long-cherished political principle, every home-nurtured instinct, every hope in time or aspiration for eternity, impelled him, —to such enrolments as these the Stonewall Brigade owed its adamantine texture, and its fame solidified for all time.

John Beall's career as a soldier was distinguished only by that unfaltering response to every demand of duty which had hitherto characterized him. He was one of those men who ever strove, and seldom failed to "do his duty in that station of life in which it pleased God to call him ;" and, after all, it must be this definition of an " honest man," which alone can constitute him " the noblest work of God."

The skirmish at Falling Waters was conducted by Jackson only with a detachment ; the eagle turned on his pursuers and struck with a single wing. The 2nd Virginia Regiment was not engaged, nor did it come into action until the 21st July, the ever memorable day on which the first grand battle of the war was fought. The 2nd Virginia was stationed with the Stonewall Brigade on the brow of the hill opposite the " Henry House," in support of the famous Washington Artillery : a detachment of it, under the gallant Lt. Col. Lackland, charged, and claimed to have captured a portion of the famous Sherman's Battery.

Beall, however, did not participate in this fight, having been absent on a short leave, and not being able to get up until the fight was concluded.

It was on the 15th of the ensuing October that he again visited the home of his mother in Jefferson, in company with a member of his company who was sick. The next day was the second anniversary of John Brown's raid into the county —the ever memorable 16th of October. A hero who, with long, flowing, black beard, erect figure, and keen death-daring black eye, mounted on a snow-white charger, had escorted

John Brown to his gallows, was now to be the principal figure in another later act of the same drama. To Lt. Col. Turner Ashby, with a few companies of raw militia, and a detachment of the cavalry regiment of which he was the second in command, had been assigned the duty of defending Jefferson, and the Valley from an advance through Harper's Ferry Gap. The task was not an easy nor encouraging one, but Ashby knew nothing but to obey orders. On the day in question the rumbling of waggons, beating of drums, and the rapid falling back of his pickets announced to him that the enemy were in motion from Harper's Ferry towards his camp near Flowing Spring. He summoned his small, irregular force, and went down to meet them. His cavalry were not remarkably well drilled, but were gallant and devoted to their commander; the militia were like all raw, untrained troops, inefficient; to these were still to be added a motley crowd of farmers, mechanics, cow-boys and other civilians—incumbrances to military operations. The news of an impending battle soon spread through the county, and among others reached young Beall. He forthwith proceeded to the field of action, threw himself at the head of a militia company, and volunteered to lead them in a charge upon the enemy. The latter had been driven back; they had no artillery; while the Confederates had brought into play an old piece of ordnance, one of the old Fourth of July *orators*, whose brazen lungs had never injured any one but those who fired it, and was not likely to do much more execution on this occasion. The Federals, however, had retreated before it. A party of them were lodged behind a large dismantled, deserted brick house, —one of the many *sign-boards* which everywhere marked the advance of the Federal army. To dislodge this party was John Beall's aim, and, seizing a musket, he encouraged the militia to fellow him, which they did right manfully until he fell. In squads of three and four the Federals were leaving the shelter of Mrs. Wager's brick house, spoken of above, and firing as they retreated. Beall had emptied his musket twice, and had it raised to his shoulder in the act of aiming to fire again when a shot from the retreating party passed under his gun, and, striking him obliquely in the right breast, broke three ribs and passed around the body. He discharged his own gun and fell. When consciousness returned, his musket lay by his side, but the enemy were gone—so were the militia! He rose, tottered back to Ashby's line, and again sank, exhausted. Among the citizens assembled to witness, or take part in the fight, was the Hon. Andrew Hunter of Charlestown. But not to play the part of an idle spectator, he had brought down his own spring waggon, with his carriage horses, as an ambulance to carrry off the wounded. Recognizing Beall, he promptly took charge of him, and carried him to the house of his mother.

The dread of his mother, and the universal apprehension of his friends were not realized, although the right lung was penetrated. Tender nursing, aided by a strong will, enabled him to survive the injury, and a few months found him sufficiently recovered to travel South,—a course which his physicians advised, owing to the implication of the lung, rendered the more dangerous by an hereditary predisposition to phthisis. In the later part of November he proceeded to Richmond, and thence to Tallahassee, the capital of Florida. Remaining here a short time, he fell in with a wealthy gentleman, Gen. R. W. Williams, who with his wife resided on Pascagoula Island in Louisiana. A strong attachment sprang up between the young soldier-invalid, and Mrs. and General Williams, and upon their urgent invitation he accompanied them to their plantation in Louisiana, where he remained for several months a welcome recipient of their hospitality.

Two young ladies, refugees from Nashville, were at the same time guests of Gen. Williams, and between the youngest of these, and the young wounded soldier, whose condition still appealed loudly for sympathy, there sprang up a degree of

interest which ripened into the highest and holiest bond which
the unmarried can know – they were betrothed. John Beall
was by nature silent, reserved, and the most undemonstrative
of men; he confided little in human nature, and was oft wont
to quote with a smile, more sad than cynical, the lines of
Burns, one of his favourite poets:

> " A' mankind are unco weak
> Aud meikle to be trusted,
> Whenever self the balance shake
> 'Tis rarely right adjusted."

It was then with a sense of *rest*, a pleasure unknown
to natures more confiding, and a tenacity equally foreign to
characters more susceptible, that John Beall clung to those
in whom he felt he could trust. His mother—his small
charmed circle of friends—his betrothed! In these he confided with a love deep, pure, silent, tender; and to their
every demand he responded with a faith as true as steel.
After his exchange, and return from imprisonment in Fort
Delaware, he visited Georgia where his betrothed was at that
time residing. Hear his own account of this visit: " I went
on furlough to Columbus, Ga., and spent there, at Col.
Chambers's, the happiest two weeks of my life."

His visit South in 1861-62, after his wound, was thus
rendered auspicious, not more by the improved condition of
his health, than by his good fortune in forming the acquaintance of one in every way worthy of his confidence. He
returned to Richmond in the following Spring. Johnson had
already fallen back from Manassas and Centreville to the line
of the Rappahannock; while Jackson, defeated at Kernstown,
was slowly retiring up the Shenandoah Valley, and forming
his plans for that brilliant series of victories unprecedented
in the war, unsurpassed in history, which were to free the
Valley of an invading army.

John Beall, after remaining in Richmond about a fortnight,
went on a visit to an aunt, living in Madison County. While
here the news reached him that Jackson, having defeated

Banks at Winchester, was pursuing him down the Valley. Beall immediately took horse, and, overtaking the advancing columns, accompanied the army into Jefferson. Here he remained while Gen. Jackson occupied the county; and, upon his retreat, which was sudden and rapid, he started to rejoin the army. In this he was not successful. His failure, and subsequent progress into Iowa are thus related in his diary: " Leaving home, I rode the first day to Mansfield [the residence of his uncle in Clarke County], and spent the night with my aunt and uncle and cousins,—heard many reports which we did not credit; next morning, after bidding, as I thought, a temporary adieu, started to see my brother and friends [in Co. G., 2nd Virginia regiment, Stonewall Brigade], rode all day, which was an exceedingly warm one, —stopping at several places of note, and at last turning off the road, staid at Mr. Kaufman's all night, avoiding a heavy rain. Next morning, resuming my route, came to a little village which I found full of troops, and heard that the high rains had swept away the bridges, and raised the streams so high as to render fording both difficult and dangerous. I was compelled, therefore, to retrace my steps, as I could not stay there. I rode all day, and met Messrs. Timberlake, Larue, and Kennedy. At night I stopped at Mr. Lewis', who put me on my route,—severe rains all night. Next day I rode, and, crossing the creek, made for Grantham's or Kitchins', (Back Creek Valley, Berkley county,) but though it was warm I got to Tomahawk Springs, and staid all night at Mr. Griffiths' on recommendation of Mr. Devany. It rained all night, and in the morning, recrossing the creek, I went through rain, &c., and succeeded in crossing the river at a ferry—(it was past *fording*, and indeed a surging torrent). Had I delayed much longer, I could not have crossed at all. After crossing, I rode only a few miles, when, the rain still falling, I stopped over night and tried to dry my clothes,—I partially succeeded. My next day carried me to the Six-mile house, where I stayed all night, and heard some of the particulars of Gen. Banks' retreat, and also of the battle of Fair Oaks near Richmond................ ....I then came on to Uniontown (Maryland), where, transacting my business, and selling my horse, I concluded to come West. I came to Chicago and thence to Dubuque, and then concluding a bargain with Mr. ————, I have taken the Cascade mill, and am running it."

Thus it will be seen his first visit North was, as he afterwards remarks in a letter to Mrs. Gen. Williams, a voluntary visit, instead of the *involuntary* one which his certain capture, had he returned home, or attempted to go forward, would have involved.

The small village which he found full of troops was some small town further up the Valley than Winchester, most probably Newtown, on the Valley turnpike leading from Winchester to Staunton. Upon finding his progress likely to be arrested, upon reversing his direction, he behaved with characteristic coolness. He rode into a barn-yard along the road, and commenced busying himself with the cattle therein; he answered all questions asked by the passing soldiers as though he were the proprietor of the farm-yard, and requested the Federal soldiers who followed him into the inclosure to close the gate after them, and not allow his cattle to stray out. Thus warding off suspicion, he introduced himself to the real owners of the establishment, and finding them loyal to the South, he left with them his papers, and everything of a suspicious character, and struck out for the Potomac river.

We find from his diary that he remained in charge of the mill at Cascade from about the middle of July until the 2nd September of the same year; when suspicions being aroused as to his real character, through the imprudence of his friends, he was obliged to flee the country. He took refuge in

c

Canada, and settled down at Riley's hotel in Dundas, C. W. We find him here on the 20th of November, 1862, resuming his diary.

About the 5th of January, 1863, we find him preparing to make his way back to the South. His intention seems to have been to break through the lines in Kentucky; but in this design, after reaching Cincinnati, he was destined to disappointment for reasons which we find explained, upon the resumption of his diary in 1864.

" John Morgan had played such havoc in Kentucky with the railroads and communications, that it was deemed impossible for me to go South by that route. I then thought of Western Virginia, but the steamboats were seized to carry subsistence to Rosencranz's army, and I took the cars to Baltimore. After a false start I got on a pungy owned and run by blockaders, and about the last of February landed in Virginia. My comrade, Mr. Schluder, of St. Louis, Mo., had escaped from the Yankees—was from Price's army. We got to Richmond, and find Dan. Lucas and all the boys right at Fredericksburg," &c.

J. Y. BEALL.
In disguise in Canada, 1862.

CHAPTER II.

WHILE in Canada in 1862, the idea occurred first to Beall to attempt the rescue of the Confederate prisoners confined at Johnson's Island. This island is situated at the southern extremity of Lake Erie, on the Ohio side near the mouth of Sandusky Bay. Upon Beall's arrival in Richmond he set about to make a digest of his views. 1st. In regard to privateering on the Northern lakes, and levying contributions on the adjacent cities ; and 2ndly, by privateering on the Potomac and Chesapeake. It is the belief of the author, that Beall was *the first* to suggest to the authorities in Richmond the feasibility of successful attack on Johnson's Island, and the rescue of the prisoners there held in confinement. In conjunction with a gallant young officer of the Confederate army, then on the retired list owing to ill-health, Beall submitted his project to the President, embracing both of the above-named objects. His ideas were bold, but not visionary. A privateer, secretly armed and manned, once set afloat on the lakes could, he maintained, sweep their waters, and lay their cities from Chicago to Detroit in ashes, unless redeemed by heavy contributions; or could surprise the steamer off Johnson's Island, release the prisoners, and with this steamer sweep Erie from Toledo to Buffalo, and burn these cities, or lay them under contributions. Beall, and the young officer above alluded to, laid this project before the President, and it was by him referred to Hon. S. R. Mallory, Secretary of the Navy. Mr. Mallory, after due consideration, informed Beall that his scheme upon the lakes was regarded as feasible, but did not think it could be accomplished without endangering our neutral relations with England. The project upon the Potomac was approved, and Beall was handed a commission as acting master in the Confederate States navy. He was assured that if at any time in the future, the Secretary should conclude to execute the Lake scheme, he (Beall) and the young officer who was acting in conjunction with him, were to be assigned positions in the enterprise. Whether the honourable Secretary kept his promise or not, may interest the future historian to inquire !

Thus held in abeyance as to his favourite enterprise on the lakes, Beall and his colleague, with their naval commissions in their hands, set about organizing an expedition for privateering on the waters of the Lower Potomac and York rivers, and on Chesapeake Bay. Meantime it should have been mentioned that Beall had gone before a medical examining Board, and received a final discharge from the military service on the ground of disability arising from a wound received on the 16th day of October, 1861, which penetrated the right lung, and increased a hereditary tendency to consumption. Wounds are disagreeable companions. Beall, while in Canada, had made his arrangements to sail for England, and embark on board of a privateer ; his wound broke out afresh, and his physician prohibited his adventuring upon the life of a seaman.

Nothing daunted, however, by his health or other obstacles, he and his companion worked faithfully to organize a company for service on the theatre before spoken of. The conscription was now being rigorously enforced in the Confederacy, and Beall was restricted in recruiting to those not liable to military duty under existing law. Among his earliest recruits were two young Scotchmen ; one was a stout, round-shouldered, deep full-chested man of two and twenty, with brown hair, blue eyes, quick with intelligence, and a fair beardless face— this was Bennet G. Burley, afterwards Beall's lieutenant

in the famous Lake Erie expedition, and subsequently delivered up on the requisition of the United States authorities, by Chief Justice Draper of Canada West; delivered up on a charge of robbery to be tried for piracy; a rendition illustrative of what Junius so much admired as represented in Lord Mansfield—*the independence of the English judiciary in political trials.* Burley, even at this early day, had not been without his experience in prison life. The son of a master mechanic of Glasgow, he had left the land of the pibroch and thistle, landed in New York, and finally strayed into the Confederacy with a sub-marine battery in his pocket. It was on paper,—the invention of his father. But neither a paper gun, nor a smiling Scotch face were sufficient introduction to rescue Burley from the Richmond Bastile, Castle Thunder. The Italian brigand (for such in outward appearance was Capt. Alexander) who presided over this famous prison, held him for some time on suspicion, until finally his gun blew the manacles off his hands and released him. He was taken from Castle Thunder to the War building, and ushered into the presence of a tall, slender, abstracted looking man in a blue naval frock coat; this man was he who, without leaving Richmond, with one ship drove back the blockading fleet off Point Comfort, sank the Cumberland, afterwards discomfited the iron-clad fleet with three guns just mounted under the casemates of Fort Drewry, and finally pierced the sides of the Ironsides, and sank the Keokuk before Charleston, and helped to defend that city against Gilmore and his fleet successfully for eighteen months...............
This man was John Brooke, the inventor of the Deep-Sea Sounding lead, of the Brooke Gun, and the planner of the iron-clad " Virginia," or " Merrimac." Burley had taken his diagram before him for his examination; he ordered Burley's release from prison, but thought his invention liable to some objections in practice. He had also a *torpedo* which required *to be attached to the side of the vessel attacked, by*

screws, and then ignited by a fuse; such attachment could only be effected by approaching the vessel by night in a small boat with muffled oars, and swimming the remainder of the way, and screwing the torpedo to the vessel,—returning to the skiff or small boat, and thence igniting the fuse. Brooke thought that Diogenes with his lamp might as soon find the object of his search, as he a man willing to swim to an enemy's vessel, screw on a torpedo, and light the fuse ! One such man, however, was found, who afterwards swam to a war vessel in the————, screwed on the torpedo, retired and sprung the lanyard, but the fuse would not ignite ; in this way the torpedo found its way again to New-York ; from Burley's pocket in Castle Thunder, corner of 21st and Carey, Richmond, to the northwest corner of Fulton and Nassau streets, New-York, whence in the columns of the *Herald* it duly issued in large capitals—"*Curious infernal machine, found attached to the bottom of the war steamer ————on————River !*" The look-out declared he had heard oars as of a bateau dipping near the ship that night, and next morning the officer found the infernal machine fastened to her prow…. A few drops of water, more or less, on the fuse enabled the man on watch to make this statement.

The Scotchman who fastened this torpedo on the vessel of war was John Maxwell, accompanied by Burley, whose companion he was when he enlisted with Beall. Maxwell was the larger of the two—he was full six feet, with broad square shoulders, black hair, moustache, and whiskers. If Burley would have done to set for Lydon the supple Pompeian gladiator, Maxwell on the other hand would have represented the almost Herculean Niger. Burley was the Lowlander from Glasgow and the banks of the Clyde, but Maxwell looked for all the world as though he might just have stepped from the side of Ben Lothian with bare legs, the plaid upon his shoulder, and the purse about his waist.

The subsequent history of this man was an explosion ; a painter could concentrate it in a few bold dashes of the brush; let him paint a human arm, torn from the socket, bloody, mangled, and terrible; and in the distance, at three miles, a vast column of smoke, with the explanation that it marks the scene of the most fearful explosion since the Kremlin.

Such were specimens of the non-conscripts who composed the first privateering expedition on the waters of the York, Potomac, and Chesapeake, which Beall originated, but, in command of which, at his own request, he was ranked by the gallant young soldier before alluded to. This expedition met with but partial success. Their numbers only reached nine or ten, and they were not armed or equipped in a style which would justify extensive operations. They started from Richmond about the 1st of April, 1863, and proceeded to Matthews Court House. Beall returned to Richmond about the 15th June, to procure cutlasses, and other necessary equipments. The company was of a partizan character, the Government furnishing nothing but arms, uniforms, and equipments, while the party furnished their own boat, received no pay, but were entitled to all they should capture. In the first month nothing more was done than to surprise a camp of armed " Contrabrands," killing one, capturing one, and putting to flight the remainder. This exploit occurred on Back River, in Elizabeth City County, Virginia, and within ten miles of Fortress Monroe.

Upon his return to Richmond Beall's superior in command received an appointment with the rank of colonel of cavalry, and, accepting it, Beall was left thenceforth in command of the adventurous squad upon the Potomac. His aim was to render his command upon the waters of the Peninsula, in the bays, and inlets of the eastern shore of Virginia, what Mosby's was on land, in the fastnesses of the Blue Ridge, and in the forests of Piedmont, and the Northern Neck. Had he been properly supported by the Chief of the Navy

Department, beyond doubt, he would have become the Mosby of the Chesapeake, cutting communication, burning light-houses, severing sub-marine telegraph wires, capturing schooners, transports, and steamers, and otherwise doing immense damage to the enemy. But he was left to furnish boats for himself, and received but little aid or encouragement from Mr. Mallory.

He again, however, about the 5th or 6th of July, with a company better equipped than heretofore, commenced operations on the waters of the Chesapeake in open boats, making Matthews County his rendezvous and point of departure. Plying between Cherrystone and Old Point Comfort was a United States steamer, the *George W. Rodgers*. Beall sent a squad of his men under Roy McDonald, a gallant young Virginian, to capture this vessel. He set out from Matthews and first struck Marapamosis Island; thence he proceeded to Cherrystone, but arrived twenty minutes after the *G. W. Rodgers* had departed; he therefore contented himself with cutting the submarine telegraphic cable between Cherrystone, and Old Point, twenty-five miles from the latter fort, and directly opposite New Point Comfort. Beall made a brief report of this exploit to Mr. Mallory, inclosing therewith a small piece of the telegraphic cable.

About the 1st of August Beall and his party again set sail from Matthews. He crossed Chesapeake Bay and struck Devil's-Ditch Inlet in North Hampton County; thence he made for Smith's Island for the purpose of destroying Cape Charles Light House. He arrived at the latter at ten o'clock in the day, and concealing his party, took with him McDonald, and accosted the good "*Union Man*" who attended to the light-house. The latter, who (like the large majority of the small number in Eastern Virginia who sympathized with the North) was an illiterate, and rough specimen, treated his visitors rather impolitely, telling them they had better be in the army than "loafing about the country."

Beall, however, succeeded in conciliating him, and got him to explain, and expose fully all the wonders and treasures of his institution. " My friend "—said Beall—" I am highly pleased with the light-house, and your management of it, and I have a party of friends belonging to the Confederate States Navy who, I think, would like to look at it ! " Upon this he gave a shrill whistle, and as promptly as his clan obeyed the summons of Rhoderick Dhu, did Beall's band spring from their covert, and rush to the light-house. In obedience to his orders they destroyed all the machinery, appurtenances, and fixtures, and brought off three hundred gallons of oil, at that time of great value in Richmond. Beall seized the large yawl attached to the light-house, and after paroling the keeper, who was terribly frightened, not to leave the Island for twenty-four hours, the party returned to Matthews.

On the 18th of September Beall again set out from Matthews. His party now numbered eighteen. Roy McDonald had been promoted to the rank of Acting Master. Beall himself was generally known as " Captain Beall," from the time he assumed entire command of the party ; though he never at any time during the war held any other commission than that of Acting Master, dating from the 5th of March, 1863. His two gallant little boats, one black, the other white, were christened respectively the *Raven* and the *Swan*. Dividing his party, taking half in the *Swan* with himself, and assigning McDonald to command the *Raven* with the remainder, he left Horn Harbor, Matthews County, and proceeded first to Racoon Island near Cape Charles ; lying off here he found a Yankee sloop, the *Mary Anne,* and two fishing scows, all of which he captured. Thence with his prizes, he proceeded to Watch Sprig Inlet on the Coast of Accomac. On the night of the 21st of September, notwithstanding the equinoctial storm had set in, and a heavy north-wester was blowing, he boarded, and captured the *Alliance*, a large sloop, Capt. David Ireland, Staten Island, New York, bound from

Philadelphia to Port Royal, South Carolina, laden with sut-
ler's stores. McDonald with the *Raven* was to tackle the
sloop on the starboard, and Beall on the port. The night
was fearfully dark and stormy; the hour selected was
eleven; the crew had turned in; the captain and mate were
playing dominoes in the cabin. The *Raven* was dashed
against the side of the schooner, her tiller broken, and
McDonald thrown headlong into the water. He regained
the boat, which was washed back by the heavy sea, and came
up with the Swan on the port; Beall and McDonald therefore boarded on the same side; the former conducted his
crew to the forecastle to capture the schooner's crew, while
the latter struck for the cabin, where he found the Captain
and mate unsuspicious of danger, quietly enjoying their game.
Capt. Ireland was a bold, brave man, and, watching his opportunity started for his own state-room to get his arms; in
doing so, however, he had to pass McDonald, who, observing
the movement, called him to halt, with a cocked pistol, and
told him to go back to the cabin; the Captain promptly
obeyed.

The next day, September 22nd, the equinox continued,
and, all hands being brought on board the *Alliance*, both an-
chors were cast away to keep her steady. That night, however, they again took boat, and just out the inlet captured
three Yankee sloops, the *Houseman, Samuel Pearsall*, and a
third, name not remembered, commanded by Capt. Rushman
Craft. On the night of the 23rd they ran these three vessels,
last named, out of the inlet, stripped them of all valuables,
scuttled them, and sent them to sea. On the 24th all hands
took to the large schooner *Alliance*, and sailed westward to
Cobb's Island. Here Beall obtained a reliable pilot, and announced his intention, hazardous as might seem the undertaking, to run his prize through the blockade, and up the
Pianketank River to North End or about that point, where he
would be enabled to land his whole cargo, and transport the

same to Richmond. Accordingly he paroled the crews of the *Mary Anne* and fishing smacks, sent McDonald with the other prisoners to Matthews, and set out for the mouth of the Pianketank with the *Alliance*. His pilot was a Canadian, experienced, and true; but whether owing to the presence of a Federal gun-boat within a mile of the mouth of the Pianketank, or some other, cause, on this occasion he missed the channel by twelve feet, and grounded the vessel. Beall promptly landed what goods he could run ashore in boats, and burnt the schooner to the water's edge. He reached Richmond with what remained of his cargo, about the same time that McDonald arrived there with seventeen prisoners. From the sale of the cargo the party realized a handsome dividend, as the goods captured were at this time very valuable in the Confederacy.

Capt. Beall's operations now began to attract attention, and to call down heavy denunciations upon him in the North. Brig. General Wistar was sent down to Matthews and the neighbouring counties for the special purpose of capturing Beall and his marines. Wistar's force for this purpose consisted of one regiment of negro infantry, two of white cavalry, and one battalion of artillery; also three gun-boats in North river, three in East river, two in the Pianketank, and one or two off New Point Comfort. Doubtless General Wistar did not know that he was sent with this formidable army to contend against an Acting Master, whose force, all told, consisted of eighteen marines, backed by a fleet of two small sailboats! Unaware of the extensive preparations made for their reception, McDonald left Richmond on the 4th of October, and reaching Matthews on the 5th was incontinently "gobbled," (to use a phrase of the day), by Genl. Wistar; only two of the party were taken with him. Beall, with the remainder of the party, narrowly escaped. He found the Peninsula, for the present, too hot for him, and, dispersing his party through the country, he returned to Richmond.

Nothing daunted by the capture of three of his party, his own narrow escape, and the large picket force guarding Matthews and adjoining counties, and the bays, and the inlets of the bay on both the eastern and western shores, Beall again collected his small band of marines, and, leaving Richmond about the 10th of November, proceeded cautiously, almost stealthily, to the coast, and again took boat. He crossed the bay again with his two gallant little birds, the *Raven* and the *Swan*; he struck Tangier Inlet, on the coast of the Accomac, and captured there a schooner. Daylight coming on, Beall sent a squad of his men with one boat to conceal themselves, while he remained with the captured schooner and only a sufficient number of men not to attract attention. The result was, the party sent out were by carelessness captured, and one of them in terror disclosed who they were. Forthwith the enemy armed all the small boats and pungies in the neighbourhood, and with four or five hundred men went in pursuit of Beall. The latter could have escaped, but waited so long to see what was the fate of his detachment, that escape became impossible, and he found himself surrounded Recognizing the fact that he was no longer master of the situation, Beall threw overboard every thing of any value, and surrendered. His capture was heralded throughout the North as an achievement of no small moment, and was the subject of a special despatch from Genl. Wistar. The "*notorious Captain Beall*" was at last caught, and the enemy proposed to deal out summary, or as the Neapolitans call it "*economical*" justice to him and his band of "*pirates*." They were taken first to Drummondtown, Accomac County, where, by order of the provost marshal, they underwent the usual search, and deprivation of all valuables, money, watches, &c. From Drummondtown they were taken to Fort McHenry, and thrown in a dungeon, heavily ironed. On the vessel which conveyed them from Drummondtown to the Fort, Beall tried to induce his men to seize the boat, and attempt its capture, and their escape; but his men prudently declined, and as it turned out very wisely, for in the hold of the vessel were concealed a company of Federal soldiers.

A characteristic anecdote is told of the effect produced on Beall's spirit by the irons with which he was manacled. The prison-keepers, whoever they were, had a habit of relieving those who were in irons by unlocking them at certain hours, and allowing the unfortunate prisoners an opportunity to exercise. Beall's whole party availed themselves of this occasional act of humanity on the part of the guard. Not so, however, with himself; he would not at any time for a moment allow the manacles to be removed! "No!" said he, "let them alone! until your *Government* sees fit to remove them!"............... He and his party remained in irons for forty-two days. At the end of this time they were released, and placed upon the footing of other prisoners of war. Beall was allowed to write a communication to Richmond, which being laid before Mr. Mallory and Commissioner Robert Ould, was speedily followed by a reprisal by placing in irons seventeen captive Federal marines, and two commissioned officers as hostages. This "*taste of retaliation*" soon had the desired effect. General Benjamin F. Butler himself gave the subject his attention, and ordered these so-called "pirates" to be released from their irons, and placed on the footing of other prisoners of war. This being done, Beall was forwarded along with other officers from Fort McHenry to City Point on the 20th of March, where he remained until the 5th of May ensuing, when he was duly exchanged, and returned to Richmond. McDonald, however, and the balance of the party, among whom was Beall's brother William, were not exchanged until the following October, when a general exchange of naval prisoners took place between the respective Governments.

Upon his return to Richmond, Beall spent his time in recruiting his health and furlough, and in visiting his friends.

It was during this interval of inactivity that he visited Columbus, Georgia, and spent, as he himself informs us, " *the happiest two weeks* " of his life—he was with his betrothed.

Upon returing to Richmond again, he immediately called
around him his friends, and by their aid addressed himself to
the Secretary of the Navy to further the new schemes which
he now had on hand.   Mr. Mallory replied, that a new
bureau for Secret Service had been organized, and referred
Beall to its chief; the latter endorsed his views favourably,
but having no authority for independent action, referred him
in turn to the Secretary of War, Hon. James A. Seddon.
The latter offered him a lieutenancy in the Secret Service ;
but this he declined for reasons which reflect honour on his
memory, and shed light upon his character ; he would have
been subject to the command of superiors whom he did not
know, in a service where disobedience would have been insubordination, while obedience might have demanded a sacrifice
of his own moral convictions ; hence, without hesitation,
he promptly declined the offer of the Secretary.

Meanwhile the War was thickening around Richmond,
the devoted capital of the Confederacy.   Grant, crowned
with the laurels of Big Black, Vicksburg, and Chickamauga,
had hurled his legions against the worn, but still defiant columns
of the immortal army of Northern Virginia.   On the very
day on which Beall was exchanged commenced the battle of the
Wilderness ; in three days the estimated loss of the Federals
was greater by fifteen thousand than the French loss at
Waterloo.   The two armies like two mad bulls with locked
horns, bent their way in parallel lines from Piedmont to Tidewater, from the Rappahannock to the James.   On the 12th
day of May, 1864, Richmond was wending its way to
church at six o'clock in the morning ; the Catholics to mass,
the Protestants to prayer-meeting.   There is no sermon like
the roar of cannon at the city gates.   Phil. Sheridan had
been thundering since five a.m., on the Mechanicsville road :

Gordon was brought in on one litter, and on another Jeb. Stuart, the Immortal Chevalier; the sad cortège which escorted " our dear dumb warrior " met a man with a drooping shoulder, compressed lips, and long brown hair with cartridge-box, and musket, wending his way to the fortifications to aid in driving back the foe,—this man was John Beall, less a warrior, but equally Christian and not less a hero than had been Stuart himself. True to his character, which was never to fail at the call of duty, he entered the ranks with his musket, and participated in Gregg's repulse of Sheridan on the Mechanicsville road. On the succeeding day he temporarily attached himself to the Engineer corps under charge of Lieutenant Henderson, a friend; and being thus enabled to draw rations, &c., he remained near the defences around Mechanicsville for some days. When, however, both armies were sufficiently exhausted to require rest, and Grant, repulsed with great slaughter at Cold Harbor, had sat down before Petersburg, (declaring to his army that " the *siege* of Richmond " had commenced,) Beall, his patience exhausted by the neglect of the department, and his spirit chafing for that action which his health denied him on the field, suddenly left the camp on the Chickahominy, reappeared on the coast in Matthews County, crossed over to the eastern shore, and came leisurely on through Baltimore to New York, and thence to Canada West.

On the 14th of August, we find him in Dundas resuming his diary, " after an absence of nineteen months." Meanwhile his friends in the South had lost sight of him; no one knew whither he had gone, or on what errand.

Beall's correspondence discloses the fact that on the 14th September he was at Windsor, Canada West, whence he writes to a friend in a certain other city of that Province in language which, but for the light of subsequent events, would appear entirely enigmatical; his letter is as follows:

DEAR SIR,—This will be handed to you by —— Esq,
who will explain what I want. Please render him every
assistance in your power.

We want 3 dozen hatchets, also 4 grappling hooks.

Please see Mr. B. If he has met with any success—*we
need that.* If there are any letters for me forward them
by him.

Truly your friend,

J. Y. BEALL.

Again on the 16th we find him writing thus :

MY DEAR SIR,—In ——'s letter was a message from
Mr. —— that every thing was ' all right and satisfactory.' If he has got the article, I want it here by 7 o'clock
a.m. Monday morning—indeed by Sunday in order to meet
me. I stop at Windsor Castle House, No. 1.

Everything is fair, and I believe he will be successful
in business. I hope you saw Mr. —— The letters I
referred to, —— sent by post.

As we may not meet again, let me thank you for your
kindness again; for a homeless exile and outcast can appreciate such.

Truly your friend,

JOHN Y. BEALL.

Interpreted in the light of events now rapidly ripening, we
can understand the objects of the " *hatchets* " and " *grappling hooks* " ; while that the " *business,* " which promised
such success, was somewhat out of the ordinary routine, we
may well infer from the impressive manner in which the
" *homeless* exile and out-cast " bids his friend farewell.

CHAPTER III.

THE LAKE ERIE RAID.

Unsuccessful attempt to rescue the Confederate prisoners confined on Johnson's Island.

On Sunday evening, the 18th of September, Bennet G. Burley, the same who had enlisted under Beall two years before in Richmond, stepped on board the Philo Parsons, a steamer of about 220 tons burden, lying at the wharf of Detroit. This steamer plied regularly between Detroit, Michigan, and Sandusky city, Ohio. Burley inquired whether the boat stopped regularly at Sandwich, a small town on the Canada side of Lake Erie : upon being informed that it did not, he requested the clerk, and part owner of the boat, W. O. Ashley, to stop there the next morning, and take on board three friends of his, who, with himself, were bound on a short excursion to Sandusky city, Ohio. Accordingly eight o'clock the next morning found Burley on board of the steamer swinging off the dock of Detroit. At Sandwich the boat did not properly *stop* at all ; Captain S. F. Atwood, in command of her, touched at the wharf, and three active young men sprang aboard of her while she was in motion. A detective might have discovered something peculiar about them ; the unsuspecting Ashley, and eighty miscellaneous passengers, failed, however, to do so. One of them, at any rate, was rather *Southern* in his appearance ; he was stoutly built, with broad shoulders, flat chest, and measuring about five feet seven and a half inches in height ; he wore grey pants with black cloth sack coat, buttoned closely over the breast, just showing a little of the white shirt below the loosely tied black silk cravat, and rolling collar. His hair

D

was brown, and half covered the ear; the forehead high, the nose straight, and regular, the complexion pale, the lips thin and compressed. He wore a light moustache, and whiskers coming to a point under the chin. His smile was exceedingly gracious and pleasant, his voice low, musical, his eyes a light blue, rather small, but at times very brilliant.

The Philo Parsons continued quietly on her way until she touched at Amherstburgh; here sixteen more passengers jumped aboard; there was no baggage among the party, save an old trunk tied up with a rope, which was thrown in the after-gangway of the boat by two of the party. The boat again resumed her passage to Sandusky, leaving Amherstburgh about half-past nine a.m., and touching at Kelly's Island at about four p.m. Scarcely had the boat left this island, which is situated near the head of Lake Erie, five miles north of Sandusky, when a sudden commotion is seen on the main deck. The person above described who had gotten on board with two others at Amherstburgh, and who had been engaged for some time in conversation with the mate, who was at the time at the helm, suddenly, at a preconcerted signal, presented a pistol to the head of the helmsman, and exclaimed —" I take possession of this boat in the name of the Confederate States! Resist at your peril!"—or words to the same effect. At the same moment three others of the party levelled their pistols at Ashley (who was now in command of the boat, Captain Atwood having gone ashore at North Bass Island, where he resided); and before the astonished clerk had time to ask an explanation of this conduct, Burley came aft, followed by fourteen or fifteen of his party, and exclaimed to Ashley—" Get into that cabin, or you are a dead man!" At the same time, with his cocked revolver in his hand, and his finger on the trigger, he commenced counting " *one! two! three!*" The clerk did not wait for a second invitation, but promptly obeyed orders. The passengers also were quickly stowed away in the cabin, and a guard of two men stationed

J. Y. BEALL.
Dressed as on board the Philo Parsons.

on each side of the door to secure them and prevent egress.
The mysterious old trunk was now brought up on deck, the
rope cut from around it, and the grappling-hooks and hatchets
taken out ready for use. Such of the crew as were not
needed to manage the boat were imprisoned in the hold, and
the boat taken entire possession of, and the Confederate flag
hoisted over her. While Beall kept his eye upon the helmsman, assuring him he had only to obey orders to escape injury, Burley commenced to clear the decks, and lighten the
boat for service ; he threw all the heavy freight, comprising
a considerable quantity of iron, overboard, and cleared the
deck for action. Beall then demanded, and received the
papers and books of the boat from Ashley, at the same time
explaining to him the meaning of the capture, and his own
relation to the Confederate States Government. He next
had the boat turned, and headed for Middle Bass Island,
where he ran into a wood, and landed the prisoners. This
island is on the Ohio side of the lake, ten miles from shore,
and about the same distance from Johnson's Island.

Scarcely had the Philo Parsons touched the wharf, when
the Island Queen, a screw propeller, Capt. George W. Orr,
plying between Sandusky and this island, came alongside the
captured steamer, and made fast to her. Beall, followed by
fourteen or fifteen of his party, armed with hatchets and
revolvers, sprang on board of her, and repeated the *coup de
guerre* of the Philo Parsons. There was a slight show of
resistance, and some shots fired, one of which inflicted a
wound in the neck of Mr. Haynes, the engineer of the
steamer. With this exception, no blood was spilt during the
whole adventure. The passengers, crew and officers of the
Island Queen were now removed to the Philo Parsons, and
confined on board for the space of an hour, when they were
landed with the private baggage, and sent on their way
rejoicing. Among the passengers on the Island Queen were
twenty-five or thirty Federal soldiers, belonging to the 130th

Ohio regiment, " hundred-day men," on their way to Toledo
to be mustered out of service. These were paroled not to
take arms against the Confederacy till duly exchanged, while
to the civilians, it is stated, an oath was administered not to
reveal the extraordinary events which had taken place until
twenty-four hours should have elapsed. Beall's treatment of
all on board these vessels was spoken of universally as kind
and courteous, though firm and determined. *Not one particle of private property was by order or with his knowledge
disturbed.* This important fact is testified to by the commanders of both vessels. A statement of the affair to the
Cleveland Leader, made on the authority of Captain Orr,
declares that "*no private property was taken, but the books,
papers and money of both boats were seized ;*" while in his
testimony before the Military Commission, Ashley testifies
that all the property which he claimed as "*personal*" was
restored to him. (See Trial, page 111.) One passenger
alone had in his possession near eighty thousand dollars ; he
approached Beall as the commandant of the party, and
demanded to know how much of this he would be permitted
to retain on condition of surrendering the remainder. He was
instantly assured by being told by Beall that none of his
property should be disturbed. The property and funds of
both boats, however, along with the boats themselves, were
taken possession of, and appropriated as legitimate prize.

It was now night, and a clear, calm moon looked down,.
from a serene sky upon the waters of Lake Erie. The passengers, Ashley, and the soldiers, and such of the crew as
were not needed had been landed, as before stated. Captain
Orr was still a prisoner in the hold of the Philo Parsons.
Beall lashed together his two prizes, and directed the helmsman to steer for Johnson's Island. One vessel was of course
sufficient for the matter in hand, and the Queen, therefore,
after being towed about five miles, was stripped, scuttled,
and sent adrift ; the next morning her smoke stack was seen.

protruding above Chickanolee Reef, where she lay a fathom
and a half below water. Meanwhile Beall continued his
course with the Philo Parsons until he reached the mouth of
Sandusky Bay. Here let us leave him and turn our attention to what had transpired on shore, and on board the United
States Steamer, which lay, like a huge watch dog, off the
coast of Johnson's Island.

On the 16th day of September we find Beall, as before
stated, at Windsor, C. W., writing to a friend to bring on
the "hatchets" and "grappling hooks." Not a great while
before he had been to Sandusky City, Ohio, where he was a
long time closeted with a certain wealthy Philadelphian, by
the name of Cole. The latter was a dashing young "swell,"
who had put up at the West House some five or six weeks
before, whose prodigality in expenditure attracted the cupid-
ity of the civilians in Sandusky, while his fine wines, and
costly dinners won, with still greater rapidity, upon the United
States officers in the vicinity. He especially cultivated the
society of the latter, and was particularly attentive to the
naval officers on board the Michigan. They invite him on
board, and show him the ship ; they dine him, and he in turn
fêtes them. He goes ashore on the Island itself, and is
allowed to converse with the Confederate Officers confined
there. That he should enjoy their conversation is natural,
since generally they are men of intelligence, and many have
been the heroes of adventures, and deeds of daring worthy of
the age of chivalry. There are Brigadier-General Jefferson
Thompson, "the Swamp Fox," Brigadier-Generals J. J.
Archer, J. R. Jones, W. N. R. Beall, and Frazer, and Major-
General J. R. Trimble ; Colonel Scales, colonel of the 30th
Mississippi, Major Thompson of General Morgan's command,
Colonel Richard Henry Lee of the Stonewall Brigade,
Captain J. Cabell Breckenridge, son of John C. Breckenridge,
Colonel J. Lucius Davis who participated so largely in the
John Brown war ; Captain Robert Cobb Kennedy, of the

1st Louisiana Infantry, who afterwards, escaping from the Island, was executed in New York for an attempt to burn that city, and many other gallant officers of lower grade, numbering in all from twenty-five hundred to three thousand. The Barracks in which they were confined were surrounded by a high enclosure, forming a yard or court in which the prisoners were permitted at certain hours during the day to exercise.   In this delightful pen, however, the mud was generally knee deep.   Three shallow pits furnishing water at the rate of four gallons per hour each, were expected to supply the prisoners with muddy water ; they consequently suffered much from thirst, while the waters of Erie, rolling within fifty yards, but as inaccessible as if they were one hundred miles distant, strongly suggested the punishment inflicted by Divine anger upon Tantalus.   Of food the day's allowance sufficed for one meal, being much less than one day's ration.   Petty tyranny and low meanness displayed themselves on the part of the Federal officials, in rank luxuriance..............
At the distance of a few rods from the main prison were the dungeons, each somewhat larger than a coffin, in which were confined officers condemned to death by court-martial.   They are chained hand and foot, and, in addition, some of them drag an iron ball of sixty pounds weight.   Most of them have been condemned by General Burnside's Draconian order, denouncing as *spies* all Confederates found *recruiting* in Kentucky, and certain other specified districts.   These young officers, destined for military mock judicial murder, are allowed a few hours' exercise each day to preserve life ; at stated hours they may be seen, shackled, handcuffed, with their iron balls thrown over their shoulders, moving slowly between the stakes which mark the bounds within which they are permitted to exercise.   Such was the prison of Johnson's Island.

To return now to Cole.   This fortunate speculator, or youthful heir of a vast fortune, or luxurious and extravagant tourist, or whatever might be his real character, was as indiscriminate in his political association, as in the objects of his prodigal liberality ; among his intimates are found officers both Federal and Confederate, prisoners, and guards, " copperheads," and Republicans. He is particularly intimate with the engineer of the *Michigan*, and they are often engaged in private, and confidential conversation. He visits frequently at the houses of some half dozen leading " Copperheads," (as members of the State-Rights party are now called in the North,) in the city. When a boatman rows him over to the Michigan, or the Island, he throws him a half dollar, and does not wait for change ; and in a thousand other ways are yellow eagles and sovereigns changed to silver, and thence disappear from his hand, as orange clouds fade into grey, and thence into mist, and impalpability. On the very night of the 18th of April, upon which we left Beall, in the Philo Parsons, hovering about the mouth of Sandusky Bay, this colleague, with whom he had been closeted at the West-House, and doubtless had been keeping up constant communication ever since, had invited the officers of the Michigan to a supper at the hotel in Sandusky. At this entertainment the officers of the Michigan were to be present ; and Cole, while in his assumed character of a Philadelphia millionaire, entertained them, in his *real character* of a *Confederate Soldier*, formerly a captain on John Morgan's staff, was to *drug* them so as to incapacitate them for duty. The party on shore acting in concert with him, were then to send up signals from Johnson's Island to Beall, who should, thereupon, advance, seize the Michigan, turn her guns on the guard, overcome them, and release the prisoners.

It was, therefore, with the most intense anxiety that Beall stood on the deck of the Philo Parsons, straining his gaze into the moonlight to see the signal-rocket glare up from Johnson's Island. He looks, however, in vain ; no signal appears : but he does not despond, nor turn back. He may still win, or losing, the sacrifice is only what thousands are making daily in the same sacred cause—life. He bears on his course unmoved, cautiously and slowly, until the lights of the Michigan are seen marking her length upon the smooth lake : men's voices are heard upon her deck ; even the dark contour of her fourteen guns can be discovered as they lie in the moonlight, silent, and as it were, asleep. Suddenly a danger besets him where least expected—*his men mutiny !* Burley and two others only, three out of twenty, stand by him ; the remainder resolutely refuse to go forward. They allege that the signal has failed, and the enterprise must have been betrayed, or otherwise discovered. In vain Beall pleads, argues, threatens, expostulates. He tells them they are all strangers to him, but he relied upon them as Confederate soldiers, and Southerners. He points out to them the immortal glory which awaits success, and the disgrace which will attend failure, if success should prove to have been possible. Finally he loses patience ; turning fiercely upon his mutinous command, he orders them into the cabin, and commands them to reduce to writing their resolve, as a memorial of their own insubordination, and a vindication of himself, and the three gallant comrades who are willing to stand by him, and attack the Michigan. He is obeyed ; here is the paper :

"On board the 'Philo Parsons,' Sept. 20th, 1865. We the undersigned, crew of the boat aforesaid, take pleasure in expressing our admiration of the gentlemanly bearing, skill and courage of Capt. Beall as a commanding officer, and a gentleman ; but believing, and being well convinced that the enemy is informed of our approach, and is so well prepared that we can not by possibility make it a success, and, having already captured two boats, we respectfully decline to prosecute it any further."

This paper, signed by seventeen of his crew, and placed in Beall's hands, furnishes the key to the mysterious movements of the Philo Parsons when so near the professed object of attack. To the hour of his death Beall believed that with-

out this mutiny, which he stigmatized as " cowardly," his
success in the capture of the Michigan was certain ; he believed that his capture of the two vessels, and rapid approach
was undreamed of ; that the officers of the Michigan were
nearly all absent in Sandusky, buried in carousal, and drunk-
enness, while the prisoners were on the alert, and in readiness,
—everything propitious.   Sadly, angrily, gloomily, therefore, did the young soldier submit to the exigency of the
situation.

Was Beall correct in supposing that up to the hour when
he was forced to turn back by the refusal of the crew to go
forward, everything had worked favourably on shore, and that
Cole was as yet unbetrayed or undiscovered ? The author does
not know upon what authority he based this opinion, and can
only say that his belief of its truth, after all the newspaper
reports to the contrary had been published, shows that he
based it upon evidence which carried conviction to his own
mind; and the fulness and firmness of this conviction to the
last hour of his life entitles his opinion to great weight.   His
information led him to believe that the discovery of the real
character of Cole and his arrest were *subsequent* to, and consequent upon the seizure of the Philo Parsons, and Island
Queen ; and that it was to cover up gross dereliction of duty
on their own part, that the officers of the Michigan indus-
triously circulated the statement that Cole had been arrested
on the 18th of September.   It is certain, however, that the
signal agreed upon was not given ; upon the other hand, if
the arrest were effected on the evening of the 18th, as represented in the Sandusky journals, and Cole's papers develop-
ing the whole plot, taken from him, why were Beall and Burley
allowed, two days afterwards, to carry out, without molesta-
tion, their part of the programme, and to advance under
the very guns of the Michigan, without being fired upon ? It
has even been stated that when the Michigan *attempted* to
pursue the Philo Parsons, her engines were found in such a

condition that she could make no headway, and their derange-
ment was attributed to the treachery of the engineer whom
Cole had bribed.   The author does not pretend to be able to
eliminate the truth from this maze of contradictory statements, as to the time, and circumstances of poor Cole's
arrest; certain it is he was arrested, and made a confession
of his real character and purpose; and thus ended in failure
the second attempt to release the prisoners on Johnson's
Island, confined there, as they were, by the Federal Government from motives of policy, and in violation of the cartel for
general exchange previously agreed upon by the two Governments.

Beall, being compelled to abandon the attack upon the
Michigan, turned from Sandusky Bay up Detroit river; about
eight o'clock on Tuesday morning he reached Fighting Island
on the Canada side, and, after landing there Capt. Orr and
other prisoners, he proceeded to Sandwich, Canada, and there,
having first removed everything of value from the Philo Parsons, scuttled her, cut her steam-pipes, and abandoned her to
her fate.   His party, all of whom were citizens of the Confederate States, either native or adopted, were disbanded; out
of the twenty composing it not one was arrested, save the two
commissioned officers, Beall and Burley, and both of these
had only to thank their own extraordinary temerity for the
unfortunate consequences to themselves which followed upon
the Lake Erie raid.

The career of Burley since the severance of his connection
with Beall, on the Potomac, had been full of adventure.   He
had received an appointment as acting master in the Confederate navy, and had been engaged in several partizan expeditions on the waters of the James, York, and Chesapeake.
In one of these he was severely wounded, and captured with
nearly the whole of his party.   Two of the latter were wan-
tonly murdered after their surrender, and the facts of the
case, substantiated by the testimony of citizens of Matthews

BENNETT G. BURLEY.

County, Virginia, who witnessed the outrage, were put on file in the archives of the Confederate Government. Burley's severe wound probably saved his life ; he was, however, subjected to great indignity and hardship, and finally, after being, according to the usual custom of the federal captors, " *gone through*," that is to say, searched and robbed, he was sent to Fort Delaware, a Federal bastile situated in Delaware River, near its mouth, which is forty miles below Philadelphia. From this prison, after a confinement of many weeks, he effected his escape in the following remarkable manner :—conducting from the large court of the fort, to which the prisoners were at certain times allowed access, to the bay in which it emptied, was a large drain or sewer. It was covered with plank, which rested on huge log sleepers, and to the level of these sleepers reached the water itself; the length of the drain was about twenty-five yards from the open court to the Delaware. Burley and five companions determined to attempt an escape by passing under this drain to the river, and thence swimming to the shore ; the distance was not over one mile and a half, but the actual stretch to be accomplished, owing to the tide, and the difficulty of landing, was not less than three miles and a half. Some idea of the hazard and difficulty attending the task may be arrived at, when the fact is remembered that before reaching the river, the dark narrow drain, twenty-five yards in length, had to be passed through ; the water being upon a level with the sleepers rendered it necessary to *dive under* these successively, and rising in the interspaces between them, to inhale such a supply of air as could penetrate through the plank covering over the sewer. When at length the river should be reached, three and a half miles of swift water and heavy surf remained before the hardy swimmer, before reaching the opposite shore, where he would find himself in the land of the enemy, dressed in Confederate grey, and subject to the almost certain liability of re-arrest and return to the Bastile.

Nothing daunted by these obstacles, of whose existence and

nature they were thoroughly informed, Burley and his companions determined to make the attempt. The former is an expert swimmer and an athlete in physical strength and endurance ; he not only felt small apprehension about his own safety in the attempt, but agreed to assist a companion who was less muscular and expert. They started in pairs, having first tied around the waist as many canteens as they could procure for the purpose, in the fort. Burley and a companion were the first pair who started, the former in advance, and these two were the only ones so fortunate as to effect their escape ; about midway to the shore they encountered a vessel bound to Philadelphia, whose master, whatever may have been his suspicions as to the real character of his cast-a-ways, accepted their story that they had been upset in a fishing excursion, and conveyed them safely to Philadelphia. Of the other four prisoners, two were drowned and two recaptured at the end of the drain, by the guard, before embarking on the waters of the Delaware.

From Philadelphia, Burley proceeded to New York, whence he wrote to his companions in prison, and informed them of his good fortune; from New York he proceeded to Canada, where, to their mutual surprise, he and his old friend Capt. John Y. Beall met in Toronto. With what success they accomplished the part of the expedition against Johnson's Island, with which they were intrusted, has already been related.

After the incidents in connection with the Lake Erie expedition, already related, Burley returned to the house of a relation in Guelph, where he had previously been staying. Here he practised little or no concealment, and soon after drew upon himself the attention of the public by some experiments which he instituted in ordnance, or gunnery ; the consequence was his arrest by the Canadian authorities. He was at first taken for Beall, but his identity was easily established, however, and his final rendition to the United States constitutes a chapter in British state-trials, which all who esteem judicial purity and independence might well wish to have left unreported ;—standing as it does in direct conflict with the English authorities, as indicated by the law officers of the Crown at home ; also, by the decision in the case of the Roanoke ; likewise in that of the Chesapeake, and finally in that of the St. Albans raid.

After Burley's arrest, Beall consulted long and seriously with his friends whether he should not deliver himself up to the Canadian authorities, but was advised not to do so, as no good could result from such a step. He, however, during Burley's confinement, spent some time in Toronto, where the latter was imprisoned; and it has even been stated, with what truth the author cannot determine, that on one occasion he travelled from Toronto to Hamilton with a detective, and discussed the Lake Erie affair with him, and the probable whereabouts of the leader, and other participators therein.

He had still most fervently at heart his own cherished scheme of launching a privateer on Erie, Huron, or Ontario. He writes from Toronto, on the 11th of October, 1864, as follows :

DEAR SIR,—I got here last night to find all of my enquiring friends departed.

We will need Mr. B.'s friend this week or so. You know that I am not one of the giving-up kind. We are going to try again on my plan. Send me any letters, &c.

We had a week's hunting out near Balsam Lake, not being very successful on account of want of good equipments.

Remember me kindly to all enquiring friends, and believe me truly your obliged friend,

JOHN Y. BEALL.

It is not deemed expedient here to enter into the particulars of the preparations made to carry out his " plan," or the causes connected with its failure ; suffice it to say that such failure was due in no degree to Beall. All who have any knowledge on the subject concur in testifying to his boldness and energy in executing every responsibility devolved upon him. He braved, when necessary, the Argus eyes of the whole herd of United States detectives, (or " Federal Spies " as the Canadians call them,) moving about through the Province without disguise, wherever his schemes demanded his presence.

CHAPTER IV.

Raid on the Dunkirk and Buffalo Railway.—Capture and imprisonment.

IT was on the 16th day of December, 1864, that John Y. Beall fell into the hands of the enemy. His capture was effected by two of the local police * at Niagara city, in the State of New York, and was due to that care and consideration for the safety of friends which distinguished him. He had, in company with a number of other Confederates, all in citizens' dress, taken the cars at Buffalo. The train reached Niagara at the usual hour. Just before their arrival at this point, Beall warned his companions against waiting in the depot for the Great Western train which was to connect at Niagara, after an interval of some hours, and on which the expectation of the party was to take passage for Hamilton and Toronto. Beall's advice was, that instead of waiting they should *immediately walk across* the Suspension Bridge and

---

* During the progress of Beall's trial, one Yonng, a detective of New York city, published a Report, in which, unless he was misrepresented by the New York dailies, he claimed that Beall's arrest was brought about by information obtained by said Young from "Larry MacDonald," whom he had enticed into a conference at or near Niagara Falls. The falsehood of this claim is shown by the facts connected with his arrest as above related, and substantiated by Constable Thomas in his evidence to be found in the published trial. Beall's arrest was an accident, as absolutely independent of any agency of Chief Detective Young and his corps, as was that of Burley. Out of *twenty* who composed his party in the Erie Raid, but *two* (himself and Burley,) were ever arrested, and both arrests were effected by the local authorities. Of the St. Albans Raiders *four* only have been arrested in Canada, and *none* in the United States. Of the eight said to have been engaged in the attempt to burn New York city one only was captured, and he (poor Kennedy!) while drunk, spilt a bottle of phosphoric fluid on the

thus reach Canada, and avail themselves of the security of
Clifton to await the Great Western train. All of the party
adopted this advice except Beall himself, and a boy named
George S. Anderson. This boy was an escaped prisoner, a
native of Pitsylvania County, Virginia, and one of Morgan's
men. Being young and inexperienced, he had been placed
especially under Beall's charge by Colonel Martin of the 14th
Kentucky Calvary, who was the leader of the raid from
which they were now returning. It was owing to his fidelity
to this trust that Beall was captured. He indeed waited on
the American side for the train, but upon its arrival was so
prompt that he had secured his seat, and the cars were nearly
ready to start when, missing the boy Anderson, he returned
to the waiting-room to look for him; he found him asleep
on a settee, and sat down a moment by his side, when an
officer attached to the train, cried out, *"All aboard going
East!"* when the two started for the door, but were suddenly seized by two policemen, Thomas and Saule. Had
resistance been possible, or had the chances for escape been
sufficient to justify the attempt, Beall no doubt would not
have surrendered without a struggle. He had upon his

---

floor of Barnum's Museum in broad daylight, in presence of one hundred
people! The whole burning party, be it remembered, came from Canada
in the same train, all being Confederates, and (what is still less credit-
able to Dix, Young, McDougall and Company!) all left New York in the
same manner, and reached Canada without interruption! Kennedy
returned to the United States, and, except him, the whole party escaped
arrest. The facts, when ventilated, therefore, prove that with the
exception of the interception of a few straggling and escaped prisoners, and the manufacture of an ingenious tissue of falsehoods in relation
to the assassination of the President, the Detective Corps in Canada
have done absolutely nothing. Their own countrymen, disgraced by
them, have been taxed to support a set of whiskey-drinking, utterly un-
reliable loungers, for the mere luxury of annoying not more the Southern
Refugees in Canada than all right feeling Canadians themselves, who
have felt justly indignant at what they have considered a violation of
the sacred right of asylum by a system of foreign espionage.

person his own faithful revolver, with which long practice and great natural steadiness of nerve had rendered him so expert, that an adversary at eighty yards had but little security against his deadly aim. On the present occasion, however, resistance to an officer whose cry for help would have summoned instantly a hundred by-standers, was clearly impossible, and Beall submitted with the best grace possible. He and his companiou were taken for escaped prisoners making their way to Canada, and this idea Beall encouraged, hoping thus to conceal his real identity.

Such were the circumstances of Beall's arrest; but the question remains—how came he on the soil of New York, and in the territory of the United States ? The story is soon told. *Raids* from Canada into the territory of the United States were the order of the day. Lieut. Bennet H. Young, at the head of ten or twelve Confederates, had ridden into the town of St. Albans, robbed one or more banks, attempted to fire the town, and finally galloped over the border into Canada. The raid on Lake Erie has already been described. The relations between Canada and the United States, were becoming more and more precarious. Major General John A. Dix, an officer of the United States army, who, though removed from the field in 1863, for real or supposed incompetency, is possessed of acknowledged administrative and police ability, was now in command of the " Department of the East," with head-quarters at New York city. Exasperated by the Erie raid, he was beside himself at St. Albans, and issued an order declaring that in all future cases the raiders should be *pursued across the border*, captured, and brought back to the jurisdiction of the outraged territory. This exasperated the Canadians in turn, and President Lincoln had to interpose, and rescind the obnoxious order. It was about this time that Beall, in conjunction with several escaped Confederate prisoners then in Toronto, conceived the plan of the raid which resulted in his capture as above described.

E

The party, however, when the scheme became ripe for execution, comprised many Canadians, and numbered in all from twenty-five to thirty persons. The scheme was to capture a military train on the New York and Erie Railroad, between Dunkirk and Buffalo, in the State of New York. The party was to rendezvous at or near Dunkirk, some proceeding thither directly by rail, and others were to cross Lake Erie in boats from the Canadian shore. Many disappointments ensued from the unfavourable weather, and other causes, and many of the party failed in getting to the rendezvous, being disheartened by repeated failures, or deterred by prudence and timidity. Finally the party dwindled down to five, who found themselves about the 10th of December, in and near Buffalo, and proceeded thence towards Dunkirk, and made an ineffectual effort to remove a rail from the track. Failing in this they crossed lake Erie, and proceeded to Port Colburn in Canada. The next night a second attempt was made, and a second failure ensued. On the third evening the party were again too late to fasten any effectual obstruction upon the railway; unfortunately for themselves at least, Col. Martin of the 14th Kentucky cavalry, who was in command, took an iron rail which he found, lying in the vicinity and fastened it upon the track. Scarcely has he done so, when the train is seen approaching; the party have only time to conceal themselves; nothing is broken, only a temporary stoppage occurs, and the train resumes its course. The raiding party get into their sleigh, return to Buffalo, and the next day proceed thence to the Suspension Bridge. The unfortunate accident by which Beall, to whom the boy Anderson had been committed by Col. Martin, was captured by over-fidelity to his charge, has been sufficiently dwelt upon. This poor frightened youth, on whose account Beall sacrificed his liberty, afterwards purchased his own life by the betrayal of that of his too faithful friend. We should not judge too harshly, however, of this treachery, under the cir-

MEMOIR OF JOHN YATES BEALL.

cumstances; Beall himself, though alluding to his betrayal in a letter written before his trial, did not speak harshly of its author, and in the end freely forgave him.

Thus on the 16th of December, 1864, we find Beall once again a prisoner in the hands of the Federal Government. His identity, however, is not established; the police officer who arrests him accuses him of being an escaped prisoner of war—" that," replies Beall—" I will acknowledge, —I am an escaped prisoner from Point Lookout." But this *équivoque de guerre* did not avail long to prevent his recognition, or identification. Anderson, as already related, informs the police officer, that he is " Captain Beall ;" it is remembered presently that the man who captured the Island Queen, and Philo Parsons, was called by a similar name, and other links in the chain of identity, are supplied from Canada, and elsewhere ; finally, Ashley, the clerk and part owner of the Philo Parsons, is sent for, and upon being confronted with the prisoner, fully identifies him as the leader of the Lake Erie raid.

First upon his capture, he was taken to the police headquarters in New York city ; here he remained from the 18th of September until the — day of January. His own diary, kept during his stay in this prison, furnishes the best account of his accommodations, companions, and frame of mind. This " little book " was taken from him by the authorities to be used as evidence against him on his trial; I deem it best to transfer it from the trial to this point in this imperfect memoir.

" I was arrested Friday, December 16th, in the New York Central Railroad station house, at the Suspension Bridge (junction with the Great Western Railroad of Canada). I was brought to this city Sunday evening (18th), and lodged here. I have been taken out some half a dozen times to be shown men, whose houses have been attempted by fire, or property otherwise attempted. The *modus operandi* is this :

The prisoner, unkempt, roughly clad, dirty, and bearing marks of confinement, is placed among well dressed detectives, and the recognizer is shown in. As a matter of course he can tell who is the stranger. My *home* is a cell about eight feet by five, on the ground floor. The floor is stone ; the walls brick ; the door iron, the upper half grated, and opens into a passage running in front of three other cells ; this passage is lighted by two large windows doubly grated, and has an iron door ; at night it is lighted with gas. The landscape view from my door, through the window, is that of an area of some 30 feet square. By special arrangement I have a mattress and blanket. There is a supply of water in my room, and a sink. My meals are brought three times a day, about 9, 3 and 7. My library consists of two New Testaments. I am trying to get a Book of Common Prayer. The first week there were brought to this place ten persons, charged with criminal offences : men, women, and children. At first I took an interest in their cases, but now I do not ; they all have been guilty, I believe, and they all wished me a speedy riddance. Nearly every one I have met with seems to regard society as his enemy and a just prey. They look on an offence simply as a skirmish. Profane, lying and thieving, what a people ! Nearly all recommend me to take the oath of allegiance, and enter the army and desert. But some are opposed to betraying comrades ('going back on 'em'), while others, more liberal, advocate any means as legitimate to save oneself from severe punishment. The Christmas of '64 I spent in a New York prison ! Had I, four years ago, stood in New York, and proclaimed myself a citizen of Virginia, I would have been welcomed ; now I am immured because I am a Virginian *tempora mutantur, et cum illis mutamus.* As long as I am a citizen of Virginia, I shall cling to her destiny and maintain her laws as expressed by a majority of her citizens speaking through their authorized channel, if her voice be for war or peace. I shall go as she says. But I would not go for a minority carrying on war in opposition to the majority, as the innocent will suffer and not the guilty; but I do not justify oppression in the majority. What misery have I seen during these four years, murder, lust, hate, rapine, devastation, war! What hardships suffered, what privations endured! May God grant that I may not see the like again! Nay, that my country may not! Oh, far rather would I welcome Death, *come as he might;* far rather would I meet him than go through four more such years. I can now understand why David would trust to his God, rather than to man.

"Since I have been placed in this cell I have read the Scripture, and have found such relief in its blessed words, especially where it speaks of God's love for man; how He loved him, an enemy, a sinner, and sent His Son into the world to save His enemy; how He compels the wretched from the hedges and highways to come in to the feast; how any may come, and how he bids them, entreats them. Though it may seem unmanly to accept offers in our adversity which we neglected in prosperity, yet it is even so that with His assistance I will go up and beg forgiveness, and put my trust in the saving blood of Him who died for man. Aye, I pray Him to grant His grace to my mother and sisters and my loved one. If He is with them, who can be against?

"What pleasure I take in the hymns I learned in boyhood! They come back to me now in my manhood and in my sorrow, and with God's blessing have wiled away and comforted many a weary and lagging hour.

"*Dec. 30th.* Last evening the doorman bought me a 'Book of Common Prayer' for $1.00, and it was and will be a source of great comfort to me. I read over the familiar services and oft-heard hymns, and committed two—'Rock of Ages,' and 'Sinners turn, why will ye die?'—to memory. There were four accused in the three cells last night. As yet I have heard but one give good advice to another. They all with one accord exhort one another to be good soldiers in warfare *vs.* society, not to give up stolen property ; and, above all, not to trust to the detectives, who are their natural and mortal enemies.   Such is life ! ! !

"*Dec. 31st.* The year is gone ; begun for me in ——— ; it sees me, as it dies, a prisoner in New York.   To-day I complete my twenty-ninth year.   What have I done to make this world any wiser or better ?   May God bless me in the future ; be it in time or eternity.   May I be enabled to meet my trials with resignation, patience, and fortitude, as one who serves his country and home and people.   The year went out in rain—drizzling rain.   Will I see the year 1865 go out ? or will I pass away from this world of sin, shame, and suffering ?

"*Jan. 1st.* 1865.   Sunday, first day of the week and first day of a new year.   To-day I enter my thirtieth year of pilgrimage.   According to the calculation of my father's family, I am more than half-way down life's stream, even if spared by war and sudden death.   But in prying into the future, I can see nothing to induce me to think that my days will be lengthened to that age of fatality, fifty-six.   Has my life been so crowded with pleasure or good deeds, that I need desire to prolong it ?   Alas ! no.   Though well reared, and surrounded with very many advantages, I have not done anything to give me particular pleasure ; nor, on the other hand, have I been remarkable for the opposite.   I am truly thankful that I always stayed with mother and the girls, and tried to do my duty by them ; that is one consolation at least, and also that I never voluntarily left them.   They know not where I am to-day ; and every one of them is this day thinking of me.   Little do they know where I am.   Indeed, I doubt if they have heard any thing definite from me for many a weary month.   Oh this war !

"This far on life's way I have lived an honest life, defrauding no man.   Those blows that I have struck have been against the society of a hostile nation ; not against the society of which I am a member by right, or *vs.* mankind generally.   To-day

the thought has obtruded itself again and again to become an
'Ishmael.' Your country is ruined, your hopes dashed—make
the best bargain for yourself. 'Remember the history of
the civil wars of France, of England—the examples of Talleyrand, Josephine, &c. ; of Shaftesbury, Carmarthen, Marlborough,' &c. To-day my hands have no blood on them
(unless of man in open battle) ; may I say so when I die. I
saw grandfather and father die ; they both took great comfort
from the thought that no one could say that they had of
malice aforethought injured them. Better the sudden death,
or all the loathsome corruption of a lingering life, with honour
and a pure conscience, than a long life with all material comforts and the canker-worm of infelt and constant dwelling
dishonour ; aye, a thousand times. O God, our Creator,
Preserver, and Saviour! I pray give me strength to resist
temptation, to drive back the thick-coming fancies brooded of
sin and dishonour, and to cling to the faith of Jesus, who said,
' Do unto others as you would that they should do unto
you.'

"*Jan. 2d.* Last night was called out, and a search made
of my room and my person. The captures consisted of two
knives. Poor Grimes! your gift and keepsake was duly
declared contraband and confiscated. They gave me two
newspapers, which do seem to bear out the statements of
Southern loss, &c. Savannah, indeed, is fallen ; but its garrison was saved, so that Hardee and Beauregard have an
army. And Butler did not take Wilmington, though the fleet
did storm long and heavy. Poor Bragg has some laurels at
last. Oh that Gen. Lee had 50,000 good fresh veteran
reënforcements! But what are these things to me here! I
do most earnestly wish that I was in Richmond. Oh for the
wings to fly to the uttermost part of the earth!

" What would I do without the Bible and Prayer-book, and
the faith taught in them, best boon of God, the fount of every
blessing ? That faith nothing can take away save God."

On the 5th day of January, Beall was removed from the Police Head-quarters to Fort Lafayette, 'a military prison situated 8 miles below New York City in New York Harbour. The ostensible cause of this removal was an attempt on his part to bribe the turnkey of the police prison, an account of which will be found in his trial. In regard to this attempt we may remark that Beall properly regarded himself as a prisoner of war ; as such he was held, and as such only was he tried, and condemned by a military Commission. He thought himself entitled therefore to effect an escape if practicable, and doubtless the subtlest of casuists will not feel disposed to dispute his right to use such means as he adopted to effect his object. Allowing for some little inaccuracies in the recollection of the turnkey, every statement made by Beall to him, the author knows, or has the highest authority for believing to have been true. The thousand dollars which he promised was a part of a mortgage for double that sum due him in Canada ; while the information worth $30,000 to the police authorities doubtless related to the arrest or conviction of certain parties for which the Federal government had offered $60,000. His conversations with the turnkey, although introduced as evidence against him by the prosecution, in reality illustrate the prudence and discretion of the man, and his fidelity to the cause which he had espoused, and for which he in the end sacrificed his life. Just before his death, speaking as a dying man, he said to a friend— " *Tell my friends in ——— that every secret of which I have been the depositary dies with me !*"

In the room in which he was confined on his removal to Fort Lafayette, were some four or five other Confederate prisoners, including Brig. Gen. Page, and Roger A. Pryor. The latter, it will be remembered, was captured by a *ruse de guerre* near Petersburg, which was so base in its character, that it has been asserted by the friends of Secretary Stanton, that even he disapproved it. A warm friendship sprang up between Beall and Pryor, and among his dying requests he desired a memento to be presented to Gen. Pryor.

While in this prison he occupied himself in preparing his own defence. What became of this production, which is said to have been most able and complete, is not positively known, though doubtless a very probable conjecture could be given if deemed important; at all events it has never been permitted to meet the public eye.

Beall was first arraigned for trial on the 20th day of January, 1865, before a military Commission, sitting at Fort Lafayette, consisting of six United States officers appointed by Major Gen. John A. Dix, commanding the Department of the East. He protested against being tried by any military Commission, though he did not object to any of the members thereof individually. His protest was entered on the record. When asked whether he was ready to proceed to trial, he rose, and in a manner perfectly composed and respectful, replied substantially as follows:

" I am a stranger in a strange land; alone and among my enemies; no counsel has been asssigned me, nor has any opportunity been allowed me either to obtain counsel, or procure evidence necessary for my defence. I would request that such counsel as I may select in the South be assigned me, and that permission be granted him to appear, and bring forward the documentary evidence necessary for my defence. If this can not be granted, I ask further time for preparation."

The application for Southern counsel, however reasonable it may appear, was referred to Gen. Dix, and by him at once refused; further time, however, was granted by the Commission for such preparation as a prisoner, confined in a dungeon, with irons on his wrists and ankles, and in whose behalf as yet not one friend had had the hardihood to step forward, could be expected to make. A report of the arraignment, and the prisoner's remarks appearing in the New York journals, was brought to the attention of the

author, whereupon the following letter was addressed to
Gen. Dix:

"TORONTO, C. W., January 26th, 1865.

MAJOR GEN. DIX,

    Commanding Department of New York, &c.,

    GENERAL,—I enclose you a slip copied from the *N. Y.
Herald,* January 19th, which has just met my eye.

I think it most probable that I am the 'Southern Gentleman' alluded to by Capt. Beall, as we are very dear friends,
and I am most likely to be the person whom he would desire
to assist him in preparing his defence. I have just arrived
here, and have come with no other purpose than to serve
Capt. Beall, if indeed he be your prisoner. I am a practising
lawyer of Richmond, Virginia. I have come here entirely
on my own responsibility, and at my own expense, and have
no connection of any sort, character, or description with the
Government of the Confederate States.

The Northern papers stated that Beall had been arrested
in Canada, and was to be tried here on a requisition by the
U. S. authorities under the *extradition treaty ;* it turned out
to be not Beall, but Burley, who was so arrested ; but *supposing it to be Beall* I came on here to defend him, and to
bring on documents absolutely essential to a fair trial. After
my arrival the inclosed slip attracted my attention.

I respectfully apply to you for permission (under such
restrictions of parol, &c., as you may think proper) to come
on to New York and appear for Capt. Beall, and to bring
with me such papers as I may deem pertinent to his case.

I again repeat that I am in no way whatever connected
with the Government of the Confederate States, nor are any
of their agents or representatives cognizant of my action in
this matter ; not being subject to military duty, I was free
to leave the Confederacy at will, and did so, prompted solely
by my desire to serve Beall, who has long been a bosom
friend ; and in response to an appeal from his widowed mother,
and his sisters.

Mr. George D. Prentiss, of the Louisville Journal, was allowed, under parol of both Governments, to attend the trial of his son before a Court Marshal in Abingdon, Va.; this precedent, and the firm conviction that you will not allow any man to suffer, while on trial under your jurisdiction, for want of opportunity to bring forward evidence so easily accessible, and for want of counsel who only awaits your permission to appear, encourage me to believe that you will respond favorably to my application.

If it be thought proper on your part to refer my application to the Department, or other authorities at Washington, I hope you will do so with a favourable endorsement. If the application be granted, please inclose me such authority as will enable me to obtain a passport, and inform me at what point I shall report to an officer who will parol me, or conduct me to your head-quarters if this be regarded as necessary."

[. .... Here follow some *references*, which were sufficient to indicate the character, and *bona fides* of the author, but which it is not now deemed necessary to insert.]

Of this letter Gen. Dix took no notice, and to it deigned no reply. If left to this humane and Christian officer, the trial would have proceeded without counsel, or evidence on behalf of the unfortunate officer on trial. It happened also that Gen. Dix had no need of reference to the parties, whose names from motives of delicacy are not inserted in the above extract, but to whom he was with confidence referred by the author; he (Dix) had in his own possession, intercepted, and not allowed, though in a manner intrusted to his sense of justice, to proceed on its mission in quest of evidence absolutely necessary to Beall's defence, the subjoined letter addressed to the author, which at once confirmed the truth of many statements made in the above letter, and fully avouched the good faith of its writer:

Exhibit A.

[One U. S. Stamp enclosed.]

FORT LAFAYETTE, N. Y., *Jan.* 22*d*, 1865.

Mr. D. B. LUCAS,

     173 Main St., Richmond, Va.

DEAR DAN,—I have taken up board and lodging at this famous establishment. I was captured in Decr. last, and spent Xmas in the Metropolitan Hd. Qrs. Police Station. I am now being tried for irregular warfare, by a Military Commission, a species of court.

The acts are said to have been committed on Lake Erie and the Canada frontier. You know that I am not a " guerrillero" or " spy." I desire you to get the necessary evidence that I am in the Confederate service, regularly, and forward it to me at once. I shall write to Cols. Boteler and Holliday in regard to this matter. I 'must have this evidence. As the Commission so far have acted fairly, I am confident of an acquittal. Has Will been exchanged ? I saw that Steadman had been killed in Kentucky. Alas ! how .they fall ! Please let my family know if possible of my whereabouts. Where is my Georgia friend? Have you heard any thing from her since I left ? May God bless her. I should like so much to hear from her, from home, Will, and yourself. Be so kind, therefore, as to attend at once to this business for me. Remember me to any and all of my friends that you may see.

    Send me some postage stamps for my correspondence.

      Hoping soon to hear from you,

          I remain your friend,

            J. Y. BEALL, *C. S. N.*

If Mr. Lucas is not in Richmond, will Mr. HUNTER ATTEND to this AT ONCE.

This letter, together with one addressed to Col. Jacob Thompson, a commissioner of the Confederate States at Toronto, Canada West, and another to Hon. Alexander R.

Boteler of Richmond, all of which were entrusted by Beall to the Commander of the Department, Gen. Dix, were held by order of the latter to be used against him on his trial, instead of being allowed to proceed on their way in quest of evidence most palpably of great importance to the defence. The other two letters referred to are in like manner abstracted from the published trial, and inserted here :

Exhibit B.

[I enclose a U. S. Stamp.]

FORT LAFAYETTE, N. Y., Jan. 22nd, 1865.
Col. A. R. BOTELER,
      Richmond, Va.

DEAR SIR,—I am on trial before a Military Commission for irregular warfare, as a " guerrillero" and " spy." The acts are said to have been committed on Lake Erie and at Suspension Bridge, in Sept. and Dec. last.

As I cannot in person procure any papers from Richdmond, I have to rely on my friends, and therefore I request you to procure evidence of my being regularly in service, and forward such evidence at once to me. I have also written to Messrs. Hunter and Lucas. Please call on them in regard to this, and also Mr. Henderson if necessary.

Very truly, your friend,

J. Y. BEALL, *C. S. N.*

Exhibit C.

FORT LAFAYETTE, N. Y., Jan. 22nd, 1865.
Col. JACOB THOMPSON,
      Toronto, C. W.

SIR,—I was captured in Decr., and am on trial before a Military Commission for irregular warfare, as a " guerrillero" and " spy." The acts are said to have been committed on Lake Erie and at Suspension Bridge, N. Y., in September and December last.

I desire to procure from my Government and its authorities evidence of my being regularly in service, and of having been acting under and by authority. Please procure and forward me, as soon as possible, certificates or other evidence confirming this fact.

The Commission so far have evidenced a disposition to treat me fairly and equitably. With the evidence you can send, together with that I have a right to expect from Richd. and elsewhere, I am confident of an acquittal.

Please attend at once to this, acknowledging at any rate the receipt of this letter.

Very respectfully,
J. Y. BEALL.

The world, and that future which will try, condemn, and crucify all of those heroes who, in the great civil conflict, shrank from the field of danger, and chose the safer position of police officer, jailor, tyrant, and military butcher at home, or hundreds of miles from the scene of conflict, should have on record the evidence that *Gen. Dix did not desire a fair trial to be accorded his prisoner ;* and no other proof of this fact is necessary than that which he himself has furnished in the suppression of these letters, and his refusal to allow the prisoner an opportunity to obtain such documentary evidence as his friends or his Government had in their possession.

It is proper to state further that Beall did succeed, through counsel, or otherwise, in communicating with Colonel Thompson, and that the latter responded, inclosing to General Dix, and also to Beall's counsel, a certificate from Lieut. Colonel Martin, who commanded the raiding party, in which the latter stated that the real object of the interception of the cars between Dunkirk and Buffalo was to release from their guard Confederate prisoners, viz., Brig.-Genls. Cabell, Marmaduke, and other officers, who were being transported from Johnson's Island to Fort Warren ; that he (Martin) did not explain the real object of the attack on the train to any of his command but his brother officer, Beall, but left the others to their own conjectures upon the subject. This certificate of Colonel Martin was not allowed in evidence by the Commission; nor had Beall opportunity to prove, as he could have done under the usual facilities for obtaining evidence, and preparing his defence, that when the train was stopped there was on board thereof the prisoners above mentioned, and that the want of time to make the obstruction effective, was all that prevented an attack upon the guard, and an attempt to release the prisoners; this latter fact was contained in the certificate of Colonel Martin already alluded to.

Thus, without counsel, and debarred from those opportunities for defence which, before civil tribunals, are allowed to those charged with the highest crimes known to the law, was Beall being hurried to his preadjudged doom. At this juncture James T. Brady, Esq., *although not permitted by law to receive any compensation for his services*, generously came forward, and undertook the defence. Those who had long admired the intellect, were now taught to appreciate, with equal admiration, the courage and generosity of James T. Brady. 'Tis something to be a great lawyer, but a much higher attribute to be a good man. This is a truth which history has continued to illustrate from the career of the first *Public Accuser* of the French Revolution to that of the present *Judge-Advocate-General* of the United States.

Printed with this volume will be found the authorized edition of the trial of the subject of this imperfect memoir, including Mr. Brady's defence, and the reply of the Judge-Advocate, and General Dix's orders for carrying out the sentence of the Commission. Any facts which I have stated additional to those elicited on the trial are given under a sense of responsibility as high as the oath administered by any tribunal could inspire.

CHAPTER V.

Last Hours and Death.

HAVING thus traced the career of John Yates Beall from the cradle to the bar of a military tribunal, from his birth to his condemnation to death, we approach now the last act in his dramatic life. Having exhibited no small degree of acquaintance with the " art of living," the question remains,—does he know how to die ? His doom is pronounced ; will his nerve give way ? Will he change his ground ? Thus far, the steadfast soldier of duty—will he now go over to the banner of policy ? A darer of death hitherto, will he now become a suppliant for life ? Will he purchase freedom for himself by divulging secrets which will expose his friends to imprisonment ? In fine, will he have the Spartan courage, with a hand not tremulous, and a cheek unblanching, to accept the crown of martyrdom which heaven or destiny holds out to him ?

What efforts have been resorted to to break his resolution and impair his will, we cannot in full relate. With his jailors, while under military authority, his friends have no particular cause of complaint. Every bastile has its own secrets ; and it may be difficult to justify the irons which manacled both the ankles and wrists of a military prisoner before any charges have been preferred against him, or even his identity fully established. It is certain, also, that the same expedient which shattered the nerves of Captain R. C. Kennedy,* and sent him into eternity blaspheming in the incipient stages of mania-potu, was tried upon Beall ; but the cup had no charm for him, and he waived it aside.

---

* Capt. Kennedy was executed for an alleged attempt to burn New York city.

Having been condemned by the Commission on the 8th of February, by order of General Dix, issued on the 14th, he was to be executed between the hours of 12 m. and 2 p. m., on the 18th of the same month. Accordingly, and with a view to his execution, he was removed from Fort Lafayette to Fort Columbus, the latter being situated on Governor's Island, immediately off New York city. Here he was placed in a dungeon, narrow and gloomy, in the interior of the fort. Into this cell no gleam of God's sun had ever penetrated. A little pine table was his escritoire. Papers were allowed to be brought him by the guard. Through the same channel he obtained writing material; while with books his friends supplied him. Over all fell his only light from the solitary gas-burner. His health, we have seen, was delicate; a suppurating wound is not a well of life, nor are Lafayette and Columbus very good *hôtels des invalides.*

It was thus under adverse circumstances that this soldier was subjected to his ordeal, and all but himself must have doubted his ability to sustain the test. Perhaps his mother, whom he dared not hope to see again, did not doubt that her boy would meet death in a manner higher than the "high Roman fashion."..............It was only on the 13th of February that he was notified of the finding of the Commission. At what period, during the four days which General Dix allowed him to prepare for death, he was notified of the order for his execution, I am not informed, nor under what circumstances this announcement was made. It was accompanied by a recommendation on the part of General Dix to the prisoner to make his will, and facilities were afforded accordingly. How he met the announcement has not been made public. We are at no loss, however, to infer his bearing from the account given by Mr. Brady, who saw him on the eve before his intended execution........There is a string in the human heart which the mother alone holds in her hand. The mother of Coriolanus touched it before the gates

F

of the Imperial City. Tiberius Gracchus felt it thrill when Cornelia exclaimed : " How long shall Rome know me only as the mother-in-law of Scipio !"......If Mr. Brady, therefore, had taxed his ingenuity or his deep skill in human nature to its utmost, he could not have hit upon a severer test of Beall's nerve than when—" after taking his hand, and bidding him farewell, he turned back as if he had forgotten something, and asked him if he (Beall) would favour him with the address of his mother, in order that he might communicate with her. He watched him keenly, but he saw no tremulousness of the fingers, no twitching of the nerves, and no emotion. But he had told me before this, ' I care nothing for the judgment of mankind, and nothing for the punishment I have to suffer, because *I know my mother thinks her son is right, and my sister will honour my memory.*' ".. ......All unconscious as Beall afterwards declared himself to be of the close, keen scrutiny of Mr. Brady, he still, as yet, betrayed no symptoms of fear—no tremulousness.

On this same evening, preceding the day first fixed for his execution, he occupied himself in writing farewell letters to his friends and relations.

The following to his faithful friend, James A. L. McClure, Esq., of Baltimore, was forwarded to President Lincoln, and is characteristic ; as also the succeeding one to his younger brother, a private in the " Stonewall Brigade."

FORT LAFAYETTE, 14th Feb., 1865.

MR. JAMES A. L. McCLURE,
          Baltimore, Md.,

DEAR SIR,—Last evening I was informed of the finding and sentence of the Commission in my case. Capt. Wright Rives, of Gen. Dix's staff, promised to procure you a copy of the record of my trial.

I am solicitous for you, who represent my friends, to have one, and to attach this statement to it : " Some of the evidence is true, some false. I am not a spy nor a guerrillero. The execution of the sentence will be murder:" and at a convenient season, to forward that record, and statement to my friends.

I wish you to find out the amount of the expenses of the trial, and forward it to me at once, so that I can give a check for the amount.

Capt. Wright Rives assured me that my friends could have my body. For my family's sake, please get my body from Fort Columbus after the execution, and have it plainly buried, not to be removed to my native State till this unhappy war is over, and my friends can bury as prudence, and their wishes may dictate.

Let me again thank you for your kindness, and believe me to be now, as in days of yore, your attached friend,

JOHN Y. BEALL.

FORT LAFAYETTE, Feb. 14th, 1865.

DEAR WILL,—Ere this reaches you, you will most probably have heard of my death through the newspapers; that I was tried by a military commission, and hung by the enemy; and hung, I assert, unjustly. It is both useless and wrong, to repine over the past. Hanging, it was asserted, was ignominious; but crime only can make dishonour. "Vengeance is mine, saith the Lord, and I will repay;" therefore do not show unkindness to the prisoners—they are helpless.

Remember me kindly to my friends. Say to them, I am not aware of committing any crime against society. I die for my country. No thirst for blood or lucre animated me in my course; for I had refused, when solicited, to engage in enterprises which I deemed destructive; but illegitimate; and but a few months ago I had but to have spoken, and I would have been red with the blood, and rich with the plunder of the foe. But my hands are clear of blood, unless it be spilt in conflict; and not a cent enriches my pocket.

Should you be spared through this strife, stay with mother, and be a comfort to her old age. Endure the hardships of the campaign as a man. In my trunk and box you can get plenty of clothes. Give my love to mother, the girls too. May God bless you all now and evermore, is my prayer and wish for you.

JOHN Y. BEALL.

The following extract from the eloquent letter of Albert Ritchie, Esq., to Mrs. Beall, which will be found published entire in the " Correspondence," furnishes a most interesting and reliable account of the unavailing efforts made in her son's behalf between the day first fixed for his execution, and the period when the final order therefor was carried into execution.

" On Wednesday morning preceding the day first fixed for the execution of his sentence, Mr. McClure, who had previously been permitted to see him at Fort Lafayette, received the information by telegraph of the finding of the Commission, and of the order to carry into execution the sentence on the following Saturday.

He immediately retained the professional services of Mr. Andrew Sterrett Ridgely, of Baltimore, for the purpose of having the case presented to the President, that he might procure if possible at first a respite, and then a commutation of sentence. Mr. Ridgely entered upon the case with the utmost possible zeal, and we three having passed the day, and most of the night in such preparation, as we deemed the emergency required, Mr. Ridgely went to Washington on Thursday morning. In the afternoon of Wednesday Mr. McClure received a telegram from Daniel B. Lucas, urging him to use every possible means, and spare no efforts to prevent the execution of the sentence. Several dispatches of a similar character were received from Mr. Lucas during the succeeding days.

On Thursday morning Mr. McClure received a letter from John in which he announced his conviction and sentence.*

. . . .

. . . .

This letter was answered by telegraph through Capt. Rives. —He instantly thought that nothing could give to the President a clearer idea of the polished character, and manly tone that John possessed, than the simple reading of this letter —and I went at once to Washington to have it presented through Mr. Ridgely. Mr. Ridgely, however, had returned to Baltimore before I reached Washington, so that I was obliged also to return the same night. We had immediately an interview with him, to ascertain the result of his visit, and efforts. He brought us no encouragement. Friends at Washington had interested themselves, and had appealed to the President even before Mr. Ridgely's arrival; and in his interview with that gentleman, he was positive in his determination not to interpose against the order, and judgment of Gen. Dix, with whom, without the active interference of the President, the case entirely rested.

At a late hour of the night we roused from his bed one of our personal friends, Mr. Francis L. Wheatly, a gentleman of influential associations in Washington, and told him that we wished him to go over in the morning. He responded with the most willing promptitude, and throughout the whole period of anxiety and effort, down to the last moment, manifested the utmost interest and zeal.

Mr. Wheatly and myself went to Washington on Friday morning. We there met at once with the co-operation of several gentlemen from New York, who had come on to Washington, representing the anxiety felt by a number of

---

* This letter having been given entire, Mr. Ritchie's abstract is omitted. See page 87.

their friends in the former city. Acting together we secured the additional professional services of Mr. O. H. Browning, Ex-Senator from Illinois, and an intimate personal friend of the President. In the meantime, we learned that many others, very few of the names of whom we were able to ascertain, had taken a deep interest in the case, and that several interviews had been had with the President. We learned, however, that among those who saw the President, were, Mr. Mallory of Kentucky, in company with several ladies, and Mr. Hendricks of Missouri. Mr. Browning, like Mr. Ridgely, entered upon the case not only with his professional ability, but with his personal feelings zealously enlisted. While he prepared in his office a statement to be laid before the President, we invoked the influence of our friends in Congress, and immediately placed in their hands an application asking a commutation of punishment. To this application we secured the names of more than ninety members during the day. The Rev. Dr. Bullock, of Baltimore, had also come over to use his influence in John's behalf. We heard through every hour of the day, also, of the interest manifested, and exertions made by others—strangers to us, and strangers to John, except so far as he was known to them by the appreciation they had formed of his character, and by those sympathetic ties which unite the generous, and high-toned, no matter what may be the differences of political or religious creed.

Late in the afternoon Mr. Browning, two gentlemen from New York, and myself went to the President.

Mr. Browning had an interview with him of more than an hour's length. He told us when he returned, that he felt assured the sentence would not be carried into execution on the next day; but could give us no idea of the probable period of the respite, which he thought would be granted.

Mr. Ridgely came over from Baltimore late in the evening, and in company with several other gentlemen who were deeply interested, we consulted, in Mr. Browning's office, in regard to the further measures it was desirable to adopt.

On Saturday morning, we received the gratifying intelligence, that a respite had been granted, but whether for any particular length of time, or indefinitely, we could not tell. Mr. Browning endeavoured to see the President during the day, that we might be informed in this particular, but was not successful. In our final interview with Mr. Browning, on Saturday afternoon, we asked to know fully and frankly his opinion of the prospect before us in endeavouring to secure a commutation of sentence. He told us that he had little hope that we would be able to accomplish more than the respite but added that if we could obtain the approval of Gen. Dix he felt assured the President would commute the sentence.

Mr. Wheatly and myself returned to Baltimore, leaving Mr. Ridgely in Washington with the assurance from him, and from Mr. Browning that nothing there should be left undone. From Baltimore, we immediately proceeded to have such measures taken in New York, and such considerations connected with the case presented to Gen. Dix, as would, we trusted, induce him to recommend, or, at least, approve a commutation.

On Monday morning, Mr. McClure went to Washington to advise with Mr. Ridgely, and Mr. Browning, while I remained here to procure letters to Gen. Dix, and to others, whose counsel and influence we deemed valuable, should it be found necessary to go on to New York. On Monday evening I received a telegram from New York which brightened our hopes ; on Tuesday evening, after the return of Mr. Ridgely and Mr. McClure another, which was discouraging. It was then thought best that I should go to New York to ascertain, if possible, the exact position of the case there, we having been still unable to learn the precise character of the respite.

Hearing at a late hour that you were in Baltimore, Mr.

McClure and myself at once endeavoured to find you, but only to learn that you had left the city. I went to New York on Wednesday night, and soon after my arrival Thursday morning, I was startled by the rumour that the sentence was to be carried into execution on Friday, the following day. The announcement was made, I believe, in but one of the morning papers, and in that one not officially. I immediately inquired at the office of that paper the authority upon which the statement appeared ; but receiving no clear information, went to the Head Quarters of Gen. Dix. I there found that the fact confirmed the rumour, and that the order actually had been issued. I presented my letters, and had an immediate interview with Gen. Dix, the result of which convinced me that as far as we relied upon him, " there was not"—in his own words—" a gleam of hope," and that there was no hope but in Washington. Other appeals to Gen. Dix continued, I believe, through the day, but I felt that my own personal resources were exhausted, and that I was helpless for the accomplishment of any other service than the discharge of those offices of friendship, which the most trying hours of our life require. Gen. Dix tendered me a pass very promptly, adding at the same time, that while he had been strict, in order to prevent intrusion, any one whom Capt. Beall wished to see, would be permitted to go to the Island.

I at once telegraphed to our friends in Washington the information I had received, and to Mr. McClure in Baltimore, telling him to send Mr. Ridgely and Mr. Wheatly to Washington, and himself to come on to New York, that we might both be prepared, when the last hope died, to carry out what had been our purpose from the beginning—which was, should it be impossible to arrest the coming of that hour, to at least share it with him if permitted. Those gentlemen went instantly to Washington, and in common, with many anxious and earnest friends, laboured to the last, as if for a brother or a son. Mr. John S. Gittings, of Baltimore, who, from the beginning had manifested the most active interest and kindest feeling in behalf of John, went in company with Mr. Ridgely. Mrs. Gittings, Mr. Montgomery Blair, and Mr. Ridgely called upon the President at a late hour on Thursday evening. The President, by his messenger, inquired of Mr. Blair the purpose of his visit, sending word at the same time that if it related to the case of Capt. Beall, he could not give an interview. Mr. Brady went on from New York Thursday night—Mr. Grafflin, of Baltimore, went also to Washington on Thursday afternoon. Mr. Brady, in company with Mr. Francis Blair and Mr. Stabler of Montgomery County, personal friends of the President, and Mr. Wheatly, called upon Mr. Lincoln at an early hour on Friday morning. There had already been two companies of gentlemen to see him on the same mission; whether they procured an interview or not, I can not say,—but Mr. Brady and the gentlemen with him were informed by the President's private secretary, that the case of Capt. Beall " was closed," and that he could not be seen any further in reference to it.

Mr. McClure, in company with Mrs. Basil B. Gordon, reached New York, from Baltimore, on Friday morning. Mrs. Gordon, at a very early hour, had an interview with Gen. Dix, and appealed to him in John's behalf, in the most earnest manner."......

It will thus be seen that no stone was left unturned to obtain a reprieve, and to the extent of a short respite these efforts were successful: during this respite every legitimate means was resorted to to influence the President or Gen. Dix, either of whom had the power to interpose between the sentence and its victim, but all intercessions were vain. For days before the execution the President closed the doors of the Executive palace against all suppliants, male or female, and his ears against all appeals, whether with the tongue of men or of angels, in behalf of his unfortunate prisoner.....
From the first Mr. Lincoln had responded to all applications

for his interposition,—" Gen. Dix may dispose of the case as
he pleases—I will not interfere"....Gen. Dix, on his part,
replied, " All now rests with the President,—as far as my
action is concerned there is not a gleam of hope !"...Thus
they stood as the pillars of the gallows, on which Beall's fate
was suspended, and between them he died....The credit, if
any, in resisting all appeals for mercy belongs jointly, in
whole or in part, to both; and in the same manner, the
infamy, if such attach to the execution, pertains in the same
undivided, indivisible estate to both....There was one
expedient which might have proved successful had it been
adopted : that was to have purchased the more influential
of the Republican journals of New York over in favour of
mercy.   There was one influence to which President Lincoln
never failed to yield when strongly directed against him—
the voice of his party; this he did upon principle, as the
head of a popular government....It was in response to such
partizan appeals that Fish, Ex-provost Marshal of Baltimore,
who on conviction of open and shameless bribery, and pecula-
tion was sentenced to the penitentiary, obtained pardon;
while Gen. Paine, found guilty before a military tribunal of
ontraging all the proprieties of war upon the persons, and
property of women, children, and other defenceless non-com-
batants, succeeded by similar means in propitiating executive
clemency....Unfortunately neither Beall nor his friends
belonged to the Republican party ; hence the doors of mercy
were closed against him.

At some period during the respite granted, Mrs. Beall
having come on from Virginia, had an opportunity of visiting
her son..............It would be an error to suppose, in
accordance with the current conjecture in the journals of that
day, that the respite was granted for the purpose of allowing
this opportunity to the heart-stricken mother. Its real object
was to give the Commission an opportunity to amend their
finding in accordance with a suggestion made to them by

Gen. Dix. The discovery of a supposed error, in regard to which it may still be doubted whether the Commission were not originally entirely right, and the Gen. commanding entirely wrong, was fortunate, inasmuch as it allowed Beall an opportunity to see his mother for the last time.

The character of this interview, which took place in the presence of officers, was naturally affecting, though both exhibited that degree of composed fortitude which might have been expected by those acquainted with their characters. The son derived from it great comfort, for, said he, " I saw the moment she entered the cell that she could bear it, and that it made no difference to her whether I died upon the scaffold, or fell upon the field." He gave her no ground to indulge the hope of final pardon for himself.......... " No !" said he, " they are thirsting for my blood !"....... And thus parted mother and son to meet again only in that realm where the changed and spotless are clothed in the transcendent beauty of immortal and incorruptible spirits.

Thus we find Beall in Fort Columbus, face to face with his doom, all hope extinguished, every avenue of mercy or escape closed. His friends tell him there is still a faint gleam of hope. He responds that he himself entertains none ; nor would he exchange, he declares, the penalty of death for the living death of perpetual or indefinite imprisonment ; he prefers an open grave to a vault.... .....Gen. Dix allows his friends to visit him freely.............Ministers of his own church bring him the holy unction of their message, and Catholic priests call on similar errands................On Thursday the 23rd, two of the latter are at the door of his cell just before his friend Mr. Ritchie asks admittance :— " If they come through sympathy," said Beall, " admit them, if through curiosity I do not care to see them." They were admitted, being holy men on a catholic errand....... The Rev. Joshua Van Dyke visits him on the day before his execution, and writes : " I found him to be all that you had described him, and much more. He was confined in a narrow and gloomy cell, with a lamp burning at midday ; but he received me with as much ease as if he were in his own parlour, and his conversation revealed at every turn the gentleman, the scholar, and the Christian. There was no bravado, no strained heroism, no excitement in his words or manner, but a quiet trust in God, and a composure in view of death, such as I have read of, but never beheld to the same degree before. He introduced the subject of his approaching end himself, saying that while he did not pretend to be indifferent to life, the *mode* in which he was to leave it had no terrors or ignominy for him ; he could go to heaven, through the grace of Christ, as well from the gallows as from the battle-field, or his own bed ; he died in defence of what he believed to be *right ;* and so far as the particular things for which he was to be executed were concerned, he had no confession to make or repentance to exercise. He did not use one bitter or angry expression towards his enemies, but calmly declared his conviction that he was to be executed contrary to the laws of civilized warfare. He accepted his doom as the will of God ....

"I left his cell," exclaims this distinguished divine,— "saying to myself—the chamber where the good man views his fate is privileged above the common walks of life !"

Dr. Weston, chaplain of the 7th New York regiment, visited him on the 18th of February, the day whence a respite deferred his execution, and Beall received him with "marked courtesy." He has a Bible, but no Prayer-book ; yet, (as he tells us in his diary), as early as December the 29th, the doorman of the Police head-quarters had bought him a "Book of Common Prayer for $1.00.".............

What then had become of it, that on the morning first appointed for his execution, he has no prayer-book ?.......

It is almost too sadly sacred to relate..........he had sent it, a gift of life from the hands of death, to his betrothed !

. . . . He does not tell Dr. Weston . . . . only the friend knows it, who has received it from his hand before the knowledge of the intervening reprieve.

His Bible has been obtained in prison ; upon opening it at random his eyes fall first upon these sublime verses : " For our light affliction, which is but for a moment, worketh for us a far more exceeding and eternal weight of glory, while we look not at the things which are seen, but at the things which are not seen : for the things which are seen are temporal, while the things which are not seen are eternal !"

He has written on the margin of his Bible several hymns, —old hymns which stand in relation to the prayer-book collection as the essential oil to the remainder of the plant : among them were, " Rock of Ages cleft for me !"—" Jesus, Saviour of my soul !" and

> " I would not live always,
> I ask not to stay !"

His friend, Mr. Ritchie, visits him on Thursday, the day preceding the execution. The jailor, Major Coggswell, U.S.A., exacts a promise that he will not furnish the condemned man with any instrument by which he can take his own life ; Mr. Ritchie relates this promise to Beall, who replies—(throwing his left foot over the right knee, and tapping it with his finger),—" In my left shoe here I have had all the time a little steel saw, with which I could have opened a vein at any moment, had I wished to do so—and I would like you to remind me of it in the morning."

This little saw, made of a steel watch-spring, and which was found on experiment to go through iron with rapidity and ease, was cut from between the double upper leathers of Beall's shoe after his death ; indeed, *two* of them were so found . . . . One of them his mother now has, the other his enemies . . . . *How they came there* is not a mystery, but a secret . . . . For what use destined, would have been

demonstrated, but for the *ice* encircling Fort Lafayette.
..........Thus the season, no less than the fates, opposed
Beall's deliverance.

The morning of the 24th of February opened fairly.   Mr.
Ritchie had spent the preceding night in the fort, and until
midnight had remained in the cell with Beall. On Wednesday
night he had slept soundly, and happy dreams of home
and childhood had visited him ; but on Thursday night, the
tooth-ache, to which he was subject, and with which he
was suffering when arrested, attacked him again, and to
some extent robbed him of his last night on earth. He would
have liked some laudanum, he said, to still the pain, but
declined to ask for it for fear of being misunderstood.......
Nothing, however, disturbed the tranquillity of his soul.

The execution was ordered between twelve and two......
Messrs. McClure and Ritchie were left in the cell with
the prisoner alone uninterruptedly for about an hour.......
this time was spent in calm, quiet, pleasant conversation
.......Old friends were inquired after..   ..old scenes
recalled......and the circumstances connected with his own
participation in the raids upon Lake Erie, and on the Dunkirk
and Buffalo railway are gone over......At some passages in
these conversations he rubbed his hands, (an old familiar
habit), and laughed in his old gleeful manner......this was
more than self-possession—it was absolute cheerfulness.....
He spoke of his approaching death, and gave directions for
the disposition of his body.. ...dictated his epitaph, which
was to be—" *Died in defence of his country!*"........
As the hour waned, McClure looked at his watch ; Beall
noticed the movement, smiled, and inquired the hour......
it was after 12......The execution, by the order, was to
be carried out between 12 and 2......his voyage was therefore rapidly drawing to a close......the sails could be seen
coming up from the under-world.......Destiny was making

the last entry in the log-book of life......the harbor, and the steeples of the city were in sight.

Very soon Major Coggswell came in to bid his prisoner farewell ; this officer himself had once been held in Richmond as a hostage, with the sword of Damocles above him, and he could therefore sympathise with a soldier under similarly trying circumstances......like all around him also he had been drawn into the magnetic circle of Beall's friendship.

After partaking of some nourishment, which Dr. Weston and Mr. McClure shared with him, Beall is left alone with his spiritual adviser and attendant : after him the officers of the law enter, and mantle him with the sad paraphernalia of death—intended to be ignominious, but with such a soul beneath it absolutely radiant, and luminous with light......
While the officers are performing their mournful duty, Beall addresses them : " All I ask," said he, " is that there be no unnecessary consumption of time in the execution ; for after all it will be to me but a mere muscular effort !"

His friends return to find him hooded, and a black mantle thrown over his shoulders. Mr. McClure, not observing that his hands are fastened behind him, offers his hand. " I can not shake hands" said he, smiling—" I am pinioned !"

His picture presented the reader was taken three hours before his death. He had dressed himself upon this morning with unusual care and neatness......his linen was white and clean, and his black silk cravat was gracefully tied beneath a rolling collar. He wore a new pair of dog-skin gloves of saffron colour.....just the extremities of his fingers protruded from the military blue-black cloth cape which some officer had considerately thrown over his shoulders, and which entirely concealed the manacles on his wrists, and the circle of death about his neck......Upon his head was placed the fatal cap ; but the bag with its long tassel fell gracefully and romantically to one side, while in front it was rolled up turban-like above the brows... .....its blackness lent additional lustre

to the whiteness of the martyr-face beneath it......this face, naturally colourless, was blanched by long and solitary confinement....it was smooth, white and almost transparently clear....the humors of the eye, whose tell-tale congestion always betrays weeping, restlessness, or nervous agitation through the night, bore now a different testimony....they were as white, as seamless as an infant's.....as he stepped from the threshold of his cell they began to beam, until (in the language of a friend from whom this description is taken) they shone with an "unusual, and unearthly splendour"....
As he passed out he turned to Messrs. McClure and Ritchie, and said—"Good-bye, Boys,.....I die in the hope of a resurrection, and in defence of my country!"

His friends Messrs Ritchie and McClure are admitted to his cell, as Dr. Weston, the minister appointed to attend him in his last moments, is leaving it.....he has partaken of the sacrament of the body and blood of Christ.

Mr. Ritchie has remained all night with him....Mr. McClure has never seen him since his removal from Fort Lafayette....When McClure asked permission of Genl. Dix to visit the prisoner, the General demanded to know why he wished to see him. Mr. McClure explained that they were old college-mates, and long-tested intimate friends; taking advantage of this opening he gave to the Federal General the truth as to the prisoner's principles, position, morals and general worth, blending the whole account in the warmly tinted colours which friendship in this instance had a double warrant to employ......When he had concluded, the General replied...."I believe him, sir, to be all that you have stated, —and something more,—he is a *Christian*."

"And how, General, did you learn this?"

"I have his Diary," responded the General.

Gen. Dix did not hesitate, therefore, to allow Mr. McClure to visit Fort Columbus. He arrived about eleven o'clock. The gallows was erected on a gentle slope at the lower extremity of Governor's Island, facing to the South, within one hundred yards of the sea ; it was a contribution from the civil authorities.....on it they had executed a negro for murder (Hawkins), a Yankee slave-trader (Gordon), and a pirate (Hicks)......the civil magnates envied the military the éclat of a political executioner, and contributed an instrument of death which would, as they supposed, lend its ignominy to the victim ; just as the Jews imagined the cotemporaneous execution of thieves would add to the shame of the Crucifixion........That nothing might be wanting to make the execution *national*, that is, characteristic of the nation, the gallows itself was a specimen of Yankee mechanical ingenuity : " There was no drop, but a chair was placed directly under the rope, which ran through an aperture, and along a groove or series of pullies in the beam above, the other end falling into a rude box, or shanty where it had connection with a heavy weight, which by the severance of a subordinate line would bring the noose up with a swift jerk to the top of the gallows-tree. Up and down in the interior of the inclosure containing the weight paced the man whose business it was to cut the short line, [supporting the weight], at the signal." ......The executioner himself was no ordinary Abhorson.. ....he was (it is stated) a *deserter*, long confined on the Island, whose pardon was promised as a reward for the faithful discharge of the hangman's office.........It is to pourtray the temper of the times, to commemorate the genius of a people, that History demands these details.....they are due to the executioners, not to the victim....for the latter the memory of his character, and the lesson of his martyrdom were sufficiently preserved by the simplest recital of the manner in which he " fell to sleep."

At a little past one o'clock the cortège passed out of the stern, arched sallyport of Fort Columbus ; the order of the procession was as follows :

G

Front.

Right.   LIEUT. TALLMAN,   *Left.*
          Provost Marshal of Governor's Island.

Company ⎫   *Centre.*   ⎧ Company
          ⎬   THE PRISONER.   ⎨
   of   ⎬   REV. DR. WESTON.   ⎨   of
          ⎬   MARSHAL MURRAY,   ⎨
Regulars. ⎭   and   ⎩ Regulars.
                 Aides.

The other prisoners of the Fort were ordered to their cells.
and the doors of the Fort were closed......The band struck
up the death-march, and the solemn procession moved forward.

Beall caught the step of the regulars, and moved with
them ; he was a soldier, and knew how to keep step even to
music of his own death-dirge ...... But his step was lighter
than that of the heavy soldiers....it was as light, as free, as
tameless as Tell's in the mountains of Switzerland.....as
proud and firm as McGregor's on the skirts of Ben Lomond
......Here was no malefactor at all .....Here was a groom
leaping to the bridal-chamber......or a conqueror passing
under the triumphal arch of an ovation !

Suddenly, upon a little eminence overlooking the spot and
instrument of execution, the procession calls a halt. What
does it mean ? The victim's face is turned full upon the
gallows......and upon the rough pine coffin at its foot....
....." *Oh ! this, this is cruel, and cowardly !* " exclaims one
of his two faithful friends who are following afar off. Beall
might avert his face....but he is a soldier, and will not do
it. For *nine solid minutes* by the watch is he kept face to
face with the gallows.........*tête-à-tête* with his own
coffin.

For once,—just for a second, or a fraction of a second,
there is a change in his countenance....... he had asked
only that there might be no unnecessary delay...... here

is an unexplained, an apparently causeless, a probably wanton delay..........for a single instant the thought sinks
in his heart of love, and the waters from the fountains of
bitterness well up to his face.   However, it is the last struggle—the articulus mortis—the death-spasm of the natural
man......it is nature turning back on philosophy......
sin's farewell ejaculation on the cross of faith.   There was
at all times something very stern—something " mysterious "
(as the friend expressed it who witnessed it on this occasion),
in Beall's frown......but now this expression is so transient,
so momentary that it escapes the priest, and all the reporters ;
only the friend who knows him so well detects it.   There is
no discomposure, no blanching, no dismay, no revived hope
of life, no relaxation of indifference to death, depicted in this
brief change of expression......it is simply the dislocation
of a smile.   For eight minutes and fifty-nine seconds, that
this unaccountable and unaccounted for suspense lasts, the
face of the victim, as the sea breeze sports up and down the
tassel of his picturesque cap, is serene, and peaceful. 'The
eager multitude who, to the number of from three hundred
and fifty to five hundred, had assembled to witness the execution, are appalled at this delay......But now Beall himself no longer regards it ; he does not see the crowd around
him.......once or twice he has smiled at their eager
curiosity ....now he no longer sees them at all.
.....He asks the direction of Fort Lafayette, remarks
that he has many kind friends there......he looks
smilingly over the gibbet across the waters of the Bay to
the hills of Staten Island, and the mountains of New Jersey
beyond......thence to the soft, blue sky on which they are
projected......and finally up to the glorious god of day
himself; then he exclaims—" *How beautiful the sun is!
I look upon it for the last time!*" ....There is heroism
in his mien, romance in his attire and appearance, religion in
his smile of peace ; and this exclamation is an inspiration
from nature—it is poetry itself.

Again the march is resumed, and the victim passes into the hollow-square around the scaffold. Before stepping upon it he turns with a smile to Dr. Weston, and remarks, "*As some author has said, we may be as near God on the scaffold as elsewhere !*" He may be thinking of the sainted Abbott of Aquila, " who wished to be buried under a gallows, and it was done."

Mounting to the platform, the prisoner takes his seat upon the chair immediately under the fatal rope. The adjutant of the post, (Lt. Keiser of the 2nd U. S. Infantry), commences to read the charges, specifications, and the orders of General Dix for his execution. Beall, little dreaming of the test to which he is to be subjected, rises respectfully when the reading is commenced ; but finding that, instead of the *last*, and briefest order for his execution, the whole prolix, and unmilitary, and unsoldierly pronunciamento of General Dix is to be gone through with,—he deliberately draws up a chair with his foot, and resumes his seat. When he hears himself designated as a citizen of the—" *Insurgent* State of Virginia "—his smile grows intensely sad and significant; he sees now the men before him no longer as his own murderers only, but as the executioners of a sovereign State—his own beloved Virginia, and he smiles not in derision, but in protest and remonstrance........Again when they denounce his heroic attempt to rescue from a vault the souls of three thousand fellow-soldiers—" *piracy,* " he smiles ; but when they accuse him of an attempt as a " guerrillero " to " destroy the lives and property of peaceable, and unoffending inhabitants of said State" (New York), he ceases to smile, and mournfully shakes his head in denial. But finally, when the adjutant reaches the concluding passages of the order, in which General Dix descants thus :

" The Government of the United States, from a desire to mitigate the asperities of war, has given to the insurgents of the South the benefit of the rules which govern sovereign

States in the conduct of hostilities with each other; and any violation of those rules should, for the sake of good order here, and the cause of humanity throughout the world, be visited with the severest penalty. War, under its mildest aspects, is the heaviest calamity that can befall our race; and he who, in a spirit of revenge, or with lawless violence, transcends the limits to which it is restricted by the common behest of all Christian communities, should receive the punishment which the common voice has declared to be due to the crime. The Major General commanding feels that a want of firmness and inflexibility, on his part, in executing the sentence of death in such a case, would be an offence against the outraged civilization and humanity of the age"—

Beall laughs outright; it is at this point that the reporters declare that the "prisoner seems to be reminded of some amusing incident in his military experience "......the reporters do not understand the joke......the truth is, Beall hears this homily upon the proprieties of War *coming from a Federal Officer! He* hears it, whose home is in the Valley of the Shenandoah! There rises up before him his own homestead......its desolated fields......its level forests......the ash-heaps which now mark the positions of its once beautiful, and cottage-like out-houses; and the thousand other vestiges of rural beauty despoiled by the brutality of Federal soldiers, in its unrestrained career of pillage, plunder, wholesale robbery, and wanton destruction.....he hears the protests of his helpless mother, and her appeals for protection heeded only by the God of the widow, and fatherless......he remembers the deep burning insults which Federal officers have heaped, in their language, upon his own sisters. He hears in the hypocritical cant of General Dix that officer's own self-condemnation; and knows that every breath which the commanding General draws is in default of the penalty which he himself attaches to the violation of the laws of civilized warfare........He hears a sermon on the

" rules which govern sovereign States in the conduct of hostilities with each other," by the man who, through his unlicensed, ill-disciplined, unrestrained, and unpunished soldiery, laid in ashes William and Mary College,—an institution whose associations were hallowed by the literary nurture of the fathers of the Republic, and whose venerable walls were whitened by the frosts of a century.......a General who, after an arduous campaign, succeeded in capturing a lunatic asylum, and who is *said* to have tendered to its patients the oath of loyalty to the United States, and who is *known* to have treated its refractory and unfortunate inmates with cruelty and inhumanity........a profound publicist, whose knowledge of international law, and regard for international obligations, have been illustrated by his celebrated Canadian Order, which a prompt repeal by the President alone prevented from resulting in a war with Great Britain! No wonder that Beall laughs outright, when this doughty warrior, whose only ambition has been to vie with the hero of Big Bethel, and Fort Fisher in the infamy of being the Del Carretto of the Revolution,—delivers a lecture to a man upon the scaffold, on the mitigation of the asperities of war, and appeals to " the civilization, and humanity of the age "!....
..Even the executioner himself grows impatient, and can not endure this ordeal: " *Cut it short! cut it short!*" cries he— " *the Captain wishes to be swung off quick*" ! The crowd murmurs, and the reporters call his eagerness to perform his office—" *brutality*".....they mistake—he means it in mercy and kindness........he is protesting *against* brutality.

The reading over, Beall promptly rises, and announces his readiness : then reverently turning towards Dr. Weston, bows his head, while over him falls, from the lips of the minister, like a spotless mantle, the inspired benediction of his Church's ritual—" The grace of our Lord Jesus Christ, the love of God, and the fellowship of the Holy Spirit, be with you and sustain you ! "

His manner has been throughout one of respectful attention; but when he mounts the scaffold, and sits down under
the fatal coil, he *turns his back* upon the adjutant while he is
reading, and faces in the opposite direction . . . . this attitude he does not change . . . . What does it mean ? . . . .
His face is turned upon his own beloved South! Far over
waters, mountains, valleys, and intervening hills, through the
deep azure sky, travel his thoughts to the land of tobacco, and
cotton,—of orange and palmetto, of moss and magnolia,—
of chivalrous deeds, and political ideas, which, rightly understood, gather in their scope the eternal years of God's own
truth, and for which no man should hesitate to die! . . . . .
As the martyr sets his face towards Jerusalem, or the Mussul-
man toward the shrine of Mecca, so this hero, dying for the
faith of his fathers, turns his face upon the South. Thus he
faces when the last duty save one of the executioner is performed ; and while standing thus, the provost-marshal asks
him whether he has anything to say. Turning upon the
officer of the day, he speaks in a calm, firm voice :

"I protest against the execution of this sentence. It is
a murder! I die in the service and defence of my country!
I have nothing more to say."

A moment afterwards a sword-flash is seen behind him,
which is the signal to the executioner, and the soul of the
hero springs upward with his body.

Thus died in the thirty-first year of his age, on the scaffold, John Yates Beall. Shameless women, who had long
lost the sense of an emotion, save the curiosity which brought
them to the island on this occasion, were now awed by the
grandeur of this death . . . . rough "machines" (regulars), rebuked this title by the tribute of a silent tear ; while
Federal officers, some of whom would have given a right arm
to have saved this heroic life, were not ashamed to weep
freely, tears both of pity and admiration.

His body, when dead, was given to his two faithful friends

whose devotion had halted at no sacrifice in their efforts to
save him while living, and they laid it privately to rest in
Greenwood Cemetery, near New York city. Dr. Weston
read the burial service of the Episcopal Church, and poured
over the dead hero the full-tide flood of inspiration which
flowed from the lips of Paul as he described the victorious,
stingless, and eternal triumph of those who " die in the hope
of a resurrection." . . . .
. . At this moment, on Fern Hill, in Greenwood, a plain
marble slab is to be seen inscribed—" John Y. Beall, died
February 24th, 1865 "—marking a green turf *covered daily
by the hands of strangers with fresh, blooming flowers.*

For the cause of his death the nation which took his life,
may differ with the world as to its justification ; as to its
manner, they themselves have given the testimony, that it
was one of the sublimest spectacles ever witnessed. As a
huge telescope gathers in its lens the half of heaven, so
this death brings down half of history in its grandeur ; it
adds Phocion to St. Stephen, Curtius to Marshal Ney . . .
in reading it, the Englishmen thinks of André, the Irishman
of Robert Emmet, the Frenchman of Eustache de St. Pierre
. . . . " Tell my mother," said he, a few moments before
his death, " That you saw her son die without bravado, and
without *craven* fear !" Here was confidence, for the hour
of trial was not yet over ; here was modesty, for he does not
disclaim fear . . . . Well might Dr. Vandyke exclaim that
he had read of heroes, but never before had he seen one !
. . . . While James T. Brady declares, " I never before
saw a human being whose composure in meeting his doom
was equally perfect, while at the same time he displayed
nothing of the bravo."

His death-scene exhibits courage without bravado, tenderness without weakness, resignation without stoicism, a protest
against the murder, without resentment against the murderers ; it united to ease dignity, to manliness a sense of respon-

sibility, composure to freedom ; it combined at once firmness,
self-possession, inflexibility, patience, intellectuality, fortitude,
cheerfulness. It was all that his friends could hope, or Christianity demand ; all that his country could be proud of in
chivalry, or his enemies dread in the example of martyrdom.

Standing on the brink of the grave, he turned a pale, pure
face full and persistently upon his native land ; nature herself, as if catching the thought, indulged its tenderness, and
flattered its grandeur ; for though the wind was blowing,
and the cord twisting, the dying face, and the dead face, as
the living had done, turned still upon the South ; the very
breeze of heaven, and the gravitation of the Earth combined
to immortalize the poetry,—the profound sentiment of his
death.

For twenty minutes Beall's lifeless body hung facing to
the South ; and for twenty minutes might History point to
his corpse, and say—" there hangs a man who died for
Liberty ; there perished a man who espoused a great principle taught him by his fathers, and being baptized into it
with the baptism of blood and fire, died for it bravely, and
without one tremor ; there has expired a soldier who bears upon
his breast the rose of the legion of honour *cicatrisé* by a minnie
ball ; who, a prisoner on the Chesapeake, was chained at
Lafayette, and embraced the manacles as badges of honour ;
—who ' fought with beasts ' at Harper's Ferry under Turner
Ashby, and marched through the Shenandoah Valley, under
Stonewall Jackson in the Immortal First Brigade . . . . . there
is suspended a Christian, who under a sentence of death
which he believes to be unrighteous, and whose execution he
believes will be murder, writes to his brother:—" ' Vengeance
is mine saith the Lord—I will repay' ; therefore do not be
unkind to prisoners—they are helpless " . . . . . . there is a
patriot who died in the service and defence of his country . . . . .
there a philosopher who could anatomize death, and pro-
nounce it a ' mere muscular effort ! ' "

If this man were wrong, he perished at least on the side of *defence*, and in obedience to the voice of his State whom his fathers had taught him it was religion to obey; neither he nor his State asked aught *but to be let alone;* and dying thus, he perished nobly and bravely. But if this man were right, and his executioners wrong...... Oh! *If* he were right! Woe, woe to his executioners! Woe! woe! to those who rendered these things possible! They are now but sowing to the wind—the whirlwind sleeps in the caves of the deep, and in the hollows of the mountains. The children of Anarchy are never let loose alone. These architects of a national Babel must soon cease to understand each other;— these graspers after continental empire, now insolent with victory, must one day learn what History has failed to teach them, that Republics cannot afford aggression; that no principle of cohesion but their own volition can hold together the members of a free Confederation; and that our National Mother Rachel can not survive, while her sons are encouraged to struggle in the womb!

When these lessons have been taught, and Virginia, conquered now in all but her soul, shall again become free, then, from his tomb in Greenwood will some freeman reverently lift the dust of John Yates Beall, and bearing it back from the banks of the Hudson to those of the Shenandoah, carry the urn to his mother, that she may write upon his tomb— " Died in the service, and defence of his country!"

Till that time let him sleep among his foes; History will claim his memory as God has his spirit; and devout pilgrims from every clime, kneeling at his shrine, will sing with the poet:

" What is worth living for is worth dying for too,
And therefore all honour, brave heart, unto you
Who have fallen, that freedom, more fair by your death,
A pilgrim may walk where your blood on her path,
Leads her steps to your grave!
         Let them babble above you!
Sleep well! where no breath of detraction may move you,
And the peace the world gives not is yours at the last."

PROCEEDINGS

IN THE

CASE OF JOHN Y. BEALL.

———o———

SPECIAL ORDERS,
> No. 14.
>> HEADQUARTERS DEPARTMENT OF THE EAST,
>> NEW YORK CITY, Jan. 17th, 1865.

6. A Military Commission, to consist of the following named officers, will assemble at Fort Lafayette, N. Y. H., at 11 a.m., on Friday, January 20th, 1865, or as soon thereafter as practicable, for the trial of such cases as may be brought before it, by orders from these Headquarters, to sit without regard to hours, and to hold its sessions in New York city, if the convenience of the service require it; four members to constitute a quorum, for the transaction of business.

DETAIL FOR THE COURT.

Brig. General FITZ HENRY WARREN, U. S. V.
      "   W. H. MORRIS, U. S. V.
Colonel M. S. HOWE, 3d U. S. Cav.
    " H. DAY, U. S. A.
Brev. Lieut. Col. R. F. O'BIERNE, 14th U. S. Infant.
Major G. W. WALLACE, 6th U. S. Infantry.
Major JOHN A. BOLLES, A. D. C., is appointed Jge. Adv.
By command of Major Gen. Dix.
D. T. VAN BUREN,
Assistant Adjutant General.

FORT LAFAYETTE, NEW YORK HARBOUR,
11 o'clock a.m., Friday, Jan. 20th, 1865.

The Commission constituted and convened by the foregoing order, met in obedience thereto.

Present, all the members, namely :

Brig. General FITZ HENRY WARREN, U. S. V.
"   W. H. MORRIS, U. S. V.
Colonel M. S. HOWE, 3d U. S. Cav.
Colonel H. DAY, U. S. Army.
Brev. Lieut. Col. R. F. O'BIERNE, 14th U. S. Infantry.
Major G. W. WALLACE, 6th U. S. Infantry.

Present, also, the Judge Advocate, and JOHN Y. BEALL, the accused, who was brought in for trial.

The foregoing order was read aloud in presence and hearing of the accused ; and he being asked if he objected to any member named in the detail, answered that he did not, but that he desired to protest against being tried by any Military Commission.

In presence and hearing of the accused, the Commission was then duly sworn by the Judge Advocate, the Judge Advocate by the President, and JAMES E. MUNSON as Stenographer and Clerk to the Commission, by the Judge Advocate.

The Judge Advocate inquired of the accused if he was ready to proceed to trial, and he answered that he was not, but desired time to procure counsel and prepare for his defence. At his request the Commission granted him until 11 o'clock a.m., Wednesday, January 25th, and the trial was postponed accordingly.

The Commission then adjourned to meet to-morrow, January 21st, at the Department Headquarters, New-York City, at 12 o'clock m., for the purpose of commencing the trial of Harris Hoyt.

JOHN A. BOLLES, Maj. and A. D. C.,
Judge Advocate.

FORT LAFAYETTE, NEW YORK HARBOUR,
11 o'clock a.m., Wednesday, Jan. 25th, 1865.

The Commission met pursuant to adjournment. Present, all the members.

Present, also, the Judge Advocate, and the accused, John Y. Beall, who was brought in for trial.

The record of the proceedings of January 20th was read by the Judge Advocate, and approved.

The Judge Advocate asked the accused if he was ready to proceed to trial, to which the accused answered that he had written for counsel ; that he had handed the letter to Colonel Burke, but had received no answer.

The Judge Advocate said that the letter referred to by the accused was delivered to him on the 20th of January, by Colonel Burke ; that he carried it that day to Mr. Brady's Office, it being addressed to that gentleman ; that Mr. Brady being out, he handed it to Mr. Traphagen, who said that if it was possible Mr. Brady would attend to the case ; if not, Mr. Brady or he (Mr. Traphagen) would endeavour to procure competent counsel to come down and consult with Capt. Beall ; and he then wrote a pass for Mr. Brady, or any other member of the bar, to visit the fort at any and all times, as counsel for Capt. Beall, and that he had this morning received the following note from Mr. Brady :

January 23, 1865.

Major JOHN A. BOLLES,

MY DEAR SIR,—I am very much obliged to you for your courtesy and consideration in regard to the case at Fort Lafayette. Unfortunately the trial I have in the Superior Court has commenced, and I must attend to it from day to day. I have sought to procure other counsel for Mr. Beall, but cannot at present obtain any whom I can in all respects commend. I trust it may not be inconsistent with the public interest to postpone the trial at

Fort Lafayette for a week. I send this by my friend William H. Ryan, Esq.

Yours truly,

JAMES T. BRADY.

Mr. Ryan being present, the Commission inquired of him if Mr. Brady would be able to be present and act as counsel for the accused, in case the trial were adjourned for one week ; and Mr. Ryan answered that he would.

The Judge Advocate exhibited to the accused three letters which purported to come from him, and which were addressed to persons in Toronto, Canada West, and in Richmond, Va., and informed the accused that, if he would reduce to writing in the form of an affidavit a statement of the facts he expected to prove by the persons or documents named in those letters, he should probably admit that the witnesses or documents, if presented in Court, would so say, and thus save the Government the delay, and the accused the trouble and expense of getting them here.

The accused stated that he wrote the letters, and that he would prepare the statement suggested, and so far as Mr. Brady was concerned, would be ready for trial on Wednesday, February 1st.

On motion of a member of the Commission, the application of the accused for delay was granted, and the trial was postponed until Wednesday at 11 o'clock a.m., February 1st, 1865, with the understanding that at that time the trial should proceed.

The Commission then adjourned until to-morrow, January 26th, at 12 o'clock m., to meet at Department Headquarters for the transaction of other business.

JOHN A. BOLLES, Major and A.D.C.,

Judge Advocate.

FORT LAFAYETTE, NEW YORK HARBOUR,

11 o'clock a.m., Wednesday, Feb. 1st, 1865.

The Commission met pursuant to adjournment.

Present all the members.

Present, also, the Judge Advocate, and the accused John Y. Beall, who was brought in for trial.

By leave of the Commission James T. Brady, Esq., appeared as counsel for the accused.

The Judge Advocate inquired of the accused if he was ready to plead to the charges and specifications, and the accused answered that he was.

The accused was then arraigned on the following charges and specifications, which were read aloud in his presence and hearing, and to which after they were so read the accused pleaded that he was not guilty.

CHARGES AND SPECIFICATIONS AGAINST JOHN Y. BEALL.

CHARGE 1st. *Violation of the laws of war*.

Specification 1. In this that John Y. Beall, a citizen of the insurgent State of Virginia, did on or about the 19th day of September, 1864, at or near Kelley's Island, in the State of Ohio, without lawful authority, and by force of arms, seize and capture the steamboat *Philo Parsons*.

Specification 2. In this that John Y. Beall, a citizen of the insurgent State of Virginia, did on or about the 19th day of September, 1864, at or near Middle Bass Island, in the State of Ohio, without lawful authority, and by force of arms, seize, capture, and sink the steamboat *Island Queen*.

Specification 3. In this that John Y. Beall, a citizen of the insurgent State of Virginia, was found acting as a spy at or near Kelley's Island, in the State of Ohio, on or about the 19th day of September, 1864.

Specification 4. In this that John Y. Beall, a citizen of the insurgent State of Virginia, was found acting as a spy on or about the 19th day of September, 1864, at or near Middle Bass Island, in the State of Ohio.

Specification 5. In this that John Y. Beall, a citizen of the insurgent State of Virginia, was found acting as a spy on or about the 16th day of December, 1864, at or near Suspension Bridge in the State of New York.

Specification 6.　In this that John Y. Beall, a citizen of the insurgent State of Virginia, being without lawful authority, and for unlawful purposes, in the State of New York, did in said State of New York undertake to carry on irregular and unlawful warfare as a guerilla ; and in the execution of said undertaking, attempted to destroy the lives and property of the peaceable and unoffending inhabitants of said State, and of persons therein travelling, by throwing a train of cars and the passengers in said cars from the railroad track. on the railroad between Dunkirk and Buffalo, by placing obstructions across said track ; all this in said State of New York, and on or about the 15th day of December, 1864, at or near Buffalo.

CHARGE 2d.　*Acting as a Spy.*

Specification 1.　In this that John Y. Beall, a citizen of the insurgent State of Virginia, was found acting as a spy in the State of Ohio, at or near Kelley's Island, on or about the 19th day of September, 1864.

Specification 2.　In this that John Y. Beall, a citizen of the insurgent State of Virginia, was found acting as a spy in the State of Ohio, on or about the 19th day of September, 1864, at or near Middle Bass Island.

Specification 3.　In this that John Y Beall, a citizen of the insurgent State of Virginia, was found acting as a spy in the State of New York, at or near Suspension Bridge, on or about the 16th day of September, 1864.

JOHN A. BOLLES, Major and A.D.C.,
Judge Advocate.

New York, 17*th January*, 1865.

HEADQUARTERS DEPARTMENT OF THE EAST,
NEW YORK CITY, January 17th, 1865.

The above-named Beall will be brought for trial before the

Military Commission of which Brig. Gen. F. H. Warren is President.

JOHN A. DIX,

Major General.

To these charges and specifications the accused pleaded not guilty, and thereupon the Judge Advocate called WAL-TER O. ASHLEY, a witness for the prosecution, who, being duly sworn, in presence of the accused, testified as follows :—

Question by Judge Advocate. State your name, place of residence, and occupation.

Answer. My name is Walter O. Ashley. I am clerk and part owner of the steamboat *Philo Parsons ;* residence, City of Detroit, State of Michigan.

Q. Look at the accused ; have you ever seen him before ?

A. I have. On the 19th day of September last I saw him the first time.

Q. State the circumstances under which you saw him. State the transaction which brought you first into company with the accused, beginning on the 18th of September.

A. On Sunday, the 18th of September, about six o'clock in the evening, I was on board the steamboat *Philo Parsons,* in the cabin alone, at the boat's dock in Detroit ; she being a boat sailing from Detroit to the city of Sandusky, touching regularly at the Canadian port of Amherstburgh, and occasionally at Sandwich. On the evening of Sunday, Mr. Bennett G. Burley came aboard the boat, and inquired for Ashley. I told him my name was Ashley. He then said he intended to go down as a passenger, in the morning, to Sandusky ; that three friends were going with him ; and he requested that the boat would stop at Sandwich, a small town on the Canada side of the river below Detroit, and take on those three friends as passengers. I remarked that it was not customary for the boat to stop at Sandwich. He then asked it as a personal favour that the boat would stop and take on his friends. I then agreed, providing he, Burley, would take the boat himself at

H

Detroit, and let me know for sure that his friends would be ready to come on board at Sandwich, that the boat would call for them. He then went away. The next morning, being Monday the 19th of September, the boat left Detroit at eight o'clock in the morning, with freight and passengers. As the boat was swinging away from the dock, Burley came to me and reminded me of my promise to stop the boat at Sandwich. At the time the boat left Detroit, Capt. S. F. Atwood was in command of her, but he stepped off at Middle Bass Island, where he resides. I told Capt. Atwood that the boat would have to stop at Sandwich, and he stopped and took these three friends of Burley at Sandwich.

Q. Who were they?

A. The accused was one, and there were two others.

Q. Coming on board, did they report their names?

A. They did not. I did not record the names; it has been my custom sometimes to record passengers' names on long routes, but I did not on this.

Q. What was the dress of the accused when he came on board, civil or military?

A. They were all dressed in citizens' clothes, the entire party; they had no baggage; they were very gentlemanly in their appearance; they said they were taking a little pleasure trip—might stop perhaps at Kelly's Island; did not know exactly where they would go; paid their fare to Sandusky. The fare is the same to Kelly's Island as it is to Sandusky. The boat then proceeded to Malden, Canada West, about fifteen miles further down the river; about twenty-five men came on board there at Malden, and they all paid their fare also; that port is the same as Amherstburgh; all the baggage brought on board by the party was a very old trunk tied up with cord, a rope tied around it. It was taken in at the after gangway of the boat by two of the roughest looking subjects in the party; most of the party were roughly dressed in citizens' dress.

Q. If the contents of that trunk became afterwards known, state what they were.

A. It afterwards became known, and it contained revolvers and hatchets.

Q. Leaving Amherstburgh, where did you go ?

A. The boat proceeded on its way to Sandusky. Everything passed off quietly during the day. It was about half-past nine in the morning when we left Amherstburgh. Everything passed off quietly until about four o'clock in the afternoon. The boat stopped at a number of islands transacting business and taking on passengers. At four o'clock in the afternoon she had just left Kelly's Island. She was two miles from Kelly's Island. Kelly's Island is in the State of Ohio, six miles from the American shore on Lake Erie. In sailing from Kelly's Island to Sandusky we sail nearly south ; we were about two miles I should judge from Kelly's Island toward the American shore, and some four miles off the Ohio main shore.

Q. State what then occurred.

A. I was standing on the main deck of the boat ; Captain Atwood was ashore.

Q. Who was in charge of the boat ?

A. I was in charge of the business of the boat ; I am not a sailor ; the mate was sailing the boat ; he was sailing master in charge of the sailing of the boat, and I was in charge of the affairs of the boat. As I said before, I was standing on the main deck in front of the office and the ladies' cabin ; the passengers at this time—there were about eighty, nearly half of whom were ladies—were in the upper cabin. Three men came up to me, drew revolvers and levelled them, and said if I offered any resistance they would shoot me.

Q. Who were the men ?

A. They were three of the party ; the accused was not one of those three, neither was Mr. Burley at this time. Bennett G. Burley came from the forward part of the boat aft, followed by fifteen or twenty. Burley had a revolver in his hand, and levelled it at me, and said, " Get into that cabin," meaning the ladies' cabin, " or you are a dead man." The parties that followed him were not armed at this time. He commenced counting " one, two, three," at the same time. He had not counted a great many, probably, before I was inside the door; two men were stationed outside of the door. I stayed inside of the door, and they were stationed outside the door, for the purpose of keeping me in the cabin, I suppose. One stood one side of the door, and the other the other, with revolvers in their hands; the party gathered around this old trunk I spoke of before; the cords were cut, the lid taken off, and they armed themselves from that with revolvers and hatchets; most of them had two large revolvers, and a portion of them hatchets; they then took forcible possession of the boat, and made prisoners of all on board. I was kept in the cabin for about one hour. I could look out through the door on the main deck and see everything that was going on. Bennett G. Burley had charge of this deck at the time. Burley, with an axe which he found on board, smashed the baggage room door open—I don't know for what purpose—then went forward and smashed the saloon door; he then went with the axe, smashed the trotting sulky to pieces, which was thrown overboard; he then, with the men under him, commenced to throw the freight overboard, consisting of household goods, tobacco and iron; the iron was thrown overboard first. I won't say that I saw the household goods thrown overboard; the iron was thrown overboard, perhaps the household goods were not; about an hour I should judge after the capture of the boat, the accused, Capt. Beall, came to me and asked me if I was in charge of the office. I told him I was. He then asked me if I was in charge of the boat's papers. I told him I was. He then said he was in charge of the party, and wanted the boat's papers, and I went into the office and gave him the papers, and he took them and carried them away.

Q. At the time he asked you for the papers, did he make
any statement to you as to who or what he was, or what his
purpose was ?

A. He did not say directly. I made a request that he
would not destroy the steamboat. He did not say directly
whether he should destroy the boat or should not. He said
something to the effect that if I was a United States soldier,
or United States officer, and had seized any of *their* vessels,
or something to that effect—I won't say the exact words—
that I would probably destroy the vessel. He did not say to
me that he was a Confederate States officer—some of the
others did say so ; said the party were Confederate States
soldiers, and that the expedition was in charge of Confederate
States officers. Directly after the capture of the boat, she
was headed down the lake ; not towards Sandusky ; directly
off from her course for Sandusky. She ran down the lake
for half an hour, I should judge, and then turned around
and ran up the lake to Middle Bass Island for the purpose of
wooding, and also for the purpose of putting the passengers
ashore.

Q. She ran to Middle Bass Island and there *did* wood,
and there the passengers *were* put on shore ?

A. Yes, sir. Middle Bass Island is in the State of Ohio,
about ten miles from the shore. She had been lying there
about fifteen minutes when the steamboat *Island Queen* came
alongside of the boat ; she is a steamboat that runs from
Sandusky to these islands with freight and passengers both,
making the round trip every day. She came alongside of
the *Philo Parsons*, and made fast alongside. The party that
were then in charge of the *Philo Parsons* went aboard the
Island Queen, seized her, made prisoners of all on board,
and brought them all on board of the *Philo Parsons* as prisoners ; part of them were put in the cabin of the *Philo
Parsons*, and part of them were put into the hold. The
passengers of both boats were afterwards all put ashore on

Middle Bass Island.   When the boat had been lying at this
island I should judge about an hour—I was in my office ; I
was allowed to go there ; there were two ladies and a gentleman in the office—Captain Beall came to the door, and said :
" Ladies, you will have to go ashore now, as we are agoing to
use this boat."   He gave the young man permission to go
also.   They started out and I followed them ; I went back
for the purpose of picking up my books and papers ; Capt.
Beall came back and Burley with him ; I stood at my desk
with Capt. Beall at one side, and Mr. Burley on the other ;
I asked if they were going to put me ashore ; they said they
were going to allow me to go ashore ; I asked permission to
take the boat's books ; Capt. Beall said I should not take
them, that I should not take any thing belonging to the boat ;
I then said I had some private promissory notes in an
envelope and requested leave to take them ; Burley said :
" Let me see them."   I produced them ; he looked at them,
said he " could not collect them," and gave them to me.
Capt. Beall then said : " We want your money."   I opened
the money drawer, in which there was very little money :
perhaps eight or ten dollars ; they took that out.   Burley
then said ; " You have more money ; let us have it."   I put
my hand into my vest pocket and took out a roll of bills of
about $100, and laid it on the desk ; I then requested again
that I might be allowed to take the books, but they refused
to let me take them : I was then put ashore.

Q. If you saw what became of that roll of bills, state what
was done with it.

A. The roll of bills was taken between them ; Capt. Beall
and Burley took the roll of bills, and also took the money
out of the drawer ; they took it between them ; they both
made a demand for the money ; Capt. Beall made the demand
first, and Mr. Burley afterwards made the demand.

Q. Which of the two took the roll of bills after you laid it
on the desk ?

A. They took it between them; I will not swear w ich one positively: they took it between them; they both made the demand; they said, "Give us the money." I then went on shore.

Q. After you went on shore state what you observed was done with either or both of the boats—the boats, I understand, both remained in the possession of the seizing party?

A. Yes, sir. After I went on shore and had been on shore about half an hour, the boats were started in the direction of Sandusky; they were alongside lashed together. It was a moonlight night, and when about two or three miles out I noticed the *Island Queen* drifting from the *Philo Parsons*; it afterwards proved that she was scuttled; she drifted about four miles, and drifted on to a reef, and was afterwards raised; she was nearly full of water when she was raised.

Q. Are you able from your own inspection to state that she was, and how she was scuttled?

A. Not from my own observation.

Q. You state from your own observation that you saw her drifting?

A. Yes, sir.

Q. How much else can you state from your own observation as to what became of her?

A. I can state that I saw her the next morning on my way to Sandusky; on what is called Chickenolee Reef; there was nine feet of water on the reef; she drew about four feet of water, and she was sunk on the reef where the water was about nine feet deep.

Q. How far was that from the point where you saw her drifting the evening before?

A. About five miles.

Q. When and where did you next see the accused?

A. I next saw the accused in the city of New-York after his arrest.

Q. Have you stated all that passed between you and him on board the *Philo Parsons* on the 19th of September ?

A. I think I have stated everything that would be of any account : I saw him considerably.

The Judge Advocate said he had no further questions to ask the witness.

Cross-examination by Accused.

Q. How long were you clerk of the *Philo Parsons ?*

A. Two seasons ; it was my second season.

Q. What was your occupation before that ?

A. I have been clerk on steamboats about nine years : clerk and part owner.

Q. In what other boats ?

A. The steamboat *Dot*, a steamboat that ran from Detroit to Port Huron, as a freight and passenger boat.

Q. Have you had any other occupation at any other time previous to that ?

A. Previous to that I was clerk in stores from the time I was 13 or 14 until about the time I was 20.

Q. Have you now stated all the occupations you have had at any time in your life ?

A. Previous to my going into a store which I think was when I was about 14—I might have been 15, I cannot tell exactly now—I was attending school ; I was also with my uncle assisting him as clerk in a Post-Office ; that is all, I think.

Q. Had you ever seen Burley or Beall before they came on board the *Philo Parsons* as you have stated ?

A. I have no recollection of ever seeing them before, either of them ; I saw Burley the 18th of September and Beall the 19th ; I have no recollection of seeing either of them previous to that to know them.

Q. When the twenty-five persons came on board at Sandwich, which of them was it that made the remark about the pleasure-trip ?

A. The twenty-five did not come on board at Sandwich, and the remark was made about the pleasure-trip when the three came on at Sandwich; Burley was the man who had something to say about that; I had more acquaintance with Burley than any of the rest of them; he was spokesman for the whole party; the other three I don't remember; Burley had something to say about the pleasure-trip the night before, on Sunday.

Q. Was Beall present at the time when Burley made the observation?

A. I cannot say whether he was or not; I did not pay any particular attention to Beall until after the capture of the boat; I don't remember that he was present.

Q. Did Burley in any of these conversations with you state that he was a Confederate States officer, what his rank was?

A. No, sir; he said nothing on that subject at any time to me.

Q. You said that some of them did say that they were in the Confederate States service?

A. Yes, sir. The two men that were guarding me directly after the capture of the boat that stood outside of the door. I asked them what they intended to do. They said that they were Confederate States officers and soldiers, and that they intended to capture the United States steamer *Michigan*, and release their friends on Johnson's Island; and others said the same thing.

Q. You say that Burley was the spokesman of the party. Did he give all the orders that were executed in regard to the boat by the persons with him?

A. I saw more of Burley for the first two hours after the capture of the boat than of the accused; I did not see the accused for an hour or an hour and a half; I had supposed that Burley was in charge of the whole party, and in fact I supposed he was until Captain Beall came to me and requested me to give him the papers; he then said he was in charge of them; I supposed that Burley was in charge of the party up to that time.

Q. Give as nearly as you can what was the language of Beall when he made the announcement to you that he was in charge of the party.

A. He asked me if I was in charge of the office; I told him I was; he then asked if I was in charge of the boat's papers and I told him I was; he said, " I am in charge of this party, and I want the boat's papers." I went into the office and gave them to him ; I then said to him that I was part owner of the boat, and I hoped he would not destroy the boat. He said something to the effect that if I was a United States officer—I will give you the words as nearly as I can —that if I was a United States officer and had seized one of their vessels, that I would probably destroy it. He did not say that he should destroy the boat.

Q. Was the language he used this : If you were a United States officer and had seized one of our boats, you would probably destroy it ?"

A. Yes, sir. " Our boats," that is the language.

Q. Did he use any language to indicate what he meant by " our"?

A. No, sir, nothing but that.

Q. Up to this time had any one stated in Beall's presence that this was a party of Confederates ?

A. Not in my hearing; as I said before I saw but very little of Captain Beall for an hour and a half or two hours after the capture of the boat.

Q. You have stated that revolvers were presented at you. Did any person actually make an attempt upon your life?

A. There were no shots fired; they were presented at me, and they said if I offered any resistance they would shoot me.

Q. Did Beall at any time or in any way interfere with you personally, either to threaten your life or to save it ?

A. At the time the money was taken from me they had

revolvers with them.　I won't say that the revolvers were pointed at me.

Q. Are you sure that you saw Beall have a revolver at the time he was in the office when the money was delivered?

A. I am, sir.

Q. Have you a sufficient recollection of the weapon to describe it?

A. I have not, any further than that it was a revolver; it had the appearance of being a revolver.

Q. Are you acquainted with the different kinds of revolvers, so as to identify it in any way?

A. No, sir, I could not identify that revolver,

Q. Did Burley threaten to shoot you?

A. He did, sir.

Q. For what?

A. At the time of the capture of the boat, before they had made the general seizure of the boat, and made prisoners of all on board, he drew his revolver and told me to get into that cabin—meaning the ladies' cabin—or he would shoot me.

Q. At no other time?

A. No, sir, I think not.

Q. Did not Burley ask you for the key of the room where the baggage was kept, previous to smashing the door in; and did you not refuse, and say you had not the key?

A. I have not thought anything in regard to that; just after I had stepped inside the door I heard some one, whether it was Burley or not I cannot say, call for the key. Burley said, " I will make a key." He found an axe on board and smashed the door open; some one called for the key; I was not asked for the key; I do remember now, I heard some one call for the key to the baggage-room, and I remember Burley taking an axe and smashing the door in.

Q. Did Burley at any time threaten to shoot you because you did not deliver the key to him, or did not obey his order, or comply with some request that he made?

A. The only time he threatened to shoot me was before the general seizure of the boat, as I stated ; I think that was the only time.

Q. Did any person make such a threat to you other than Burley ?

A. Three others that I spoke of in the first place, just previous to Burley making the threat.

Q. Was Beall present on either of those occasions ?

A. No, sir ; I did not see Beall for an hour or an hour and a half after the capture of the boat.

Q. Did you see him before the trunk was opened ?

A. Not that I know of ; as I said before, I have no recollection of seeing him until the time he had made the demand for the boat's papers.

Q. Was there any occasion while Beall was in your presence that any person either threatened or made a movement as if to shoot you, Beall interfering and preventing it ?

A. I don't recollect of anything of the kind.

Q. Did any such circumstance as this happen, that you being asked for the key, and either refusing or hesitating to give it up, a pistol was presented at you, and the threat made to shoot, and Beall remarked, " Don't kill him, I will make a key myself," or anything of that character.

A. I don't recollect of anything of that kind. It is possible that I might have seen Captain Beall, the accused, before the time that I allude to that he took the boat's papers, but I have no recollection of seeing him after the seizure of the boat, until that time.

Q. You say he was in citizen's dress like the other two persons who came on board ?

A. Yes, sir.

Q. Had he a hat or cap on ?

A. I won't swear positively. I don't pay very close attention to people's clothing.

Q. Was there anything peculiar about any part of his dress that you observed ?

A. No, sir, nothing peculiar.

Q. Did you hear any conversation between Beall and Burley, or Beall and any other person, in which they spoke of their design except what you have already stated to the Court?

A. No, sir.

Q. Had the small sum of money which was in the drawer been collected from the passengers ?

A. The whole of it had been collected from passengers, or in payment of freight.

Q. Was there any money collected from any person, as if they were passengers, after the party took possession of the boat ?

A. No, sir, not to my knowledge ; I collected none.

Q. Can you now state what you have not answered specifically to the question put by the prosecution, which of these two persons it was that actually took into his hand the money that you produced ?

A. I can swear that Captain Beall took some of it.

Q. As to the hundred dollars in the roll, I mean ?

A. They both of them made the demand, and I laid the money on the desk.

Q. Who took it up?

A. The money was taken between them ; I am not going to swear positively ; I took the money out of the drawer ; they both made the demand for the money.

Q. When Captain Beall asked you for the papers, as you say, did he say anything about wanting such papers as showed the nationality of the steamboat ?

A. I think he did ; he asked for the boat's papers ; I asked him if he wished the enrolment and license. He said he did ; something to show what kind of boat she was, or something to that effect ; that she was a United States vessel ; and I produced the enrolment and license, and I stood by in the office when he read them ; he read them in my presence, or a portion of them.

Q. Did he state any reason why he wanted the papers ?

A. No further than he said he was in charge of the party, and wished the papers.

Q. When he asked you for the money, or when the money was demanded, were you asked if you had any public money in your possession, or money that belonged to the United States ?

A. I don't recollect that those words were used at all.

Q. Did any one of them designate the money asked for as money belonging to the boat ?

A. Capt. Beall said in the first place : " We want your money ;" and Burley said : " You have more money, and let us have it."

Q. Did either of them in any way designate or specify what money they were asking for, whether it was the money belonging to the boat, or all the money in your possession ?

A. I think they did not designate. All the money I had, however, was the property of the boat, of myself and others interested in the boat.

Q. Did either of them say anything to the effect that they did not want any private money that belonged to you personally ?

A. No, sir, they did not, not to my knowledge ; the word private or personal I don't think was used ; they gave me my personal papers—some personal notes ; I did not claim any of the money as personal ; I claimed the notes as personal, that was all I claimed as personal.

Q. Did they take any papers except such as belonged to the boat ?

A. No, sir. I made a demand for these notes as my personal papers, and they gave them up.

Q. When the *Island Queen* attached herself to the *Philo Parsons*, were there any soldiers on the *Island Queen ?*

A. There were about twenty or twenty-five unarmed United States soldiers going to Toledo to be mustered out of the service ; they were in uniform.

Q. What became of them ?

A. They were taken as prisoners with the rest of the passengers, and were put into the hold with the rest of the passengers.

Q. What was the last you saw of them ?

A. I was in the office ; they were put ashore before I was ; they were put ashore at Middle Bass Island, the place where I was put ashore.

Q. Where did you see Mr. Beall when you saw him in New York as you state ?

A. I saw him at the Police Station in the City of New York.

Q. Who took you to see him ?

A. I was taken by Colonel Ludlow.

Q. Was he alone when you saw him ?

A. No, sir ; there were about twenty-five or thirty in the room with him.

Q. Had he a hat or cap on then ?

A. I don't think he had anything on at that time ; I think not.

Q. Were you asked to point him out ?

A. No, sir.

Q. Did you speak to him ?

A. I did not at that time.

Q. Did he wear his hair and beard as he does now, when you saw him in New York ?

A. The same as it is *now ?* yes, sir.

Q. How was it when you first saw him ?

A. He had a moustache without whiskers.

The accused said he had no further questions to ask the witness.

Examination by the Commission.

Q. State whether there was any military or naval mark òr badge on the accused while he was on board the *Philo Parsons*.

A. There was not ; they were dressed as citizens, in citizens' dress, and paid their fare as passengers, and were treated as passengers.

Q. Did Burley and Beall divide the money in any way, which you took and laid in a roll of bills on the desk ?

A. They were taking the money when I left ; I laid it on the desk, and they were taking the money ; they both made the demand, and were both taking the money between them. I saw them taking the money between them and dividing it. I don't know anything about how much either one of them took ; there was an actual division of the money, and I saw it.

Re-examination by Judge Advocate.

Q. At the time the boat was captured, how far was she from Johnson's Island ?

A. Johnson's Island is in Sandusky Bay, inside of the main shore. I should judge the boat was captured about six miles from Johnson's Island.

Q. How far is Kelly's Island from Johnson's Island ?

A. About eight miles.

Q. How far is it from Middle Bass Island to Johnson's Island ?

A. I should say thirteen or fourteen miles.

Q. Have you ever seen the United States war steamer *Michigan* ?

A. I have seen her, but I never have been on board of her.

Q. Do you know where she was at the time of this affair ?

A. She was lying off Johnson's Island, I should say about a mile. I stated that I had never been on board the steamer *Michigan*. I was on board her six or seven years ago. I have not been since the war.

Re-cross-examination by Accused.

Q. You said the soldiers on board the *Island Queen* were unarmed ?

A. Yes, sir.

Q. Do you know whether there were any arms on board of this vessel ?

A. There were not ; not to my knowledge.

Q. Did you examine to see whether there were or not ?

A. I did not examine.

Q. During any part of the time you were on board after the capture of the *Philo Parsons*, was any flag displayed by this party ?

A. Not while I was on board.

Q. Did not they display a flag afterwards to your knowledge ?

A. Not to my recollection.

No further questions were asked ; his testimony being read to the witness, he affirmed the same.

———

The Judge Advocate then called WILLIAM WESTON, a witness for the prosecution, who being duly sworn, in presence of the accused, testified as follows :

Examined by Judge Advocate.

Q. State your name, place of residence, and occupation.

A. William Weston, Sandusky City, Ohio. I have been fireman for the last five years.

Q. Have you ever seen the accused, Capt. Beall, before ?

A. Yes, sir.

Q. When for the first time, and where ?

A. The first time I saw him was on board the *Philo Parsons*, on the 19th of last September.

I

Q. State what you saw him do, and what you heard him say.

A. After the capture of the boat, and we got a little excited, he came forward and told us what they were going to do with us, and the boat; I was a passenger on board; he said they were not going to hurt or harm any of us, and that they would land us as soon as they thought fit; he also stated that he was an escaped rebel prisoner from Johnson's Island, and that they had taken the boat for the purpose of capturing the United States vessel *Michigan ;* he said they were going to liberate the prisoners on Johnson's Island, and were going to destroy the commerce on the lakes; that is all I recollect he said.

Q. Did you see what was done with any of the freight on board the *Philo Parsons* after the boat was seized ?

A. I did not see them do anything with the freight, only they threw out one of my boxes, that I got afterwards on the beach, that was pitched out; that was after they landed us on the Island; they pitched one of my boxes into the water.

Q. Will you state whether Beall, the accused, had any arms about him or not, while on board the *Philo Parsons?*

A. I could not state; I did not see.

Q. How was he dressed ?

A. He was dressed in citizens' clothes.

Q. Do you remember whether he wore a cap or a hat ?

A. He wore a kind of a low-sized hat; a low-crowned hat.

Q. Where did you next see him after you were landed ?

A. I did not see him after I was landed on the Island until I saw him here, at Fort Lafayette, when I was brought down to the fort to indentify him.

Q. Did you hear on board the *Philo Parsons*, from himself or others, what was the name of the accused; what they called him ?

A. Captain Beall.

Q. You heard him called Captain Beall ?

A. I could not say whether he was the person or not ; I heard somebody called Captain Beall.

Q. Can you state who appeared to be in command, or charge of the party who seized the *Philo Parsons ?*

A. I could not state.

The Judge Advocate said he had no further questions to ask the witness.

Cross-examined by the Accused.

Q. When you were brought down to Fort Lafayette to point out Captain Beall, did you point out this man?

A. Yes, sir, when I saw him.

Q. Who was with him ?

A. I could not state who was with him ; I am a stranger ; I don't know any of the men around.

Q. Didn't you point out another and a different man, who proved to be a man named Smedley ?

A. No, sir.

Q. What was the first you saw of this person ; who told you he was a rebel prisoner ; where was he ?

A. He came forward stating what they were going to do with us ; that was the first time I saw him.

Q. Did you know then that the boat had been captured ?

A. Not until he spoke.

Q. Who was he speaking to ?

A. He was speaking to the passengers.

Q. Were you a passenger on board ?

A. Yes, sir.

Q. Did you notice what kind of a cord or string he had round his hat ?

A. I could not state.

Q. Was there any tassel on it ?

A. I could not say.

Q. Was there any gold in it ?

A. I don't know.

Q. Did you notice what kind of buttons he had on his coat or vest ?

A. No, sir, I don't recollect.

Q. Did the man who said he was a rebel prisoner, say that he was an officer in the Confederate army ?

A. I don't recollect.

Q. Where were you put ashore. ?

A. On Middle Bass Island.

Q. Did these persons in possession show any flag at any time while they were aboard ?

A. I did not see any.

Q. Have you ever seen a secession flag ?

A. No, sir.

Q. What kind of a box was this of yours that they threw overboard ?

A. A large box containing bedding.

Q. Who threw it overboard ?

A I could not state who threw it overboard, but I saw the man pitch it out.

Q. Did either of them say any thing at the time as to why they threw it out ?

A. No sir, they were out six or seven rods from the shore.

The accused said he had no further questions to ask the witness.

No questions were asked by the Commission.

The testimony being read to him, he affirmed the same.

The Judge Advocate then called DAVID H. THOMAS, a witness for the prosecution, who, being duly sworn, testifies as follows :

Q. State your name, residence, and occupation.

A. My name is David H. Thomas ; I reside at Niagara city, Niagara County, New York ; occupation, a police officer, by authority of said village.

Q. You arrested the accused ?

A. I did, sir.

Q. When and where ?

A. In the depot of the New York Central Railroad Company at Niagara City, on the 16th day of December last, at about 9 or 10 o'clock at night.

Q. Did you arrest any other person at the same time ?

A. I did, sir, a young man calling himself Anderson.

Q. Were the two in company ?

A. They were. There was another police officer with me at the time of the arrest, Mr. Saule.

Q. What baggage if any, had these men ?

A. They had a small carpet bag—contents, a dirty shirt, a shirt that had been worn, a pair of socks, some five or six tallow-candles that had not been burned, some matches done up in a paper, and a box partly full of paper collars. The accused had a bottle of laudanum in one of his pockets.

Q. What was the dress of the accused ?

A. I should judge the same clothes that he has on now, with the addition of an overcoat and cap.

Q. He had on citizen's dress ?

A, Yes, sir, all citizen's dress, with an overcoat and cap.

Q. Had he any arms about him ?

A. He had one of Colt's navy revolvers in a sheath attached to his body by a belt under both his coats, outside of his pants on his hips.

Q. Was the revolver loaded ?

A. Yes, sir, it was fully loaded—it was a six-shooter.

Q. Did you inquire his name.

A. I did, sir—while searching him I asked him his name, and he said Beall. A few minutes afterwards I asked him again, with a view of learning his initials ; he then said his name was W. W. Baker. I attempted to correct him by stating that he formerly told me his name was Beall, and he denied it. I insisted upon it that he did say Beall, and I told him I should

make the record Beall or Baker—I should put his name
down Beall or Baker.

Q. If he had any money, state what it was.

A. He had two ten-dollar American gold pieces, two four-
dollar Canada notes, one two-dollar Canada note, and he
had some five or six dollars in American money or scrip, the
exact amount I disremember. By scrip I mean fractional
currency. I think he had some little silver with him. I did
not get the correct amount of the money.

Q. Did he give you any account of himself at any time ?
and if so, what did he say ?

A. When I arrested him he asked me what I arrested him
for ? My reply to him was, that he knew probably as well as
I did what I arrested him for. He said he did not. I finally told him I arrested him as an escaped rebel prisoner. He
asked me from where. I told him that mattered not, as long
as he was an escaped rebel prisoner. Finally he wanted to
know from where. He asked if it was from Point Lookout. I
told him it was ; that he was an escaped prisoner from
Point Lookout. Said he, " That I will acknowledge. I am
an escaped prisoner from Point Lookout."

Q. Did you make any inquiry of him how he got that
Canada money ?

A. I did, sir. His answer was, that after he escaped from
Point Lookout he made his way to Baltimore, and he had
friends in Baltimore who had furnished him with this money
to go to Canada.

Q. In regard to the carpet-bag of which you have spoken,
and the contents, what are the facts within your knowledge as
stated by the two parties you arrested, that will enable the
Court to judge to whom it belonged ?

A. When we arrested the two men, his bag was between
them on the seat, and carried, I think, by the prisoner Anderson into the room where we took them to search them. It
was into the adjoining room, the telegraph office, that we took

them to search them. We asked which of them owned that bag, and the young man said that the accused owned the bag.

Q. The accused being present and hearing the remark?

A. Yes, sir; I asked him if the bag was his, and he said it was not. The accused said it was not; but the other man said it was.

Q. Did you make any inquiry as to the purpose of the candles or matches?

A. I asked them what they were doing with those candles. They said they were sometimes a necessary article to use when they could not get other lights. This young man, Anderson, I think, answered in that way. I would not want to say which of them; it was between them. They were both present. In regard to the laudanum, I asked the accused what he was doing with that; and his answer was that he was subject to the toothache.

Q. If the accused said anything to you in regard to the mode of his arrest in connection with the fact of his being armed, state what he said.

A. Yes, sir. During the evening or night, when we were conversing over the subject, he said it was fortunate that I arrested him suddenly as I did; that he had been in prison so much that he had made up his mind, whenever he was attempted to be arrested again, and on this particular occasion, had I not taken him as quick as I did, that one or the other of us would have been a dead man—that he had fully resolved never to be taken alive.

Cross-examined by the Accused.

Q. Was Beall alone when you arrested him?

A. No, sir; they were together sitting on a settee, he and Anderson, in the depot of the Central Railroad at that place.

Q. Was it day or night?

A. Night, somewhere between 9 and 10 o'clock—about 10 o'clock.

Q. Was any person with you ?

A. Mr. Saule, another policeman.

Q. Did he take any part in making the arrest?

A. He put his hand on Anderson and I mine on Beall.

Q. How large was this vial of laudanum that he had ?

A. I believe what they call a two-ounce vial.

Q. Was it full ?

A. There was a very little out of it.

Q. In this conversation that he had with you, did he tell you any thing about his being a Confederate officer ?

A. He said that he belonged to the Second Virginia Infantry, was a sergeant in the ranks. I asked him if he held any other position, and he said, No.

Q. Did he tell you when he escaped from Point Lookout ?

A. He did not give me the dates, but it was several days previous to his arrival at Buffalo.

Q. What kind of a cap was he in ?

A. It was a cloth cap—a citizen's cap.

The accused said he had no further questions to ask the witness.

No questions by the Commission. His testimony being read to the witness, he affirmed the same.

The Commission then adjourned until to-morrow at 11 o'clock, a.m.

JOHN A. BOLLES, Major and A.D.C.,

Judge Advocate.

———

FORT LAFAYETTE, NEW YORK HARBOUR,

Thursday, February 2nd, 1865.

The Commission met pursuant to adjournment.

Present all the members.

Present, also, the Judge Advocate, and the accused, John Y. Beall, who was brought in for trial ; and James T. Brady, Esq., his counsel.

Yesterday's proceedings were read and approved.

The Judge Advocate then called EDWARD HAYS, a witness for the prosecution, who being duly sworn, in presence of the accused, testified as follows :

Q. State your name and occupation ?

A. Edward Hays, doorman at the Police Headquarters, Mulberry street.

Q. You see the accused sitting here ; have you ever seen him before ? and if so, where ?

A. Yes, sir ; at the Police Headquarters in Mulberry street.

Q. State whether he ever said anything to you, and if so, what, in regard to his escape from Mulberry street ?

A. He asked me to carry a letter out for him and have it mailed; I asked him where he wanted to send the letter to ; he said he wanted it to go to Canada; I asked him if he could get it through easily there ; he said he did not think he could very easily, as the Government were opening all letters which were going there now ; he said he thought if he could get a letter to Canada, and word could be sent to his Government that he was in prison, they might do some good for him to get him out. I then went to get him the paper to write the letter; at the same time I reported to Mr. Kelso, who was then in charge of the Detective Office, what he had told me, and I went back to the prisoner and told him that there were several detectives in the office at the time, that I could not very easily get the paper ; that I would wait for a start to get the office cleared of those detectives, and then I would have a better opportunity of getting it in without being seen. He then said to me : "Hays, I tell you what you can do for me ;" I said, "What ?" he said, "You can let me go ;" I said I could not ; he said, "If you do I will give you $1,000 in gold." I asked him if he had that amount of money with him ; he said no, but if I would take his word, his word was good for the money when he would get to

Canada; that a man there had that amount of money and more belonging to him; that it would surely be given as soon as he would get there. I asked him if he had any hand in the fires here in New York; he said no, but that he knew the parties, and that they were then in Canada. I told him I did not think I could let him go for the money, as it would place me in a bad position; that I did not like to do it; that it would be too much risk for me to run. He said that I knew his position; how he was placed; that he thought he would be found guilty, and that I should run a little risk to save him. He said he was arrested before, some time ago, and that he got a letter through by some of his friends, and the Confederate Government, hearing of his imprisonment here, put in prison a son of one of General Meade's head officers, together with eleven more officers, and kept them there until he was released. I then said to him, "I suppose if your Government found out that you were in prison here now that they would try to get you out in some way." He said he did not think they would, because he was arrested under a different charge now from what he was then, and that he did not think his Government was as strong now as it was then. I then told him I would see if I could let him go; that I could not say whether I could or not; I asked him if he did not want to write a letter out, and he said no, that it would take too long before the letter could do any good, but that I could release him without getting myself into any trouble; and said he, "You know you can." I then left him and came into the office; I told him that I would see what I could do, and I reported to Mr. Kelso and Inspector Carpenter what he had told me. I again went back to him and told him that I thought it was pretty hard for me to do it, but if I did it, what time in the night would he like to get away. He said he would like to get away in the fore part of the night; that he had two friends living up, he thought, in Thirtieth street; that if he could get to their house, he wanted to get out in time so he could get there, so nobody would hear him make a noise around the place ; he thought he could get arms there, and then it would take somebody to arrest him if he could get arms after he got out ; for, said he, " I know well what would happen to me if I was to be caught and brought back again." I then asked him if those friends of his could not furnish him the money before he would leave New York ? He said that very probably they could furnish a part of it, probably half of it in greenbacks, if not in gold, before he would leave New York ; if not, that he would leave me an order that would positively get it in Canada. I asked him how did he think he could get clear from New York, and if he had any friends that he thought would get him clear on the way going. He said first he would go to this man's house in Thirtieth street, and then he would start for a friend of his in Jersey, about five miles from Jersey City, who did business in New York, who came every morning and went back at night, and by getting there he knew he would be safe. I then asked him if he would not tell me the number of the house where those men lived in Thirtieth street, or what were their names, who were willing to assist him. He would not tell me their names ; said he did not know exactly the street they lived in, or the number of the house. I asked him what his own name was, or if he gave the right name in the detective's office when they brought him in. He said he did not ; that they did not know his name, and could not find it out. I then said to him : " I think you are a very smart man, and you must have done a good deal of harm to our Government since this war commenced ;" and he said : " Yes, I have taken hundreds and hundreds of prisoners ; I have done Lincoln's Government a good deal of harm, and they know it." I asked him if it was on land or sea that he took those prisoners, and he said it was his secret. I asked him to tell me his right name, and he said he would not. He said he knew something that would be worth $30,000 to any

one in the detective's office, if he would tell, and things that
would be worth millions of dollars to the Government if he
would only come out and discover ; but he said he would
die first ; he said he knew he could not live long, as he had
got a ball through his side, and he knew that would come
against him and cause death anyhow.   I told him, " I am
very glad you are not very fond of telling or discovering, for
you would have to keep a good record if I let you go.   He
said he knew many things that he would not tell ; he said,
" You can rest assured that you can get the $1,000, and get
it in gold, as I own more than that myself."   I then told
him I would see what I could do, and if I could let him out
that night I would, if possible, but I could not exactly say ;
and that, if not, I would come back and see him the following
evening ; and I then left him, and when I came back he was
gone, and I have not seen him since ; he was taken to Fort
Lafayette the next day.

No further questions by Judge Advocate.

The accused objected to the testimony of the witness in
which he narrated the statement of the accused, as irrelevant,
not relating to any charge or specification, but did not wish
any ruling on the point.

Cross-examined by Accused.

Q. How long have you been doorkeeper at the Police
Headquarters ?

A. Since the 11th of April last.

Q. What was your business before that ?

A. I worked in the Navy Yard at labouring work.

Q. Where did you reside when you were appointed doorkeeper ?

A. At 17 Lewis street, New York.

Q. What was your business, if any, before you worked in
the Navy Yard ?

A. Liquor business, at 157 Madison street.

Q. About what was the date at which you first saw Beall, the accused?

A. It must have been a week before New Year's, I think. I think it was New Year's Day that I was to come here and see him. It was the night before New Year's that this conversation occurred. I am not positive, but I think so.

Q. Did all the conversation you have stated occur on the night before New Year's?

A. It all passed in one night.

Q. In what part of the headquarters was Beall confined at that time?

A. Down stairs in the cell.

Q. Who had charge of the cell?

A. Mr. Kelso was then in charge of the office, in the absence of Mr. Young.

Q. Who had the key of the cell?

A. The keys are generally left in the office. When I would be on duty as doorman, I would take the keys when I wanted to go into the cell for anything, to feed them, etc. I am doorkeeper one day, and another man the next day.

Q. How did you happen to begin this conversation with Beall?

A. Mr. Kelso asked me if I could not find out what Beall's name was; and if I could get him to tell his name, to try and find out what charges he was arrested on, and what was against him.

Q. Where were the Police Commissioners at that time?

A. I don't know, sir, if they were not gone home from Headquarters. I don't know if they were up-stairs or not.

Q. At what hour of the night was it that Kelso asked you to find out Beall's name?

A. I think it must have been about 7 o'clock.

Q. Did Kelso say that he did not know what Beall was charged with?

A. No, sir, he did not say any such thing.

Q. Did he say that he did not know what his name was?

A. He did not say so.

Q. Did he speak of him as a person named Beall?

A. No, sir, not at that time.

Q. I want you to repeat what Kelso said to you, when he expressed a wish that you should see this man and ascertain his name.

A. Mr. Kelso said to me when I would get time to go into the cell to him, to see if I could not draw on with him to get him to tell me what his name was; and if so, to see if I could not get from him to tell me what charges he was arrested on. That was all Mr. Kelso said to me.

Q. How did Kelso describe or make you understand what person you were to ask this question of?

A. Baker; he told me to go in and see Baker—which name he then went under; I called him Baker always when he was there; he went by the name of Baker; he told me to go in and see Baker, and see what I could learn from him.

Q. Before Kelso spoke to you, did you know that there was any such person as Baker confined in any cell there?

A. I knew that he was there, and that he went by the name of Baker—that he was called Baker.

Q. Who told you that he was called Baker?

A. I heard it from the detectives first when they first brought him in there.

Q. Had you seen him before the time when Kelso asked you to go and inquire about his name?

A. Yes, sir; several times.

Q. Did Kelso tell you what object he had in finding out this man's name?

A. No, sir.

Q. What was Kelso's position there at that time?

A. He was then acting as sergeant.

Q. Did you say to him that if he wanted to know what

this man's name was, or what he was charged with, he could ask the Commissioners ?

A. No, sir.

Q. Did you know who brought Baker in ?

A. Not at that time.

Q. Did Kelso state that he had asked the Commissioners what Baker was charged with, and that they would not tell him ?

A. No, sir.

Q. Then he gave no reason whatever for wishing to obtain this information?

A. No, sir ; not that I know of.

Q. Did you, at Mr. Kelso's request, go immediately to the cell where the accused was ?

A. Not immediately—I waited some time until I had leisure ; I had a good deal of work to do.

Q. Was it a part of your general instructions that you should or should not converse with prisoners there ?

A. I never got any instructions to that effect as to whether to converse with them or not.

Q. What time of night was it that you went to the accused and began this conversation with him ?

A. I should think it must be about eight o'clock—I think so, I'm not sure—between seven and nine.

Q. Was that the first time you had ever spoken a word with him ?

A. I had spoken to him previously to that while feeding him, and everything of that kind.

Q. Had you done any thing before that to get his confidence, or had he done any thing to get yours ?

A. No, sir ; not that I know of.

Q. Had you in any way before that night said or intimated to him that you were willing to help him to escape ?

A. No, sir.

Q. Can you state any reason growing out of what had

passed between you and the accused why he should place any
confidence in you particularly ?

A. I did not know of any reason why he should have
done it.

Q. When you went at 8 o'clock to his cell to obtain for
Mr. Kelso the information Kelso said he wanted, what was
the first remark that you made to the accused that you now
remember ?

A. There was a man in the cell that day, an old man, who
wanted me to take a letter for him, and I would not take it;
he said he would pay for taking it; I asked how much he
would pay, and he said "so much"—I forget how much
he did say ; I said I could not send it for that ; that evening
when I went in at 8 o'clock in the cell, there was no one
there at that time but the accused ; I said to this man, the
accused : " It is pretty cold in here this evening ;" he said
" Yes, it was pretty cold ;" I said, " The old man had good
luck to get out of there before night, as it was so cold ; " he
said " Yes ;" I said he wanted me to send a letter for him,
and I could not do it; he would not give enough to have
it sent, and I could not get anybody to take it for that
amount; the accused said, " I wish you would take a letter
for me and I will pay well for taking it ;" I told him, " There
is a good deal done for money—money does a good deal ;"
I then asked him where he wanted to have the letter sent;
that was how it commenced.

Q. Had you any instructions whether to permit any letter
to be sent by a prisoner without its being examined by any of
the public officers of the Government or city.

A. Yes, sir ; I was instructed not to take a letter out for
him without first showing it to the officer in charge of the
detectives' desk.

Q. Did you know that the accused when first taken to the
head-quarters of the police had been searched, and that

he had no money about him or under his command at the time this conversation took place ?

A. I don't know ; they did not tell me they searched him ; I know it is customary to search prisoners when they come here.

Q. Up to the time when you returned the first time to his cell that night and said that you could not get the paper for him to write on, had you said anything to him about his name ?

A. I don't think I had.

Q. Up to that time had you asked him what he was charged with ?

A. I don't think I had.

Q. Did you, during any part of this conversation, ask him what he was charged with ?

A. Yes, sir.

Q. What did he say ?

A. He said that was his secret.

Q. Do you mean to say that he stated that what he was charged with by our Government was his secret ?

A. What he was charged with—the charge he was arrested on ? Yes, sir.

Q. Did he state that as the reason why he could not tell you what he was charged with ?

A. He did not state what was the reason ; he would not tell me.

Q. Did you tell Kelso that he had refused to tell you what he was charged with ?

A. Yes, sir ; I think so.

Q. Did you bring him paper to write on ?

A. No, sir.

Q. Did he write, or attempt to write any letter ?

A. No, sir ; not that night.

Q. Did you pretend to him that if he wrote a letter you would have it sent for him to Canada ?

A. I told him I would have it taken, and try and send it to Canada.

Q. Did you intend to send it to Canada when you said so?

A. I first intended to give it to Kelso, who was in charge, to let him act on it as he saw fit.

Q. Did Kelso during that night give you any instructions about the subjects about which you should talk to the accused?

A. After I first came in and reported, he told me to try to find out the charges he was arrested on, and to get from him all I could.

Q. Did you report to Kelso, from time to time that night, what the accused said?

A. Yes, sir; I reported.

Q. Did Kelso suggest to you to get the accused to tell you he wanted to escape?

A. He told me no such thing.

Q. Before the accused said to you, " You can let me go," what, if anything, had you said or done to make him believe that you were his friend and would let him go?

A. Nothing that I could think of, more than I would see and have that letter forwarded as much as possible.

Q. Do you mean to say that although he refused to tell what his name was, he wanted you to take his word for $1,000 in gold to let him escape?

A. He wanted me to take his word. Yes, sir; he was to leave me an order for the money on that man in Canada.

Q. Did you ask him whether he would sign his real name to that order?

A. No, I don't think I did.

Q. Did you say to him that he could not expect you to take his word when he would not give his name?

A. I don't think I said so.

Q. When you asked him about the fires in New York, did you do that of your own suggestion, or because Kelso mentioned it?

A. No ; I thought I would find out if possible who the parties were, as I would like to know it at that time.

Q. When he told you that he thought he would be found guilty, did he say what he would be found guilty o

A. No, sir.

Q. When he told you that he had been arrested before, did he tell you where he was arrested or what he was arrested for ?

A. He did not say.

Q. Did he tell you the name of one of General Meade's head officers whose son had been imprisoned by his Government?

A. He told me the name, and I have forgotten it.

Q. When he spoke of his two friends who resided in 30th street, did he say in what part of the street they lived, or what their business was, or any thing of that kind ?

A. He said he did not know in what part of the street they lived in, or if they lived in 30th street or not ; he said they did business down town in the lower part of the city.

No further questions by the accused.

No question was asked by the Commission. His testimony being read to the witness, he affirmed the same.

The Judge Advocate then called GEORGE S. ANDERSON, who being duly sworn, in presence of the accused, testified as follows :

Q. What are your name and age ?

A. George S. Anderson ; I will be eighteen some day this month.

Q. Have you been in the Confederate military service ?

A. Yes, sir.

Q. You saw and spoke to the accused as you came in ; when did you see him the last time before ?

A. I saw him yesterday, and the last time I saw him before that was in prison in New York city.

Q. When and where did you first see Captain Beall, the accused ?

A. I first saw him on the railroad out from Buffalo, several miles west towards Dunkirk ; I don't know what day it was ; it was five or six days before my arrest at Suspension Bridge.

Q. Were you and the accused arrested at Suspension Bridge at the same time ?

A. Yes, sir.

Q. State the circumstances which led to your seeing the accused on the railroad, and all that followed after you saw him in connection with your movements and his.

The accused inquired if this testimony would relate to the sixth specification of the first charge. The Judge Advocate answered that it would.

The accused objected to any proof in regard to that specification, on the ground that it related to a transaction which, if perpetrated as stated in the specification, would be an offence cognizable by the laws of the State of New York, and not within the jurisdiction of any military tribunal ; he consented that the objection be overruled for the present, but he wished to reserve the point. The question being repeated, the witness answered as follows :

A. I got to Buffalo on the Sunday preceding my arrest ; I got there an hour or two before daylight on Sunday morning ; I went into a hotel and got a room and went to bed ; I was in citizen's dress and had no arms ; in the morning, I suppose it was 8 o'clock when I got up, I went into the street and then came back to the hotel.

Q. Did you meet any one at the hotel whom you had known in the rebel service ? and if so, whom ?

A. I did ; I met Lieutenant Headley ; he belonged to Morgan's command when I knew him ; I saw him, but I did not speak to him, and he did not speak to me ; he got up and went out on the street, and I went out after him after a while ; he signified to me to follow him out ; I went out after him, and he told me to follow him up stairs in the same hotel, which I did ; I also saw Colonel Martin there who had been an officer in the rebel service.

Q. What passed between you and them ?

A. They said they were glad to see me ; they said they had a plan in view then, and they wanted more men, and they would like to have me with them.

Q. What did they say about their plan, if any thing ?

A. They said they intended to capture a train ; they told me to remain there that day ; that they were going to. Dunkirk the next day to capture the train from Dunkirk the next night after that.

Q. Where did you get the pistol that was found upon you when you were arrested ?

A. Lieutenant Headley gave it to me.

Q. On this Sunday or afterwards ?

A. No, sir ; it was afterwards at Dunkirk.

Q. Did they tell you where they had come from ?

A. No, sir ; they did not.

Q. Whether from Canada or any other place ?

A. I think they said they were from Canada.

Q. What, if any thing, did they say to you in regard to their intended movements, after they had accomplished their plan ?

A. They did not say any thing ; they expected to go back to Canada, but what they intended to do they did not say anything about.

Q. Go on with your narrative of what was done.

A. On Tuesday evening I went to Dunkirk, and they were to capture the train that night coming from Dunkirk to Buffalo.

Q. Who went to Dunkirk ?

A. I went to Dunkirk, and these two officers went.

Q. Anybody else that you know of ?

A. Not that I know of ; at Dunkirk they told me that they were not going to try to take the train that night ; they told me to be at the depot in Buffalo the next day at 2 o'clock ; that was Wednesday. I was there at the depot the next day at 2 o'clock, and I saw those two officers there, and they told me to follow them out along the railroad towards Dunkirk, which I did ; followed them out, I suppose, three or four miles from the town, when we overtook Captain Beall, the accused, on the railroad.

A. State whether Beall became one of the party from that time in their movements.

A. Yes, sir, he was one of the party. We went on the railroad to a point I suppose five or six miles from the city— we four ; we tried to get a rail off the track.

Q. How did you try ?

A. We tried with a large sledge-hammer and a cold chisel.

Q. In whose possession did you first see that sledge-hammer ?

A. I saw it in Capt. Beall's possession.

Q. Who used it in trying to lift the rail from the track ?

A. Colonel Martin.

Q. Who else ?

A. I don't think that anybody else used it. We tried to get a rail off the track and could not do it—did not succeed in the attempt, and went back to town. We then went to Canada that night, to Port Colburn. We remained there two nights and one day. We then came back to Buffalo. There was five in the party then.

Q. The same four with one additional man ?

A. Yes, sir.

Q. Who was he ?

A. I don't know who he was.

Q. Do you know what he was from his own statement or otherwise ; whether he was a soldier or officer in the rebel service ?

A. He was a soldier.

Q. How do you know ?

A. All I know about it was, he told me he was an escaped prisoner from Rock Island.

Q. You five came to Buffalo, and what was then done ?

A. The Colonel told me to go with this Capt. Beall and stay with him, and he would meet us at a bridge with a sleigh —which I did.

Q. Did Col. Martin meet you there ?

A. Yes, sir, and Lieut. Headley was with him.

Q. Where was the fifth man ?

A. The fifth man went with Capt. Beall and me, and we parted. We missed the bridge—went the other side of the bridge, and we took one end of the road and came back to the bridge, and he took the other end of the road, and the sleigh had got by when we arrived there. But the sleigh found us at last.

Q. And then there were five of you ?

A. Yes, sir, five of us—the same five as before.

Q. What did you do then ?

A. We went to a point on the railroad, I suppose five miles from the city.

Q. And did what ?

A. We did not do any thing ; the train passed about the time that we got there.

Q. What did you do that night and the next day ?

A. We went back to Buffalo, and I and Capt. Beal and this fifth man stayed together at the hotel until the next day at 2 o'clock.

Q. What did you do then ?

A. Then we met the Colonel and Lieut. Headley in a sleigh at the same bridge, the next day at 2 o'clock.

Q. The same party of five, and the same sleigh ?

A. Yes, sir ; it was a two-horse sleigh. Then we went back to the same point on the railroad that we went to on the day before.

Q. What did you do there ?

A. Three of the party went up the track to get the sledge-hammer, I think, and I and the Colonel were in the sleigh.

We hitched the horses and got out, and went up the railroad a piece, and we saw the train coming, and the Colonel had taken up an iron rail and taken one end and laid it across the track. He got the rail by the side of the track.

Q. How far had he got it on the track?

A. He laid it across the track.

Q. Was it then light or dark?

A. It was then just about dark.

Q. What happened, so far as you saw, to the train?

A. I saw it strike the rail; and the whistle blew just then, and it stopped, I suppose, some two or three hundred yards from there. I don't know what damage was done.

Q. What did your party do, or what did the people in the cars do?

A. Somebody came back with a lantern—two or three came back. We went back to the sleigh and went to Buffalo.

Q. What became of the sledge-hammer?

A. It was thrown away; I don't think they got it.

Q. What became of the cold chisel?

A. It was thrown away.

Q. What had the cold chisel been carried in?

A. It had been carried in a carpet-bag.

Q. In the carpet-bag that was taken when you and the accused were arrested?

A. Yes, sir.

Q. In whose possession did you first see that carpet-bag?

A. I saw it in Lieut Headley's possession.

Q. How came it to be in your possession or Capt. Beall's at the time of your arrest?

A. It belonged to the party, I suppose.

Q. Who brought it away from the place of the railroad collision with the rail?

A. It was in the sleigh.

Q. On getting back to Buffalo with the sleigh, what became of the party?

A. They determined to leave and go to Canada ; we took the cars for Suspension Bridge.

Q. Who brought along the carpet-bag ?

A. I think I had it most of the time.

Q. By whose direction ?

A. By direction of the party.

Q. On getting to Suspension Bridge on the train from Buffalo, what was done ?

A. I and Captain Beall were arrested.

Q. What became of the other three ?

A. I don't know ; I never saw them after I left Buffalo.

Q. You and Captain Beall stopped at the depot, and were arrested there ?

A. Yes, sir.

Q. Did you hear the statement that Captain Beall made to the police officers who arrested you and him as to where he came from, and who he was ? State as near as you can recollect all that was said and done at the time of your arrest.

A. Captain Beall told the officer that we were from Point Lookout ; he said that we had escaped from Point Lookout, and were making our way to Canada. I have most forgotten what was said there at the time.

Q. What time in the evening was it that you were arrested ?

A. We were arrested about 9 or 10 o'clock at night ; I and Captain were in the depot seated near together.

Q. How many officers were there who made the arrest ?

A. There were but two officers, I think.

Q. Were you and Captain Beall wide awake when they came in and made the arrest ?

A. I was asleep ; I don't know how he was.

Q. What awoke you ?

A. The officers awoke me ; they pulled me off my seat.

Q. Where was the carpet-bag at that time ?

A. It was on the bench that I was sitting on.

Q. Between you and Captain Beall ?

A. Yes, sir; I think it was.

Q. When Captain Beall stated that you were from Point Lookout, did you say any thing? and if so, what?

A. I think that I assented to what he said, but I did not give any account of myself.

Q. Did Colonel Martin, or Lieutenant Headley, or the accused, at any time in your presence state whether they were under orders, or were acting by anybody's directions?

A. No, sir; I don't thing they did.

Q. What, if any thing, did they tell you they intended or expected to do or accomplish at any or all times when you were with them in or near Buffalo?

A. They did not tell me any thing except about the train.

Q. What did they say about that?

A. The Colonel told me that he expected to capture the express and the money that was on it.

Q. Is that all you recollect?

A. That is all I recollect.

No further questions by the Judge Advocate.

Cross-examination by Accused.

Q. In what part of Virginia were you born?

A. I was born in Pittsylvania County.

Q. How long have you known Captain Beall?

A. The first time I ever saw him was on the railroad.

Q. When did you first enter the service of the Confederate States?

A. I entered it last May, I think.

Q. What corps were you in, and in whose command?

A. In Morgan's; as a private in the cavalry.

Q. When did you become acquainted with Col. Martin?

A. I got acquainted with him when I was with the command.

Q. Was he a Colonel in Morgan's corps?

A. He was with Morgan.

Q. Did you attach yourself to Martin as courier or otherwise ?

A. Yes, sir ; I was courier for the Colonel.

Q. How long did you remain his courier ?

A. I think it was a week or two.

Q. Then what became of you ?

A. I went back to my company.

Q. At what place ?

A. It was about three miles above Rogersville in Tennessee, I think, where I joined my company.

Q. Had you ever seen Lieut. Headley before you joined him at Buffalo ?

A Yes, sir ; he was with Colonel Martin.

Q. You had seen him and knew him personally ?

A. Yes, sir; he was attached to my company about three weeks.

Q. When you went into the hotel with Col. Martin, and it was said that there was a plan in view—who said that there was a plan in view ?

A. It was the Colonel ; I think both of them were speaking of it at the time, and spoke to me.

Q. Did the Colonel introduce you to Headley ?

A. No ; I was acquainted with Headley before.

Q. Was anything said about there being three or some other number of Confederate generals on the express train of the Lake Shore Road, and who were being removed from Johnson's Island to Fort Warren, Massachusetts ?

A. No, sir ; there was not.

Q. Colonel Martin had command of this expedition ?

A. Yes, sir.

Q. And Headley and Capt. Beall acted under his orders ?

A. Yes, sir ; all that I saw acted under his orders.

Q. Was Captain Beall present at the time when it was said what this plan was they had in view about the capture of the train ?

A. No sir; he was not.

Q. Was the accused present at any conversation between Headley and Martin, when you were also present?

A. I don't think that he was; I don't think that we had any conversation in his presence.

Q. Had you ever seen Capt. Beall before the time that you overtook him on the railroad?

A. I never had; not that I know of.

Q. Who told you what his name was?

A. They told me that he was one of the party, and they gave me some name.

Q. Who told you?

A. Lieutenant Headley told me.

Q. Did they tell you that he was an officer in the Confederate service, or about his rank, or any thing of that kind?

A. I don't think they did.

Q. Did they call him Captain, or how did they address him?

A. I have forgotten how they did address him.

Q. Did Captain Beall give you any orders in regard to the attempt to get the rail off the track?

A. No, sir; I don't think he did.

Q. Who gave those orders?

A. Colonel Martin was the principal; I think he gave the orders; it all went by his directions.

Q. When the train struck the rail which Colonel Martin had laid across the track, was your party concealed somewhere?

A. Yes, sir, we were in the woods; I and the Colonel were in the woods; the others, I think, were up the road apiece; I don't know whether they were concealed or not.

Q. Did you all come together again after the train struck?

A. Yes, sir.

Q. Was that at the place where the sleigh had been left?

A. Yes, sir.

Q. And went back to Buffalo?

A. Yes, sir.

Q. Arriving there about what time ?

A. Well sir, we got there, I suppose, an hour after dark; it was about dark when this thing happened, and we went on to Buffalo.

Q. Did you go into the hotel together, or did you separate outside after you got back to Buffalo ?

A. I don't recollect whether we went into any hotels or not.

Q. You say the party determined to go to Canada ?

A. Yes, sir.

Q. What arrangement was made, if any, about your meeting in Canada, you five people ?

A. There was not any arrangement made about meeting; they were all to go, I think, to Toronto.

Q. Why did you not all go together ?

A. There was nothing said, that I recollect, about the reason why we did not go together.

Q. In going from Buffalo to Niagara you were all on the same train ?

A. I suppose we were, but I don't recollect seeing them after we left Buffalo.

Q. When you and Beall were in the depot at Niagara, what were you waiting for ?

A. We were waiting for the train— the eleven o'clock train that night; I think it was the eleven o'clock train.

Q. Was that the only reason why you were in the depot at that time—waiting for the train ?

A. Yes, sir, that is all the reason that I know of.

The accused proposed no further questions.

Examination by the Commission.

Q. What do you mean by Express ?

A. The Express and the money in it.

Q. What do you understand to be the meaning that they were to take the Express train, or the Express in the train ?

A. The Express that I understood was the Express safe.

Q. What did the accused do at the time Col. Martin laid the rail across the track ?

A. He did nothing: there was nobody that did any thing except Colonel Martin.

The Court proposed no further questions; his testimony being read to the witness, he affirmed the same.

The Judge Advocate then read in evidence the three letters of the accused, and acknowledged by him to be his, which were placed by him in the hands of Colonel Burke: one addressed to Colonel Jacob Thompson, Toronto, Canada West, dated January 22, 1865 ; one addressed, by Flag of Truce, to Messrs. Hunter & Lucas, 173 Main Street, Richmond, Virginia, same date , and the third addressed to Col. A. R. Boteler, Richmond, Virginia, by a flag of truce, same date ; which three letters are hereto annexed, and marked Exhibits A, B and C.

The Judge Advocate also read in evidence a pocket diary, which the accused said was kept by him, and was in his own handwriting, and taken from him at Fort Lafayette, commencing Thursday, December 29, 1864.   It is hereto annexed and marked Exhibit D.   The Judge Advocate announced that the prosecution rested here.

The accused being asked if he was ready to proceed with his defence, answered that he was not, and asked for an adjournment until next week.

On motion of a member of the Commission, the further hearing of the case was postponed until Tuesday, February 7, 1865, at 11 o'clock, a.m.

The Commission then adjourned util to-morrow at 11 o'clock, a.m., to meet at Headquarters, New York City.

JOHN A. BOLLES, Major and A.D.C.,
Judge Advocate.

FORT LAFAYETTE, N. Y. HARBOUR,
Feb. 7, 1865, 11 o'clock, a.m.

The Commission met according to adjournment.

Present, all the members, the Judge Advocate, the accused, J. Y. Beall, and his counsel.

The proceedings of the two last days of this trial were read and approved.

The accused then introduced the papers hereto annexed, marked Exhibits E and F, purporting to be copies of the warrant of the appointment of the accused as Master in the insurgent navy, and of a manifesto of the President of the so-called Confederate States ; and there the defence rested.

By leave of the Commission, the counsel for the accused, James T. Brady, Esq., then delivered in behalf of the accused the address hereto annexed, and marked Exhibit G.

Upon the conclusion of the address of the accused by his counsel, the Judge Advocate, in behalf of the prosecution, delivered the address hereto annexed, and marked Exhibit H.

The Commission then adjourned to meet to-morrow, Feb. 8, 1865, at the Department Headquarters, New York City, at 12 o'clock noon.   ●

JOHN A. BOLLES, Major and A.D.C.
Judge Advocate.

————

DEPARTMENT HEADQUARTERS, NEW YORK CITY,
Feb. 8, 1865, 12 o'clock noon.

The Commission met pursuant to adjournment.   Present all the members, and the Judge Advocate.

The Commission was clear for deliberation upon the case of the accused, John Y. Beall.

Upon careful consideration of the evidence adduced, the Commission find the accused, John Y. Beall, as follows :

Of Specification 1, Charge I., ...   Guilty.

"   "   2,   "   . . . .   Guilty.

"   "   3,   "   . . . .   Guilty.

"   "   4,   "   . . . .   Guilty.

"   "   5,   "   . . . .   Guilty.

"   "   6,   "   . . . .   Guilty.

Of CHARGE I, ...   Guilty.

Of Specification 1, Charge II., ...   Guilty.

"   "   2,   "   . . . .   Guilty.

"   "   3,   "   . . . . . . Not Guilty.

On the day alleged in this specification :

Of CHARGE II, ...   Guilty.

And the Commission do therefore sentence him, the said John Y. Beall, to be hanged by the neck until dead, at such time and place as the General in Command of the Department may direct, two-thirds of the members concurring therein.

     FITZ HENRY WARREN, Brig.-Gen. U. S. Vols.,

                          President.

     JOHN A. BOLLES, Major and A.D.C.,

                       Judge Advocate.

Exhibit A.

[One U. S. Stamp enclosed.]

     FORT LAFAYETTE, N. Y., Jan. 22d, 1865.

Mr. D. B, LUCAS,

     173 Main St., Richmond, Va.

DEAR DAN.,—I have taken up board and lodging at this famous establishment. I was captured in December last, and spent Xmas in the Metropolitan Hd. Qrs. Police Station. I am now being tried for irregular warfare, by a Military Commission, a species of court.

The acts are said to have been committed on Lake Erie and the Canada frontier. You know that I am not a " guerillero " or " spy."

I desire you to get the necessary evidence that I am in the Confederate service, regularly, and forward it to me at once. I shall write to Cols. Boteler and Holliday in regard to this matter. I must have this evidence. As the Commission so far have acted fairly, I am confident of an acquittal. Has Will been exchanged? I saw that Steadman had been killed in Kentucky. Alas! how they fall! Please let my family know if possible of my whereabouts. Where is my Georgia friend? Have you heard any thing from her since I left? May God bless her. I should like so much to hear from her, from home, Will, and yourself. Be so kind, therefore, as to attend at once to this business for me. Remember me to any and all of my friends that you may see.

Send me some postage stamps for my correspondence.

Hoping soon to hear from you,

I remain your friend,

J. Y. BEALL,

C. S. N.

If Mr. Lucas is not in Richmond, will Mr. HUNTER ATTEND to this AT ONCE?

Exhibit B.

[I enclose a U. S. Stamp.]

FORT LAFAYETTE, N. Y., Jan. 22d, 1865.

Col. A. R. BOTELER,

Richmond, Va.

DEAR SIR,—I am on trial before a Military Commission for irregular warfare, as a " guerillero " and " spy." The acts are said to have been committed on Lake Erie and at Suspension Bridge, in September and December last.

As I cannot in person procure any papers from Richmond, I have to rely on my friends, and therefore I request you to procure evidence of my being regularly in service, and forward such evidence at once to me. I have also written

L

to Messrs. Hunter and Lucas. Please call on them in regard
to this, and also Mr. Henderson if necessary.

Very truly, your friend,

J. Y. BEALL,

C. S. N.

Exhibit C.

FORT LAFAYETTE, N. Y., Jan. 22nd, 1865.

Col. JACOB THOMPSON,

Toronto, C. W.

SIR,—I was captured in December, and am on trial
before a Military Commission for irregular warfare, as a
" guerillero " and " spy." The acts are said to have been
committed on Lake Erie and at Suspension Bridge, N. Y.,
in September and December last.

I desire to procure from my Government and its authorities evidence of my being regularly in service, and of
having been acting under and by authority. Please procure
and forward me, as soon as possible, certificates or other
evidence confirming this fact.

The Commission so far have evidenced a disposition to treat
me fairly and equitably. With the evidence you can send,
together with that I have a right to expect from Richmond
and elsewhere, I am confident of an acquittal.

Please attend at once to this, acknowledging at any rate
the receipt of this letter.

Very respectfully,

J. Y. BEALL.

Exhibit D.

THURSDAY, Dec. 29th, 1864.

I purpose to keep in this little book a daily account of my
imprisonment as far as I can.

First. As to my incarceration :

I was arrested Friday, December 16th, in the N.Y. Cen-

tral R. R. station house, at the Suspension Bridge (junction
with Gr. Western R.R. of Canada). I was brought to this
city on Sunday evening (18th), and lodged here. I have
been taken out some half dozen times to be shown men, whose
houses have been attempted by fire, or property otherwise
attempted. The *modus operandi* is this : The prisoner, unkempt, roughly clad, dirty, and bearing marks of confinement,
is placed among well-dressed detectives, and the recognizer
is shown in. As a matter of course he can tell who is the
stranger. My *home* is a cell about 8 feet by 5, on the ground
floor. The floor is stone ; the walls brick ; the door iron, the
upper half grated, and opens into a passage running in front
of three other cells ; this passage is lighted by two large
windows doubly grated, and has an iron door ; at night it is
lighted with gas. The landscape view from my door, through
the window, is that of an area of some 30 feet square. By
special arrangement I have a mattress and blanket. There is
a supply of water in my room, and a sink. My meals are
brought three times a day, about 9, 3 and 7. My library
consists of two New Testaments. I am trying to get a Book
of Common Prayer. The first week there were brought to
this place ten persons, charged with criminal offences ; men,
women, and children. At first I took an interest in their
cases, but now I do not ; they all have been guilty, I believe,
and they all wished me a speedy riddance. Nearly every
one I have met with seems to regard society as his enemy
and a just prey. They look on an offence simply a skirmish.
Profane, lying and thieving, what a people ! Nearly all
recommend me to take the oath of allegiance and enter the
army and desert. But some are opposed to betraying comrades (" going back on 'em "), while others more liberal
advocate any means as legitimate to save oneself from severe
punishment. The Christmas of '64 I spent in New York
prison ! Had I, four years ago, stood in New York, and
proclaimed myself a citizen of Virginia, I would have been

welcomed ; now I am immured because I am a Virginian *tempora mutantur, et cum illis mutamus.* As long as I am a citizen of Virginia, I shall cling to her destiny and maintain her laws as expressed by a majority of her citizens speaking through their authorized channel, if her voice be for war or peace. I shall go as she says. But I would not go for a minority carrying on war in opposition to the majority, as the innocent will suffer and not the guilty ; but I do not justify oppression in the majority. What misery have I seen during these four years, murder, lust, hate, rapine, devastation, war! What hardships suffered, what privations endured! May God grant that I may not see the like again! Nay, that my country may not! Oh, far rather would I welcome Death, *come as he might;* far rather would I meet him than go through four more such years. I can now understand why David would trust to his God, rather than to man.

Since I have been placed in this cell I have read the Scripture, and have found such relief in its blessed words, especially where it speaks of God's love for man ; how He loved him, an enemy, a sinner, and sent His Son into the world to save His enemy ; how He compels the wretched from the hedges and highways to come into the feast ; how any may come, and how He bids them, entreats them. Though it may seem unmanly to accept offers in our adversity which we neglected in prosperity, yet it is even so that with his assistance I will go up and beg forgiveness, and put my trust in the saving blood of Him who died for man. Aye, I pray Him to grant His grace to my mother and sisters and my loved one. If He is with them, who can be against?

What pleasure I take in the hymns I learned in boyhood! They come back to me now in my manhood and in my sorrow, and with God's blessing have wiled away and comforted many a weary and lagging hour.

Dec. 30th. Last evening the doorman brought me a

" Book of Common Prayer " for $1.00, and it was and will be a source of great comfort to me. I read over the familiar services and oft-heard hymns, and committed two—" Rock of Ages " and " Sinners, turn, why will ye die ?"—to memory. There were four accused in three cells last night. As yet I have heard but one give good advice to another. They all with one accord exhort one another to be good soldiers in warfare *vs.* society, not to give up stolen property ; and above all, not to trust to the detectives, who are their natural and mortal enemies. Such is life ! ! !

Dec. 31*st.* The year is gone ; begun for me in ——; it sees me, as it dies, a prisoner in New York. To-day I complete my twenty-ninth year. What have I done to make this world any wiser or better ? May God bless me in the future ; be it in time or eternity. May I be enabled to meet my trials with resignation, patience, fortitude, as one who serves his country and home and people. The year went out in rain—drizzling rain. Will I see the year 1865 go out ? or will I pass away from this world of sin, shame, and suffering ?

Jan. 1*st*, 1865. Sunday, first day of the week and first day of the new year. To-day I enter my thirtieth year of pilgrimage. According to the calculation of my father's family, I am more than half-way down life's stream, even if spared by war and sudden death. But in prying into the future, I can see nothing to induce me to think that my days will be lengthened to that age of fatality, fifty-six. Has my life been so crowded with pleasure or good deeds, that I need desire to prolong it ? Alas ! no. Though well reared, and surrounded with very many advantages, I have not done anything to give me particular pleasure ; nor, on the other hand, have I been remarkable for the opposite. I am truly thankful that I always stayed with mother and the girls, and tried to do my duty by them ; that is one consolation at least, and also that I never voluntarily left them. They know not

where I am to-day; and every one of them is this day thinking of me.   Little do they know where I am.   Indeed, I
doubt if they have heard anything definite from me for many
a weary month.   Oh this war!

This far on life's way I have lived an honest life, defrauding no man.   Those blows that I have struck have been
against the society of a hostile nation; not against the
society of which I am a member by right, or *vs.* mankind
generally.   To-day the thought has obtruded itself again and
again to become an "Ishmael."   Your country is ruined,
your hopes dashed—make the best bargain for yourself.
"Remember the history of the civil wars of France, of England—the examples of Talleyrand, Josephine, &c.; of
Shaftesbury, Caermarthen, Marlborough," &c.   To-day my
hands have no blood on them (unless of man in open battle);
may I say so when I die.   I saw grandfather and father
die; they both took great comfort from the thought that no
one could say that they had of malice aforethought injured
them.   Better the sudden death, or all the loathsome corruption of a lingering life, with honour and pure conscience, than
a long life with all material comforts and the canker-worm of
infelt and constant dwelling dishonour; aye, a thousand times.
O God, our Creator, Preserver, and Saviour! I pray give me
strength to resist temptation, to drive back the thick-coming
fancies brooded of sin and dishonour, and to cling to the faith
of Jesus, who said "Do unto others as you would that they
should do unto you."

Jan. 2d. Last night was called out, and a search made of
my room and my person.   The captures consisted of two
knives.   Poor Grimes! your gift and keepsake was duly declared contraband and confiscated.   They gave me two newspapers, which do seem to bear out the statements of Southern loss, &c.   Savannah, indeed, is fallen; but its garrison
was saved, so that Hardee and Beauregard have an army.
And Butler did not take Wilmington, though the fleet did

storm long and heavy. Poor Bragg has some laurels at last. Oh that Gen. Lee had 50,000 good fresh veteran reinforcements! But what are these things to me here! I do most earnestly wish that I was in Richmond. Oh for the wings to fly to the uttermost part of the earth!

What would I do without the Bible and Prayer-book, and the faith taught in them, best boon of God, the fount of every blessing? That faith nothing can take away save God.

Exhibit E.

[COPY.]

CONFEDERATE STATES OF AMERICA, NAVY DEPARTMENT.
Richmond, March 5th, 1863.

SIR,—You are hereby informed that the President has appointed you an Acting Master in the Navy of the Confederate States. You are requested to signify your acceptance or non-acceptance of this appointment; and should you accept, you will sign before a magistrate the oath of office herewith, and forward the same, with your letter of acceptance, to this Department.

Registered No. ——.

The lowest number takes rank.

(Signed)   S. P. MALLORY.
Secretary of the Navy.

Acting Master JOHN Y. BEALL, of Va., C.S.N.
Richmond, Va.

(ENDORSED.)

CONFEDERATE STATES OF AMERICA, NAVY DEPARTMENT.
Richmond, 23d December, 1864.

I certify that the reverse of this page presents a true copy of the warrant granted to John Y. Beall, as an Acting Master in the Navy of the Confederate States, from the records of this Department.

In testimony whereof I have herewith set my hand and

affix the seal of this Department, on the day and year above written.

(Signed)   S. P. MALLORY,
                    Secretary of the Navy.

Exhibit F.

BY AUTHORITY—CONFEDERATE STATES OF AMERICA.

Whereas, It has been made known to me that BENNETT G. BURLEY, an Acting Master in the Navy of the Confederate States, is now under arrest in one of the British North American provinces, on an application made by the Government of the United States for the delivery to that Government of the said BENNETT G. BURLEY, under the treaty known as the Extradition Treaty, now in force between the United States and Great Britain; and whereas it has been represented to me that the said demand for the extradition of said BENNETT G. BURLEY is based on a charge that the said BURLEY is a fugitive from justice, accused of having committed the crimes of robbery and piracy in the jurisdiction of the United States; and whereas, it has further been made known to me that the accusations and charges made against the said BENNETT G. BURLEY are based solely on the acts and conduct of said BURLEY, in an enterprise made or attempted in the month of September last, 1864, for the capture of the steamer *Michigan,* an armed vessel of the United States, navigating the lakes on the boundary line between the United States and the said British North American Provinces, and for the release of numerous citizens of the Confederate States, held as prisoners of war by the United States at a certain island called Johnson's Island; and whereas, the said enterprise or expedition for the capture of the said armed steamer *Michigan,* and for the release of the said prisoners on Johnson's Island, was a proper and legitimate belligerent operation, undertaken during the pend-

ing public war between the two Confederacies, known
respectively as the Confederate States of America and the
United States of America, which operation was ordered,
directed, and sustained by the authority of the Government
of the Confederate States, and confided to its commissioned
officers for execution, among which officers is the said BEN-
NETT G. BURLEY ;

Now, therefore, I, JEFFERSON DAVIS, President of the
Confederate States of America, do hereby declare and make
known to all whom it may concern, that the expedition aforesaid, undertaken in the month of September last, for the
capture of the armed steamer *Michigan*, a vessel of war of the
United States, and for the release of the prisoners of war,
citizens of the Confederate States of America, held captive by
the United States of America at Johnson's Island, was a belligerent expedition ordered and undertaken under the authority of the Confederate States of America, against the United
States of America, and that the Government of the Confederate States of America assumes the responsibility of answering
for the acts and conduct of any of its officers engaged in said
expedition, and especially of the said BENNET. G. BURLEY,
an Acting Master in the navy of the Confederate States.

And I do further make known to all whom it may concern,
that in the orders and instructions given to the officers engaged
in said expedition, they were specially directed and enjoined
to " abstain from violating any of the laws and regulations of
the Canadian or British authorities in relation to neutrality,"
and that the combination necessary to effect the purpose of
said expedition " must be made by Confederate soldiers and
such assistance as they might (you may) draw from the
enemy's country."

In testimony whereof I have signed this manifesto, and
directed the same to be sealed with the seal of the Department of State of the Confederate States of America, and to
be made public.

Done at the city of Richmond, on the 24th day of December, 1864.

JEFFERSON DAVIS.

By the President,

J. P. BENJAMIN, *Sec. of State.*

Exhibit G.

Address of James T. Brady, Esq., Counsel for the Accused.

MR. PRESIDENT AND GENTLEMEN OF THE COMMISSION,— Since I had the honour of appearing before this Court on the last day, there has, been a publication in all our newspapers relating to the activity and success of a number of our detectives in ferretting out, as is supposed, the perpetrators of the attempt to fire the city of New York. That, of course, you gentlemen have all read, and being gentlemen of intelligence, reading it has made some impression on your mind. In ordinary cases an advocate seeking every advantage for an accused party, lays great stress on the fact that a person called a juror may have had his mind impressed by the publication of a statement affecting him, and it is, as you know, a reason frequently for setting a juror aside; I have never, either as a lawyer or individual, attached much importance to that suggestion. I should be very sorry though, if any man claiming to be intelligent, should read any account of the transaction, and say it did not produce some kind of impression on his mind, and I only allude to it now for the purpose of saying that Captain Beall's name was mixed up in that, with a great many inaccuracies, and so far as there is any hint or suggestion there that he was either connected, or could be connected with that incendiary attempt, it is without foundation. He spurns any such suggestion; and he has spent most of the time since I came into this room in vindicating himself from such an aspersion; and he begs, that if the Court have any idea that he had the least concern in that transaction, he may be put upon

his trial for that.   He talks like a soldier and like a gentleman, and expresses the most unlimited confidence in the fairness
and integrity of this Commission ; but he has the natural apprehension that every man would have in like position, that
these out-door publications may insensibly affect the mind of
some persons—though he feels from the profession, and the
dignity and professional honour of the Court, that he is hardly
warranted in entertaining that idea, however remotely.   I
wish to assure him, and to say to the Court, that I have no
such fears.   And I can say to the Court, what they may have
ascertained—what the Government can be informed of if
necessary and proper, that Mr. Beall is of highly respectable
origin.   His ancestors emigrated many years ago from the
north of Ireland.   He was a man of considerable property in
the South, and he entered into the fight which is now going on
from such motives as had impelled men of high intelligence,
and men who, however delusively influenced to such an opinion,
really think as sincerely as we believe in the sacred cause that
we sustain, that they were acting from the most laudable
motives.   And while I presume that all the gentlemen in this
room, like myself, feel that this battle should never cease on
our side until we have imposed again the authority and power
of our Government over all the territory we ever possessed,
and even feel, as I certainly do for one, that when that shall
have been accomplished, the power of this Government should
be felt in other directions, whenever the justification arises ;
yet we would be false to our Maker if we supposed that all
the men who fought on the other side were hypocrites and
fanatics, or were impelled by such bad motives as impelled
men to perpetrate crime.   It would be inconsistent with my
views of the majesty and justice of the Almighty that he
should permit such men, led by such intellects, to act entirely
from unreasonable and blind and wicked impulses.   That we
have justice on our side is undoubtedly in our belief certain.
But soldiers, whatever civilians may do, will never look at an

enemy like the one we are contending against, as utterly
bereft of reason, as utterly inferior to us, and not exactly
level with the brutes.   The accused has been, as the gentlemen of this Court have learned from his diary, I think intelli-
gently educated ; and whether it makes for him or against him,
he has received sound moral culture.   The mother and the
sister to whom he so affectionately refers in that diary, have
exercised over him—the mother first, and the sister afterwards
—those ennobling influences which in the homestead exercise
their great power over all of us in childhood and after life.
And being a gentleman of education, a graduate of the
University of Virginia, he has his own views about this case,
and has communicated them to me, and I will present them to
you.   I have never had the pleasure of addressing, except as a
private citizen, any of the honourable members of this Court;
and my friend Major Bolles—I am sure he will permit me to
call him so, as he has acted as such towards me—and myself have never been associated or opposed in any matter.
And for that reason, at the risk of being considered, for the
moment, egotistical, I wish to say to this Court, on the honour
of a gentleman, that I never have supposed that Lord Broug-
ham's definition of the duties or right of an advocate was
correct.   I have never entertained the idea that it proceeds,
in the view of refined society, or in the view of any instructed
conscience, further than this, that an advocate may fairly
present honourably whatever any man who is accused would
have a right in truth to say for himself, and no more.   With
that view of the duty which I am attempting to discharge on
this occasion, I present in the first place the prisoner's proposition that this Court has no jurisdiction of the matters which
are here being investigated ; that the trial of these offences
should take place in a general court-martial, organized according to the well-established principles of the laws of war ; and
that a Military Commission, though it may exercise power over
the citizens of the Government which establishes it, cannot,

according to the law of war and of nations, take cognizance of
the specific accusations presented here. I have never examined this question at all until this trial arose ; and I say to
you, that the questions involved in this case, except so far as
I have derived my knowledge from my general reading as a
lawyer, are new to me. Some of them seem to be novel even in
reference to the large experience of the Judge Advocate
General, whose opinions are contained in the Digest of his
decisions recently published.

I find by looking through the history of jurisdiction, especially as to spies, that by an Act of Congress of 1808, it is in
terms declared that a person charged as a spy shall be tried
by a general court-martial. The Act of the 13th of February,
1862, contains the same provision ; but the Act of 1863
provides that persons embraced in the description of spies as
there given, may be tried by a court-martial or military commission ; and of course it would seem that if it were within the
power of Congress to make such a law, there is a specific
warrant for trying this party before a military commission on
the charge of being a spy. How much further it extends is
a little questionable. But there is this peculiarity, to which
I must call the attention of the Court. I refer to the Revised
United States Army Regulations of 1863, page 541. In the
Act of 1863 it is provided in the first Section, that so much
of the law of July 17th, 1862, as requires the approval of the
President "to carry into execution the sentence of a court-
martial, be, and the same is hereby repealed, as far as relates
to carrying into execution the sentence of any court-martial
against any person convicted as a spy or deserter."

You see, therefore, that unless there is something to modify
this, a peculiarity arises from this legislation if a man be tried
before a court-martial.

[The Judge Advocate called the attention of the counsel
for the accused to the Act of July 2d, 1864, chapter 215,
passed at the last session of Congress, which extends the

provision to sentences of military commissions as well as court-martials on the trial of spies, guerrillas, &c.   Mr. Brady resumed as follows:]

I am very much obliged to you, and I am confident that something has occurred in legislation on that subject, or in the decisions.   I believe one of the decisions of the Judge Advocate General was to the effect that in equity, that provision would be extended to the cases of conviction before a military commission.   But I had not in my library the Act of the last session; and that being explained to me, I have said all that I wish to present on the subject of jurisdiction, and pass from that to another proposition, and that is, that Capt. Beall in these charges and specifications seems to be treated in two aspects: one as a mere individual, engaged in the perpetration of an offence against society at large; and the other in the character of a military man, offending against the laws of war.   If what is here presented against him in the proof shows that he has only committed some offence against general society cognizable in the ordinary courts of judicature, then he would be entitled under the Constitution of the United States to a trial by jury. That right accompanies him as a citizen of the United States, without any reference to what any revolting States may declare; and whatever the South may say or think, we have not given up a single provision of our Constitution in regard to those matters, although we have heard of, and the Government has acted on the idea of the suspension of the habeas corpus, and done other acts incident and proper to a state of war, so that some of the provisions of the Constitution have been to a certain extent interfered with.   The Court, of course, perceives at once that I am correct in saying he is so treated.   I will refer to this Digest of the opinions of the Judge Advocate General, at pages, 79 and 81.   I read first the 11th paragraph:

" Where a military commission was invested by the original

order of the general convening it, ' with jurisdiction in all cases, civil, criminal, and in equity, usually triable in courts established by law'—held that such a tribunal was not authorized to be created, either by law or usage, and *recommended* that it be ordered by the Secretary of War to be dissolved." Very properly, because in that case it would seem, that in organizing the court the order grasps all kinds of jurisdiction incident to the ordinary tribunals, and that was an assumption of power which the Government through its proper officers, very properly reprehended. I then read paragraph 16, which is as follows :

" The murder of Union soldiers, for the disloyal and treasonable purpose of resisting the Government in its efforts to suppress the rebellion, is a military offence, quite other than the ordinary offence of murder, cognizable by the criminal courts ; and citizens who have been guilty thereof, though in a state where the courts are open, may be brought to trial before a military commission. In such case, the circumstances conferring jurisdiction should be indicated in the charge, and distinctly set forth in the specification." That will commend itself to every member of this Court. It is quite possible that a man in the Confederate service, ordinarily engaged as a soldier by his Government—I shall use their phrase of course—might come within our lines and perpetrate a murder as an individual, in a way and under circumstances wholly divested of any relation with his military character, for private gain or personal revenge. The mere fact that he was a Confederate soldier, that he was within our lines, and that he murdered one of our citizens, would not render him amenable either to a court-martial or a military commission, if the circumstances indicated nothing giving it the quality of a military offence. That you very well understand. That is illustrated in this case of murder, where the Court and Judge Advocate must state the special circumstances which give to that murder of Union soldiers the quality and character bringing it within the jurisdiction of a military tribunal.

Now, in the expedition of Lake Erie, with which the accused is connected, and the other attempt on the railroad, offences were committed cognizable by the laws, in one case of Ohio and in the other of New York ; punishable by those laws.   And if the evidence should establish that the persons engaged in either of those acts were acting irrespective of character as soldiers of the Confederate Government, then we respectfully submit that neither this Court nor a Court-martial would have authority to try the accused.   If one of our soldiers should straggle and go into Richmond, or into any of the towns along the path of Sherman's army, and remain there and secrete himself and commit larceny or burglary, he would not be amenable to any court-martial in the South for any such act, as we understand it.   And we apply the same principle to the same act perpetrated in our lines by a Confederate soldier.

In regard to the offence of the attempt to throw this railroad train off the track, wholly irrespective of the design avowed, according to the testimony of the witness Anderson, to take possession of the safe and money, we have a statute in New York, passed in 1838, which distinctly makes it an offence to do any such thing in regard to railroad trains, and subjects the offender to five years' imprisonment in the States Prison, or one year in the penitentiary, according to the judgment and discretion of the court.

The Act of March 1863, section 30, provides this : " *And be it further enacted*, That in times of war, insurrection, or rebellion, murder, assault and battery with an intent to kill, manslaughter, mayhem, wounding by shooting or stabbing, with an intent to commit murder, robbery, arson, burglary, rape, assault and battery with an intent to commit rape and larceny, shall be punishable by the sentence of a general court-martial or military commission, when committed by persons who are in the military service of the United States, and subject to the articles of war." Congress deemed it necessary thus to provide for the authority of a court-martial to punish our own citizens when in the military service for the crimes of murder, robbery, &c.

But the accused and myself respectfully submit that the perpetration by a man who happens to be a Confederate soldier, within our territory, of an offence, in the consummation of which he acts not in any military capacity or quality, is not an offence which a court-martial or military commission can take cognizance of.   And if you look at this man who is here now, as here amongst us without a uniform, acting as a mere aggressor against general society, the punishment of his offence belongs to the ordinary tribunals and not to this. I will consider that again in connection with the specific charge of his being a guerrilla, where it is supposed that the due authority for taking cognizance of this case will be found. I pass it for the present, having closed what I intended to say on the subject of the tribunal which should investigate this case, and the principles by which they should be governed.

The accused also insists through the medium of his own reason and his reading and reflection, that the charge—particularly the first charge—" violating the laws of war," is too general and vague, and does not conform to the requirements of the law applicable to cases of this character.

When I was first consulted in this case, it was suggested that the objection to the generality of this charge should be made at the outset, and that is the usual course.   But I said that so far as that objection was worthy of any consideration, the honorable members of this Court would consider it quite as much in their ultimate action as if the objection was specifically made.   And I must say to my client, with your permission, that usually the objection to anything on account of its generality is not of practical value, because if it be

M

erroneous, it is only informing your adversary to make it more specific. It is of no advantage to the accused ; and I hope the accused, in this instance, will feel, as I do, that this Court has acted with the greatest possible courtesy—certainly to me and I think to the accused ; and the Judge Advocate has not done anything in this case not eminently professional and honourable, and I am certain he will do nothing prejudicial to the accused except in such manner as becomes an officer and a gentleman. I lay no stress, therefore, upon this objection as to the generality of the charge, because I don't see that there is any substance in it, except the one that naturally suggests itself to the accused that he might be tried again, and the charge, " Violation of the laws of war," would not show what specific offences were presented against him. I leave this part of the case with just that remark, and come directly to what I understand to be the substance of the two accusations, without reference to the language of the specifications. And we have ourselves met with the charge, in the first place, that he was a spy : and, in the second place, a guerrilla.

This charge of being a spy seems, from the language of these specifications and the tenor of the proof, intended to apply to him during all the time that he was in the condition which, for the present, I shall call *within our lines*, though I presently may have to ask this Honourable Court to inform themselves what that phrase means, as applied to the particular war now being waged between the two sections of our country. What are lines ? Now, as to his being a spy, I may deceive myself, but I see no proof whatever to justify that accusation. And if, in what I am now about to say, I shall accidentally bring my mind in conflict with any settled opinions which you gentlemen of the profession of war may have in your own minds, you will be good enough mentally to pardon me and wait till I get through with the demonstration I attempt to offer. And not to appear pedantic, as any man may become, who looks through encyclopædias and dictionaries, and gets the reputation of being learned without the merit,—for as the poet has said :

> " Digested learning makes no student pale;
> It takes the eel of science by the tail,"—

let me come to the definition of the word *spy*. We know it comes from the French word *espionner*—to observe with the eye.

That definition is certainly not broad enough, because a blind man might be a spy and a very good one. He may roam through the country as a blind beggar, and through his ear receive intelligence to his side of the greatest service.

And, if actual observation with the eye were necessary, Major André was not a spy, for he made no observation within our lines that could be of any possible service. He was not there for that object. He came there to meet Arnold, to get despatches with a view to deliver them to Sir Henry Clinton. He was convicted of being a spy because he was within the enemy's line to receive intelligence, and deliver it to the Commander-in-Chief of his own army, that it might be used against the Colonies.

That is a very clear case of being a spy ; just as clear as the case of Davis who was convicted the other day, a man who was carrying despatches from Canada to the South, and passing through our lines for the purpose of communicating that intelligence. And I cannot imagine how all this sympathy is wasted upon André, which I am sorry to say has found its way into the excellent work of Phillimore on International Law. It is true that André had on a uniform, but it was covered over with an outer coat. There was an actual concealment of the true character of the man, and he was travelling with a false pass, I may say, from Arnold ; and Arnold had the impudence to insist that André should be surrendered to Sir Henry Clinton, because he was travelling under this traitorous pass given by him.

And André the less deserves our sympathy, because one letter of his addressed to Col. Sheldon is in existence, mentioned in Irving's Life of Washington, showing that he intended to take advantage of a flag of truce for the purpose of holding his communications with Arnold. And if any thing on earth known among men, recognized by society, and sustained by humanity, is deserving of veneration, it is a flag of truce—that Divine aspect of Heaven amidst the grim and bloody horrors of war.

Now the definitions of the term *spy*, which I will take the liberty to mention so as to recall your memories to the nature of the word, are, first, from Webster. He gives three : 1st. " A person sent into an enemy's camp to inspect their works, ascertain their strength and their intentions, to watch their movements, and secretly communicate intelligence to the proper officer. By the laws of war among all civilized nations, a spy is subjected to capital punishment. 2nd. A person deputed to watch the conduct of others. 3rd. One who watches the conduct of others."

Of course, the first is the only one important in reference to the word *spy* as used in these charges and specifications. Bouvier, in his Law Dictionary, says a spy is " one who goes into a place for the purpose of ascertaining the best way of doing an injury there. The term is mostly applied to an enemy who comes into the camp for the purpose of ascertaining its situation in order to make an attack upon it."

Bailey gives, I think, the best definition of spy that I have found anywhere ; but of its excellence, of course you will be the judge. He says a spy is "one who clandestinely searches into the state of places and affairs."

Major General Halleck, in his most valuable treatise on International Law and the Laws of War, at page 406, says this : " Spies are persons who, *in disguise, or under false pretences*, insinuate themselves among the enemy, in order to discover the state of his affairs, to pry into his designs, and then communicate to their employer the information thus obtained...........................The term *spy* is frequently applied to persons sent to reconnoitre an enemy's position, his forces, defences, &c., but not in disguise, or under false pretences.   Such, however, are not *spies* in the sense in which that term is used in military and international law, nor are persons so employed liable to any more rigorous treatment than ordinary prisoners of war.   It is the *disguise* or *false pretence*, which constitutes the perfidy, and forms the essential element of the crime, which by the laws of war, is punishable with an ignominious death."

We see, therefore, that irrespective of the Acts of Congress, from the nature and signification of the word *spy ;* from the definitions which have been given to it by intelligent writers; from what is said here by the General, who is certainly an excellent authority, there must, to constitute the crime of a spy, be something in the nature of a disguise, and the purpose of it to clandestinely obtain information to communicate it to the enemy.   Now, let us see what Congress has said on the subject.   I refer to page 502 of the Army Regulations, and this is somewhat interesting to me, whatever it may be to the Court—I mean the character of the legislation on this subject.   In 1806, Congress provided : " That in time of war all persons not citizens of, or owing allegiance to, the United States of America, who shall be found lurking as spies in or about the fortifications or encampments of the armies of the United States, or any of them, shall suffer death, according to the law and usage of nations, by sentence of a General Court-Marshal."

It related, you see, exclusively to persons not citizens of the United States, and did not owe it allegiance ; and no other persons, by the definition of Congress, could be regarded as spies.   So matters remained, for we had no occasion to legislate on the subject at all, until the act of 1862 was passed, which provides " that, in time of war or rebellion against the supreme authority of the United States, all persons who shall be found lurking as spies or acting as such, in or about the fortifications, encampments, posts, quarters, or headquarters of the armies of the United States, or any of them, within any part of the United States which has been or may be declared to be in a state of insurrection by proclamation of the President of the United States, shall suffer death by sentence of a General Court-Martial."

That, you will perceive, is a provision made to reach the case of persons acting as spies in the South, or in such portions of the States, or in such States as were in rebellion; and Congress seems to have considered that special legislation was necessary for that object; and that won't apply to the accused; but, in 1863, the last legislation that I know of on this subject contains the provision : " *And be it further enacted,* That all persons who, in time of war or of rebellion against the supreme authority of the United States, shall be found lurking, or *acting* as *spies* in or about any of the fortifications, posts, quarters, or encampments of any of the armies of the United States, or *elsewhere*, shall be triable by a general Court-Martial or military commission, and shall, upon conviction, suffer death.'

All persons—there is no longer the distinction that they shall not be citizens or owe allegiance to the United States. The term is now large and comprehensive ; but they must be lurking or acting as spies in or about the fortifications, camps, &c. ; and I would respectfully submit to the Court that the words " or *elsewhere*," only mean elsewhere in reference to something of the same character. They cannot mean any place in the wide world, because, according to that definition, if a man were out in the middle of the prairies on his way, or if he were in any state in the South, if he were near any fortification that we had there, or was away from any fortification, if he were lurking, it would reach him. Therefore it seems that so far as Congress has legislated upon this subject, they only treat as a spy a person who is lurking, acting specifically as a spy, in or near some place where the army is, with a view to detect its movements and inform the enemy; and the question will be whether the prisoner stands in that category. Now, of course I heard when I was a boy, before I had ever looked at a law book, that there was a traditional idea, and it seems to have prevailed to this moment, that the mere fact of an enemy's being found within the lines of an adversary, without a uniform, constitutes the offence of being a *spy*. We find that that is not strictly correct, or else it becomes correct by reason of his appearing without a uniform being equivalent to assuming a disguise.

Well, of course, it is just as much a disguise to take off a dress by which you are ordinarily characterized, as to put on one different from your ordinary garb. That I concede, and it is very plain ; but in the case of the accused, there is no proof that he ever had a uniform, that he ever owned one or wore one ; and I suppose you, gentlemen, know that, as a general thing, if not almost invariably, there is no such thing as a uniform in the South, and has not been for two or three years, except in the general resemblance that their clothes have ; and I believe you know that, in almost every case, if I am correctly informed, where an officer of the Confederate Government has been captured by our side, he has not had on any buttons or other insignia to denote his rank or condition. There may have been many cases to the contrary ; but if I am correctly informed, General Johnson, when captured by Hancock, had no uniform on. He had a round hat, and was very ordinarily attired. He was found in our lines, and in citizen's dress. Where he got that dress; how long he had worn it ; whether he had had any other for the last five years, we know nothing about. But whatever may have been his dress at any time while within our territory, when will this Honourable Court say that the accused was within our lines, which is essential to constitute his being a spy? What are, in a military sense, the lines of the United States Army for the purpose of determining the question of one's being a spy, or any other question? Now, even if I felt so disposed, I have not the capacity to give this Honourable Court any information. That is a matter which military gentlemen understand perfectly, and they must determine for themselves. All of us who have been educated at all have some general idea of it; but when we seek for definitions from the lexicographers, we derive very little assistance. I find Mr. Webster, in his dictionary, only gives one: "A trench or rampart; an extended work in fortification," for which definition he cites Dryden. Now, I respectfully ask you, what are the lines of the United States Army, the being within which, in disguise, would constitute being a spy, if there were nothing to take that character away from the accused party? Do you mean all of the United States not in rebellion? Why any more or less than all the territory that the United States ever occupied or governed? We have never consented to the idea that we have parted with one inch of that territory for any purpose. We claim that the United States exist now as they always did, and exist under the same Constitution as ever, for there is no other Constitution; and whatever moral progress, whatever intellectual progress, we may have made, however far we may have advanced toward any philanthropic or other result, we have had no other Constitution, and we never can have, until we change it in the mode prescribed in the Constitution itself, and by which we have just taken a step toward the abolition of slavery. So that, in a general sense, if the United States now should get into a war with France or England, according to what seems to be claimed here in the case of Capt. Beall, the whole of our territory would be the lines of the United States Army. Is that so? Or has this word *lines* a particular signification in military law and practice more restricted than that? If it have, you can say to one another what it is;

and when this Court shall have disposed of its duties in this case, if I have the pleasure of meeting one of you gentlemen, and there is nothing improper in it, I shall ask you to construct a definition which may be of service to me in the future. But I had supposed the word lines had some reference in general parlance to a camp. You may make a city a camp or an entire district, but I don't know that you can make a whole country a camp. I don't know whether Cæsar, Hannibal, or Alexander, in any of their extensive marches, could have established as their camps the whole country through which they went. I don't suppose that General Sherman could claim the whole of the State of Georgia as his camp. All this may be of very little consideration to you, because you know so much more about it than I; but I respectfully submit that the word lines must mean some imaginary or prescribed territory relating to, and directly affected by the government of the army as such; and in that sense I don't see how Beall was within our lines in a military sense, because he happened to be in the State of Ohio taking passage in a steamboat, or up at Niagara in the State of New York; the State of New York never for one moment being subject to any kind of military occupation. I don't see how the State of Ohio or the State of New York could be within our lines. But that proposition I submit to your intelligence and judgment.

But suppose it should appear that the accused was in disguise, or without uniform, and within our lines; what was he here for? Was he here to lurk as a spy? Why, not at all. The evidence not only fails to show that, but it directly establishes that he was not. A man belonging to the Confederate service might come within our lines without his uniform, for a very lawful purpose. He might come to perform an act of humanity; he might come to see a friend or relation, not to speak one word on the subject of war. I think I may say I know the fact that officers of the armies on both sides who have had the acquaintance of ladies before this war have crossed the lines to visit them. And if you could to a certainty prove that a Confederate officer came within our lines, or they could prove that one of our officers went within their lines for a mere social purpose, it instantly divests him of the character of a spy. I will now refer you to the Digest of the opinions of the Judge Advocate General, page 127 : " That an officer or soldier of the rebel army coming within our lines disguised in the dress of a citizen, is *primâ facia* evidence of his being a spy. The disguise so assumed strips him of all claim to be treated as a prisoner of war. But such evidence may be rebutted by proof that he had come within our lines to visit his family, and not for the purpose of obtaining information as a spy."

And then this is stated : " The spy must be taken in *flagrante delicto*. If he is successful in making his escape, the crime, according to a well-settled principle of law, does not fathom him, and, of course, if subsequently captured in battle, he cannot be tried for it.

" Merely for a citizen to come secretly within our lines from the South, in violation of paragraph 86, of General Order 100, of 1863, does not constitute him a spy. A rebel soldier, cut off in Early's retreat from Maryland, and wandering about in disguise within our lines for more than a month, and seeking for an opportunity to join the rebel army, but not going outside our lines since first entering them : *held* not strictly chargeable as a spy."

Now, on this subject we find that the accused did not come here as a spy, nor for any such purpose. He came on one occasion, if you believe the testimony in this case, to assist in a demonstration for the relief of the prisoners on Johnson's Island ; a specific purpose of war if he acted in a military capacity. And in the other case, he was in the State of New York engaged in the capture of a railroad train, so as to get possession of the mails and money in the

express safe ; and coming for either of those purposes, he
did not come to lurk or make himself a spy in any way.
And on that subject the Judge Advocate has been good
enough to present the letters and diary of this young man to
prove his declarations.   Now, on the subject of declarations,
the law is this, and it has always been the law : If I prove
in reference to a man, in any proceeding, civil or criminal,
his statements, they must always be taken together ; what
exculpates you as well as that which proves you guilty. That
is a rule of the soundest reason.   If you should happen
to shoot a man, and another person should arrest you, and
should ask, " Who perpetrated this ?" and you should say,
" I killed that man, but I did it in self-defence," by no law
of reason or justice could the first part of that statement be
proved against you and the rest reserved.   And more than
that ; when you prove a man's statements or declarations, as
they are called technically, they must be taken as true,
unless they are in their nature incredible, or unless they are
disproved by some other testimony.   Now, we have here the
letters written by this man, to which I shall refer—written
while he has been in custody ; and for what he writes, and
states, and does, the accused holds himself responsible.

[Mr. Brady read extracts from the three above-mentioned
letters, which are in evidence, and from the diary of the
accused, which is also in evidence, and proceeded as follows :]

Now, bearing upon this question of whether he was one
who intended to engage in the business of being a spy, I
invite your attention to this diary, so impressively read by
my friend the Judge Advocate, the other day, where the
accused declares in regard to himself, that although he has
been imperfect—and which of us has not—that although his
life has not been one unvarying progress of what is pure and
good, he only reproaches himself as a Christian reproaches
himself ; as any one of us reproaches himself in the silent
watches of the night, when we are apt to suppose ourselves

more completely in the presence of our Maker, and we are
compelled to acknowledge the weakness, and imperfections,
and folly which have disfigured our lives. It is only in this
sense he has reproached himself. But he takes credit to
himself, and thanks the Lord that he can say: " I never
stained my hand with the blood of my fellow man, except in
lawful battle ; and I cling to my mother and sister, and never
left them voluntarily." I cite these things—fortunately in
this case—as showing who it is you are trying, and as
bearing upon the general probability of this young man, just
thirty years of age, having forgotten the principles that he
learned at the fireside, and by hereditary transmission from
honoured and honourable parents— the probability of his doing
anything except what he intended to be, and regarded as
honourable warfare, according to the civilized customs of
mankind. And I can assure you that there is nothing in that
man's nature which does not make it abhorrent to him, if I
am a judge of human nature at all, to do anything than what
a misled Virginian would think was just and manly, on the
side to which his conscience, conviction, education, and
military attainments, led him.   I think, therefore, that I am
warranted in saying, that the charge of being a spy is not
only not sustained, but entirely disproved.   He did not come
as a spy ; he did not lurk as a spy ; he sought no information ;
he obtained none ; he communicated none.   He was arrested
at Niagara on his way to Canada, having, according to his
declaration to Mr. Thomas, a witness of the Government, and
whose statement the Government must act upon, reached
Baltimore after the failure of the expedition on Lake Erie,
been provided there with funds, and was making his way to
Canada.   He was just exactly in the condition of that soldier
in Early's army who had been wandering about in our lines
in disguise, waiting for an opportunity to return to the rebel
force.   And that is precisely what this man was engaged in
doing, irrespective of the assault upon the railroad train to

which I am about to refer. Under those circumstances he
was not a spy—he was anything and everything but a spy.
He was acting under a commission; he was in the service of
the rebel Government; he was engaged in carrying on warfare; he was not endeavouring to perpetrate any offence
against society. And if he were not acting under a commission or with authority, but was acting upon his own
responsibility and from the wicked intent of his own heart for
motives of personal malice or gain, he is not amenable to this
tribunal, but must answer to the ordinary courts of the State
within which the crime was committed.

I now proceed to the second subject—the accusation that
he was acting in violation of the law of war as a guerrilla.
On that subject the Judge Advocate General says, at p. 66:

" The charge of being a guerrilla may be deemed a
military offence, *per se* like that of ' being a spy,' the character
of the guerrilla having become, during the present rebellion,
as well understood as that of a spy, and the charge being
therefore such an one as could not possibly mislead the
accused as to its nature or criminality if proved, or embarrass
him in making his plea or defence. The epithet ' guerrilla'
has, in fact, become so familiar, that, as in the case of the
term ' spy,' its mere annunciation carries with it a legal
definition of crime."

I have the pleasure of knowing the Judge Advocate
General well. He is a very able lawyer, and perhaps not
surpassed for genius and eloquence by any man alive—
certainly in forensic efforts there is no man living who, in my
judgment is equal to him; and those who have not heard him,
have been deprived of what is a great intellectual treat. I
can understand that his intelligence has exhausted that particular subject to which he refers, of the sufficiency of the
charge against an accused that he is a guerrilla. But I do
not find that he has given his opinion authoritatively on what
is the real meaning of that term, nor to what kind of warfare

it relates. I shall, therefore, look at other authorities in connection with that subject. Originally, we find from looking to history that an enemy was regarded as a criminal and an outlaw, who had forfeited all his rights, and whose life, liberty, and property were at the mercy of the conqueror. That was softened down from such rugged asperity by the advance of civilization and Christianity, but essentially the principle remains. The soldiers who surrounded Captain Beall on his way to this Court, and unknown to their superior officer, when the opportunity presents itself, murmur out in his hearing words that would denote that he was contemplated by them as a murderer, an outcast, and a villain, have not brought themselves to understand, to contemplate the dreadful fact, that war is nothing but legalized deception, and fraud, and murder. If I slay my fellow-being upon a provocation or insult,—if he should assail the reputation of my mother, or offer insult to my sister in my presence, and in a moment of passion I slay him, by the law of the land I am guilty of murder, although the circumstances might recommend me to the clemency of the Court. And yet, if in obedience to the call of my country I go against the phalanx of men who have done me no personal wrong, do not I always gain my military triumph by the massacre of those innocent men? If you march your battalions against the conscripted armies of the South, who suffer but the innocent? while the guilty leaders —the wicked men who set this rebellion on foot, have thus far escaped, and seem destined to escape, whatever may be the issue of the war. Soldiers like you are not to be horrified by the fact that men engaged in a warfare, who treat you, and consider you to be their enemies, take possession of your steamboats, or obstruct railroads, or endeavour to throw railroad trains off the track. It is very horrible to contemplate, when you look at it through the lens of ordinary society. A man who in times of peace lays obstacles upon the track for the purpose of throwing off a train in which

there may be innocent women and children, not to speak of
full-grown men, is regarded as a fiend. But has it not been
a customary thing in this war, in all these expeditions called
raids, for leaders to earn brilliant reputations by, among other
things, tearing up rails, removing them, intercepting and
stopping railroad cars, without reference to the question of
who happened to be in them? Would a general officer, or
any one in command, who sought to interrupt the communication by rail between two of the enemy's posts, let a train
pass through or stop it? If he seeks to stop it he must
apply to it the means necessary to accomplish it. Before the
days of railroads, when soldiers were transported by means
of animals attached to some kind of conveyance, did a
General engaged in warfare, who wanted to stop the soldiers,
whether they were in stage-coaches (if soldiers ever travelled
in that manner) or in caravans, ever stop to see how many
innocent people would suffer by assailing them with weapons
of destruction? Certainly not. It is death, desolation,
mutilation, and massacre, that you are permitted to accomplish in war. And you look at it not through the medium of
philanthropy, not through the Divine precept that tells you
to love your neighbours as yourself, but through the melancholy necessity that characterizes the awful nature of war.
You must change your whole intellect and moral nature to
look it as it is, the *ultima ratio regum*—the last necessity of
kings. This being so, legalized war justifying every method,
every horrible resource of interrupting communication, where
do you draw the line of distinction between the act of one
you call a guerrilla and the act of one you call a raider, like
Grierson? Where do you make the distinction between the
march of Major-General Sherman through the enemy's
country, carrying ravage and desolation everywhere, destroying the most peaceable and lawful industry, mills and machinery, and everything of that nature,—where do you draw the
line between his march through Georgia and an expedition

of twenty men acting under commission who get into any of
the States we claim to be in the Union, and commit depredations there ?   And what difference does it make if they act
under commission, if they kill the innocent or the guilty ?
There are no distinctions of that kind in war.   You kill your
enemy ; you put him *hors de combat* in any way, with some few
qualifications that civilization has introduced.   You may say it
is not allowed to use poisoned weapons, and yet we use Greek
fire.   You may not poison wells, but you may destroy your
enemy's property.   Even Cicero, in his oration against Verres,
when the question arose whether the sacred things were to be
preserved in warfare, said : " No, even sacred things become
profane when they belong to an enemy."   Now, I don't
perceive that this term " guerrilla" has been interpreted so
fully as one would seem to think, from a hasty glance at the
Judge Advocate General's opinion to which I have referred.
At the outbreak of this war the Savannah privateers were
captured ; they were held and tried as pirates.   I was one
of the counsel for the accused.   The jury in the city of New
York disagreed.   In Philadelphia they convicted some of
them ; and as the honourable members of this Court remember, the Confederate Government proposed retaliation, and
took an equal number of our men, their lot being determined
by chance, and secured them, to be executed in case death
were visited upon any of the privateers ; and one of the men
who was so held was Major Coggswell, who has just left this
room ; and for the first time in my life I had an involuntary
client, because the life of my friend Coggswell was dependent
upon the result.   Very soon, however, the Government set
aside that idea and gave up the notion that privateers were
pirates.

You remember the case of the "Caroline," which occurred
in 1840, when the British Government sent its officers within
our lines and took a steamboat from one of our citizens and
set fire to it, and sent it over the Falls ; and you remem-

ber the diplomatic controversy that arose, in which it was claimed by England that the principle of *respondent superior* must apply ; that it must be settled by the Government whose agents the perpetrators of that offence were.   And although McLeod was tried in New York and escaped by the strange defence of proving himself a liar—by proving that he would not have done the things that he boasted he had done, the idea has not yet been removed that it was something to be settled in the international relations of the two Governments.

We see that there may be transactions which do not seem at the first flush to belong to those of war ; and yet on a closer examination of them they prove to come within that description. I refer you to General Halleck's book, at page 306, and I beg your attention to this, as I know you will give it :

" Partisans and guerrilla troops are bands of men self-organized and self-controlled, who carry on war against the public enemy, without being under the direct authority of the State. They have no commissions or enlistments, nor are they enrolled as any part of the military force of the State ; and the State is, therefore, only indirectly responsible for their acts. * * * * If authorized and employed by the State, they become a portion of its troops, and the State is as much responsible for their acts as for the acts of any other part of its army. They are no longer partisans and guerrillas in the proper sense of those terms, for they are no longer self-controlled, but carry on hostilities under the direction and authority of the State. * * * It will, however, readily be admitted, that the hostile acts of individuals, or of bands of men, without the authority or sanction of their own Government, are not legitimate acts of war, and, therefore, are punishable according to the nature or character of the offence committed."

If that be so, you cannot convict any man as a guerrilla who holds a commission in the service of the Confederate Government, and perpetrates any act of war in that capacity.

N

He is not self-organized with his command, nor self-controlled. He is acting under authority of our foe, and he is regarded as under so much protection as belongs to the law of war. If he has a commission, and do any thing which no man may do belonging to the army under any circumstances whatever, and commits offences which military courts have cognizance of, they will take jurisdiction and award the punishment he deserves.

You will find that in this case Captain Beall was acting as an officer of the Confederate Government, either in command himself of Confederate soldiers, or under the command of some Confederate officer, as in the attempt on the railroad where Colonel Martin of the Confederate service was in command. Commissioned officers of the Confederate Government engaged in depredations for the purposes of war within our territory, are not guerrillas within this definition of General Halleck, or any definition recognized in any book that I have had occasion to refer to. So far as that definition and the like is concerned, that it is ratified by this Government, is shown from this proclamation of Jefferson Davis, referred to in specific terms showing that it was done by authority of the Government. Now permit me, in this connection, to refer you, Mr. Judge Advocate, to Phillimore on International Law, 3d volume, p 137 :

" If the unauthorized subject carry on war, or make captures, it may be an offence against the sovereignty of his *own* nation, but it is not a violation of international law.

" The legal position that no subject can lawfully commit hostilities, or capture property of an enemy, when his sovereign has either expressly or constructively prohibited it, is unquestionable. But it appears to be equally unquestionable, that the sovereign may retractively ratify and validate the authorized act of his subject." He says on page 145 : "Guerrillas are bands of marauders, acting without the authority of the sovereign or the order of the military commander—a class

which, of course, does not include volunteer corps, which have
been permitted to attach themselves to the army, and which
act under the commands of the general of the army."

So that a guerrilla must be a marauder, self-controlled, not
acting by the authority of his Government, without a commission—a mere self-willed and self-moving depredator. The
question is, whether there is any proof of any such character
in regard to Capt. Beall. As to the transaction on Lake Erie,
I accept all the proof which has been given by the Government. It was an expedition to take possession of that steamboat,
at a distance of some six miles from Johnson's Island, to *run
down the United States armed steamer Michigan*, then lying
at about the distance of a mile from Johnson's Island, and
thus give the prisoners on Johnson's Island an opportunity to
escape.

[The Judge Advocate said there was no evidence to prove
that the purpose was to run down the *Michigan*.]

Mr. Brady resumed. Oh yes ! you have proved the declarations of the parties engaged in it on board the boat, by Mr.
Ashley. Ashley states expressly that that was the purpose.

[The Court said that the witness said the object was stated
to be to capture the *Michigan*.]

Mr. Brady again resumed. That was the purpose of the
armed expedition of Confederate soldiers or officers, to take
possession of, or capture the *Michigan*, and thus aid to release
the prisoners on Johnson's Island. That I call a military expedition ; and that I call an expedition which being carried
on by men under commission from the Confederate Government, is legalized warfare and not the conduct of guerrillas.
That, however, must be submitted to your judgment.

Now, what was undertaken at Niagara is proved here by
no witness except Anderson. What the accused said to Mr.
Thomas, within the rule that I have already announced, that
the whole must be taken together and all believed unless it
conflicts with other proofs, has no relation to any such thing as

this charge. When Capt. Beall was arrested by him, the Captain asked him for what he was arrested, and Thomas said in substance—I don't profess to give the very words—"You know as well as I do."

And then it was stated that he was arrested as an escaped rebel prisoner : and Beall said, " From Point Lookout?" "Yes." "Well," says he, " I confess that I am an escaped prisoner from Point Lookout."

The records of this Government show, I presume, and therefore I am warranted in alluding to the fact, that Capt. Beall was a prisoner, and at Point Lookout, was taken by our forces and exchanged. In his conversation with Thomas he was acting the part of human nature.   He wanted to be released if possible. He got the officer to suggest that he was an escaped prisoner ; a thing involving no kind of turpitude or wrong, for every prisoner is entitled to escape, civil or criminal. It is the right of every man in society to escape the consequences of his actions ; it is the right of society to punish him. But what is the proof ? He did not say any thing to him except what I have already narrated.   Now, who is Anderson ?   He is an accomplice.   And what is the law as to accomplices ?   They are competent witnesses.   They are often employed from the necessity of public justice.   Their testimony, as an old writer says, is tolerated rather than approved.   The act of turning traitor to your associate involves what we have regarded from boyhood as the meanest kind of perfidy.   And although upon his testimony alone you can convict a party, it is always stated, and it is stated by McArthur on Court-Martials, that he must be corroborated in something tending directly to implicate him.   There is the only proof.   Now, what was the object of the capture of the express train ? There is no person from the railroad to testify in regard to it. We don't know what happened to that train. Somebody went back with lights. We don't know whether any person was injured or not. Certainly, according to Anderson's testimony, there was no attempt made

to take possession of any thing on board. I have not gone into
any minutiæ of the testimony; it is not necessary. I shall not
follow the wanderings of the statements made by Weston and
Hays, who come from the station-house, or as to the details of
what was in this carpet bag, holding it to be entirely immaterial
who owned it. Anderson said it belonged to the accused, and
the accused said it did not. There were candles. They said
they were serviceable when they could not get any other light
There was a bottle of laudanum in the pocket of the accused,
which he said was for the toothache. Whether he had the
toothache, or intended to poison himself, does not concern us.
He had a right to poison himself, except as between Capt. Beall
and his Maker, or Capt. Beall and his Government; but it is
wholly immaterial what that was for. And then as to the proof
which my friend deemed it proper and necessary to give, to
which I made no objection, emanating from this Hays, as to what
occurred in the station-house; at the very worst, if Hays reported it accurately, it was an attempt to escape. What would
either of you gentlemen do if you were captured by the enemy? Get away if you could. I know I was very much rejoiced when my friend, General Franklin, made his escape so
adroitly. And whether the accused did or not offer $1,000
to this man, whom he immediately took into his confidence
without any reason for bestowing that confidence; whether this
man is correct in saying Capt. Beall, when he would not tell
him his name, asked him to take his word for $1,000; all this
does not bear upon this case. Now this escape, which in the
law books is sometimes called flight, is sometimes given in
evidence as a circumstance tending to fix crime. If a man
should fall in the street, and should be discovered to be dead,
and two or three others run away, and there are circumstances
tending to prove that they murdered him, the fact that they
run away is an item of evidence against them; but only an
item of evidence. But in warfare if a man is taken prisoner
and afterwards escapes, his escape is sometimes the most

poetical transaction in his life ; and his daring in getting away entitles him to as much glory as courage on the battle-field. We read it in romance and poetry, and it stirs our hearts as much as any thing in the record of battles.

Therefore, I think, we have two distinct questions here, and only two : Is the accused proved to be a spy ? And is he found to be a guerrilla ? What proof is there for the purpose of establishing these charges ? In the one case we say he was shown to be within our lines, if within our lines at all, not for the purpose of acting as a spy, but for other developed and proved objects inconsistent with his being a spy. In the other case it appears that he was not a guerrilla because he was a commissioned officer in the Confederate service, acting under authority of that government during war, in connection with other military men, for an act of war. If so, then he is not amenable to this jurisdiction. If I were before a tribunal who had not been accustomed to look at war with its grim visage, with the eye of educated intelligence, I should apprehend that the natural detestation of violence and bloodshed and wrong would pursue this man. But however wrong the South may be—however dismal its records may remain in the contemplation of those who have the ideas of patriotism that reside in our minds—yet not one of you, gentlemen, would even be willing to acknowledge to any foreigner, hating our institutions, that you did not still cling to the South in this struggle, wrong and dreadful as it has been, and award them the attributes of intelligence and courage never before perhaps equalled, and certainly never surpassed, in the annals of the human race.

Bad as their act may be in our contemplation, have you any doubt that in the conscience of that man, in the judgment of his mother, in the lessons he received from his father, he has what we may think the misfortune of believing himself right ?

That mother and those sisters who are watching the course

of this trial with their hearts bleeding every instant to think of the condition of the son and brother, who would not care if he should be shot down in one hour in open battle, contending for the principles which they, like him, have approved ; if he were borne back to that mother like the Spartan son upon a shield, she would look at his corpse and feel that it was honoured by the death he received. But she would be humiliated to the last degree if she supposed that he had departed from the legitimate sphere of battle, and turned his eyes away from the teachings of civilization, and become a lawless depredator, and deserving and suffering ignominious death.

I leave his fate in your hands. I have endeavoured to avoid any attempt to address to you any thing but what becomes the sober reason of intelligent men. There are occasions when the advocate may attempt, if he possesses any endowment of that nature, what is commonly called eloquence, what is known as oratory. But I never consider that in a court like this any address of that nature is appropriate in any sense or degree. This is a thing to be reasoned upon. You will view it through the medium of reason with which the Almighty has endowed you. And I think I may say to my client, that whatever conclusions this Court reaches, it will be that of honourable and intelligent gentlemen, who would convict him, if at all, not because he is a Southern officer, but because it is the imperious necessity of the law that they deem to be sufficient.

Exhibit H.

Address of the Judge Advocate, Major John A. Bolles, A. D. C.

Mr. President and Gentlemen of the Commission : It would be entirely improper, if it were at all possible, for me to imitate the example and follow the course of the elo-

quent counsel for the accused. He has a right to be eloquent.
He could not help being so even if it were wrongful. I
have no such right. He is the *advocate;* I am the *Judge*
Advocate. It is my pleasant duty to represent, not one side
but both sides of the case ; absolute and entire justice ; the
law as it is, and as it affects the case ; the facts as they are,
and as they affect the Government and the accused. It is
the duty of the advocate for the accused to seek for his acquittal. It is never the duty of the Judge Advocate to seek
for the conviction of the accused ; but simply to take care
that the facts and the law are spread before the Court and
that strict justice be done.

In order that justice may be done in this case, I shall,
before proceeding to the body of my address, ask the attention of the Court to one or two preliminary observations suggested by the remarks of the counsel for the accused.

No reference has been made by the prosecution, and none
will be made, to any supposed connection of the accused
with the November attempt to destroy the city of New York
by fire, or with any other matter, which is not described in
the charges and specifications on which he is tried. The
Court cannot, and would not, go beyond the case thus presented and the evidence adduced by the prosecution.

Allusion has been made in the argument—but I must remind the Court that there is no fact in evidence to warrant
any allusion—to the wealth, family ancestry, and university
education of the accused. These are matters quite outside
of the case, and have nothing to do with the real inquiry
before this tribunal.

Something was said of the accused, as appearing by government records, to have been at some time a prisoner of
war at Point Lookout. But no such record is shown. The
only evidence in the case that connects him with Point Lookout, is his false statement to policeman Thomas in December, that he had escaped a few days before from that place,

in company with Anderson ; whereas we prove him to have
been at large in September, and to have been passing to and
from Canada during the week of his arrest.

It has been argued to you that the accused is honourable,
devout, and of tender conscience ; and appeals are made to
his diary for proofs. What *shall* we, what *must* we, think of
his conscience who within a fortnight of that atrocious attempt upon the railroad, could devoutly thank God, as he
does in that diary, that he has never commited any outcrying
sin ?

You are asked to show some forbearance toward him on
account of his hearty and conscientious belief that the cause
in which he has been engaged, the rebel cause, is a righteous
and just cause. But on page 11 of that diary, he states
amongst his "consolations" that he never, of his own accord,
left the home circle of his mother and sisters,—"I never voluntarily left them." Such is his real relation, involuntary,
to the rebel service. I cannot regard him, therefore, as a
firm believer in the justice of the insurgent cause.

Two papers have been put in evidence by the accused,
without objection on my part,—his letter of appointment as
master's mate in the rebel navy, and the " manifesto" of Mr.
Davis in regard to Burley and the Lake Erie expedition.
I was willing to admit that Beall was a rebel officer, and that
all he did was authorized by Mr. Davis; because, in my
view of the case, all that was done by the accused, being in
violation of the law of war, no commission, command, or
manifesto could justify his acts. A soldier is bound to obey
the lawful commands of his superior officer. Our 9th article
of war punishes him for disobedience to such commands, but
none other. His superior officer cannot require or compel
any soldier to act as a spy, or as an assassin. If, then, such
unlawful command be given and obeyed, its only effect is to
prove that both he who gave and he who obeyed the command
are criminals, and deserve to be gibbeted together. When

did a spy ever seek to justify himself by pleading the command of his general ? How can the manifesto of the archrebel screen any of his subordinates who has trampled under foot that law of war—for war hath its laws no less than peace —which is binding upon all alike, from the rebel president to the rebel raider?

In this connection I will read some extracts from the opinions of the Chief Justice of the Canadian Court of Queen's Bench and of his associates, in the case of Burley, who was concerned, with the accused, in the seizure and plunder of the Lake Erie steamboats. The Chief Justice said : " But, conceding that there is evidence that the prisoner was an officer in the Confederate service, and that he had the sanction of those who employed him to endeavour to capture the *Michigan*, and to release the prisoners on Johnson's Island, the manifesto put forward as a shield to protect the prisoner from personal responsibility does not extend to what he has actually done ; nay, more, it absolutely prohibits a violation of neutral territory or of any rights of neutrals. The prisoner, however, according to the testimony, was a leader in an expedition embarked surreptitiously from a neutral territory ; his followers, with their weapons, found him within that territory, and proceeded thence to prosecute their enterprise, whatever it was, into the territory of the United States. Thus assuming their intentions to have been what was professed, they deprived the expedition of the character of lawful hostility, and the very commencement of their enterprise was a violation of neutral territory and contrary to the letter and spirit of the manifesto produced."

In the same case Judge Haggerty observed, that " had this prisoner been arrested on the wharf in Detroit, as he stepped on the *Philo Parsons*, and avowed and proved his character of a Confederate officer, he would have been in imminent danger of the martial rule applicable to a disguised enemy. Had he been secretly joined there by twenty or thirty persons starting over from the neutral shores of Canada, and then by a sudden assault destroyed some national property, or seized a vessel lying at the wharf and taken the money from the unarmed crew, I think they would, if captured in the act, have great difficulty in maintaining their right to be treated as prisoners of war, with no further responsibility.

"In the Russian war, I think, we should hardly have allowed such a mild character to a like number of Russians coming over stealthily from the friendly shores of Detroit to burn, slay, and plunder in Windsor.

"All the prisoner's conduct, while within our jurisdiction during this affair, repels the idea of legitimate warfare. A British subject, without the Queen's license and against her proclamation, in the service of one of the belligerents, acting in concert with persons leaving her ports on the false pretence of peaceful passengers, to wage war on a friendly power— no act of his raises any presumption in favour of his being in good faith a soldier or sailor waging war with his enemy."

Mr. Justice WILSON made use of the following language :

"The evidence returned to us shows, *primâ facie*, that the prisoner committed a robbery in the State of Ohio, one of the United States. But, it is answered, first, that the prisoner held a commission as Acting Master in the navy of the Confederate States. The holding of this or any other commission, does not authorize him, *mero motu*, to wage warfare from a neutral territory on the unoffending and non-belligerent subjects of the country at war with the nation whose commission he holds. He says he seized the *Philo Parsons* as an act of war, with intent to liberate the prisoners on Johnson's Island ; but for this act he produces no order of any superior officer, and the evidence does not show that he had any such order. He says this robbery was at worst an excess of a belligerent right, which was merged in the principal act. Now, what was the principal act of war performed ? Under the pretence of being

a passenger, he went on board a freight and passenger steamboat at Detroit. As a favour, he requested the master to
touch at Sandwich, a British port, to take in three persons
as passengers, which was done. The boat proceeded on its
regular voyage to Amherstburgh, a town in this Province,
near the mouth of the Detroit River, about fourteen miles
below Sandwich. Here about twenty men, dressed in the
ordinary attire of the farming people of the United States,
with one rough trunk, tied round with a cord, and no other
baggage, supposed to be citzens of the United States returning
to their homes, after an absence, to escape the draft for the
recruiting of the army of the United States, came on board
the steamer. The prisoner and his three fellow-passengers
affect no knowledge of the last twenty. The course of the
vessel to Sandusky, from the mouth of the river, is southeast.
She had to pass a number of islands. The northerly are
British, the southerly American. The boundary line of this
Province was north of the Bass Islands, and thence between
Pele Island and Sandusky Island. Johnson's Island is said
to be fourteen miles from the Middle Bass Island, and two
miles from Sandusky. Nothing occurred to excite suspicion,
or cause alarm, until the boat was clearly within the territory
of the United States. Suddenly the prisoner presented a
revolver at Ashley, and drove him, at peril of his life, into
the ladies' cabin. Beall, one of his confederates, overcame
the mate in a similar manner. The other twenty, more or
less, rushed to their trunk, armed themselves with revolvers
and hatchets which it contained, acted under the orders of
Beall and the prisoner, and the boat became at once under
their control. So far, neither of the leaders declares his
reason for this proceeding. It was rumoured that their object
was to liberate the prisoners at Johnson's Island. After some
hours, the boat landed at the Middle Bass Island, having
taken possession of a small steamboat, the *Island Queen*. At
this island, just before Ashley was put on shore, Beall and the

prisoner, with revolvers to enforce the command, demanded his money. After getting what was in his drawer, the prisoner insists he has more, and Ashley took from his waist-coat pocket a roll of bills, about $90 he supposes, which the prisoner and Beall shared between them. These proceedings, so mean in their inception, and so ignoble in their develop-ment and termination, we are asked to consider as acts of war, and to accord to the prisoner belligerent rights. What is there in all this which constitutes the act of war? If the object were to release the prisoners, from all that appears they never were nearer than fourteen miles to Johnson's Island. Was the seizure of this unarmed boat *per se* an act of war? for it has been argued that the robbery was merged in the higher act. The seizure of the boat, for whatever purpose, was one thing, the robbery of Ashley quite another, and in no way that we see, in furtherance of the design now insisted upon, necessary for its accomplishment. But is not the *bonâ fides* of the enterprise matter of defence which a jury ought to try? Such a trial can only be had where the offence was committed, and we cannot doubt but that justice will be fairly administered.

" Then we are told that although the prisoner has no orders to show authorizing what he did, he has the manifesto of the President of the Confederate States, avowing the act and as-suming it, and therefore he is not subject to this charge at all. We accord to that Confederacy the rights of a belligerent, as the United States has done from the day it treated the sol-diers of the revolted States as prisoners of war; but there is an obvious distinction between an order to do a belligerent act and the recognition and avowal of such an act after it has been done. The one is an act of war, the other an act of an established government. The one is consistent with what Great Britain acknowledges, the other is not. For as judici-ally to give effect to the avowal and adoption of this act would be to recognize the existence of the nationality of the Confederate States, which at present our Government refuses to acknowledge.

"Giving for the moment this manifesto its full force, it distinctly disclaims all breaches of neutrality; but it is clear that this expedition took its departure and shipped its arms from our port. But does it assume the responsibility of this seizure and all that was done upon it throughout? If not, it is neither justification nor excuse. I see no authority for the doing of the act, and as an assumption of what was done, therefore the whole justification fails.

"The attitude of the United States towards us is no concern of ours. Sitting here, whatever they do, while peace exists and this treaty is in force, we are bound to give it effect. We can look with no favour on treachery and fraud, we cannot countenance warfare to be carried on except on the principles of modern civilization. We must not permit, with the sanction of law, our neutral rights to be invaded, our territory made the base of warlike operations, or the refuge from flagrant crimes. Peace is the rule, war the exception of modern times; equivocal acts must be taken most strongly against those who, under pretence of war, commit them. For these reasons I think the prisoner must be remanded on the warrant of the learned Recorder."

Mr. Davis' manifesto in terms forbids all violations of neutral rights, and proposes to ratify only "a proper and legitimate belligerent operation," to wit, the capture of the United States armed steamer *Michigan*, and the release of rebel prisoners at Johnston's Island.

But whatever had been its language, the manifesto could not have justified any violation of the laws of war committed for the sake of accomplishing "a proper and legitimate belligerent operation," such as robbing, stealing, and plundering in disguise; and, as matter of fact, the acts of the accused had no reference to that "operation," not one particle of proof is in the case that any design was formed, or effort made, by the plunderers of the *Philo Parsons* and *Island Queen* to effect that " operation."

You have been asked to reject as unworthy of credit the testimony of George Anderson, in regard to the outrage near Buffalo, because he was an accomplice ; and it has been said that the laws regard such evidence with suspicion. There is no arbitrary rule of law on this subject. According to *Benet's Military Law*, pp. 242, 243, you are at liberty to believe or disbelieve the testimony of an accomplice according to your own convictions ; and upon his testimony, with or without corroboration, you may convict the accused.

The rule of law is equally reasonable in regard to the admissions of the accused, oral or written. If the prosecution puts in a part it must put in the whole ; but when such evidence is actually before you,—so says *Benet*, p. 264,—it rests with you to either believe or disbelieve either the whole or a part. If, then, you look at the letter of the accused to Mr. Lucas, and find that it describes the accused as an officer in the rebel navy, you may believe it ; and if you find it asserting " you know that I am not a guerrillero or a spy," you may believe, or disbelieve that the accused so thinks. But you will never commit the error of supposing that what he asserts on that point is any thing more than his opinion ; and upon the same facts which led the accused to that mistaken opinion, you may be compelled by the law and the evidence to find him guilty.

At this stage of the case, as well as at any time, I may answer the remarks of the learned counsel upon the legitimate scope and meaning of the phrase " within our lines." He has quoted an Act of Congress, which, as he thinks, and thinks correctly, punishes spies that are found in the insurgent States, and he has also referred to the later Act which punishes them wherever found ; in an Act to which the word " elsewhere" was introduced for the purpose of covering all possible cases ; and yet he is anxious to have your definition of the words " within our lines." Those words do not appear in this case in charge, specification or evidence. But there can be no doubt of their meaning in the military mind. Every man is within our lines who enters a loyal State by sea or land, with hostile purposes. Any rebel emissary who has first violated the rights of Canadian neutrality, and then in the guise of a peaceful citizen crossed into our territory, along the whole northern frontier of which are military posts and garrisons, is within our lines; and if he be a rebel officer or soldier, the law pronounces him to be a spy; and unless he can prove that he is not, he will be hung as a spy just as certainly as he is caught and brought to trial.—*Judge Advocate Holt's Digest, p.* 127.

" Within our lines," means any spot within the loyal States where an enemy could do us a mischief, be it the Lake Shore Railroad, where the accused attempted his last enterprise, or the city of New York, in which the November incendiaries endeavoured to destroy the commercial metropolis of the country, or Boston or Portland Harbour, into which rebel pirates or privateers might seek entrance, or a traitor spy might try to pilot them. There is no shore or border so remote that it is not now within our lines, and lines that bristle everywhere with bayonets, and frown everywhere with forts and cannon. The phrase " within our lines" is as comprehensive as is the word " elsewhere" in the Act of Congress of March 3, 1863, sec. 38, as given on page 542 of the Revised Army Regulation, which provides that " all persons who in time of war or of rebellion against the supreme authority of the United States, shall be found lurking, or *acting* as spies, in or about any of the fortifications, posts, quarters and encampments of any of the armies of the United States or *elsewhere*, shall be triable by a general court-martial, or military commission, and shall, upon conviction, suffer death."

The section thus quoted, I beg leave to say, shows that a spy, whoever he may be, and wherever found within the broad limits of the United States, " lurking or acting," is amenable to a military commission like the Court which I now have the honour to address, as well as to a court-martial; and thus I furnish an answer to that question of jurisdiction which was raised by the accused, and which his counsel suggested in the beginning of his address as the first proposition of his client's, and not as his own.

There can be no doubt upon this question of jurisdiction. It is true, as was decided by the Judge Advocate General on p. 79 of *Holt's Digest*, cited by Mr. Brady, that a military commission cannot lawfully be clothed with power " in all cases civil and criminal, and in equity."

But the same authority, on the same page, has decided that " many offences which in time of peace are civil offences, become in time of war military offences, and are to be tried by a military tribunal, even in places where civil tribunals exist."

Major General Halleck, who is himself, as the counsel for the accused admits, of great authority in matters of public law, proclaimed the same doctrine in his celebrated Missouri Order, No. 1, quoted by *Benet*, p. 15.

Will the Court permit me here to answer the claim set up by the accused to be tried by a jury for the crimes now charged against him in connection with the seizure of the steamboats and the attempt upon the train of cars ? It is true that if these enormities had been committed in time of peace, or by ordinary citizens, rogues, and desperadoes, they would have been mere municipal or civil offences, and the perpetrators would be amenable to the civil courts and entitled to the trial by jury. But the accused is not prosecuted for a civil offence. He is, by the theory of this case, a military offender, a violator of the law of war.

Mr. Brady himself admits, and quotes *Holt's Digest*, p. 79, par. 16, to show that murder, which is a civil offence under ordinary circumstances, may and does, in time of war, when committed for disloyal and treasonable purposes, become a military offence, and may then be tried by a military

court, without the interposition of a jury. In time of
war, the offender being a rebel officer in disguise, the
question of intent, the *quo animo*, is very easily determined.
In this case it is very clear that personal advantage was not
the motive that led to the seizure of the steamboats, or the
attempt on the railroad.   To destroy the commerce of the
lakes was one of the objects avowed by the raiding party on
Lake Erie ; to inflict great injury upon great numbers of their
Yankee enemies, and not the crazy expectation that a gang
of five rebels could overcome and plunder a thousand passengers, was the purpose of the railroad attack.

The acts charged and specified being military offences are
triable by a military court, and the accused has no constitu-
tional right to a jury trial.

" The amendment of the Constitution," says the Judge
Advocate General (*Digest*, p. 79, 80, sec. 18), "which gives
the right of trial by jury to persons held to answer for capital
or otherwise infamous crimes—except when arising in the land
or naval forces—is often referred to as conclusive against the
jurisdiction of military courts, over such offences when committed by citizens.   But, though the letter of the article
would give force to such an argument, yet in construing the
different parts of the Constitution together, such a literal
interpretation of the amendment must be held to give way
before the necessity for an efficient exercise of the *war
powers* which is vested in Congress by that instrument."

The Judge Advocate General further says : " A striking
illustration of the recognition of this principle by the legislation of the country since an early period of our history is
furnished by the 57th Article of War, in the fact that it
has, from the beginning, rendered amenable to trial by court-
martial for certain offences " holding correspondence with or
giving intelligence to the enemy), " not only military persons,
but all persons whatsoever."

I will add, that by the act of Congress of 1806 in regard to *spies*, the same jurisdiction of courts-martial was extended to that class of offenders, that they might suffer death " according to the law and usage of nations."

If *citizens* may thus be subjected to trial by such courts, *à fortiori*, may *enemies* and armed rebels be deprived of the trial by jury.

Pending a war like this, not less than in all ordinary wars, that branch of the law of nations of which Congress speaks in the act of 1806, already quoted, as " the law and usage of nations" in regard to spies, *i. e.*, " the law of war," that law of war exists and takes effect everywhere within the territory of the belligerents, and everywhere by the instrumentality of military tribunals, and without a jury, punishes every offence against natural right and justice which is committed by soldiers or citizens, for disloyal and treasonable purposes.

The accused, not his counsel, is of the opinion, as Mr. Brady informs us, that the 1st charge does not set forth with sufficient particularity the offence alleged against him. By the well-settled rule of law, the charge is always thus brief and general.

The Judge Advocate General (*Digest,* p. 66) has decided that the charge of " being a guerrilla" is sufficient. It is in the specification which follows the charge, that the circumstances constituting the offence, and describing its perpetration, are to be fully and clearly set forth.

Dehart, p. 145. *Benet*, p. 52.

Neither the accused nor his counsel can complain that the specifications under the 1st charge are not sufficiently explicit.

I come now, Mr. President, to the inquiry, what are the true legal character and definition of the offences with which the accused stands charged ?

 I. What is it, in law, to be a spy, and do the facts proved come up to the legal requirements ?

II. What is it, in law, to carry on irregular warfare, and
has the accused been found guilty of this ?

I. The learned counsel for the accused is dissatisfied with
every definition of a spy that is comprehensive enough to
cover the case on trial ; and is a little inconsistent in the
matter.

Bouvier, in his Law Dictionary, defines a spy to be *" one
who goes into a place for the purpose of ascertaining the best
way of doing an injury there."*

Why is not the counsel for tho accused content with that ?

The accused was an enemy, who came with hostile intent
into both Ohio and New York, to ascertain the best way of
injuring their peaceable and unsuspecting inhabitants.

Bailey, in his dictionary, presents a definition which
almost seems to satisfy the counsel for the accused. According to that venerable lexicographer a spy is one who " clandestinely searches into the state of places and affairs."

The accused came aboard the *Philo Parsons* clandestinely, with the heart and hate of an enemy, but in the dress
and with the profession of a friend ; so did he clandestinely
enter the *Island Queen ;* so did he clandestinely visit Buffalo.
Deception, disguise, concealment, falsehood, stamp their
guilty image and superscription on all his acts, and on all his
declarations.

His dress belies and disguises his real character. If André
in uniform was rightly held to be in disguise because of his
citizen's overcoat, is Beall not disguised when clad as a
citizen throughout, from hat or cap to boots ?

His story to officer Thomas was a tissue of falsehoods, for
he denied his real name and assumed another : he asserted
that he was in the rebel infantry, and not in any other branch
of the service, when he *was a naval*, and was *not a military*
officer : his account of his recent escape with Anderson from
Point Lookout, and all its details, was untrue.

Do I say that his dress disguises his real character? It did so at the time of his coming within our lines; but now every disguise is a proof, an exposure, a demonstration, of his genuine character, because he is a spy.

The counsel for the accused believes that Major André was a spy. He also believes that Davis, whose case I do not remember, was properly held to be a spy. According to Mr. Brady's statement, Davis was a rebel officer who was on his way from Canada to the South, carrying despatches, and proceeding without delay through the intervening loyal States, holding communication with no one on his way. According to this admission the true definition of spy includes a class of men who come within the limits of the loyal States from a neutral and friendly territory, not to obtain information, but simply to cross our territory as errand boys, carrying papers which contain information.

Is the learned counsel quite consistent, then, when he goes on to quote as entirely satisfactory to him, Major General Halleck's definition of a spy; a definition which requires that the spy should have come within our limits not only to *make* discoveries, but "to *communicate* to their employers the information thus obtained?"

This definition does not cover the case of Davis; nor does it cover the case of those who come of their own accord and have no employer; nor of those who are directed, or are determined, to act on the information they gather, instead of communicating it to any one.

Gen. Halleck himself very properly says, that "it is the disguise or false pretence which constitutes the perfidy and *forms the essential element of the crime*."

It is very clearly immaterial whether the spy comes as principal or agent, to get information for his own guidance or that of others, or whether the information is to be communicated, or to be retained and acted on without communication or consultation; and the true definition of a spy would include any man who comes in disguise, or clandestinely, into his enemy's territory, to obtain and use, or to obtain and transmit information with hostile intent; or who, being within that territory, treacherously seeks information to be used by himself or others for hostile purposes.

In the General Orders of the War Department, No. 100 (April 24, 1863), paragraph 88, it is said that " a spy is a person who secretly, in disguise or under false pretences, seeks information with the intention of communicating it to the enemy." If to this definition had been added the words " *or of using it as an enemy*," it would, I think, have been exact and all comprehensive.

But why linger and dwell on dictionaries and definitions, when, so far as this case is concerned, the legal character of the accused as a spy is settled by authority beyond all question?

The learned Dr. Lieber, in his letter on guerrilla parties, thus states the law :

" *A person proved to be a regular soldier of the enemy's army, found in citizen's dress, within the lines of the captor, is universally dealt with as a spy.*"

The learned Judge Advocate General, at the head of our Bureau of Military Justice, has again and again decided that *the fact that " an officer or soldier of the rebel army comes within our lines disguised in the dress of a citizen, is* PRIMA FACIA *evidence of his being a spy,*" *and that " the disguise so assumed strips him of all claim to be treated as a prisoner of war.*" (*Digest*, p. 127.)

It is true, as the Judge Advocate further says : " that such evidence may be rebutted by proof that he had come within the lines to visit his family, and not for the purpose of obtaining information as a spy." (*Digest*, p. 127.)

" It is also true, that if the spy succeeds in making his escape, the crime does not follow him; and if he be subsequently captured *in battle*, he cannot -be tried for it." (*Digest*, p. 127.)

2. The second branch of this first inquiry is now to be considered, viz. : what are the facts proved to which those rules of law are to be applied ?

It is proved and admitted that the accused was in the military and naval service of the rebel authorities. He produces his warrant as master's mate in the navy ; he told officer Thomas that he was an infantry officer. His counsel contends that in the railroad enterprise he was serving under Col. Martin.

It is proved, in the second place, that he came three several times, in the disguise of a citizen, from Canada to Ohio and New York ; *first*, as a passenger in the steamer *Philo Parsons* ; *next*, as a railroad operator, when the brave party of four— Martin, Headley, Beall, and Anderson—attempted in vain to lift a rail from the track ; and *finally*, when that heroic band, enlarged by one new recruit, and refreshed by two nights of sleep at Port Colborn, returned upon their chivalric errand, and attacked the Dunkirk train.

If, as the counsel for the accused argues, the statement of Anderson the accomplice in this railroad enterprise, is not to be believed—and all that you know in regard to the accused in New York, are the facts sworn by Thomas, who arrested him—that he was in disguise, that he gave a false name, and that he made divers untrue statements in regard to himself; then is his character as a spy still more strongly proved, according to Mr. Brady, because he is here, a rebel officer, in disguise, practising deception, and without any assigned pretext or excuse.

Are these two facts and the legal conclusion therefrom, met by any explanation, by any rebutting testimony ?

Has any evidence been offered to change this fatal *primâ facies* of the case ?

The accused came to Ohio, says Mr. Brady, to perform a belligerent act. Unfortunately there is no such proof.

He *might*, says Mr. Brady, have come to Ohio and to

New York on some innocent errand, or some errand of humanity. He *might*, indeed. But where is the proof that he *did?*

Has he purged himself of his criminality as a spy in Ohio or New York? Has he, in the language of the authorities which I have read, returned to the belligerent army, or to the navy in which he holds rank, and been captured in battle?

This is not even claimed or argued. He *did* go back to Canada, whose neutral rights he had violated, in September. He *did* attempt to go back to Canada in December. But he did not return to the insurgent States, nor was he taken prisoner in lawful or honourable warfare.

Now, Mr. President and gentlemen of the Commission, I do *not* ask you to set aside, but I *do* ask you not to enlarge or to disregard the narrow limits of that rule of law which discharges from guilt a spy who, having returned to the field of legitimate warfare, has been captured on the field of battle.

This rule is arbitrary. It is an exception to the general rule of civilized war, which inflicts ignominious death on all who violate its humane regulations by acts of perfidy, baseness, and treacherous hostility. It is your duty to see that this exception is not enlarged.

II. I now proceed, may it please the Court, to the inquiry as to the law and the evidence in support of specifications 1st, 2d, and 6th, under Charge I. As matter of law, do the facts alleged in these specfications constitute violations of the laws of civilized warfare, and, as matter of fact, are those allegations proved?

I shall not spend much time in answering what was so ingeniously argued by the learned counsel in regard to the legal meaning of the word *guerrilla*. That word occurs only in the 6th specification, and is there quite immaterial—mere surplusage—and might be stricken out and leave that specification as complete as are the 1st and 2d specifications.

I might admit, for the purpose of argument, that if the word guerrilla had now, and in our service, the same signification which belonged to it at the time when Gen. Halleck published, in San Francisco, his work on International Law, there would be weight as well as ingenuity in Mr. Brady's argument; though even then I should ask you merely to omit the word in your finding of guilty on the 6th specification. But, as the Judge Advocate General (*Digest*, p. 66) informs us, this word guerrilla, during this unhappy war, has acquired a peculiar and well-settled meaning, so that it is as idle to go back to Gen. Halleck, or the old dictionaries or treatises, for its present significancy, as it would be to go back to Cicero for the laws of modern warfare.

If the evidence in this case shows that the accused engaged in hostile acts which are forbidden by the law of war, you may call him brigand or raider, guerrilla or guerrillero, prowler or robber,—he is still amenable to this Court, whatever may have been said by writers of a former and less civilized period. We do not go back to Cicero, nor even so far as Puffendorf, Bynkershoeck, or Grotius, to discover precisely what is now the law of war. We may go back to our Divine Master and His teachings in Judea, to discover the pure fountains of that law of love which has now found its way into the very code of war, and we may thence follow downward to our own day the course of Christianity in its influence upon Government, social institutions, and rules of civil conduct, and at last discover what are to-day the rules of civilized warfare. And in that code, as it now exists, we shall learn that warriors are not allowed to lay aside their uniforms, and the badges of their profession, to assume the disguise of peaceful citizens, to creep insidiously into the midst of peaceful and unsuspicious communities, and assassinate leading individuals, set fire at night to crowded theatres and hotels, or lay obstructions across railroads, and hurl men, women, and children indiscriminately to destruction; and that for atrocities and infamous attempts of this description, no command, no commission, no public manifesto, can be pleaded or proved in justification, extenuation, or mitigation.

President Woolsey, in his *Introduction to the Study of International Law* (2d Ed., p. 214), observes, that among the rules which lie at the basis of a humane system of war, is the rule that "war is waged between Governments by persons whom they authorize, and is not waged *against the passive inhabitants of a country.*"

And, as he says, the reasons why " guerrilla parties do not enjoy the full benefit of the laws of war, are, that they are annoying and insidious, that they put on and off with ease the character of a soldier, and that they are prone themselves to treat their enemies who fall into your hands with great severity."

In the enunciation of these humane doctrines all the recent text writers on public law are in harmony. But there is no work in existence devoted specially to the subject of irregular warfare, except the little treatise of Dr. Lieber, from which I have already quoted in speaking on the subject of spies, and from which I beg leave now to read a few passages that bear upon this second branch of the case on trial :

" There are cases in which the absence of a uniform may be taken as very serious *primâ facia* evidence against an armed prowler or marauder." . . . . " It makes a great difference whether the absence of uniform is used for the purpose of concealment or disguise in order to get by stealth within the lines of the invader for the destruction of life or property, or for pillage " . . . . " nor can it be maintained in good faith, or with any respect for sound sense and judgment, that an individual—an armed prowler—shall be entitled to the protection of the laws of war . . . . because his government or chief has issued a proclamation by which he calls upon the people to infest the bushes and commit homicides which every civilized nation will consider murders." (Pp. 16, 17.)

"The armed prowler is a simple assassin, and will thus always be considered by soldiers and citizens." (P. 20.)

"Armed bands that arise in the rear of an army are universally considered, if captured, brigands, and not prisoners of war. They unite the fourfold character of the spy, the brigand, the assassin, and the rebel, and cannot expect to be treated as a fair enemy of the regular war." (Pp. 20, 21.)

"No army, no society, engaged in war...... can allow unpunished assassination, robbery, and devastation, without the deepest injury to itself, and disastrous consequences, which might change the very issue of the war." (P. 22.)

I have received from Dr. Lieber, and now propose to read as an authoritative exposition of the law which is to control this part of the case, a letter addressed to myself, and bearing date:

"NEW YORK, February 5th, 1865.

"DEAR SIR,—There is no work which treats in a clear and full manner like a law book, on spies, and so-called guerrillas, nor on the law and usages of war in general. In no war previous to our present one have these subjects received that minute and candid attention which we give them, though this is a war of a lawful government with insurgents.

"Nowhere have the spy and guerrilla been treated of more distinctly than in my pamphlet on 'Guerrilla Parties,' which the Government printed and of which I would send you a copy had I one, and also of General Orders No. 100 (year 1863). I must say, however, that in my interleaved copy of this order I have added to § 88 'Enemies found in disguise or concealed, or lurking near the army, are by these facts deemed to be spies except they can prove that they are prisoners of war in the act of escaping.'

"I should certainly propose to add this were I consulted as to a new edition.

"I ought also to have given something on *enemies who in disguise come from the territory of a neutral to commit*

robbery or murder, and those who come from such territory
in uniform.

"*I don't believe that such people now called by the un-
acceptable term* RAIDERS, *have ever been treated of by any
writer.*

" The thing created no doubt in the mind of any one.
*They have always been treated as brigands, and it can
easily be shown upon principle that they cannot be treated
otherwise.*

" *Never*, so long as men have warred with one another—
and that is pretty much as long as there have existed
sufficient numbers to do so—*has any belligerent been insolent
enough to claim the protection of the laws of war for banditti
who take passage on board a vessel, and then rise upon the
captain and crew, or who gather in the territory of a friendly*
person, steal in disguise into the country of their enemy, and
there commit murder or robbery. The insolence—I use the
term now in a scientific meaning—the absurdity and reckless
disregard of honour, which characterize this proceeding, fairly
stagger a jurist or a student of history.......

" Your obedient servant,   FRANCIS LIEBER."

This, gentlemen of the Commission, is the voice of the law
speaking from the lips of the living jurist—of that learned
and eminent jurisconsult whom our Government, in the
beginning of 1863, saw fit first to consult and then to employ
in drafting that manual of " Instructions for the Government
of Armies of the United States in the Field," which, having
been " approved by the President," became the will of the
War Department, and was published as that " General
Order No. 100," from which I have already quoted in the
course of my argument.

With one reference to that order, from which I now read,
paragraph 101, I will close my citation of the authorities
which determine the law applicable to the case now on trial :

" 101. While deception in war is admitted as a just and

necessary means of hostility, and is consistent with honourable warfare, the common law of war allows even capital
punishment for clandestine or treacherous attempts to injure
an enemy, because they are so dangerous, and it is so
difficult to guard against them."

Reference was made by the counsel for the accused to the
trials in New York and Philadelphia, upon the charge of
piracy, of certain rebel privateersmen.   Let me remind this
Court, that in those cases the civil judge, as matter of law,
determined that the parties thus tried, though sheltered by a
rebel commission, were pirates.   It was executive policy,
and not the law, which led to their exchange as prisoners of
war.

The case of the steamer *Caroline* and the Canadian
McLeod, to which Mr. Brady has alluded, can shed no light
upon the present trial.   England and the United States
were friendly, not belligerent powers, and those border
difficulties were adjusted without recourse to the laws of war.

And now, Mr. President, I come to the final inquiry in
this most interesting and important trial.   What are the
facts proved by the evidence under the 1st, 2nd, and 6th
specifications of Charge 1st ?

I submit to the Court that we have proved,

1st. That the accused was and is a rebel officer.

2d. That he was within our lines in disguise.

3d. That he, at Kelly's Island, in Ohio, in September last,
with the help of other rebel officers and soldiers in disguise,
seized the American private steamboat *Philo Parsons*.

4th. That he stole the money and destroyed the freight on
board of her.

5th. That in September, at Middle Bass Island, in Ohio,
he, still in disguise, and with the same friends in disguise,
seized in like manner another steamboat, the *Island Queen*,
and scuttled and sunk her.

6th. That in December he came from Canada to Buffalo,

in New York, in disguise, and with other disguised rebel
officers and soldiers attempted unsuccessfully to throw a railroad train from the track.

7th. That he went back to Canada, and again returned in
the same treacherous manner as before, and repeated his
infamous attempt upon a night train from Dunkirk, and was
caught as he fled from the scene of his unenviable exploits.

The evidence upon these points is not contradicted, and
admits of no denial or doubt.   I respectfully submit to the
Court that the acts thus proved, having been done within our
lines by rebel enemies in disguise, upon the persons and property of peaceable, unoffending, unsuspicious citizens, are
acts of irregular warfare—call them raiding, brigandage,
robbery, theft, piracy, plunder, murder, or assassination—are
offences against the laws of God and the laws of man, against
municipal law and the laws of war, and may be tried and
punished by either municipal courts of civil jurisdiction, by
court-martial, or by military commission.   They are brought
before you for trial.   Yours is a rightful jurisdiction.   Upon
you devolves the solemn duty of determining the issues, in
this case, which, to the accused, are the dread issues of life
and death.

I have felt, Mr. President and gentlemen, oppressed, as
I know you all must feel, with the terrible responsibility
imposed upon me, and upon you, by the facts and the law in
this case.   But it is not a matter in which the dread of responsibility must be allowed to influence either your action or
mine.   It is important that you and I, sir, and our wives and
children—that all of our fellow-citizens, may feel, when they
enter a railroad car within the loyal States, that they are safe
from all perils but those of ordinary travel ; and that if any
party of rebel soldiers in disguise, enemies of the Republic
and friends of the Confederacy, attempt to place obstructions
on the track, and throw off the train, they will be punished
with the most exemplary speed, certainty, and severity.

Enormities like this cannot be justified or screened from legal vengeance by the plea or proof of a military commission, command, or ratification, no matter how exalted may be the rank of the commander ; since the law of war, which forbids and punishes the crime, is obligatory upon all.

It must have been apparent to you, gentlemen of the Commission, that in the conduct of the defence the accused was utterly embarrassed, perplexed, and at a loss to know how to protect himself ; and that he was compelled to resort to two distinct, incongruous, and contradictory lines of defence ; at one time seeking to escape from the jurisdiction of this Court by treating his acts as mere civil offences ; and at another time claiming the protection of the laws of war as a legitimate and regular belligerent, acting in obedience to the lawful commands of his superior officers. Neither of these lines of defence, I respectfully submit, can stand for one moment against the charge and pressure of the law and the facts.

The accused, knowing the terrible risk he assumed, knowing the peril under which he acted, entered upon a scheme of illegal warfare upon the lake and upon the land. Some one on board the captured steamers uttered the foolish assertion, that with the stolen boats they meant to capture the U. S. armed steamer *Michigan*. Every movement of those captured boats proves the falsehood of that pretence. Not one single mile, not a rod, not an inch, did either of those vessels move under rebel direction toward that ship of war.

An act of lawful war ! Seizing two passenger steamers, robbing the clerk, throwing overboard the freight, committing the crimes of pirates and of thieves, and not moving one barleycorn of distance toward what is pretended to be the object and end of their warlike enterprise ? Such a case does not admit of argument.

And so in regard to the defence of that scandalous attempt upon the train—that it was a simple attempt at robbery, and a mere civil offence, on the part of this " *humane and con-*

scientious" prisoner and his worthy associates, who with a force of five men, armed with five revolvers, a sledge-hammer, and a cold chisel, expected to capture a train of fifteen cars and fifteen hundred passengers, and to plunder the express-man's iron safe ! It is a glaring absurdity. Why, sir, the moment the train halted and they saw the approach of three or four lanterns, this squad of express robbers jumped into their sleigh and fled for the Canada border !

All the evidence in this case, may it please the Court, tends to show that the accused was part and parcel of a wide-spread scheme of unlawful and irregular warfare along our whole Canadian line ; whose purpose was, in any way and in every way, except by open and honourable hostility, to endanger the lives, destroy the property, and weaken the strength of those Yankee citizens whom these brigands of the border so bitterly hate.

The piracy of the lake, and the outrage on the railroad, were parts of that system of irregular warfare, under the fear of which no man, woman or child can sleep with any feeling of security in our midst. Such atrocities are attempts, on the part of the rebel officers and soldiers who engage in and countenance them, to bring back war to its old condition of barbarism—to imitate the stealthy cruelty of the North American savage, who creeps under cover of midnight upon his unsuspecting victim, and smites him to death ere the sound of approaching footsteps has roused that victim from slumber. With the accused this savage purpose takes form in the robbery of steamboats and the destruction of railroad trains and travellers. In other hands, it manifests itself in midnight attempts to burn great cities. There is nothing of Christian civilization, nothing of regular warfare, nothing of a high, noble, bold, manly, chivalrous character about it. It is an outbreak of passions so bad and violent that they have overcome all the native elements of manliness, and have led men, of whom four years ago to have suspected such things possible would have been a calumny and a crime, to indulge in atrocities from month to month and year to year, such as have not stained the pages of warfare for two hundred years. And you sit here to-day, and I stand here to-day, as the representatives of recognized law and honourable warfare, to see that such outrages, when they are clearly and distinctly brought home to the guilty party by the evidence adduced upon the trial, shall not escape unpunished.

These proceedings having been submitted to Major Gen. John A. Dix, the Major General in command of the Department, he endorsed thereon his approval, and issued the following order :

The order of Maj. Gen, Dix upon this case is as follows :

GENERAL ORDERS,
  No. 14.
     HEADQUARTERS DEPARTMENT OF THE EAST,
      NEW YORK CITY, Feb. 14th, 1865.

I. Before a Military Commission which convened at Fort Lafayette, New York Harbour, by virtue of Special Orders No. 14, current series from these headquarters, of January 17, 1865, and of which Brigadier General FITZ HENRY WARREN, United States Volunteers, is President, was arraigned and tried JOHN Y. BEALL.

. . . .

[Here follow the charges and specifications, and the finding of sentence.]

II. In reviewing the proceedings of the Commission, the circumstances on which the charges are founded, and the questions of law raised on the trial, the Major General commanding has given the most earnest and careful consideration to them all. The testimony shows that the accused, while holding a commission from the authorities at Richmond as Acting Master in the navy of the insurgent States,

P

embarked at Sandwich, Canada, on board the *Philo Parsons*, an unarmed steamer, while on one of her regular trips, carrying passengers and freight from Detroit, in the State of Michigan, to Sandusky, in the State of Ohio.   The Captain had been induced by Burley, one of the confederates of the accused, to land at Sandwich, which was not one of the regular stopping-places of the steamer, for the purpose of receiving them.   Here the accused and two others took passage.   At Malden, another Canadian port, and one of the regular stopping-places, about twenty-five more came on board.   The accused was in citizen's dress, showing no insignia of his rank or profession, embarking as an ordinary passenger, and representing himself to be on a pleasure trip to Kelly's Island, in Lake Erie, within the jurisdiction of the State of Ohio.

After eight hours, he and his associates, arming themselves with revolvers and hand-axes, brought surreptitiously on board, rose on the crew, took possession of the steamer, threw overboard part of the freight, and robbed the clerk of the money in his charge, putting all on board under duress. Later in the evening he and his party took possession of another unarmed steamer (the *Island Queen*), scuttled her, and sent her adrift on the lake.   These transactions occurred within the jurisdiction of the State of Ohio, on the 19th day of September, 1864.

On the 16th day of December, 1865, the accused was arrested near the Suspension Bridge, over the Niagara River, within the State of New York.   The testimony shows that he and two officers of the insurgent States, Colonel Martin and Lieutenant Headley, with two other confederates, had made an unsuccessful attempt, under the direction of the first-named officer, to throw the passenger train coming from the West to Buffalo off the railroad track, for the purpose of robbing the express company.   It is further shown that this was the third attempt in which the accused was concerned to accomplish the same object; that between two of these attempts the party, including the accused, went to Canada and returned, and that they were on their way back to Canada when he was arrested. In these transactions, as in that on Lake Erie, the accused, though holding a commission from the insurgent authorities at Richmond, was in disguise, procuring information, with the intention of using it, as he subsequently did, to inflict injury upon unarmed citizens of the United States and their private property. The substance of the charges against the accused is, that he was acting as a spy, and carrying on irregular or guerrilla warfare against the United States ; in other words, he was acting in the two-fold character of a spy and a guerrillero. He was found guilty on both charges, and sentenced to death; and the Major General commanding fully concurs in the judgment of the Commission. In all the transactions with which he was implicated —in one as a chief, and in the others as a subordinate agent—he was not only acting the part of a spy, in procuring information to be used for hostile purposes, but he was also committing acts condemned by the common judgment and the common conscience of all civilized States, except when done in open warfare by avowed enemies. Throughout these transactions, he was not only in disguise, but personating a false character. It is not at all essential to the purpose of sustaining the finding of the Commission, and yet it is not inappropriate to state, as an indication of the *animus* of the accused and his confederates, that the attempts to throw the railroad train off the track were made at night, when the obstruction would be less likely than in the daytime to be noticed by the engineer or conductor, thus putting in peril the lives of hundreds of men, women, and children. In these attempts three officers holding commissions in the military service of the insurgent States were concerned. The accused is shown by the testimony to be a man of education and refinement, and it is difficult to account for his agency in transactions so abhorrent to the moral sense, and so inconsis tent with all the rules of honourable warfare.

The accused, in justification of the transaction on Lak Erie, produced the manifesto of Jefferson Davis, assuming the responsibility of the act, and declaring that it was don by his authority. It is hardly necessary to say that no sucl assumption can sanction an act not warranted by the laws o civilized warfare. If Mr. Davis were at the head of a independent government, recognized as such by other nations he would have no power to sanction what the usages o civilized states have condemned. The Government of the United States, from a desire to mitigate the asperities of war has given to the insurgents of the South the benefit of the rules which govern sovereign States in the conduct of hosti lities with each other; and any violation of those rules should, for the sake of good order here, and the cause of humanity throughout the world, be visited with the severest penalty. War, under its mildest aspects, is the heaviest calamity that can befall our race; and he who, in a spirit of revenge, or with lawless violence, transcends the limits to which it is restricted by the common behest of all Christian communities, should receive the punishment which the common voice has declared to be due to the crime. The Major General commanding feels that a want of firmness and inflexibility, on his part, in executing the sentence of death in such a case, would be an offence against the outraged civili zation and humanity of the age.

It is hereby ordered that the accused, JOHN Y. BEALL, be hanged by the neck till he is dead, on Governor's Island, on Saturday, the 18th day of February, inst., between the hours 12 and 2 in the afternoon.

The commanding officer at Fort Columbus is charged with the execution of this order.

By command of Major Gen. Dix.

D. T. VAN BUREN, Col. A.A.G

On the 17th February the execution of the sentence against Beall was suspended by the following order, viz. :

HEADQUARTERS DEPARTMENT OF THE EAST,
NEW YORK CITY, Feb. 7th, 1865.

Commanding Officer Fort Columbus,
New York Harbour.

You will suspend the execution of the sentence of John Y. Beall until further orders.

By command of Major General DIX.

(Signed)   D. T. VAN BUREN,
Colonel and Assistant Adjutant General.

On the same day an order was issued reconvening the Commission. This order and the proceedings of the Commission in obedience thereto, appear from the following record :

HEADQUARTERS DEPARTMENT OF THE EAST,
NEW YORK CITY, Feb. 20th, 1865, 11 o'clock, a.m.

The Commission appointed by Special Orders No, 14, par. 6, from these Headquarters, dated Jan. 17, 1865, reassembled in obedience to the following order :

SPECIAL ORDERS,
No. 42.

HEADQUARTERS DEPARTMENT OF THE EAST,
NEW YORK CITY, February 17th, 1865.

1. The Military Commission, of which Brigadier General Fitz Henry Warren, U. S. Vols., is President, and which was convened pursuant to Special Orders No. 14, current series from these Headquarters, N. Y. City, will reassemble at these Headquarters to-morrow at 10 o'clock, a.m., or as soon hereafter as practicable, for the purpose of reconsideration of the finding in the case of *John Y. Beall,* for reasons more particularly set forth in communication herewith enclosed from the Major General Commanding the Department.

By command of Major General DIX.

(Signed)   D. T. VAN BUREN,
Assistant Adjutant General.

Present, all the members of the Commission, viz. :

Brig. General FITZ HENRY WARREN, U. S. V.
Brig. General W. H. MORRIS, U. S. V.
Colonel M. S. HOWE, 3d U. S. Cav.
Colonel H. DAY, U. S. Army.
Brev. Lieut. Col. R. F. O'BIERNE, 14th U. S. Infantry.
Major G. W. WALLACE, 6th U. S. Infantry,

Present, also, the Judge Advocate. The Commission was cleared for deliberation.

The foregoing order was read aloud by the Judge Advocate.

The President then read the following communication from the Major General Commanding :

HEADQUARTERS DEPARTMENT OF THE EAST,
NEW YORK CITY, February 18th, 1865.

GENERAL : I have suspended the order for the execution of John Y. Beall, and have reconvened your Military Commission, that I might send the proceedings in that case back to the Commission for a revision of the findings therein.

I would particularly call the attention of the Commission to the finding upon the 3d. Specification under Charge 2d.

A familiar rule of law requires that the finding should meet, and affirm or deny, every averment in the Specification. This is not done by the present finding, except by implication. The finding negatives the averment of date, and omits all mention of the other averments, leaving it to be inferred that the Commission considered the Specification sustained by the proof in every other particular. If such were the opinion of the Commission, the rule of law to which I have referred would be complied with by finding the accused " Guilty, omitting the word September, and substituting the word December ;" or, " Not Guilty as to the day averred, but guilty of acting as a spy, at or near Suspension Bridge, in the State of New York, on or about December 16, 1864."

The Commission may deem it well to consider and determine once more whether the proof under Specifications 1 and 2, charge 2d, establishes the characteristics of a spy, viz., an enemy clandestinely within our lines to obtain information to be used for hostile purposes.

I do not make this last suggestion for the purpose of raising a doubt in regard to the correctness of the finding, but that the judgment of the Commission may be placed beyond all question.

I am, very respectfully, yours,

JOHN A. DIX,
Major General.

Brig. General FITZ HENRY WARREN,
President Military Commission.

The Commission then reopened the case of John Y. Beall, and re-considered the finding upon Specification 3d under Charge 2d.

Upon careful consideration of the evidence recorded in the proceedings, the Commission find the accused, John Y. Beall, of Specification 3d under charge 2d not guilty as to the day averred, but guilty of acting as a spy at or near Suspension Bridge, in the State of New York, on or about Dec. 16, 1864.

After careful deliberation the Commission find no reason to reconsider their finding on either Charge, or any other Specification, and do therefore reaffirm their sentence, two-thirds of the members of the Commission concurring therein.

(Signed)   FITZ HENRY WARREN,
Brigadier General U.S. Volunteers, President.

JOHN A. BOLLES,
Major and Aide-de-camp,
Jdge Advocate.

These Proceedings were laid before the Major General
commanding, who endorsed thereon the following approval
and order, on the 21st of February, Tuesday:

The proceedings, finding, and sentence are approved, and
the accused, John Y. Beall, will be hanged by the neck till
he is dead, on Governor's Island, on Friday, the 24th day of
February, 1865.   The commanding officer at Fort Columbus
is charged with the execution of this order.

(Signed)   JOHN A. DIX,

Major General Commanding.

CORRESPONDENCE.

Letter from John Y. Beall to Col. J. Thompson.

FORT COLUMBUS, Feb. 21st, 1865.

Col. J. THOMPSON,

Confed. Com'r.,

SIR,—Perhaps I should have written to you sooner, but I knew that you were not inappreciative of my situation, and I hope that you did not slacken your efforts on account of the reprieve of six days. You may not succeed in your efforts, but I do expect you to vindicate my character. I have been styled a pirate, robber, etc. When the U. S. authorities, after such a "trial," shall execute such a sentence, I do earnestly call on you to officially vindicate me at least to my countrymen. With unabated loyalty to our cause of self-government, and my country, and an earnest prayer for our success as a nation, and kindest feelings for yourself,

I remain, truly, your friend,

JOHN YATES BEALL.

Col. THOMPSON,

Toronto, C. W.

(True Copy.) WRIGHT RIVES,

Capt. U. S. A.

Letter from John Y. Beall to Col. R. Ould, Commissioner of Exchange, &c.

FORT COLUMBUS, Feb. 21st, 1865.

Col. R. OULD, Com'r. Exchange,

Richmond, Va.

SIR,—The published proceedings of Military Commission, in my case, published in the New York papers of the 15th inst., made you and my Government aware of my sentence and doom.

A reprieve, on account of some informality, from the 18th to the 24th was granted. The authorities are possessed of the facts in my case. They know that I acted under orders. I appeal to my Government to use its utmost efforts to protect me ; and, if unable .to prevent my murder, to vindicate my reputation.

I can only declare that I was no " spy " or guerillero, and am a true Confederate.

Respectfully,

JOHN Y. BEALL,

Act. Mas. C. S. N.

(True Copy.)   WRIGHT RIVES,

Capt. U. S. A.

LETTERS WRITTEN DURING HIS FIRST VISIT TO CANADA, IN 1862.

Letter to Mrs. Genl. Williams.

DUNDAS, CANADA WEST,

Dec. 6th, 1862.

Since we parted in April, Mrs. Williams, very often have I thought of you, and hoped that you might not forget me. Especially after the fall of New Orleans and Memphis, and during the seige of Vicksburg, did I think of my Louisiana friends. I met your brother's brigade at the Rapidan, and, when his name appeared among those of the unreturning braves who fell on the banks of the Antietam, I assure you that you had my warmest sympathies. Alas, so many now mourn a kinsman's loss! Dr. English lost his brother at Port Republic in June last ; my brother fell in action, severely wounded, at Manassas, Aug. 30th, 1862. I can imagine the suspense and anxiety of my Tennessee friends after the battle of Perryville. Remember me most kindly to them, and tell them that they owe me several letters, and I do *wish* a reply may be started *via* underground railroad, directing to care of Samuel Overfield, Esq., Dundas, Canada West.

I will explain why I am writing from her Majesty's dominions and not from the Conft. States. I stayed in Richmond till after the battle of Williamsburg, when I went to Gordonsville, where I saw some of my friends, and, I think, Mr. Mc, who taught at Mr. Cotton's. Then I went to Madison county, where my aunt lives, not far from Cedar mountain. After some rest, I started to rejoin my regiment under Jackson, then after Banks. During this trip I completely broke down, and was unable to keep up with the army, and, following on, suddenly found myself in the midst of McDowell's corps ; but, appearing careless and unconcerned, I strolled about reconnoitering ; and, finding it impossible to go on, I took the back track, and, during the confusion, rode out of town, passing hundreds of their infantry and cavalry. By dodging, I eluded my pursuers, and finally found myself on the banks of the Potomac. I chose to go North voluntarily instead of involuntarily. I gave the Yankees a circumstantial account of Jackson whipping Fremont and McDowell at Strasburg. They thought nothing impossible to Jackson, and cursed Banks as a coward and liar.

(Some of the Pennsylvania Dutch think old Stonewall is Andrew Jackson, and the impersonation of every military virtue.) From Maryland I went into Pennsylvania ; thence to the west, and thence effected a strategic movement to this place.

I have been heretofore buoyed by the hope of soon being able to rejoin my comrades, but now doubt it. Should I, however, become able, I will join some privateer fitting out from England, where I have relatives.

I have enjoyed peculiar advantages to observe the phases of public opinion in the West and Canada. The majority of the last democratic vote was in favour of peace, and since then *many* republicans have yielded in their views, and to-day the North is divided, and they begin to feel it, but not enough yet to found hopes of peace. The majority of the Canadians are pro-Southern, and that majority is increasing. The English are more strongly Southern than the Canadians. At first the North possessed this sympathy, but by their folly and stupidity they have changed it into contempt and hatred. Recognition *will only come after more successes.* This province has many deserters from the Yankee army, and to avoid draft. They have now a fearful force to hurl against us—I think some 500,000 men, besides the navy. Of these, many are daily deserting, and many in camp stealing and oppressing. I feel that our hated foe will hurt us more than ever before, but I pray God, " who doeth all things well," to help us, and if we strive on, I hope and believe that we will yet win. Remember me kindly to the General, and the Misses Robert, to Dr. English and Charley, and any other of my friends that you may see. I would be very glad to hear from you and my Tennessee correspondent.

Believe me to be now, as ever,

Your grateful friend,

J. Y. B * * * *

Mrs. R. W. WILLIAMS,
Tallahassee, Florida.
(Mailed 17th, 1862, via Lexington, Kentucky.)

Letter to Miss E. A. Aglionby.

DUNDAS, CANADA WEST,
Nov. 19th, 1862.

DEAR COUSIN,—Yours of Augt. 6th was handed me a few days ago. I hasten at this, my first opportunity, to thank you for it, and for the expression of your sympathy for us, individually and nationally. His nature must be cold indeed

whose heart is not strengthened and energies braced when
engaged in a life-and-death struggle for all that one holds
high, sacred, and dear, by the knowledge that his motives
are understood and appreciated, and that the heartfelt good-
wishes and God-speeds of the good and generous of the world
are given for his success. We are fighting the cause of
liberty, truth, and right. I believe, aye, I hope and trust we
will win. But whether we succeed or fail, we will have fought
a good fight. Alas, many a hearth will be desolate, and
many a fireside will know it's master no more! Yet it has
ever been so; we must not complain! The path of honour,
duty, and truth has ever been watered with the tears and
blood, and strewn with the mangled bodies of the innocent,
the good and generous.

I am glad the photograph pleased you. I was dressed
plainly, and coarsely dressed to avoid suspicion and recognition. I am old, prematurely old : exposure, hardship, suffering, the drain of an unhealed wound, anxiety, hope deferred,
have done the work of time on the body,—they have not
quenched my spirit nor impaired the tenacity of my will.

Let me thank you for your kind invitation. Should I visit
England, I will come to see you. I had purposed to go
there to embark on a Confederate war-vessel fitting out
against the Abolition Yankees, but my physician advised me
not to cross the sea at present. I read a letter from home
dated Oct. 9th ; it ran the blockade ; mother had been sick,
but was better. Poor mother, 'twas unrest of spirit and illness of mind, anxiety and care which brought on sickness of
body. My brother William, a lad of eighteen, had been
wounded in the battle of Manassas, Aug. 30th, and they did
not hear from him for a long time ; he had, at last, got home,
and was better. The rest of the family were well, and so
were all your relatives. When I last wrote I was in Iowa,
whither I went when I eluded the Yankees. I stayed there
as " Mr. Yates," recuperating and working for my country.

At last I was discovered, and had to fly for liberty and life. After much trouble I got to this place. I then returned to the U. S. to get some means I had left, and have again returned to Her Majesty's dominions.

The recent elections in the North have gone for the democratic, conservative, peace-inclined party, though the new Congress does not meet for one year. I think that the recognition of the nationality of the South by England would assist that party so much as speedily to put an end to this unhappy and unholy strife. Peace would open up the South to the trade of England, and she would get cotton for her operatives, and thereby bread. Nations must consult their interest, hence an official proclamation of the fact must forward that interest to justify its proclamation.

In the meantime the struggle goes on. We, the weaker in numbers and resources, are cut off from the world. Yet we have withstood our enemies better than the ablest of our generals thought possible. In August last we gained the bloody battles of Cedar Run, Rappahannock, and Manassas in Virginia, Richmond in Kentucky, and Murfreesboro' in Tennessee. In September we captured Harper's Ferry in Va., with 12,000 men, and Munfordsville in Kentucky with 5000, and defeated the Yankees at South Mountain and Antietam in Maryland, and Shepherdstown in Va., but suffered a reverse at Corinth, Mississippi, while we defeated them at Perryville, Kentucky. Our cavalry went into Pennsylvania, and returned after performing many heroic and brilliant feats.

But enough of America and her unhappy strife. Of coarse I could not sympathize with Garibaldi. 1st. He had no business in Rome ; 2nd. He is fond of the Yankees and they of him, especially those who tore down convents and cathedrals, and insulted sisters of charity, and held meetings " to remonstrate with the Almighty for *His blunder* in permitting the success of the peace party in recent elections."

I must, however, bring my long letter to a close. Assure my other cousins, when you see or write to them, of my good wishes for them and theirs. If you can find time and inclination I would be glad to hear from you or them.

I pray God to bless you and them.

Your cousin and friend,

J. Y. BEALL.

DIARY.

July 23rd, 1862.   *Cascade, Dubuque County, Iowa.*

I purpose in this book to record passing events as I may
best understand them, and according to the best information
that I can get ; to make extracts from books, and papers, and
conversations, of any and everything that interests, amuses,
or may interest me in future. And first, how I came here.
—Leaving home I rode the first day to Mansfield, and spent
the night with my aunt and uncle and cousins—heard many
reports which we did not credit ; next morning, after bidding,
as I thought, a temporary adieu, started to see my brother
and friends ; rode all day, which was an exceedingly warm
one, stopping at several places of no note ; and at last turning
off the road, staid at Mr. Kaufman's all night, avoiding a
heavy rain. Next morning, resuming my route, came to
a little village which I found full of troops, and heard that
the high rains had swept away the bridges, and raised the
streams so high as to render fording both difficult and
dangerous. I was compelled, therefore, to retrace my steps,
as I could not stay there ; I rode all day and met Messrs.
Timberlake, Larue, and Kennedy ; at night I stopped at
Mr. Lewis', who put me on my route—severe rains all night.
Next day I rode, and, crossing the creek, made for Grantham's
and Kitchen's ; but though it was warm, I got to Tomahawk
Springs, and stayed all night at Mr. Griffith's on the recommendation of Mr. Denny. It rained all night, and· in the

morning, re-crossing the creek, I went through rain, and succeeded in crossing the river at a ferry—it was past fording, and indeed a surging torrent. Had I delayed much longer, I could not have crossed at all. After crossing, I rode only a few miles, when the rain still falling, I stopped over night, and tried to dry my clothes; I partially succeeded. My next day carried me to the *Six Mile House*, where I stayed all night, and heard some of the particulars of Gen. Banks' retreat, and also of the battle of Fair Oaks near Richmond. From all that I could learn, Gen. Jackson had about 25,000 men, veterans, well equipped, flushed with victory, and burning to re-enter their homes. By a series of skillful manœuvres he cut off and surprised a part of Gen. Banks' command at Front Royal, Virginia, say 15,000, and then, throwing himself on the main body, routed them, already confounded, pursued them to Winchester, and there again defeated them with a heavy loss of men and stores. Immediately converging his columns, he scattered them over the entire country down to the Potomac, effectually picking up the stragglers, waggons, &c. Not giving his men any time to rest, he retraced his now-converging column on Winchester, and gathering his plunder, estimated at 3,500 prisoners, 270 waggons, 8,000 arms, and $1,000,000 worth of military stores, he hurried on to Strasburg, where, placing his army between that of Fremont and that of Shields, he skirmished with both until his trains got out of danger, when he retreated slowly along, occupying the strong places, and thus retarding the progress of the main columns, while it was too dangerous to push a *small* one parallel to him, as it would be unsupported. Having finally gotten his waggon train off safely, he turned on Gen. Fremont at Cross Keys, entirely defeated him with great loss, variously estimated at from 1,500 to 3,000. The next morning he attacked Gen. Shields at *Port Republic;* he destroyed all means of junction between Genls. Fremont and Shields, and almost annihilated

Q

Shield's army. Indeed it is said that Fremont and McDowell lost from 8 to 10,000 men in the short space of ten days.

Leaving next morning, I came that night to the top of the mountain, and stayed all night, where I saw men who had heard direct from the battle of *Fair Oaks.* From them, and from admissions seen since in extracts from Richmond papers, and New York papers, I judge that Gen. Casey was thrown forward with his division on McClellan's left. Gen. Johnston, taking advantage of the heavy rains, threw a heavy column suddenly on it, and almost annihilated it before Couch's division could come up, and it and the fragment of Casey's were driven before Johnston, losing everything, such as camp equipage, cannon, and many prisoners. Gen. Heintzelman's and Sumner's corps were unable to drive back Johnston, who ran his cars out to the spot, hauled off all the spoils, and then quietly withdrew to the high ground. His loss was about 6000 men ; McClellan's was 23 cannon and 13,000 men. Johnston's men had the prestige of victory, a thing whose importance cannot be over estimated. . . . .

I then came on to Uniontown, where, transacting my business, and selling my horse, I concluded to come west. I came to Chicago, and thence to Dubuque, and there concluding a bargain with. . . . . , I have taken the Cascade mill, and am running it. When. . . . . returns I may go into partnership, but my opinion is that all business will languish, and must be dangerous. Since I have been here, Memphis has fallen into the hands of the Union fleet, and army, the Confederate gunboats being all destroyed or captured. This was a foregone conclusion to my mind, and the consequent evacuation of Corinth by Beauregard gave a wasted country to Halleck and his army. Where the Confederate forces are that were at Corinth no one knows ; but it is unsafe to send out waggon trains or detachments of troops, as a regiment of 500 men and 175 waggons have been lost in one excursion. To overrun a country is not to conquer it by any means, and this truth, the result of experience in times gone by, is now beginning to force itself into the *noodle skulls* who rule and ruin this goodly land.

On the sixteenth of June was fought the battle of James Island in S. Carolina. The Confederates had erected batteries in the centre and elevated part of the Island, which lies just back of Fort Sumter. Gen. Brenham, the commander of the Federals, had encamped on the Island, and his camp was being continually shelled by the Southern troops; whereupon he tried to carry the works, and after a severe contest was signally defeated with a loss of 1,100 men in killed and wounded. Of course his ill-success has cost him his situation, as success has ever been held to be the criterion of merit.

The battle of *Fair Oaks* or *Seven Pines* was fought May 31st and June 1st. After that, Johnston being wounded, Lee, the Southern commander, allowed Gen. McClellan to advance without much resistance to the edge of the swamp. The hard fare of an active campaign, where everything has to be hauled far, the malaria and miasma of a swamp, under a burning sun, and the effluvia of the dead, sick and wounded made the camp of McClellan one vast hospital. Gen. Stuart, of the rebel cavalry, about the middle of June, made a detour of the entire Federal army, cutting off communication, and destroying much property, and capturing some prisoners.

On the 26th of June, Gen. McClellan, whose left rested on White Oak Swamp, and right occupying both sides of the upper Chickahominy, advanced to get out of the swamp, and succeeded. The designs of the Southern commanders, Lee and Johnston, were already formed. Jackson, who had defeated Banks and prevented the junction of Fremont and McDowell, defeating both in pitched battles, with heavy loss, and had driven them helter skelter before him, now turned, and leaving a small force in front of them, marched by long and rapid marches, and joined the army of Richmond. Like an avalanche his 20,000 men fell on the right of McClellan's army, which extended over too much ground, on the 27th (Friday). After a day's struggle Porter's (F.) corps was entirely defeated, and the right wing of the Federal army defeated, driven back on the centre, which with difficulty held its position.

On the morning of the 28th, Jackson advanced and took the railroad, the only avenue of transportation, and simultaneously the conflict was renewed on the front, and the doubled up wing. Defeat that day was the result of the conflict to the Federals everywhere. The only resource left McClellan was to make a road through the swamp, and, deserting his sick and wounded, and medical stores, &c., to get to the James River under the protection of the gunboats. On Sunday, Monday, and Tuesday, the same scene was enacted —battles, defeats, retreats—until finally the James River and the gunboats came in sight and into play, and safety from ball and battle was insured to the army. McClellan now is encamped on the hills and bluffs of the James, his left on the river, his right on the swamps of the Chickahominy. This country is extremely unhealthy, being exposed to the malarious and miasmatic winds which every day blow between the rivers. His provision transports are continually fired on by the flying artillery of Stuart. Fever and ague and cholera, especially abound in this part of the world, and yellow-fever has always loved it. His army, with its strength shattered by fatigue, hunger, excitement, and dispirited by defeat, must fall by thousands before fevers and sickness. His loss in the battles of Chickahominy cannot be less than 30,000 killed and wounded, and 18,000 prisoners. His entire loss since he reached the Peninsula of York and James, in killed and wounded, has been at least 50,000, in prisoners 20,000, and 50,000 in sick—120,000 altogether, an aggregate startling, but nevertheless I believe it to be true, as his army has counted 200 or 230,000 men.

President Lincoln visited him last week, and expressed himself as highly pleased, and McClellan as " all right," but Halleck has been appointed Commander-in-Chief, thus topping McClellan who was the senior officer ; so he truly stands in Winfield Scott's shoes, honour *before* the contest, *disgrace after* it. What has Halleck done ? nothing—it is only a desperate resort, an expedient, a grasping after some saviour. It requires no genius to see that John Pope is trying to supplant both Halleck and McClellan. He has been remarkable for magnificent statements, but has really done little to justify his boasts. He has had to encounter guerillas, &c., before ; *now* he will have to meet a foeman, worthy of any general's steel, Thomas J. Jackson, better known by the soubriquet of " Stonewall Jackson," with his troops, the heroes of Manassas, Winchester, Cross Keyes, Port Republic, and Chickahominy, men who, all agree, are splendidly armed, equipped, officered and disciplined, and who are accustomed to hard fighting and constant victory. When General Pope shall have conquered *these,* he may crown himself with laurels, and none shall gainsay him. Till then, prudence, if not modesty, should dictate silence—acts, and not words. In the meantime another awful pause ensues, and I firmly believe another bloody drama will be enacted in Tennessee, between the armies of *Buell* and *Bragg.* In the West, military movements of great importance have taken place. General Curtis has been roaming about in Arkansas in pursuit of an enemy, and of a Union sentiment ; the latter he found always to take the shape of a bill for damages, ever to be where his army *was,* never where it *has been.* The former has at length been found ; Maj. General Hindman, having landed in Arkansas, has been continually worrying him by cutting off his pickets, forage-trains, communications, and in all such ways harassing and injuring him ; now his army having acquired consistency and numbers, he has grown bolder and success has favoured his boldness. He has succeeded in

destroying the navigation by water to Curtis's army ; and thus
isolating him in a wasted country, one brigade has already
been lost and a most painful suspense hangs over his destiny,
(especially as General Price has recrossed the Mississippi and
has reinforced Hindman, but to what amount no one knows,
but any force added to it will be apt to seal the doom of
his army, and open up Missouri to the invading Price, who,
it is said, will be able to get 10,000 fresh men, which, added
to his army, would make it truly formidable, and able to
drive any Federal force now there out of it.)

In the meantime General Forrest has advanced on Nashville, and captured Murfreesboro' with some 1,500 men and
a battery, and cut off communication with Buell.   This feat
may be like that of Stuart's in Virginia—a daring reconnois-
sance or only a dash to scare and injure.   In Kentucky
Colonel John Morgan, of guerrilla renown, has added to his
fame for audacity ; he has advanced, taking Tompkinsville
and four hundred cavalry, Frankfort, Cynthia, and advancing
on Cincinnati, Ohio, which he can compel to surrender by
holding the bluffs of Kentucky opposite, and threatening to
shell the town.   Morgan is represented as being largely reinforced at every step of his tour.   The Confederates also
advanced to the Ohio river and captured Henderson, and,
floating their flag over its court-house, crossed the river and
captured 3260 stand of arms, which they carried off.   The
Confederates here lately seem to have taken a good many
arms, as at Winchester, Cross Keys, Port Republic, Fair
Oaks, Chickahominy, Murfreesboro', and Newbern ; and, as
they were said to be suffering for them, they justly regard
these as highly important victories.

At Vicksburg a most fearful battle has been progressing
for many days, and as two fleets are trying in vain to pass, it
may be safely asserted that the Southern troops are so far
successful.   Even should the fleets be able to go by, no vessel
will be allowed to pass, as a small cannon would stop all

progress, and no one can doubt but that the rebel commanders
would avail themselves of such expedients.   The Mississippi
will not be open for trade until peace is restored, and confidence born again, and many years elapsed.

> Alas to think that love decays,
> And friendship wears the length of days,
> And hands disjoin and hearts dissever,
> But hate lives, grows, and lasts forever.

> " There hath arisen betwixt us
> An immortality of hate.   Old Time
> Shall sink to dotage and forget himself,
> And Pity cling unto an usurer's heart
> Ere he and I grow friends."

Sir, you may apologize to me, you offer to shake hands, you beg
pardon, but can you *unstrike me?*

The perversion of knowledge is more to he feared than the want of it.
The latter leaves man a powerless animal, the former makes him a
powerful demon.

Problem by Carlyle,—Given a world of knaves to produce happiness
out of their united efforts.

He who steals from a citizen ends his days in chains and fetters, but
he who steals from the community ends his days in gold and purple.—
Cato.

> The jars of brothers
> Are like a small stone thrown into a river ;
> The breach scarce heard, but view the current,
> And you shall see a thousand angry rings
> Rise in his face, still swelling and still growing.—*Old Play.*

Whenever any great change in society is taking place, its ultimate
effects are foreseen and foretold by one party as clearly as they are
denied and ridiculed by another.   It is not ignorance but prejudice
which is principally to be dreaded.

The most imperious of all necessities to mankind is a government.
The illusion of self-government is but for an hour, with the choice of
the demagogue which is to wile, or of the cabal to direct them.—*Alison.*

"Scelera impetu, bona consilia morâ valescere."   Speaking of the
French Revolution, one of the directors said : " Falsehood is the constant
and favourite resource of the cabals which prevail here.   It is impossible
to conceive the impudence with which the most palpable lies are pub-

lished and propagated among the people. The most positive assertions, the most minute detail of facts, the strongest appearance of probability, are made to accompany the grossest falsehoods."

The history of the past is *mutatis mutandis* the history of the present. Until we read the past, one *wonders* at the present. And if I did not live in the United States at the present time I would not, and could not believe all one reads about the French Revolution. History, like nature, but reproduces herself.

" My dear Abbé," you have loosed the bull ; do you expect he is not to make use of his horns ?"—*Mirabeau.*

Epithets and nicknames should never be despised ; it is by such means that mankind are governed.—*Napoleon.*

An unavoidable and most alarming increase in the public expenditures, accompanied by a corresponding diminution in the income. Effect of revolution.—*Alison.*

Famine, the natural consequence of the public convulsions, want of employment, the inevitable result of the suspension of credit, pressed severely upon the labouring classes.—*Ibidem.*

Words put nations in motion ; bayonets alone arrest their course.— *Lamartine.*

It belongs to God alone, in his inscrutable wisdom, to visit the sins of the fathers upon the children ; it is the first principle of *human* justice to deal with every one according to his individual deeds.   The melancholy catalogue of crimes which stain.................... .... proved too clearly that .... were unfit for liberty, and unworthy of that blessing, for they had not yet laid the corner-stone of the structure in *learning to be just.*—*Alison.*

July 24th, 1862.

" What, is this our Liberty ?   We can no longer hang whom we please !" (French mob in the Revolution)—*Epea pteroenta!* Winged Words ! Flown down through history even to our own day !

It is impossible to read the history of the French Revolution by Alison without being struck by the similarity of that of America of 1861–62 : it almost seems prediction.

Our Revolution will not in all respects produce the same results, for the circumstances are different : and while from similar causes we may expect like effects, it is also true that these results must be modified by conditions existing in this country to be found no where else in the world. The *similarity* consists in the same rottenness of human nature, the same belief in human perfectibility, the same false notions of equality ;—and these are producing the same class of demagogues, blood-thirsty,—demon-like ; the same prejudice, and ignorance, the same falsehood systematized, and used as an engine of power. Again, in this country, the *distribution of power* is different; nationalities, distinct, and in some instances hostile, are commingled, while over all broods party-spirit, which, tho' it may be smothered, " is not dead—it only sleepeth." Still another modifying circumstance is the remoteness of foreign powers, from the scene of strife, and the entirely different feeling with which they view the object and end. The French Revolution aimed at Liberty, this at Despotism. Whether the hideous effort to establish the latter aim, is to be crowned with the same amount of bloodshed, is in the future. The effort will, I have no doubt, be successful. Who will be the man to concentrate all power in himself? Most probably some one as yet unknown,—some Cromwell, Cæsar, or Napoleon. To rule this people will not require force, so much as *Humbuggery*. In *that* art are many adepts. *Nous verrons!*

The mail to-day brought me a letter from............
.... Poor Bob English! he was a kind-hearted man ; when last I saw him he seemed glad to see me ; but then we only saw each other for a moment. I pray God to bless him ;—though his account is settled long ago for better or for worse. Many more, no doubt, have also gone to that settlement. I pray God, that when my name is called, I may go to the right, even though it may be through fire—sincerely I pray so.

" Every heart knoweth its own bitterness," and out of the heart are the issues of life, and death also. The wickedness of man, who can estimate! Though God does not always punish it in this world, yet he does somewhere, unless it has been repented of, and atoned for by the blood of Jesus the Lamb of God. But nations have no hereafter, and they receive their offsets here. How tremendous must have been the sins which are calling down such scenes, and how awful the calamities which are to follow such crimes against humanity and Christianity ! It almost makes the blood run cold to hear of the barbarities, and behold the scenes daily enacted! O ! Lord what have we done to call down such ? But, Lord Thy will, not ours—Thou gavest, Thou takest away—blessed be Thy name evermore ! Give strength to bear, to forbear, and to forgive for Jesus Christ's sake !

The war news to-day is most important. The fleet at Vicksburg has been worsted by a ram steamer, Arkansas, which seems fair to rival, aye to excel the Virginia in effectiveness and in terror ; its first appearance has been most effective ; the Federal fleet seems now more intent on escape than on advance, and if it is as formidable as represented by the despatches from Memphis, it will not be long before the Mississippi will be too hot to hold the mortar-boats—and then look out for New Orleans !

From Virginia there is news. General Jackson has defeated one division of Gen. Pope, said to be under Siegel, and General Ewell has certainly defeated General Hatch, so that General Pope has boasted before his time ; and though he betrays his usual brutality in the way of orders, and impudence and faith in lies, yet he certainly has been so far worsted, and will be, I have no doubt, in future—for nearly all braggarts are *do littles*. Yet fearful are the times and trials of the people ; the troubles fall chiefly on the innocent and defenceless. I would that I were " over the hills and far away." Morgan's expedition into Kentucky seems to have been planned on a much larger scale, and has resulted in more important results than any one at first supposed. He fought quite a battle at Lexington, and advanced on Cincinnati, capturing cannon, men and horses. All the reports of his own capture by United States troops being false and not having foundation in fact. At Frederickton, Missouri, the guerrillas have been at work, and totally defeated, the home-guard killing and wounding quite a number. The entire arm-bearing population is called out, and the entire arms and ammunition, private and public, are summoned and seized. Vive la République—Vive la Liberté.

July 25th, 1862.

Gunnery and specie issuing at once and at the same value as an offset for indebtedness, both must become objects of merchandise ; and the more plentiful any merchandise becomes, the more it must decline in price. From this must necessarily result inextricable confusion—the purchase of land for a nominal value, the discharge of debts for an illusory payment, and, in a word, a universal change of property by a system of spoliation, so secret, that no one can perceive from whence the stroke that ruins him has come. Suppose the depreciation is only 10 per cent. The Treasury at that rate gains 10 per cent. on the entire debt. Is not that national bankruptcy ? If it continues and increases will not all debts be depreciated and creditors ruined ?

" They [our enemies] march with the opinion of 500,000 men !"—*Napoleon*.

July 31st, 1862.

There is the usual meagreness of news, not but that events of great importance are occurring, but the Government does not allow the knowledge of them to go forth. Bragg has advanced on Corinth, and has captured many Federals at Grand Junction, a place where the Ohio and Mississippi railroad intersects the Memphis and Charleston railroad, between Corinth and Memphis,—and Florence is also captured, being between Buell's army and Corinth and Humbolt, between Corinth and Columbus, Kentucky. Thus General Grant finds

himself surrounded, and his communications cut off.   No one
knows what is his force, and how it is posted.   An estimate
is máde thus : General Grant had, April 6th, about 42,000
men, and lost in battle about 12,000, by sickness about 5,000 ;
and then Generals Hurlburt and Sherman have been sent to
Memphis with say about 10,000—thus leaving of his original
corps about 15,000.   His reinforcements have probably
numbered about 20,000, of whom 5,000 are disabled by sickness and wounds—making his entire force not over 30,000
effective men.   General Buell has not more than 30,000.
Hurlburt, Sherman and Curtis do not probably number over
20,000.   There are scattered over the country through
Tennessee, Kentucky and Mississippi, Alabama, say 25,000
more, and in Missouri, Arkansas, Louisiana, Florida, Kansas,
say about 25,000, and in rendezvous in Illinois, Indiana, &c.,
15,000 more, making in the Western army an effective force
of 145,000—and in Virginia, Maryland, District of Columbia,
North and South Carolina, Georgia and in rendezvous, about
185,000,—making a grand total of 330,000 out of 1,000,000
—which have borne arms since the beginning of the war.
Many consider this too liberal an estimate of the number of
efficient men, and say that there have been 75,000 desertions.
If General Bragg has marched to attack General Grant at
Corinth, his force is about 45,000 men ; and unless I greatly
err in my estimates of the opposing forces, Bragg will be successful.   If he be so, the forces of General Buell will be in
a very unsafe position.   The papers are in as usual.   The
telegrams are confused and unsatisfactory ; nothing doing at
or about Richmond ; they say that about Gordonsville, and
Charlottesville are many thousand Confederates under Gen.
Jackson, who seems to be ubiquitous, and at the head of
everything which promises trouble to the authorities at
Washington.   Kentucky swarms with guerrillas, going everywhere, and doing everything, and so of Missouri, which at
this present time is not *very* peaceable, whilst armies are

rshalling there, and blood is being spilt daily. The ram
d gunboat Arkansas at Vicksburg seems to be a very for-
dable affair, having had another battle with Davis's fleet, and
en quite successful, having disabled two Federal gunboats
cording to their account, and according to the rebel accounts
e, sunk for ever at that. The telegrams also say that
errimac No. 2 expects shortly to run out from Richmond,
d say that rebeldom expects great things therefrom, such
destruction of the whole fleet at Harrison's Landing.
is is all one can know; what is past we can't find out, and
at is in the future no one can tell : we only know that the
nfederates at this time have the prestige of victory, and
results too on their side, and these are of great importance
they are now assuming the *offensive* everywhere. Re-
iting under the new call for 300,000 men seems to go on
ry slowly, and the enormous bounties do not drag men out.
t one new regiment has been enlisted; and should the
l be filled, doubtless they will not be in time to avert the
ding storm which seems to be on the eve of sweeping over
South, and destroying the invading hosts seeking to re-
re the Union. From what one sees in the papers I would
her that force is to be employed to make Iowa cast a
ublican vote, and elect war-men to Congress, as well as to
ist in a draft if found practicable. From what I can learn,
istance will be made to a draft and blood be shed, but no
led plan will be carried out, and this but little affected.
he Union is peace !"
n reading the papers again this morning I think danger
a collision is to be apprehended in Dubuque between the
vernment and the Democrats. Arms, &c., are being sent
re, and threats are being used of coercing Mahony to a
ticular policy, and he refuses most positively to go in the
r they indicate, and justly too. I hope and trust that
nis may be successful, and gain a victory over them; the
h will rise up, and, if organised, will make most bloody

work ; for nothing under the sky is as savage as a mob, and a victorious one is a monster abounding in cruelty, and ferocious beyond imagination.

August 1st, 1862.

On reviewing the history of the last month we are struck, in the first place, by the magnitude of the events which have occurred. 1st. Of the armies; 2nd. Of the acts of the Government; 3rd. Of the people ; 4th. Of the foreign world.

1st. *The movements of the armies.*—This month (July) was ushered in by the bloody contests of the Chickahominy which resulted in the complete discomfiture of General McClellan and his army. The official loss is put down at 16,000. But as the Richmond papers claim that they took 6,000 wounded, and 4,000 well prisoners, and over 5,000 wounded have come up already from Harrison's Landing, we can see at a glance that this official statement is not true. General Banks reported a loss of 1,000, and it was over 3,000 ; and Fremont of 600, at Cross Keys, when it was 2,000 ; McClellan of 5,500, at Fair Oaks, when it was 13,000. We may safely infer, therefore, that the loss of General McClellan is not less than 40,000 in those terrible battles of the Chickahominy. General McClellan secured his retreat to the James River, and there, under the cover of gun-boats, he is endeavouring to reorganize his defeated and demoralized army. General Burnside has been withdrawn to reinforce the army of McClellan, thus practically evacuating North Carolina. Concerning the movements in Western Virginia, I cannot learn anything; silence is ominous. In the Valley and along the Potomac the corps of McDowell or Banks and old army of Fremont, all under *General Pope,* seem to be doing nothing except plundering. General Halleck's division was much cut up at or near Orange Court House, and Siegel was pressed at or about Sperryville, and the cavalry of Don Piatt was defeated near Middletown in

Frederick County. The Federal army in South Carolina and Georgia is strictly on the defensive. In the West the Confederates have held Vicksburg against all attempts of the two fleets to take it; and the gun-boat "Arkansas," Confederate navy, has twice defeated the flotilla, sinking and disabling some ten or twelve Federal vessels. The siege is now abandoned, and the Mississippi is unopened and likely to remain so for all time. General Curtis' army succeeded in escaping from Arkansas to the Mississippi much cut up and demoralized, having lost nearly half of his force by skirmishes, sickness, and desertions. He is intent on retreat and not on advance. In Tennessee the Confederates have been very active and successful. General Forrest, with a large cavalry force, attacked Murfreesboro', near Nashville, and captured the force there, about 2,000, and stores, &c., to amount of $100,000. They also succeeded in taking Grand Junction and Humbolt with many men and stores. Concerning Buell's force we can hear nothing, and are inclined to believe that they are in a precarious situation. In Kentucky, Morgan has been cutting up on a grand scale, having captured cities, towns, thousands of prisoners, and arms, and millions of stores—threatening Cincinnati, Louisville, and Frankfort. In Missouri several battles, or rather skirmishes, have been fought, and many thousands have been enlisted for Price, who is moving on Rolla and Springfield. So much for military affairs. We must conclude that, during the last month, the Confederates have been successful in a high degree—defeating choice armies, capturing immense stores, and many thousands of arms and ammunition in proportion.

2nd. Acts of Government. — Congress has adjourned, having done all that it could do to embitter the South. It authorized robbery, plunder, and insurrection. It passed high direct tax bills, and an enormous indirect tax bill, known as *tariff.* The executive has called for 300,000 more men, and the work of enlisting goes on slowly, notwithstanding the enormous bounties promised to be paid, and as *men* are the necessity of the hour, drafting is to take place shortly. The republic is gone, and a military despotism is substituted in its stead, which is seizing means and men wherever they are to be found.

3rd. Conduct and temper of the people.—While these events, the defeat of the army and navy, and increase of expenditures of Government are occurring, a spirit of opposition is rising among the people, and the party clamouring for cessation of hostilities is daily becoming stronger and more bold. An attempt to put them down will be made, and will be resisted to the shedding of blood. The taxes, draft, and the natural popular inconstancy, all point to the overthrow of the republican party. In my opinion, civil commotions and bloodshed will be the result, and farewell, a long farewell to peace! The innocent will suffer with the guilty, but so it has been since the creation of the world. Hosts of witnesses attest this truth. Distrust·and suspicion are rife throughout the land, and credit has been blighted by the events of the last month. Gold is ranging from fifteen to twenty-five per cent. above currency or treasury notes. As a consequence of the depreciation of currency of the United States, prices of everything have gone up. The annihilation of the cotton·trade has raised clothing 100 per cent., and it shortly must go up another 100 per cent. This applies to wool as well as cotton. This is not confined to America, but is universal. So of sugar and molasses. The high tariff on the "decencies" of life, such as coffee and tea, has run them up nearly 100 per cent., without taking into consideration the depreciation of currency. Price of labour has gone up temporarily, but will shortly go down. Agricultural products of the West are lower and must go lower still, and that *stay* and right arm of the country must languish, debts depreciate, and shortly repudiation will take place, thus throwing off all our debts and honour at once. So goes the world.

5th. Foreign world.—I have paid but little attention to foreign affairs. The crops of Europe appear to be good, but every interest connected with manufactures and commerce languishes; and in England and France it is quite evident that intervention is not only talked about but seriously considered and decided on in certain contingencies which, I think, have occurred and are occurring, when they shall become known. Then look out for storms! The Government will try to rally the people in order to save themselves. Who may read the future? In Russia there seems to exist a spirit of insurrection which is manifesting itself in incendiarism, nearly one half of St. Petersburg having been burned, and no one knows by whom or what for. Mexico and South America generally seem to be in their normal state of civil war, and murder, and rapine.

"Si muevo." The world does move! I am afraid it is in a circle though. One thing is evident, viz., the powers of Europe are trying to get all of their property out of this country, and therefore buying flour, &c., in exchange for goods, &c.

Facilior inter malos consensus ad bellum, quam in pace ad concordiam. —*Tacitus.*

In reading the proceedings of the Assemblies of the Revolutionary times of France, one is struck with the unanimity of the votes, while doubtless many thought differently, and wished the opposite. In revolutions the fiercer overpower the more moderate, and always have done so; examples are to be found in the country of Washington in the year 1862.

The news to-day by telegrams is that the Arkansas has been victorious again, sinking two gunboats and disabling another, which has drifted down the stream. She proves herself a gigantic and formidable adversary, having defeated and destroyed ten gunboats, and raised the siege of Vicksburg, and released some twenty thousand men from that garrison to assist in active operations. There are also reports which

R

say that the Confederates have gradually bought a navy in Europe, and it has been delivered at Mobile. This seems incredible, but if so it may be considered as sealing the fate of Gen. Butler and the re-capture of New Orleans. That some vessels were bought I believe ; it was said that they bought several vessels belonging to the Australian Steamship Company, and then purchased the iron, and had them carried to Malta and other Mediterranean ports, where the vessels were iron-plated and armed. That there may be two or three I can credit, but do not for a moment believe in more. At all events it does seem that there is life in the South, and that they are far from being conquered yet, and are determined not to give in. They have the sympathy of the good and generous of all countries.

August 4th, 1862.

Received Saturday a letter from cousin Elizabeth Aglionby, of Wizton Hall, Wizton, England. She says all are well there, and that things are going on in the old even tenor of their ways. She represents the weather unfavourable for a crop, and that in the manufacturing districts great distress prevails, and fears for the coming winter when destitution must be frightful. Her sympathies are with the South, and she is but the type of the large class of the people of England. May the merry old land long remain at peace and in prosperity ! I like the English very much ; their women, though not possessing the beauty of the Americans, are still stout, good-looking, handsome lasses.

Mr.——— came out from Dubuque. He says that a draft is decided on, and that it will be resisted to the bitter end, but that there is no system yet devised in regard to it, and that the blood spilt will be in vain. This may be so, or may be not so ; blood spilt is never lost, it crieth to Heaven, and in time it is answered !

Retreat from crime is not to nations, any more than individuals, a path strewed with flowers.—*Alison.*

Dare ! that is the sole secret of revolutions !—*St. Just.*

Nemo unquam imperium flagitio quaesitum bonis artibus exercuit.—*Tacitus.*

It is the insensible gradation in violence, the experienced necessity of advancing with the tide, which renders such convulsions so perilous to the morals, as well as the welfare of nations.—*Alison.*

Of all the lessons derived from the history of human passion, the most important is the utter impossibility which the best men will always experience of stopping, if they are once led into the path of error. Men are seduced, in the first instance, by plausible theories; their heated imaginations represent them as beneficial, and easy of execution, they advance unconsciously from errors to faults, and from faults to crimes, till sensibility is destroyed by the spectacle of guilt, and the most savage atrocities are dignified by the name of state policy.—*Lavalette.*

> .... " The unconquerable will
> And study of revenge, immortal hate,
> With courage never to submit or yield,
> And what is else not to be overcome."
>
> *Paradise Lost, Milton.*

The leaders of the French Revolution were great men, some in talent, some in learning and eloquence, and some in energy and wickedness; so of the Revolution of 1861 in America—some are truly great in intellect, but alas ! almost all are so in wickedness.

August 6th, 1862.

The papers of yesterday morning brought us no tidings of a great battle, yet there are intimations of a great contest to take place somewhere along the Tennessee River, and also of important movements along the James River. I still hold to the opinion that a movement is to be, or has been made on Buell's army in East Tennessee, and the "guerrilla" movement of Forrest was made to cut off his supplies and lines of communication. An extra was received here last night to the effect that another call had been made for 300,000 men, thus calling for 600,000 men since the defeat of McClellan on the Chickahominy in the early part of July. A draft is to be made forthwith, and men are to be made to go whether or no. Thus one must suspect that news of great interest is withheld. Distrust points

to three points : to defeat and capture of Buell and army,
2ndly, another defeat of McClellan on the James ; 3rdly,
to the foreign news, such as recognition of the Southern Confederacy, and future mediation and intervention of England
and France.   Possibly all three of these things may take
place or have taken ; if so, the Government is trying to recruit
its strength, and force its people to spend everything in
ruining themselves and injuring everyone else. " The world's
a motley weare !''

The question with me now is this, shall I send my flour on
to New York or not ?   I believe the best thing I can do will
be to ship it direct to Europe and retain the gold there.
Provisions will be scarce there, and consequently high.
I will go to Dubuque to-morrow if the news turns out to be
true, and thence to Pittsburg or Philadelphia or Baltimore to
meet my friends, and consult.

Spirit of Freedom.—It dignifies and hallows all that it inspires,
and, even amidst the ruins which it has occasioned, exalts the human
soul.—*Alison.*

The worst rebellions are those which proceed from the stomach.—
Bacon.

Human institutions are not like the palace of the architect, framed
according to fixed rules, capable of erection in any situation, and certain
in the effect to be produced. They resemble rather the trees of the forest,
slow of growth, tardy of development, readily susceptible of destruction.
An instant will destroy what has taken centuries to produce ; centuries
must again elapse before, in the same situation, a similar production can
be formed. Transplantation, difficult in the physical, is impossible in
the moral world ; the seedling must be nourished in the soil, inured to
the climate, hardened by the winds. Many examples are to be found of
institutions being suddenly imposed upon a people—none of those so
formed having any duration. To be adapted to their character and
habits, they must have grown with their growth, and strengthened with
their strength.—*Alison (History of Europe), French Revolution.*

August 10th, 1862.

This Sunday evening I resume my pen.   My shoulder
predicted a storm, and the excessive heat of this morning

foretold a storm. It has come at length, and the blinding lightning, and loud pealing thunder and heavy rain are almost awe-inspiring. I went to Dubuque last Friday, and returned yesterday evening. This unhappy country, to what is it hastening!

In regard to the war news, the guerrillas of Arkansas and Tennessee are showing their usual activity and address, and it is said that they have destroyed $15,000,000 of stores within the last month. In Kentucky Morgan is trying his hand again, and he always plays trumps. But Missouri seems to be taking the lead so far, as over 2000 men have been lost to the Federals within this month. Now no Government can stand this long! Hooker has been driven from "Malvern Hill," Virginia. In the night attack on McClellan it is said that there was a loss of 100 to 500.—The Tribune says 500.

The Vicksburg siege is over, and the Confederate success is a great one, (so says the "New York World") in prestige, and in the Federal loss severe in killed and wounded, and in vessels. The Memphis correspondent of the *Chicago Times* says that there is every reason to believe that seven gunboats ironed have run in to Mobile, and that they bore by the blockading fleet boldly. A few days will disclose the truth or falsity of this.

But the *most important* thing that has occurred this month, is the certainty of the failure of volunteering; all troops henceforth are to be got by draft, and on the 15th of this month is to take place, all over the North. And any one attempting to escape is to be arrested and forced into the army; "*sic transit gloria mundi!*" This is an order of the President and Secretary of War, and not by virtue of any law, or convention, and this is a free country, where every man is presumed to be innocent until proved guilty. Henceforth the presumption is against a man. *Vive la République! Maximus innovator tempus!*

August 11th, 1862.

Evils of (the French) Revolution—Moneyed insecurity, financial embarrassment, arbitrary confiscation, general distress, plebeian insurrection, sanguinary tumult, civil warfare, and military despotism.—*Alison.*

The worst of tyrannies, the tyranny of a multitude of tyrants.—*Alison.*

It is the remembrance of the danger which is past, not the prospect of that which is future, that ever affects the generality of man.—*Alison.*

Augustus attempted the reduction of Ethiopia, and was repelled by the " heat of the climate."—*Gibbon.*

The public virtue called patriotism by the ancients is derived from a strong sense of our interest in the preservation, and prosperity of the free Government of which we are members.—*Gibbon.*

Augustus was sensible that mankind was governed by names.—*Gibbon.*

History indeed is little more than the register of the crimes, follies, and misfortunes of mankind.—*Gibbon.*

Property is the occasion of most of the disturbances of society.—*Gibbon.*

Of all of our passions and appetites, the "love of power" is of the most imperious and insatiable nature, since the pride of one man requires the submission of the multitude. In the tumult of civil discord the laws of society lose their power, and their place is seldom supplied by those of humanity.—*Gibbon.*

" Omnia fui et nihil expedit."—(*à propos* Lincoln to McClellan.)

August 13th, 1862.

Received a letter from home yesterday of date of 5th. One's troubles have to be borne ; it is both useless and sinful to repine and fret ; I pray God to infuse into *our* hearts a spirit of humiliation, and resignation, and also of faith and forgiveness.

Had a talk yesterday with a Chicago man concerning the state of the country. He says that it is the cry of every division that they need reinforcement, and that right away ; that Memphis is threatened, Curtis also, Buell and Grant are in the same box. In Missouri the guerrillas are quite brisk and active, capturing by hundreds and thousands the Federals, and destroying immense amounts of material and stores. Kentucky at present is quiet, but only that preceding the storm. From Tennessee there is no news at all, but from Curtis in Arkansas the tidings are that one division of two thousand men were overwhelmed, and another lot of waggons captured, and in short five different skirmishes in one day.

From the east, the news is of a more active character. General Pope has found the enemy at last, and discovered their lines ; there he, however, found their faces also ; a severe battle was fought near Culpepper C. H., some six miles south of the Rapidan river. From the meagre accounts furnished by telegraph, General Pope's Centre (Banks) was attacked by Jackson and Ewell, and driven back, when McDowell came up, but he did not turn the scale, and late at night Siegel came up, and he did not effectuate much—only relieved the " weary, hungry and exhausted " troops of Banks. A battle will be fought there again. The loss is said to have been heavy—General Santon of Siegel's corps is mortally wounded, General Geary of General Banks' corps is severely wounded, and Generals Augur and Prentice of McDowell's corps are wounded ; some nine colonels and majors are reported as having been killed, wounded and prisoners.

There is no report of the rebels " skedaddling."—The bravery and good conduct of " *our* " troops were conspicuous during a large portion of the fight. " *When overpowered by numbers, some regiments retreated in disorder*." " General Wilder," of the rebels is killed (I suppose General Winder is meant). The rebels are reported to be the divisions of General Jackson, Ewell, and A. P. Hill—together with Robertson's cavalry, and must amount somewhere toward 30,000 men—Banks, Siegel, and McDowell must amount at least to the same. Possibly to-day we may hear of the particulars of the fight and of the trophies.

August 21st, 1862.

I have been compelled to deceive my friends, and in concealment to live for some time, and must fly the country as quickly as possible." What a great matter a little fire kindleth!"

But I am constrained to thank my Creator for his protection and for the kind friends that have been raised up and for their discretion and care. I do thank him, and implore him to make me grateful and humble.

Yesterday was the anniversary of father's death. Seven years have only shown our loss, they have not blotted out his memory. The loss of a father is one of the greatest that a family can sustain; his strong hand would have ruled the children and made all of us more subject—he would have restrained when restraint was needed. In regard to worldly matters we would have been better off.—Though in the present state of —— hundreds of thousands fly away as readily as tens, I am rejoiced, however, that not one of our family but can make a living, even though our losses are to be counted by thousands through an unholy war, an unbridled soldiery, and licentious and roaming negroes. These losses of property are permitted by our all-governing Protector, and though we see the wicked means, yet we should remember that they are permitted to do this by One all powerful to save. We should learn humility. Have we done so? On examining myself I find that though my lips may say "Thy will be done," it proceeds rather from indifference than from humility, from carelessness rather than from resignation. No doubt exists in my mind but that our souls are in greater danger than our liberties or our moneys. And what a difference in the value of the two—our eternal and our temporal interests! We have so long and so often neglected our duty to our Creator and Preserver, that we look on this earth as the bounds of our life, and success in it as the only thing worth existing for, neglecting or rather ignoring the fact that this life is but a mere fragment of our existence.—It is difficult to forego present enjoyment however fleeting and evanescent, for the future however full of pleasure or satisfaction. Our life here,

so full of disappointment where so often called on to lament
the miscarriage or failure of best laid plans, and most carefully
and hard-laboured for objects, when hope has allured us as
seeming about to crown our toils with their calculated and
anticipated results, nourishes this feeling within us.

On making a retrospect of my life, how much is there in
it to deplore, how little to dwell on with pleasure. Born of
honest parents, with a good mind and having superior advantages of acquiring information, my parents strove ever to
inculcate into me that goodness was preferable to greatness
or wealth. What have I done? Why, candour compels me
to confess that I am a failure. I have accomplished but
little. I know that there are many whose lives are fuller of
more flagrant violations of right, more injustice and injury to
their kind. I know that I have done some things which are
useful (and will, I hope, be so for a long time to come),
wherein I was actuated by a sense of duty and enlightened
charity, but what a blank in comparison to my opportunities;
how many unknown, secret, and unsuspected sins, were
committed by me, and the opposite insinuated. They have
weighed on me; but do I repent? Would I abstain under
similar circumstances, or favourable opportunities, even after
these and similar reflections?

My present life is a cheat, and a deceit, a miserable,
cowardly, contemptible sham! This is my deliberate opinion
and judgment.

"The heart of man is deceitful above all things, and
desperately wicked." Lord be merciful to me a sinner!

In this civil war that is desolating my country can one
abstain from the struggle lawfully? Can he engage and
preserve the proper spirit? To see the most palpable
invasion of one's rights, the most wanton destruction of
property and life, stirs up all the resentment of our passionate
natures—and who may restrain passion? Can we engage
in this struggle and preserve the just equilibrium of resentment, and oppose only sufficient to repel?

How can we say " Forgive us our trespasses, as we forgive those who trespass against us," when we are animated
by hatred and a sense of injustice driving us onward, and
a thirst for revenge, disguised under the name of military
duty and patriotism ? When we are subordinates, can we do
harm and shelter ourselves under the reflection that we are
obeying orders ?

Is it consistent with justice or duty to withhold our assistance from the country that has protected us so long, when she
is in danger, aye in the very hands of her merciless enemies ?

Let us refer to our standard here, and see what it says.
I do not remember now any passage of the New Testament
which bears on this point. The spirit of His creed is against
war ; is this an exception ? This question demands an answer.
We must, therefore, content ourselves at looking at the voice
of mankind on this subject, and, after discarding passion and
all adventitious surroundings, I believe that it is the concurrent
and consentient voice of unanimous humanity, that it is the
duty as well as the privilege of a man to uphold his country
in the maintenance of its just privileges and undoubted
rights, when they are essential to the happiness of its people
or necessary to their well-being. The existence of these
privileges and rights must be decided, as all other questions,
viz : by evidence and reason. I therefore conclude that it
may be the duty of a man to take the life of his fellow-man
in the defence of his country, as much so as in self-defence
against a robber. Yet here too, he must regard the necessity, and remember that it is the measure of his warrant, and
all else is murder and sin. A danger particularly to be
guarded against is the devotion of himself to the cause of
the country, forgetting that there is one higher who claims
that. He should constantly recall to his mind that in perilling
his life and giving his time to his country, he is only proffer-
ing part of his duty, and he must not leave the other undone.

He should watch carefully his heart, for out of it are the

issues of life and death. " Love your enemies, do good to those who persecute you, and despitefully use you." God our governor commands this. It is the boast of the civilization of every age that it inaugurates a more liberal code of military law. War is a horrible trade at best, and in engaging in it we should constantly invoke God to grant us humility of heart, and his constant ever present assistance ; without that assistance we must degenerate, and become careless alike of life, justice, and judgment to come : and then in vain our toil, our care, our blood, our life and our death ! O Lord grant thy assistance, and enable us not to forget thee, nor thy counsels and command.

August 22nd, 1862. *Cascade, Iowa, U. S. Na.*

The Progress of the War.—By a careful reading of the papers which treat of the battle in Culpepper County, Virginia, I draw the following conclusion. That Pope did not expect to meet Jackson, and had his troops spread over some forty miles. Genl. Siegel's corps, consisting of two divisions, (Schenk's and Schultz) of I do not know how many brigades was encamped about Sperryville some twenty miles from Culpepper; Bank's corps of two divisions (Williams and Augur), consisting of five brigades, Green, Gordon, Prince, Crawford and Geary, were encamped in and around Culpepper C. H. ; McDowell's corps of two divisions (Rickett's and Tower), were extended toward Warrenton and Fredericksburgh. Then there are King's and Saxton's divisions, besides in addition three brigades of cavalry. Estimating each division at five thousand effective men, we have forty-five thousand *effective* men, representing ninety thousand men in all. Jackson had his division consisting of Winder's Taliaferro's, Stewart's and Johnson's brigades ; Ewell's division consisting of Trimble's, Taylor's, and Elsey's brigades ; and A. P. Hill's Division, with the formation of which I am entirely unacquainted, and Genl. Stuart's cavalry, in all

amounting to about twenty-five thousand men. Jackson, crossing the Rapidan, advanced on the centre, and, driving the
cavalry of Bayard with much loss, took position near Mitchell's
Station, on a high hill called Slaughter's Mountain. Banks
came up, thinking it a small force, attacked him with about
10,000 infantry and artillery, and 2,500 cavalry. Jackson's
whole force was not at the battle, but was disposed so as to
threaten portions of Pope's line. Banks was completely
defeated with an immense loss in proportion to the force
engaged. Indeed did we implicitly believe the incongruous
reports, two brigades (Prince's and Crawford's) lost two-
thirds of their men, and two (Gordon and Geary), half, and
Green 200 or 300; thus making a loss of some 5000 men,
at least in Banks' corps. Then part of McDowell's and
Siegel's divisions came up, and they must have suffered
severely. Genl. Augur was wounded in the *back* while turning in his saddle, calling his men forward.   Genl. Geary had
his arm broken by a *minie ball*, and Genl. *Price* is a prisoner. On the Southern side, Genl. Winder is reported to
be killed. In speaking of the dead, one paper says they
amount to 500.   In regard to the wounded, one paper says
about 1,200 were brought in to Washington, very many into
Alexandria. Many had to be left at Culpepper, and 400,
says one correspondent, were on the field Monday (battle on
Saturday) : one paper says 800 of the prisoners were sent
to Richmond. The first account of the battle was the
loss of 3,000, *now* 1,500. Let us see ; 1,200 men in Washington, 1,200 at Alexandria, and in Culpepper, and 400 on
the battle-field, makes 3,600, say this is too much, and 3,000
is nearer the mark ; one-fourth killed would be 750,—and
1,000 prisoners would make some 4,750—a pretty heavy loss.
The newspaper correspondents say that Jackson lost at least
200 killed, say 800 wounded, and 200 prisoners ; making
thus 1,200 men,—and some writer says 150 k—600 w. about
200 pr.—950. " Contrabands" say they over-heard Jackson

say it was from 1,500 to 2,000. I will do the papers the justice to say that they do not claim a victory, but brag very much that Banks acted well, and the men fought desperately. Jackson thus, at a very small loss proportionably, disabled a corps of Pope, and then resumed his old position, waiting for something to turn up. ˙His position (as I understand it) about Orange county skirting the Rapidan.*

Burnside left North Carolina after the battle of the Chicka-hominy, and came to Fortress Monroe, and thence to Acquia Creek. Now McClellan's army has left James River, and is making its way to Fortress Monroe, and it too will be sent to the Rappahannock. By these means, and hunting down the new recruits and incorporating them into the old regiments, Halleck will have under him an army of 200,000 men, all bearing on Richmond, yet this army will, though composed mostly of veterans, be collected from many defeats, the "he-roes" of Winchester, Cross-Keyes, Port-Republic, Slaughter's Mountain, Yorktown, Bull-Run, Leesburg, Big Bethel, McDowell, Alleghany Mountain, Williamsburg, Fair-Oaks, Gains'-Mill, Chickahominy, Newbern, &c., will be united and march to meet their conquerors, and to defeat again, (I hope, aye and trust!) If in the eastern armies there has been ac-tivity, in the western country too have there been many des-perate fights. At *Baton Rouge*, Breckenridge attacked the Federals, and took the town, but could not hold it on account of the gunboats.

The Federals claim a victory because Baton Rouge was not entirely held by the Confederates; they confess to burn-ing the tents, &c., of their camps. Genl. Williams, the Fed-eral commander, was killed, and Genl. Clark, of Mississippi, mortally wounded.

ᵢ In Eastern Tennessee there have been some battles, and both parties claim victories; the late Richmond papers say the

---

* Four miles from Gordonsville.—*Editor.*

entire Federal force about Cumberland-Gap has been captured; this I do not believe. They mention three brigades, Barton, Stevenson, and Bowen, all under command of E. K. Smith. There are about the Chattahooche McDonald, Leabetter, Hayne, under Pemberton, and no doubt others at both Knoxville and Dalton,—all, I believe, under Jno. B. MacGruder. Then there are Bragg, Price, Hardee, Polk, Cheatham, Villipegue, &c., &c. Genl. Theophilus Holmes has been sent to Arkansas to assume the duty of moulding the Arkansas, Missouri, and Texas guerrillas into shape, and make them formidable by reason of their discipline, organisation and numbers. Kentucky is stirred up by some news which seems contraband; she is about to be invaded, it seems, but by whom I do not know. It may be that the Confederates have cut off the army of East Tennessee. Morgan has taken Gallatin, and cut off communication between Louisville and Nashville. He caght some 200 or 300 prisoners. Buell still is in a bad predicament according to all accounts, and I expect daily to hear of his entire force being cut too pieces, and himself taken prisoner: *Sic itur ad astra!* Here, in the west, they have arrested old Mahony, and scared some of the leading secessionists, and now recruiting goes on bravely, and possibly the draft will not be needed.

The military despotism is now scarcely reviled, it is most warmly applauded by the republicans. The democrats are too frightened to oppose; they insinuate disapprobation. "They hint a fault, and hesitate dislike."

But treason now is broader than ever. Silence is treason, the purchase of specie is treason, and what is not treason now? I can't say, except villainy, robbery and abolitionism, and " the end of all these is death."

My papers have ceased, the *Herald's* subscription has run out, and the *News* has been suppressed—no cause assigned, save that it does not support the Administration. Thus we go. Forty recruits go from this little place (Cascade), under the new call. These men go forth, they know not why, nor can they tell anything about the merits of the struggle now going forward. The English papers assert that the Americans are the most inconstant of people, and truly I believe it; many of these recruits do not believe in the justice of the war, and yet they " *go volunteering*" in it. Many dark days await both sections of this unhappy country ere peace resumes its sway over it.

These new levies of 300,000 volunteers, and the reserve of 300,000 militia in themselves constitute a large army and a formidable one, for in nearly every company there are one or more old soldiers who will add to its discipline and efficiency. But before they can get into battle, it will be October, that is any considerable number, and before this day twelve months 70 per cent, will have left their banners; but the rest (90,000) will be good soldiers: so of the drafted men, ere their time of nine months expires they will not have 75,000 effective men. But what have the South to oppose this army? No more troops can be drawn from her population; yet her resources of supplies, as the cultivation of cotton and tobacco diminishes, must be greater and greater, and the struggle seems about to be extended to an indefinite period. *Now* does the North for the first time feel the ravages of war in her population. Her trade has flourished nearly as much as heretofore; but now her *sons* are going forth, and soon the lamentation will come up as of Rachel weeping for her children, and refusing to be comforted because they are not. And shortly National Bankruptcy will deluge the land, annihilating the property of debts, and depreciating every other description,—destroying confidence, and bringing misery and loss home to every one,—" punishing every one in all his ways." This seems to me to be the inevitable result, but such is the wilful blindness that few believe it,—and so we go.

There is a report that Pope, Burnside and McClellan are all retiring from " on to Richmond," and will concentrate

their troops, recruit, fill up, and then take the field again.
If so, the Yankee army must have suffered terribly at Chickahominy, and in Culpepper—far more than I thought.   And
the South-western army under Buell will be apt to be envel-
loped and destroyed,—perhaps Grant, too. I hope so, but fear
not.

Got a letter from........informing me of the purchase
of $400 in gold at 17 per cent premium, and requesting in-
structions for the future, saying that some are paying 18 and
20 for it.   Since it has reached such a height I think the
best plan will be to see whether or not it can be purchased
cheaper in Chicago.   The immense new levies will create
some successes for the Union army, but they cannot ultimate-
ly prevail; and even though they should, can that change
the final result, viz: the Bankruptcy of the country? No,
no—the credit of the country must fail, repudiation will take
place in the end.   Then gold will alone be of any exchange-
able value as money.

(I wrote to him to buy on as before.)

Paper will receive anything.—*De Stael.*

If ever free institutions are destroyed in U. S., it will arise from the
unlimited tyranny of a majority.—*De Tocqueville.*

Courtiers and demagogues not only bear a strong resemblance to each
other, but are in fact, the same men, varying in the external character
according to the ruling power which they severally worship.—*Aristotle.*

Imprisonment has ever been the great instrument of despotic power;
it is not by heartrending punishment inflicted on its victim, in presence
of the people, but by the silent, unseen operation of confinement and se-
clusion, that the spirit of freedom has in general been most effectually
broken.—*Alison.*

When vice prevails, and impious men bear sway, the post of honour is
a private station.—*Old Poet.*

Centralization of power is the most deadly enemy of a country's
freedom.

Confederate Experience.

They were totally incapable of appreciating the merit of a system of
defence which was to last for years, and in which ultimate success was
to be, purchased by a cautious system of defensive policy, and frequent
retirement before the enemy.

Their idea of war was a victory followed by an immediate advance to the enemy's capital.—(Alison) : non alia Romae, alia Athenis.

Even when the spirit of freedom had been utterly extinguished, the tamest subjects have some time ventured to resist an unprecedented invasion of their property.—*Gibbon.*

August 28th, 1862.

Got a letter from home, they are well as usual ; have not heard of William since the fight at Slaughter's Mountain. They complain of a bitter bondage of the Federal army, but it is evident that the retaliative measures of Davis have made the Yankees more cautious and less arrogant. The Yankees complain and threaten, but do not act as badly as they began—such as administering oaths of allegiance, &c. They say three Canadian deserters from Pope passed by there, and communicated much to them ; the Yankees were afraid of Jackson, and said that Banks was drunk, and had his side hurt by running against his cavalry ; that from the first Banks' army was thrown into confusion, and could only be brought up to the scratch by troops in the rear ; that Jackson had advantage of position, and his loss is not one-fourth as heavy as Banks' ; that 500 of their men have already deserted, and they look to the day of battle as to that of defeat.

The letter reports constant skirmishes between guerrillas in Clarke, Frederick, Berkley, and Jefferson Counties, and much damage resulting therefrom to the Yankee arms. This warfare seems to be more effective than I supposed it could be, many old soldiers are going into, and many persons driven from their homes by the Yankees. There are no doubt instances of treachery to our service, but it is a source of pleasure to know, that but little desertion has taken place. Two men of Jno. Henderson's company deserted and joined the enemy, and one was killed near Berryville.

The military are carrying things with high hand here ; they are arresting whom they will, and there is no recourse whatever but flight. So goes the world !

August 30th, 1862.

There has been a battle on the Rappahannock between Pope and Lee. Several reports have come to hand concerning it, such as Siegel shooting McDowell through the head on the battle field, alleging treachery; and then that Siegel had captured 2,000 Confederate prisoners and killed 400 by enticing them across the Rappahannock, and then crushing them out: that Jackson nevertheless was only thirty miles from Manassas.

Yesterday's paper ("Times") has just been read, and it by no means is jubilant over the news. Now such is the credulity of that paper that it requires only telegraphic accounts to believe the grossest and most unlikely improbabilities: yet it says nothing of the kind! I believe McDowell to be one of the ablest Federal Generals, and Siegel one of the most trifling; he doubtless is brave but not a man of genius; he is cruel, tyrannical, and an abolitionist. McDowell is not a man of genius, but one trained to war, brave, and a gentleman. This last quality renders him unpopular and odious. Siegel would gain the favour of the abolitionists by killing him, but the hatred of every other class of men. I hope for the Confederate cause that he *may* do so if he has not already done so: but fear he has too great a regard to his own life to attempt McDowell's.

In regard to the capture of the 2,000 men, the correspondent of the *New York Tribune* says that three Federal cavalry regiments charged on the advance of Lee's army at Brandy, and were repelled by two volleys "emptying many saddles." That for three days skirmishing and artillery firing took place across the Rappahannock, that now the left under McDowell, now the centre under Banks, now the right under Siegel were attacked. At last General Siegel determined to reconnoitre, and ordered Schultz across the Rappahannock, and aftering crossing, they had a fierce fight; That the rebels had twenty-five pieces artillery and the battle raged from 9 a.m. till 6 p.m. and Siegel's loss, "*till he left,*" was only sixty; but afterwards the "gray backs pursued" Schultz to the river, and the "fusilade was as sharp as any I ever heard." "Siegel made a few prisoners, and not five regiments, as was reported." This account studiously disclaims a victory, but claims some "strategic advantages," such as obstructing the march of Lee, and Jackson till the "massed forces" of Burnside at Fredericksburg, and McClellan at some other point, and the increased force of Pope, will, "within thirty days, take Richmond the rebel capital." "The best laid plans of mice and men gang aft aglee!"

From Tennessee the news seems by no means clear; Galatin has been captured, and a General Johnson captured by Morgan; Clarksville and Fort Donelson taken, and very many, no one knows how many men, surrendered; indeed mystery seems to shroud the movements and transactions of both armies; but the Federals in Kentucky and Tennessee seem to have been very unfortunate lately. The newspapers are clamouring for the disgrace of the unsuccessful officers. Their rule is, "*success*" is the only test of merit; to it will every thing be forgiven.

The Indians in Minnesota seem to be successful in their incursions, having defeated the Yankees at New Ulm, and continue to murder all who oppose them. If they had a few pieces of artillery and some union and concert, they would carry every thing before them, and "clean out" Minnesota and Iowa, and part of Wisconsin. If I could I would assist them.

Guerillas very active and successful in Missouri, great many captures made there, much suspicion of treachery. Oppression has in every age begotten treachery, and man's nature has not changed. I think therefore that it is most likely that many have, and will desert—some from all service, and many join the rebels. So goes the world.

For some time past I have been reading Alison's history of ·

Europe. The ancients said that truth was found, or to be found in the bottom of a well. What belief can we place in any history after reading Alison's narrative of Napoleon and Wellington, and of the war between this country, and England in 1812? His statements are partial resulting from his prejudice. He is a firm believer in kings and aristocracy. Now, experience proves that that order of society is as corrupt and inefficient as any other. The truth is that all governments, partaking of the imperfections of man, share his mortality. Alison looks on England as presenting the perfection of human government prior to 1800. He is proud of Scotland first, of England second, and of Ireland *subordinately* thrown in, that is to say as a make-weight in the scale of English destiny.

Very many of his principles are quite true, and many of his observations eminently just and happy. His learning is varied. He brings his politics into his history, but that is true of every one, more or less. From the perusal of his first volumes, I have derived much pleasure, and (I hope) profit; but the later volumes being full of military movements, did not interest me, as I had no maps which indicated the position of the armies. Without maps we cannot understand military movements. I have begun *the history of Gibbon.*

How any historian will be able to get at the truth of contemporaneous events in this country passes my comprehension, as *lying* is authorized, and published as truth by the Government, and the publication of *facts* is declared a high military crime. The veriest trash is telegraphed to the corrupt papers, and believed by many simple fools among the people; but these lies will go forth, and in time solidify into the foundation stones of history.

This is to be deplored. Even if the Government desired to tell the truth, and such is far from being the case, IT can not get at it, as an unsuccessful officer is cast off in disgrace, and the temper of the people is so inconstant and fickle, that they would become despondent. The freedom of the press would destroy the Government in ninety days. Thus there is no way of publishing the truth in the North.

The news is that Jackson has completely swept around Siegel and got into the Federal rear, capturing two or three regiments along the road and occupying Manassas, and that Lee is pressing Pope in front and flank, and Jackson in rear. I have not seen the papers, but hear that the above is contained therein. The result proves " Gen. Banks' fighting against time " not to have been good " strategy." In his case a " bad retreat would have been better than a good stand still." If my memory is correct, Manassas is about half way between Culpepper and Washington, say thirty miles from each. It is the summit of the ground intervening between the waters of the Rappahannock and Potomac. It will be ever memorable in the history of this country, as being the place of defence of Beauregard against Scott; the battle-ground of July 18th is nearly due north from the junction and distant three miles, and the engagement was fought between Beauregard and McDowell. That of the 21st, was to the West, and distant from three to five miles, and was fought mainly between Johnston and McDowell. If any contest takes place now it will be to the South and West of Centreville. Here is the most strongly fortified place in that part of Virginia ; a long line of forts on the high hills between the Accotink and Bull Run render it formidable, and, if manned by determined men, will keep five times their number off, especially now since all the adjoining timber has been cut down to make firewood for the winter-quarters of Johnson's army. Unless Pope has a large army, he must now be lost, as they can starve him out as well as whip him. Perhaps he had better look at the " line of retreat" for himself, as well as study that of his enemy's. Pride goes before a fall, and Pope's fall will be no easy one.

September 2nd, 1862, *Cascade, Iowa.*

Mr.———— returned from Dubuque last night, and said

that affairs had been exaggerated—of that I had no doubt. Now my time approaches, ere the cold becomes too great, to travel, or to do anything else in this inhospitable climate. I am undecided but inclined to take buggy, as the more safe and easy way of travelling.

The war news is of the highest importance ; it is no less intelligence than that of two battles, or rather of a *number* of engagements. First series were in Virginia. It seems that Jackson with a body of men swept around Pope, and took *Warrenton* and Manassas, and captured many hundred prisoners. This breaking up of the communication of Pope's army necessitated the evacuation of the " strong position of the Rappahannock," which could not have been accomplished without much loss. In the meantime McClellan's army was coming up on Jackson, who fell back towards the mountain, and a fierce battle was fought on Friday, and Pope says he lost 8,000 men, but gained a victory. On Saturday, however, the telegraph reports that another battle was fought which resulted in a Confederate victory, and Pope retreated to Centreville, and in fact this side, so that I think that Lee has soundly thrashed Pope with immense loss. And hence I conclude that the entire Federal loss since Cedar Mountain has not been less than 30,000 men. Pope says one battle was fought on old Bull Run battle ground, another account says near Haymarket, which is some ten miles from Manassas. But Pope did not know, and did not scruple to lie in that as in many other statements. Pope has ordered back all of the army correspondents. They could not make all of their lies " dovetail," and therefore Pope sent them off. The papers say that there is not so much depression in Washington and Alexandria as there was prior to McClellan's coming up from Fortress Monroe, " with his bearded and bronzed veterans, whose tread knew no disorder, and whose battalions were so often victorious at Williamsburg, Fair Oaks, Chickahominy, &c." Cedar Creek or Slaughter's Mountain is now claimed as a great victory, and Banks' stand is as much praised as his retreat! I judge one by the other. Banks is a poor show, a miserable humbug. I do trust that he may be promoted, he *deserves* it, for a grander scoundrel does not strut about in blue and gilt. The second engagement or series of engagements took place in Kentucky. Kirby Smith, with a large force, advanced into Kentucky, and fought a battle at Richmond near Lexington, defeating Nelson, and driving all before him—loss on Yankee side according to their own account, 125 killed and 350 wounded. From that we may judge that the loss is some 1000 or 1500 in killed and wounded, not to say a word about prisoners. Smith is playing sad havoc " *there and thereabouts,*" as say the Yankees.

Humphrey Marshall, who was " dead," " resigned," "disgusted," and so forth, now seems to be alive, and himself again. He is invading Kentucky on the East via the Big Sandy valley, and has already taken Piketon and Prestonburg, and is steadily advancing. His forces are said to number some 5,000 men. I suppose he and Smith will effect a junction, and try to rally a large force of recruits. Buckner is in Kentucky also, so that things bid fair to be very lively in the " Dark and bloody ground " of Kentucky.

I saw also Morgan's report of his raid into the State some time ago. He says that he marched 1,000 miles in twenty-four days, fought many skirmishes, captured seventeen towns, 1,500 home-guards, 1200 regulars, and brought back 400 more men than he took with him. He burnt many million dollars worth of Government stores, and did them immense damage in the way of stirring up the good old State. His movements were entirely independent of Forrest, who it seems devotes his time to Tennessee, Morgan to Kentucky, Stuart to Virginia, and I hope soon to Maryland.

The Federals at Cumberland Gap are not used up, but all communication with the world has been cut off by the Confederates. Bragg has gone to Chattanooga, so " they " say and " they " know.—Hindman is now well armed ; yesterday he was badly armed.

The *Missouri Republican* gives a lugubrious account of things and matters in that state.—The guerrillas have been quite successful according to its showing.

The Minnesota Indians are pushing matters to the wall: they have cut off two companies of regulars and about to take a fort.   They are stirred up by some Missouri Indians, and secession traders and agents, so the papers say.

Iowa, too, is being invaded, some dozen or so having been already killed.   The Indians are but little in advance of Yankees in barbarities.—and I think that they will shortly lose that ground, as Butler, Phelps, Hunter and Pope, all are making efforts to overcome that small start ; and, from their energy and practice, I think they will succeed.   The South never stood so well as she does now ; may she brighten and increase.   The papers also contain mention of Lieutenant Baylor performing a brilliant dash, and of Sergeant Timberlake doing some fine exploit.   Baylor must be " *Tin:*" Timberlake, " *Seth,*" wounded at Manassas, formerly of company " G."—It also says that our loss at Slaughter's Mountain was about 900 ; that of the Yankees four or five times as great.

November 20th, 1862.   *Dundas, C. W.*

I resume my journal to-day, after a long interval.   When last I wrote I was in concealment in Iowa ; now I am in a neutral country.   I was discovered to be a " rebel," and had to fly for liberty and life.   By lying concealed at first, and then making good time by both night and day, at length I got across the Mississippi into Wisconsin, and thence into Chicago and thence to Kalamazoo, and thence to Detroit and thence to *London,* Canada, and thence to Hamilton, and thence to Dundas, where I board at Riley's Hotel.   After much difficulty I got through from Dubuque $1620.00 in gold, and finally went to Galena and meeting........ got $500 in

gold and $32 in paper : thence I returned...............
and am now trying to get into business. I have written to
friends to forward to me game, &c., and I will sell it.

Mr.————, handed me a letter from *sister Mary*, directed
by————, examined by Washington authorities. It com-
plains of bondage, and mourns the loss of many men from
our country. Poor Botts* was killed.—Willie, Chipley and
Bunch Brown are wounded and all improving. Mother had
been sick, brought on by unrest of sprit and anxiety and care.
It said many hearts were made desolate. But so it has ever
been and will be.—Also got a letter from cousin Elizabeth
Aglionby, wherein she gives me quite a flattering invitation
to visit England. Mr. Wright of Dundas has just returned,
and says that there is no doubt but that vessels are being
built for the Southern Confederacy in the Clyde; some iron
clad and some not : and that at Halifax he met several C. S.
N. officers going over to England : of course they go for the
purpose of taking commands of C. S. vessels. I think I will
join them and take of their fortune for good and evil. Met
here with an escaped prisoner from Camp Morton, Indiana.
He is a Kentuckian of 2nd Regiment, Breckenridge's Brigade,
and was captured at Fort Donelson. Oliver Lee Bradley is
his name. He wants to get his father's consent to go to the
war again, and expects to do so now. I also met a gentleman who had served twelve months in Southern army ; was
in battles of Peninsula and front of Richmond; wounded
slightly in three places. He is, and was, a British subject.
His accounts of the Richmond battles vary much from the
Yankee accounts. He does not think the Yankees are such
desperate fighters as they claim to be. Also a gentleman
from Missouri who had served under Price and been confined
in St. Louis prison ; escaped and now being in London, C.
W. : health bad.

---

* Col. Botts, 2nd Va. Regiment.

Since I last wrote, events momentous have occurred both
in America and in Europe.   Those in America I will clas-
sify under head of *military* and *political*.   In Europe, those
entirely European and those bearing on America.   I. Military. 1st, Operations in Virginia and Maryland.   After the
defeat of Pope, at Manassas, August 30th, Gen. Lee threw.
forward toward Washington, his advance, left in front ; and
immediately Pope evacuated Centreville, and marched direct
on Alexandria and Arlington.   A severe engagement took
place near Chantilly, in which Genls. Kearny and Stevens
(Yanks) were killed ; the Yanks succeeded in getting
through.   Gen. D. H. Hill, commanding the 3d. army corps,
of the Confederate army, which had not participated in the
battle of Manassas, occupied Leesburg, and a junction having
now been effected with Jackson and Longstreet, Lee threw
the greatest part of his force into Maryland, threatening
Pennsylvania and Baltimore. Suddenly they enveloped Harper's Ferry, and, after some days' fighting, captured it, 12,000
men, and immense stores.   In the meantime McClellan;
having collected all the old armies from Western Virginia,
Fortress Monroe, Washington, &c., and many new levies, in
all about 150,000 men, advanced after Lee.   At South
Mountain, Md., he overtook the rearguard under D. H. Hill,
and a severe fight took place : but Harper's Ferry had fallen,
and Lee massed his forces at Antietam Creek, and waited the
arrival of Jackson and A. P. Hill.   Before they had come
up, he was attacked, and, on 17th September was fought the
battle of Antietam, or Sharpsburg. It was long, and bloody :
but Jackson and A. P. Hill coming, it ended in the repulse of
McClellan's army. On the 19th of Sept. Lee recrossed the Potomac near Boteler's mill.   The result of the Maryland Campaign, as far as I can gather : Lee's loss at Boonsboro or South
Mountain and Sharpsburg,(or Antietam,) was about 12,000 ;
sick and stragglers, 2,000 : total 14,000. McClellan's loss at
Harper's Ferry, 12,000 men ; at South Mountain, 5,000 ; at

Antietam, 20,000 ; total 37,000 ; besides immense stores of arms and ammunition, provisions and clothing. Since then the army has moved, part to Fredericksburg and part to Winchester. The Yanks were encamped in Pleasant Valley, Harper's Ferry, Fairfax C. H., &c., when Gen. Stuart, taking some 1,800 cavalry, marched around the entire Yankee force, entering Pennyslvania, capturing Chambersburg, and exciting many fears in Pennsylvania and Md. After Lee had crossed into Virginia, the Yanks followed, and A. P. Hill, turning fiercely back on them, killed, wounded and captured about 3,000 of them. Much skirmishing has been going on since.

From Norfolk, the Yankees have advanced to Suffolk, in Lower Virginia, and much skirmishing takes place, but with no decisive result : In Western Virginia the Confederates under Floyd, Echols and Jenkins have advanced, and, after much skirmishing and many affairs, drove the Federals back to the Ohio, capturing many stores, prisoners, and getting many recruits. The Yankees, having been reinforced by the new levies and some of the Cumberland Gap army, advanced again, and the Confederates fell back to Lewisburg, gathering much spoil, &c. &c. Thus the Confederate forces are again drawing back to the centre, Richmond, and the Yankees are advancing on it from Western Virginia, Norfolk, Fortress Monroe, Fredericksburg, and Washington. They claim that their force is 200,000 men, without counting the navy.

In Kentucky.—After Kirby Smith advanced into Kentucky he was joined by Humphrey Marshall, and they occupied the best part of that state, constantly attacking the enemy, replenishing their commissary and quartermaster departments, and also recruiting their ranks, threatening Cincinnati and Ohio. In the meantime General Bragg has left Chattanooga, and, eluding Buell, thrown himself between Buell and his reinforcements and supplies. He then marched north into Ken-

tucky to join Smith. His advance under Buckner attacked
Munsfordsville, and after some skirmishing, captured it with
some 4,000 prisoners, and much stores, &c. Buell followed
Bragg and Forrest. Bragg then threatened Louisville
and Cincinnati. But in the meantime Gen. Nelson at Louisville, and Wright at Cincinnati, had collected heavy armies of
new volunteers and brought some veterans from Missouri and
Arkansas, and Gen. Buell went by water to Louisville. Nelson was killed by T. C. Davis, and Buell, having recruited
his army to about 90,000 men, advanced on Bragg. This
visit of Gen. Bragg had filled the States of Ohio and Indiana
with alarm.

. Bragg, on the approach of Buell, started off his teams
(said to be 4,000) and stock (10,000) towards Cumberland
Gap, which had been evacuated by General Morgan (Yankee),
and concentrated his forces about Harrodsburg. But before
this concentration was complete, he fell with part of his forces
on General McCook's army corps of Buell's army, supported
by Crittenden's, and defeated it. He then fell back to Camp
Dick Robinson, and thence towards Tennessee. His army
is still at Murfreesboro', Tennessee. He has thus rescued
Middle Tennessee and North Alabama from the Yankees.
While he was in Kentucky, Forrest invaded Nashville, and
completely invested it, but it was relieved by Buell after the
retreat of Bragg. In the South-west, Van Dorn attacked
Corinth, Mississippi, and, after temporary success and great
slaughter, was repulsed; he, in turn, was attacked on his
retreat, but succeeded in getting off. This defeat broke up
the campaign in Kentucky, and for the capture of Nashville,
Tennessee. Since the battles of Corinth and Hatchie, the
Confederates have been reinforced by Holmes and his army
from Arkansas, and it seems probable that a heavy battle is
imminent in Mississippi.

On the Seacoast.—General Mitchell (Yankee) attacked
the Charleston and Savannah Railroad at Pocotaligo and

Coosawatchie. They were repulsed by General Beauregard with heavy loss. The Federal gun-boats occasionally go up some creek, and burn a farm-house, &c. Much skirmishing in North Carolina. Many vessels have been running the blockade, some into Mobile and some into Charleston. I think that some more gun-boats must be nearly ready at the South. The Confederates bought a vessel in England, and, under Captain Semmes, as the "Alabama," it has roamed over the ocean, destroying some twenty-four or twenty-five merchant-men, as far as known; and many more ships are said to be fitting out as vessels of war—may good luck attend them !

Political.—In its effect on the continuance of the war, perhaps the political state of the country must be considered, at the present time, to be the most important phase, if indeed we can separate the political, financial, and military one from the other. A proclamation marks oftentimes an era, as a battle does an actual contest. There have been two very singular documents published in the United States, which have entered largely into the canvass, and made the issue between parties. 1st. The proclamation of A. Lincoln promising freedom to all negroes of rebellious States on and after January 1st, 1863 ; and, 2nd. The publication of General Scott's " views " concerning the magnitude of the war, and the impossibility of ever having peace again,—one put forth by *Republicans* and the other by *Democrats*. The illegal arrests, and military despotism generally, of the Government was protested against, and finally, though many were arrested, discussion took place. The democrats assimilated to the ground of the peace party. They triumphed in Pennsylvania, Indiana, Ohio, Illinois, New York, New Jersey, Delaware, and gained largely in Iowa, Minnesota, Wisconsin, Michigan; but yet the republicans carried the day. In Missouri there was a mockery of an election, and, of course, the abolitionists triumphed there. Immediately on the defeat of the administration, McClellan was removed from chief command in Virginia, and Buell in Kentucky; Burnside and Rosecranz taking their places respectively.

In *financial* matters the condition of affairs in the United States is rapidly growing worse. Gold is worth from 33 *to* 50 *per cent.*, and per consequence, there is a corresponding rise in everything. The tax bill is now beginning to weigh heavily on the people of the North.

The progress of the idea of peace is spreading very rapidly in the North; this is evinced by the recent elections, as well as by the altered tone of the people and some of the press. A settlement is called for by these, but will not be heard for some time to come, as the present leaders know that they must *triumph, or die, or become exiles.* The prospect of a fight among the Northerners themselves is becoming brighter and brighter.

In Europe we also see evidences of the turbulence of the people, and the truth of the Napoleonic saying, " Europe must be Cossack or Republican." In England the members of Parliament have travelled their usual rounds of business and speeches. From the majority we hear the belief of the triumph of the South. In Lancashire there is much distress resulting from the cotton famine, as many as 1,000,000 operatives being thrown out of usual employment. In France there is also much distress on account of want of cotton, and the emperor has requested England to join him in mediating and eventually in opening the blockade, which was declined by England on the ground of being premature. He has not moved in it himself, but he has sent an immense force to Mexico under Forey, the hero of Montebello. In Italy Garibaldi has renewed rebellion, and was conquered, wounded, and captured, and the rebellion quelled. Garibaldi wants to join the Yankees. France still holds Rome, and will do so. In Greece the people have expelled Otho, and have a sort of provisional Government.

In Prussia the King and his Commons have quarrelled, and the King, so far, is successful. In Turkey there has been a war going on for some time, and the Turkish Government has a new lease of power. Looking in Europe, we may say that the "pot boils."

November 27th, 1862. Dundas, C. W.

The papers bring no news of any important movement or engagements between the rival armies. Jackson is represented as moving to reinforce the main Confederate army at or about Fredericksburg, but nothing certain is known about it. The Richmond papers represent that President Davis has ordered ten Union officers to be executed under certain contingencies. The cry of extermination is beginning to be heard louder and louder. The Maine papers say that the Alabama is threatening some of the coast towns of that State. The foreign papers contain the full dispatch of the French Emperor to the British and Russian Governments, of mediation, or suggesting the extreme desirability of an armistice of six months and uninterrupted possession of trade, hoping at heart to direct men's minds towards peace. England declines, thinking that the time has not yet come for that. Russia is willing to go farther than England, and will join France if the Emperor concludes to offer his services to the contending parties, and also England when she thinks that the time has come.

> "Lord of himself;—that heritage of woe."—*Lara.*
>
> ---
>
> "Nor sent nor came he till conjecture grew,
> Cold in the many, anxious in the few."—*Lara.*
>
> ---
>
> "Yet does he live?" exclaims the impatient heir,
> And sighs for sables which he must not wear.
> "Brief were his answers, and his questions none."
> "Because the worst is ever nearest truth."—*Lara.*
>
> ---
>
> "The rather to *condemn* than praise."
> "Religion—freedom—vengeance—what you will,
> A word's enough to raise mankind to kill."
> "And they that smote for freedom or for sway,
> Deemed few were slain, while more remained to slay."

" The feigned retreat, the mighty ambuscade,
The daily harass, and the fight delayed,
The long privation of the hoped supply,
The tentless rest beneath the humid sky,
The stubborn wall that mocks the leagner's art,
And palls the patience of his baffled heart,—
Of these they had not deemed : the battle day
They could encounter as a veteran may,
But more preferred the fury of the strife,
And present death, to hourly suffering life.
And famine wrings, and fever sweeps away,
His numbers melting fast from his array."

" An exile's sorrows, or an outlaw's hate."

" Nor is his mortal slumber less profound
Though priest nor bless'd, nor marble deck'd the mound."

" Why did she love him ? Curious fool !—be still—
Is human love the growth of human will ?"

—" She lies by him she loved—
Her tale untold—her truth too dearly proved."

" Let me remember, when I find myself inclined to pity a criminal,
that there is likewise a pity due to the country."—*Matthew Hale.*

November 28th, 1862.

There is nothing new by telegraph to-day. "All quiet
on the Potomac" and Rappahannock. Nothing is known
of the whereabouts of old Jackson and his corps. Some of
Stuart's cavalry have been into Maryland, capturing Pooles-
ville, &c., &c., and shortly returning. The Federal papers
report, with every approval, the account of the destruction of some saltworks and some woollen mills. They who
pretend to be fighting for " the Union, the Constitution, and
the Laws." The New York *World* is now against the war,
and out and out for peace ; it was once the strongest kind of
war paper, and of much influence in bringing it about. There
is nothing new about the " Alabama" and her assaults on
Yankee commerce. There are reports also of another vessel
out " snapping up" the commercial marine of Yankeedom.

December 1st, 1862.

There is no news from the seat of war, in the papers of this morning. Gen. Burnside has been to Washington, and has returned to Fredericksburg again. Cavalry has been scouting again, but only captured some "two or three" cavalry companies, destroying stores, &c., &c. Jackson's whereabout is not known; indeed, according to Yankee account, he is ubiquitous, being at several different places at the same time. In the South the grand army is in motion, but as yet no enemy in sight.

The extracts from European papers concerning the mediation question are quite interesting and instructive. The Emperor of France certainly desires to go into and finish up the job. England wants to go in, but is afraid to do so on account of suspicion of French motives. Russia is willing to give moral aid now, and also to support England when she thinks proper to put forward her foot. The Yankee papers say that France is ardent; England desirous, but afraid; Russia unwilling, but not unwilling to be coaxed to *assist* in American affairs. England, as a matter of course, comes in for the greatest abuse, and she seems to be able to bear it. The French papers seem to think that the Emperor will go it " solitary and alone." I hope he may go in right away, and win for his Kingdom the gratitude of the Confederate States now and forever.

In the meantime, Spain is putting in her say, inasmuch as Yankee vessels have been trespassing on Spanish rights, violating her rights of territory, in trying to seize, and in seizing, vessels running the blockade from Mobile, Charleston, &c. Her sympathies are with the South, and she is disposed to recognise the nationality of the Confederate States. Spain had at one time the foremost place in European affairs. By land and sea she was unrivalled. Her sailors and soldiers were distinguished for their gallantry, discipline, steadiness and skill. Under Columbus, Cortez, Pizarro,

T

Alva, Parma, Charles, John, Ferdinand and Isabella, their exploits will ever be memorable. For a long time, then, they were a second rate power, and but little was heard of them till the dreadful Peninsular campaigns of Wellington. After that the nation seemed still to get along slowly, but within the few late years she has reorganized her internal and domestic affairs, her army and navy, introducing the new arms, new combinations of troops ; and, in the recent contest with the Moors of Africa, her troops revived the credit of their ancestry for steadiness. They are a *stately, proud race, tenacious of their word*, quick tempered and rapid to strike an enemy. In war they have shown, on many occasions, courage, patience, and perseverance most remarkable. The sieges of Tarentum and Saragossa will be memorable as long as the art of war has any students.

December 3rd, 1862.

There is only the message of President Lincoln in the papers, and certainly it is a remarkable document. Language was meant to *convey* meaning, but certainly in this message it requires a large amount of charity to prevent a man from thinking and saying that the President uses it to *conceal* his meaning. Some of his twaddle is perfectly childish. There are no important military movements to chronicle, and no great military wonders to relate, save the route of 8,000 rebels by 500 Yankees ! and a brilliant and successful cavalry reconnoisance by General Stahl. There is also a rumour of the supersedure of General Burnside by General Hooker. This, however, has not yet been confirmed, but maybe it is only anticipating. Halleck is out in a letter replying to McClellan, convicting little Mac of great caution, and of very little reverence for the commander-in-chief, Henry Wager Halleck ; and also of overstating his losses in Maryland some 4,000— which last acquisition is, my extraordinary Mac says, some 15,000 ; Halleck says 10,000, and the New York correspondents, some 30,000. At any rate Mac is down, and it is safe to kick him, and Halleck does it.

December 5th, 1862.

The papers continue to contain gems of Lincoln's message and comments thereon, some denunciatory and others sarcastic. There is no news concerning the war of any importance save that the work of organizing the new levies is going on, and great preparations are making in the navy too. To make the new troops effective will require much drill and *marching*, and *that* Lee seems to be willing to give them. Assertions are made that over 100,000 of the Federal army are sick, and 50,000 have deserted, and the President is reported to have said that the Federal army is less than it was before the last call. Oh! how many of *our* gallant boys have perished too, and how many will be disabled forever! Damnation seize the leaders of this war!

December 6th, 1862.

The newspapers report that General Joseph E. Johnston has been sent to Mississippi to take command of the army now organizing at and about Jackson, Mississippi, now under command of Pemberton, Van Dorn, Sewell, and Price, said to number 40,000 effective men. It is also said that Holmes and his corps have been assigned to the army too. General Magruder has gone to Texas to get ready for Banks. General Beauregard has been organizing the defensive preparations of South Carolina and Georgia, and has some 6,000 or 8,000 men under him.

General H. Cobb has been assigned to the command of the department of Florida. Generals Jones and Forney command at Mobile, and are said to have done much towards its defence. I hope to God that they may burn Mobile, and Savannah, and Charleston before they surrender them to the Yankees.

December 8th, 1862.

There is no news of any important military movements to-day. Some reports of the capture of Winchester, Virginia, and Grenada, Mississippi, by Yankees, but nothing authentic or reliable.

December 9th, 1862.

In Tennessee John Morgan has surprised some four regiments of Yankee troops, and captured the entire force, some 2,000 men, besides many waggons and stores. The Yankees say that there has been a fight in North-Western Arkansas, and do not claim a victory for themselves, but state that they will be reinforced by Herron's brigade of Iowa troops. Hindman and Marmaduke had some 25,000 men under them, so they say. In Virginia, along the Rappahannock, there has been considerable skirmishing, and also along the entire coast to Savannah, and in Western Virginia. The Southern papers claim that a battle is imminent somewhere towards Suffolk, or on the road to Weldon. Seward threatens a continental war against England and France if they dare to try to cause a cessation of our war. Of course he will bully and fool them, as they are not his match in duplicity and shamelessness. "The combat thickens, on ye brave!"

December 10th, 1862.

The papers contain extracts of a correspondence between Seward and Adams which will not redound to their credit as men of judgment, or of principles,—and also Federal accounts of a "non-decisive victory" in Arkansas between Hindman and the *Yankees.* Hindman's division threw themselves between Blount, and Herron, attacked first one and then the other, and then retreated without pursuit, losing no guns and prisoners. Yankee loss, 600; Confederate, 1,500.

December 12th, 1862.

Burnside has begun the passage of the Rappahannock at Fredericksburg, bombarding it with 176 cannon, and endeavouring to cross over. He has not succeeded in getting any considerable body of his army across, and doubtless our army will compel the destruction of the town in preference to surrendering it as winter quarters to the Yankees. There are indications of a great battle in Virginia this ensuing week. The army of Pemberton and Price has eluded Grant and Hovey, and doubtless marched to reinforce Johnston and Bragg, who are pressing Rosecranz in and around Nashville. The battle of Hartsville was a decided Confederate victory, some 2,300 Federal prisoners being taken by *Morgan*. Now if Pemberton and Price and Bragg and Smith unite with Johnston, one army of the Northern force is lost to a dead certainty, and then for a race for Louisville, Kentucky.

In the fight in Arkansas it seems that Blount and Herron disagree concerning the loss of their army. Blount says 800. The Confederates, after the junction of the two armies, retreated unmolested, and left their dead and mortally wounded behind. Galveston, Texas, seems to be a skirmishing ground for Magruder and the Yankees. The Alabama has been at her work again. The crews of two more merchant-men, having just arrived, give an account of having been captured, and their vessels burned, and they sent ashore. She was being reinforced in men and guns, and now mounts some eight large rifled guns, and has a crew of 150 men. She went to St. Martinique, and, while coaling and otherwise refitting sails, the San Jacinto came in, and then sailed out again, and watched for " *the Alabama;*" but Semmes was too smart for Wilkes, and was gone two days before the Yankee knew of it.

December 13th, 1862.

No news this morning from Fredericksburg, except that the Confederates do not seem to be making a very obstinate resistance to the passage of Burnside. Nothing new from Tennessee, or Mississippi except some skirmishes, not entirely successful to the Yankees, and a report of the defeat of

Hovey who made a flank movement on Grenada,—these are Federal reports. Also the comments of English papers on Lincoln's proclamation, and emancipation and insurrection policy. The Arkansas battle does not seem to gain credit in New York, and the *N. Y. Herald* says that it has to take with many grains of allowance, especially the superiority of Confederates which it does not believe at all, in fact assigns good reasons for the contrary. The *Chicago Times* also says that the navy of "Rip Van Winkle Wells" is mostly a delusion in regard to nautical strength and effectiveness.

> I have done
> As you have done, that's what I can; induced
> As you have been, that's for my country;
> He that has but effected his good will,
> Hath overta'en mine act.—*Coriolanus.*

> Thus I turn my back;
> There is a world elsewhere!—*Coriolanus.*

> Extremity was the trier of spirits,
> That common chances common could bear.
> That, when the sea was calm, all boats alike
> Shew'd mastership in floating.—*Ibid.*

> For I will fight
> Against my canker'd country with the spirit
> Of all the under fiends.—*Ibid.*

> O! a kiss
> Long as my exile, sweet as my revenge!
> Now, by the jealous queen of heaven, that kiss
> I carried from thee, dear, and my true lip
> Hath virgin'd it e'er since.—*Shakspeare.*

> Chaste as the icicle,
> That's curded by the frost from purest snow,
> And hangs on Dian's temple.—*Ibid.*

Dundas, December 15th, 1862.

On Saturday the 13th, a battle was fought at Fredericksburg, Virginia. After much severe skirmishing, General

Burnside crossed the greater part of his army over the Rappahannock, attacked the Confederate army behind their intrenched camps about two miles back from the river. Of course we can only give Yankee accounts. They say that Sumner and Hooker attacked the entrenchment three times, and three times were driven back with loss; that Franklin on the left gained some "*partial*" success over Jackson, and that their loss of life is very great, and not very heavy on the Confederate side. They report two generals killed and four wounded and many other officers. The Confederate cavalry has been successful in getting to Dumfries, Virginia, under *Hampton* (South Carolina), on the road between Fredericksburg and Washington, capturing stores, officers, &c., &c. The papers of Saturday contained headings, " *Lee outwitted*," &c. To-day they say Burnside cannot *renew* the fight. I (and they) suppose that *Lee will now attack*, and fears are entertained for the safety of Burnside's army, and reports are freely circulated in Washington of " great disasters "—which reports " are started and circulated by the secessionists of Maryland and Washington."

December 17th, 1862.

The papers are filled with accounts of the battle of Fredericksburg. With one accord they proclaim the defeat of the Yankees with immense loss. They say that Jackson commanded the Confed. right, Longstreet the centre and left. Franklin commanded the Federal left, and was thus opposed to Jackson; Sumner and Hooker to Longstreet. The fight commenced as soon as the fog raised in the morning, and continued through the day. Franklin moved against Jackson, and the battle raged fiercely, and Franklin could not go forward beyond the first few out-posts which were entrenched. His loss was 5,932, in killed, wounded, and missing. Sumner, on the Yankee right, advanced and tried the works, and in vain; rested and tried again, and in vain; rested, and reinforced, and tried again, and in vain. Hooker, in the centre, also attempted to storm the works, and was driven back in confusion for three consecutive times. It seems that Sumner suffered most. After making allowance for high figures their loss must be not less than 13,000, and may be 20,000. The Confederate loss is said to be less than the Yankees, so they admit. Burnside stayed to be attacked by infantry, but General Lee preferred to use his artillery night and day, and finally Burnside left Fredericksburg and effected a masterly and " outwitting " retreat across the Rappahannock unmolested by Lee, bringing back all of his wounded and taking up the bridges so that Lee " might not pursue him." *Sic transit gloria mundi!* Burnside's glory has subsided as suddenly as it sprang up. Siegel and the Harper's Ferry column has been sent to Burnside, so that the Yankees have now some 50,000 or 60,000 men more than Lee. Banks has gone to the South, most probably to try Mobile and then Texas. From Tennessee the news seems to indicate that Johnston and Bragg are fortifying below Murfreesboro', and are determined to fight if a good opportunity presents ; and Major-General John H. Morgan has gone northward with some 5,000 men. Maybe he and Forrest may unite and give Kentucky another benefit.

Altogether I think the prospect seems not so dark as it was last spring, for though the enemy had advanced down the Mississippi, we have triumphed in nearly every battle, and driven them back, sometimes " over the border and far away," and when we went into Maryland and Pennsylvania, we were not driven out ; and so in Kentucky, we fought three times, and every time victorious. When we had to retreat, we came back unmolested and laden with " booty " —some 4,000 waggons, &c.

Dundas, December 19th, 1862.

The details of the Fredericksburg battle begin to come in, and, judging by them, this has been the most decisive and

bloody combat of the war. From early noon to the going
down of the sun Burnside hurled his forces against that
" crest," and everywhere did they come back shattered and
defeated. The " Union" army is divided into three grand
divisions under Sumner, Hooker and Franklin ; and each
grand division into three corps, and each corps into three
divisions, and each division into three brigades,—thus making
the entire army to consist of *eighty-one brigades* of infantry,
and, together with their batteries of artillery, must reach
162,000 exclusive of cavalry : thus Burnside commanded
175,000 men. Now Heintzelman and Siegel have not less
than 75,000 men under them. Thus we see that Halleck,
with his 250,000 well and available men, has not got farther
than the Rappahannock. The loss at this battle from present
indications cannot fall short of the enormous sum of 30,000 ;
while that of the Southern army does not exceed 5000, and
most probably 4000. Seven Generals have fallen, two to
rise no more, besides Colonels, Majors, Captains, &c., &c.
The newspapers say that not one half of our " Confederate"
troops were engaged. The plunder was pretty great, according to accounts ; one detachment of 140 six-horse waggons,
laden with ammunition, having been taken at once,—the
cavalry having gotten into their rear, snapping up sutlers,
&c., &c. Never has history recorded a greater blunder,
than was committed by the Yankees on this occasion. A trap
was set for them, and, forewarned of it, they walked into it,
and lo ! " *On to Richmond*" ceases. The arrangement of
forces on the field was exceedingly defective, and their ignorance of the actual position of the Confed. forces is laughable.

Lee seems to have had his forces much nearer the river
than they anticipated, and thus the five or six columns of
Burnside were unable to deploy at any time, and their ranks
of " fours," in long lines, afforded splendid targets for the
musket and cannon balls, shell and grape and canister,—and
sixty pieces seem to have been used for that purpose. On

the Yankee left the men seem to have been deployed in line, and were met by a comparatively small force, and driven back.

Yanks say that they lost many prisoners and some guns, and took some three hundred prisoners.

Evans (Leesburg) telegraphed under date of 14th that Foster had attacked him at Kingston, N. C., on Neuse River, on the railroad from Newberne to Goldsboro'—on the main road from Weldon to Wilmington: and that after three hours of fighting, he drove Foster to his gunboats. And the tenor of the dispatch was that he expected another fight with him. Banks has not yet been heard from. No arrivals from Europe this week. In the *Chicago Times* there are accounts of a fight in Mississipi near Coffeeville, wherein Yankee came out second best. Also some accounts of the Hartsville battle, which make it appear that there was a considerable fight there before the Yankees gave up.

December 20th, 1862.

The Richmond papers state that the Confederate loss in the battle of Fredericksburg was some 2500 in killed and wounded. Kingston, N. C., has been taken by Yankees. A fight is reported to be progressing in Mississippi between Forrest and Yankee cavalry near Corinth, and it is reported that Pemberton and Bragg are trying to effect a junction, and march against Grant.

December 23rd, 1862.

The accounts in the Northern papers still sing of Fredericksburg and its blunders; of the awful slaughter of Yankees. They also contain Genl. Lee's official report of the battle, in which he says his loss was about 1,800 killed and wounded, including Genls. Cobb and Gregg. There is also a report of Burnside claiming to have lost only 12,000 men. There has been a fight at or near Goldsboro', N. C. The Confederate cavalry have been clearing up things generally in Western Tennessee, capturing towns, regiments, &c.

Also reported that Seward has resigned as Secretary of State, and Chase of Treasury; and the hubbub seems to be going on in New York, all tending to peace.

December 24th, 1862.

Regarding all news as favourable or not as it affects the cause of peace in the United States, and the recognition of the Southern Confederacy, I look as much to the domestic history of the North as to the army movements; as a change must spring from the people themselves, and will not come from the army. Now all the parties concur that war is becoming very unpopular all through that section, first under one name and cry, and then on some different pretext. The slaughter at Fredericksburg has startled many out of their propriety, and they are now clamouring for something; some for cessation of hostilities, some for peace, all for change. In the meantime poor Burnside stultifies himself by making contradictory statements about his loss; now 13,000, now 10,000, and now 8,000; while the journalists say it is 18, 20, and 55,000 men. Thus it goes. Now the army is retreating to Washington, and therefore we may conclude that the winter-campaign in Virginia is over, as far as the Yankees are concerned, and Lee may turn his attention to other parts of the Confederacy.

From Goldsboro', N. C., we hear of armies and of movements against the railroad wherein Foster has succeeded in throwing his force against it, south of the town, and injuring it somewhat. A large Confederate force under General Gustavus W. Smith has concentrated there, and a considerable fight is imminent in that neighbourhood. I hope we may be successful there, for it would help us much to whip Foster and his myrmidons. In Kentucky the Confederates are turning up in and about the centre of the State under Morgan; and in the eastern part under Marshall; while in Western Tennessee the Confederate cavalry are doing well, routing

Yankees, capturing stations, and artillery, destroying communications, resources, &c., &c. The movements of the Western army of the Confederates seem to be a mystery to Yankeedom. They have twice the force, and seem to be trying to steal all that the people have; to insult them as much as possible, and render themselves as odious to the South as possible, and contemptible to the outside world, by cruelty, bombast and failures.

There seems to be some force at and about Harper's Ferry and Martinsburg, and through that country, so that it will he difficult to get through the lines there; but go through I must and will, somewhere or fail; *try* I must and will. Another year or season of this suspense would be intolerable, and I will at least try to end it, some way or other.

Mr. Ballard's boarding-house, Dundas, December 25th, 1862.

Christmas of 1860, I spent in Chicago; Christmas, 1861, at the railroad station, Monticello, Florida; this one in Canada,—one among strangers; the second in a friendly country, but also among strangers; this as an exile in a foreign land, though among kind persons from whom I have received kindness.

To-day's papers contain some interesting accounts of the Fredericksburg battle from the Richmond papers. The Southern papers did not realize the state of the enemy's army after that battle, thinking only some 8,000 had been hurt, whereas nearly or quite three times as many had fallen; and thus Lee has lost a fine opportunity of injuring the Yankee force, but he on the ground knows more than we can here. Stafford heights, which command the south bank of the Rappahannock on the Fredericksburg side, were crowded with heavy artillery, and Lee doubtless wished to have his victory unsullied by much slaughter. From Kentucky we receive accounts of the advance of Marshall into the State by Pound Gap—and the telegrams intimate that the Federals

intend to clean the "rebels" out of the State now and
forever. How easy to promise! Yet they are largely superior to us in numbers, and with any good General they would
succeed effectually in repelling Marshall. In Western Tennessee the Confederate cavalry have been doing good work,
having captured many posts, property, hundreds of prisoners,
&c., &c., and being well up to Kentucky, in fact, not over
fifty miles from Cairo. Van Dorn has taken Holly Springs,
capturing all of the Yankees therein, and many thousand
dollars of property, and then advancing to Grand Junction,
capturing it; and some have gone near to Memphis, capturing
miles of cattle, stores, &c., &c.: thus it goes there. In Arkansas, it is reported that Jefferson Thompson has started on
New-Madrid, hoping to capture it, and thus to blockade the
Mississippi. Things seem quiet in Missouri, but the Spring
will open up the guerrillas again.

Dundas, December 30th, 1862.

This morning's papers bring us important news from the
army, both East and West. In Virginia, Stuart has been
around Burnside, capturing 1,600 men and four cannon in
one place, and breaking up two detachments of Pennsylvania
cavalry, capturing those not killed, occupying Occoquan,
Dumfries, &c.—waggons, &c. "Prompt and forcible"
measures have been taken to capture or dispossess him!!—
In West Tennessee the Confederates, under Brig.-General
Forrest have been emulating Stuart, having taken many
hundred prisoners, much stores, &c., and got to threatening
distance of Columbus, causing the evacuation of New-Madrid,
Hickman, &c., by Yankees—effectually cutting off communications to Grant's army. But to make assurance doubly
sure, *Van Dorn* made a flank movement, and, marching
around Grant, captured Holley Springs, with some 1,500 men
and an immense quantity of stores; tore up the railroad, &c.,
whereon Grant has been necessitated to retreat, thus putting

off the evil day of Vicksburg. Some few of the cavalry got into Memphis a day or so ago, but only in small numbers. Morgan, not to be outdone, started north, and, taking Glasgow, advanced to Elizabethtown, and finally to " Muldraugh's Hill," near Louisville, capturing 150 men at one place, 600 at another, and burning bridges, trestle work, and on Louisville and Nashville railroad, effectually destroying the communication to Nashville for some time, even if no more obstruction were placed thereon. So that, taking all things into consideration, I do not see any cause for despondency on our part, as far as arms go. Concerning foreign intervention, that will not come until we do not need it, when it will come in a hurry. In South-Eastern Virginia there has been some unimportant skirmishing and so in Eastern Kentucky.

Yankees are reported to be on half rations at Corinth and thereabout, and a battle is reported at or near Murfreesboro', between Bragg and Rosecranz.

January 1st, 1863.

To-day I enter on my twenty-eighth year. Like many others, to day, I form new resolutions in regard to the future, and bewail the past. The last twelve months have indeed been productive of but little profitable, either now or hereafter, in my life. I may not rely on my own strength, for it is not enough to carry through the temptations which beset me, and to which I am too prone to yield. I do pray God to help me and protect me—and, especially in these times when wickedness flourishes, to " help mine unbelief."

January 5th, 1862.

Designing to start to Kentucky, hoping to get through to the South by that route, I will leave a few directions in this book which I expect to leave with Mr. S. O., together with some other things such as......watch, &c.

If I get to Kentucky I expect to get to Lexington to Mr. B., or to a Mr. C., between Winchester and Paris. Should I get to Louisville, I will go to K. C. In Cincinnati I will call on Dr. B. Thus if my friends do not hear of me before they get this book, they can doubtless find out something about me from those gentlemen.

The news from the seat of war to-day is an account of slaughter and of battle. But it seems to be confined to the west and south-west. Sherman landed on the south side of the *Yazoo* River, and marched on Vicksburg,—and heavy skirmishing is taking place. They report a battle and that one gunboat has been repulsed up the Yazoo; Grant has been compelled to retreat to Holley Springs, thus relieving Pemberton of them, and enabling him to precipitate quite a large force on Sherman, before Grant or Banks can come to his assistance. I sincerely wish that they may do so, and thus give a quietus to Yankees on the Mississippi.

From Tennessee we hear from Bragg, who reports that Forrest took 1,200 prisoners, and there are confused accounts of the Murfreesboro' battles, for the contest has lasted four days. The Yankees reported that they have eight Generals killed and wounded, and prisoners, and Colonels without number. " The slaughter of officers " is described as " heartrending"; also that Wheeler has got to the rear of Rosecranz, capturing 400 waggons, 700 prisoners, and an ordnance train—cutting off communication with Nashville. And most confused accounts come in concerning the struggle : now Mr. Cook is driven four miles, and now Thomas has got into Murfreesboro', and now he has not ; now that his troops have crossed the river (Stone's), and now that they have not ; and finally there comes the *news* from New York that there is nothing to be had from Nashville any more. And thus it is. In the meantime the report is that *Old Abe* thinks of entering the field in person.

The news from Europe shows that the French Emperor is very anxious to intervene, and still proposes, or purposes to propose, mediation : while from New York, New Jersey, and Ohio, there comes a cry for peace, and some mutterings also for another 300,000 men. And *Seymour* begins to show his hands against the Federal Government in defence of state rights, which will be apt to conduce much towards a revolution in Northern sentiments and feelings, and actions.

August 24th, 1864. Dundas, Canada West.

After an absence of nineteen months, I resume writing in my book, and will, before I go on with my Journal, bring up an account of my time and a sketch of events.

Leaving Dundas, I walked to Hamilton, and took the cars for Detroit and thence to Cincinnati, where I arrived all right and sound. I went to see. Dr. T. and Dr. D., from both of whom I received much kindness. John Morgan had played such havoc in Kentucky with the railroad and communications, that it was deemed impossible for me to go South by that route. I then thought of Western Virginia, but the steamboats were seized to carry subsistence to Rosecranz' army, and I took the cars to Baltimore. After a false start, I got on a *pungy* owned and run by blockaders ; and, about the last of February, landed in Virginia. My comrade, Mr. Schluder of St. Louis, Mo., had escaped from the Yankees ; was from Price's army. We got to Richmond ; find Dan Lucas and all the boys at Fredericksburg right. I went to camp, and met Wm. Dick, Chip., Ben., &c., and I felt quite at home. I also got a letter from Martha, mother, Anne, and sister Mary.

I went before the examining board, and was discharged from the army. The paper being signed by Dr. Straith & ———— also Chipley, Nadenbousch, Funk, Trimble, Jackson, and Lee.

I then entered Con. Navy as acting master, and operated on the coast with varied success, and finally captured November 16th. We were taken to Fort McHenry and treated as pirates, but a little taste of retaliation soon released us, and finally, I was sent to City Point, March 20th, and exchanged May 5th. —— I went on furlough to Columbus, Georgia, and spent there at Col. Chambers' the happiest two weeks of my life.

On my return to Richmond I became assistant Engineer for David Henderson, Topographical Engineers, and our Company participated in the Mechanicsville Road skirmish with Sheridan, May 12th,—and David, leaving me in charge of camp went to Drewry's Bluff, and participated in the action of the 16th May.

June 11th, we rode along the line of our army from the Chickahominy to Foster's. After the flanking of Grant to Petersburg, I came down to Matthews County, and thence crossing came on here through Baltimore and Eastern shore, and New York.

I will now try to give a truthful and short account of affairs in the South up to this time.

First in Virginia—The tide waters of Eastern Virginia are entirely in the Federal power, if not actual possession; this enabling them at any time to bring an army to the White House,—Fredericksburg, City Point, or Bermuda Hundreds. Western Virginia is far more easily provisioned from Ohio than from Richmond, the B. and O. R. road furnishes a fine base of supplies along the Northern part of the State. After the battle of Fredericksburg, General Lee's army consisted of two corps of infantry and artillery under Lieut. Generals Longstreet and Jackson, made up of eight divisions. Anderson's, Hood's, McLaws', Pickett's (1st, Corps) Trimble, Early, A. P. Hill, Rodes (2nd Corps,) the artillery under Pendleton and the cavalry under Stuart. In Western Va. was Sam. Jones, and in the Valley, W. E. Jones. In April, General Lee sent General Longstreet to threaten Norfolk and capture Suffolk, whereupon General Hooker crossed the Rappahannock, and a terrible battle was fought at Chancellorsville and Fredericksburg in which General Hooker was defeated : but General Longstreet was foiled after partial success. Hooker sent Stoneman with his cavalry to get to Lee's rear, and make a raid against Richmond ; this raid did cut railroads, but effected little else.

After the retreat of Hooker, an advance was determined on, and General Jackson having been killed, and reinforcements having come up, the army was remodelled. The first Corps, Lieutenant General Longstreet, consisted of the divisions of Hood, McLaws and Pickett ; second Corps, Lieutenant General Ewell, those of Johnson (formerly Trimble's) Rodes and Early ; third Corps, Lieutenant General A. P. Hill— Heth's (formerly A. P. Hill's), Anderson's and Pender's. The cavalry was increased and made more effective. In June, Ewell crossed the Blue Ridge, and, appearing suddenly before Winchester, first forced Milroy into the works and captured the place and most of the army ; the outlaw, Milroy, escaping. The third Corps re-enforcing, Ewell crossed into Pennsylvania, and gradually, the whole infantry, preceded by W. E., and S. Jones's cavalry, were across the Potomac. Stuart constituted the rear guard, and crossed the river east of the Blue Ridge. The army met with little opposition till July 1st, when the Federal army, under Meade, met it at Gettysburg, and the famous battle began. The Yankee advance was driven back, and both armies getting into position, General Lee attacked and failed to carry the Yankee centre. He then awaited an attack : then retreated to Md., and then, after a delay of several days, into Virginia. This was the first battle where the Eastern Confederate army had failed to carry the enemy's position. The enemy made a demonstration against Richmond at this time. General Lee fell back to Culpepper and the campaign of Penna was ended. Affairs had come to a head in Tennessee, and General Longstreet, with two divisions, McLaws' and Hood's, was sent there. After some delay General Lee moved against Meade, and forced him back to

Manassas, and then quietly resumed his quarters at Orange
Court House, the army holding the lines of the Rapidan.
The Yankees having refitted, started again " On to Richmond." Meade crossed the river, and, after a severe action
at Locust Grove, or Mine Run, fell back, and every thing
resumed its quiet in the army of Northern Virginia. Thus
closed the year of 1863 with the Virginia army.

The war in Tennessee.—The army of Tennessee under
General Bragg consisted of two corps under Lieutenant
Generals Polk and Hardee, with cavalry under Wheeler, Van
Dorn, Forrest, and Morgan. After the drawn battle of Murfreesboro', Bragg withdrew in a south-easterly direction, along
the railroad to Chattanooga. Rosecranz remained quietly at
Murfreesboro' until after the campaign opened in Mississippi,
when he slowly advanced toward the Tennessee river. After
heavy skirmishing, the Federal army occupied Chattanooga,
while Burnside advanced on Cumberland Gap, which igno-
miniously surrendered to him, occasioning the evacuation of
East Tennessee. Bragg, being reinforced by Buckner of
East Tennessee and Longstreet of Virginia, assaulted Rosecranz at Chikamauga in North Georgia, and defeated him
with great loss. After much delay, Longstreet was sent into
East Tennessee ; after gaining many successes, he was defeated at Knoxville, after Grant had whipped Bragg at Lookout Mountain. Cleburn, however, drove back the pursuing
army at Ringgold, and Longstreet, turning at Bean's Station,
drove back his pursuers. And this closed the war in Tennessee. Bragg was relieved, and Johnston took his place.

Morgan made a raid in the summer, and his whole force
was captured in Ohio.

The war in Mississippi.—The department of Mississippi
was placed under Lieutenant General John C. Pemberton,
who occupied the strong places of Vicksburg in Mississippi,
and Port Hudson in East Louisiana. His command was Van
Dorn's old Corinth army, and numbered some thirty-five or

forty thousand effective men. After Sherman's repulse in January, the Federal commander, Grant, accumulated a vast army at Memphis, and a powerful fleet at Cairo, Cincinnati, St. Louis, &c. After many fruitless efforts and much loss, he succeeded in running some gunboats by the batteries ; the first were captured, but finally the means of carrying his army from the western side to the eastern, were obtained, and his powerful army was landed at Port Gibson, driving back our small and badly located force. Pemberton sent detachments of his army to fight Grant's entire concentrated army, and was defeated and finally shut up in Vicksburg, which was surrendered July 4th. Johnston made fruitless efforts to relieve Pemberton, but that incapable officer did not, co-operate. Johnston fell back, and, after a severe engagement, evacuated Jackson, which was again occupied by Grant, who returned to Vicksburg, was called to Washington, and then sent to Chattanooga after the battle of Chikamauga. Port Hudson was strongly fortified by General Gardner, and resisted every water attack, but simultaneously with the investment of Vicksburg, Banks crossed from West Louisiana, and, surrounding, assaulted the works. After many repulses, and the surrender of Vicksburg, Port Hudson also surrendered July 9th. The campaign in Mississippi for 1863 ended with the Yankees in possession of the river and adjoining country.

The war in the *Trans-Mississippi Department.*—This department was in charge of Lieutenant General Holmes, who was totally unfitted for it, and only helped it on to anarchy. Price had, under him, charge of the Missouri interest, Hindman of Arkansas, Taylor of Western Louisiana, and Magruder of Texas. Early in the spring Lieutenant General C. Kirby Smith was sent over, but not in time to avert Holmes' and Hindman's difficulties. Gradually Arkansas was over-run, and into the very vitals of Western Louisiana crept the Federal armies and fleets ; not, however, without vigorous protests from Taylor, who, suddenly attacking Brashear city, captured it and its immense stores; then moving rapidly, ambuscaded the advance of Banks and repulsed it, yet he could not prevent his march when Banks crossed the Mississippi and invested Port Hudson and captured it July 9th. The campaign of 1864 opened in Eastern Florida by the Yankees under General Seymour advancing from Fernandina, along the Railroad towards Tallahassee. They were met at Olustee Station, and totally routed. In Mississippi General Sherman, at the head of a large infantry force, left Vicksburg, and marched towards Selma, Alabama, while a large cavalry force left Memphis to co-operate with him. General Polk retreated before Sherman, but so disposed his cavalry under General Stephen D. Lee as to annoy and delay the enemy's march, while General Forrest threw his cavalry against Smith's Memphis force, and utterly defeated it. This decided the campaign in Mississippi, and necessitated the retreat of Sherman. The forces of both armies were moved. Lee and Forrest remained in the Mississippi. Polk with his army went to Johnston. Sherman was appointed commander of the armies of the west, and took command against Johnston. Forrest assumed the offensive, and invaded West Tennessee, capturing Union City, and pushed up to Paducah, capturing it. He then turned suddenly, attacked and carried by assault Fort Pillow, and fell back to North Mississippi, where he turned on his accumulating enemies and utterly routed them at Tishomingo creek. Reinforcements were then sent from Memphis against him, when he and Lee, effecting a junction, repulsed the enemy, and Forrest suddenly marched on Memphis, and surprised it, and, capturing many of its defenders and stores, retreated. In Mississippi the enemy have made no progress, while Forrest has ridden triumphantly to the Ohio, captured and killed many more men than his command numbered, and recruited his force.

In the trans-Mississippi Department Banks and Porter, with an immense army and navy, advanced on Shreveport, Louisiana. They captured Alexandria, but were utterly routed at Mansfield, and forced back to New Orleans, having lost 10,000 men and many vessels. While Banks was coming up, Steele came down from Arkansas to co-operate. Price, reinforced by the victory of Mansfield, attacked and put him to flight, capturing his quarter-master and commissary stores, pursuing him North of Arkansas River. Cavalry and flying artillery inmediately began to operate on the Mississippi, effectually stopping commerce. Many gallant deeds adorn this campaign. The Confederates were triumphant.

The campaign in Virginia.—General Lee's army consisted of Ewell's and Hill's corps at Orange Court House, Longstreet at Bristol, and troops in Eastern Virginia and North Carolina. Grant has been created Lieutenant General, and took command against him.

General Lee initiated the campaign by throwing his cavalry against the forces in the Shenandoah Valley and collecting much forage, while General Pickett moved against Newberne, N. C. He swept around it, capturing many stores and prisoners, while Commander John Taylor Wood, of the Navy, entered the port of Newberne, and captured the steamer "Underwriter,"—but, the tide being out, was compelled to destroy her. Pickett then fell back, and investing, captured Suffolk and threatened Portsmouth. The enemy being distracted by these movements, suddenly Genl. Hoke, commanding several brigades, and assisted by the gunboat "Albemarle" attacked and carried Plymouth, N. C., with 2500 men and immense stores. Gen. Lee thus cleared his line of communication, and waited the advance of Grant, who, at the head of an immense army, crossed the Rapidan. The battle of the *Wilderness,* May 5th and 6th, was a great Confederate victory, but Grant, changing his course, marched towards tidewater, compelling Genl. Lee to come nearer Richmond, May 8th, 10th, 12th. The enemy tried to break his line, and failed.

Grant then flanked again towards tidewater, and Lee moved correspondingly. June 3rd, Grant tried the lines again at Cold Harbour, and again in vain. When Grant crossed the Rapidan, he sent Butler up the James, towards Petersburg, also three converging forces from Western Va., on Lynchburg. Beauregard was in command at Petersburg, and, May 16th, defeated Butler at Drewry's Bluff. In the Valley, Siegel was driven back by Breckenridge ; and the enemy, after gaining partial success in Western Va., were foiled.

Grant suddenly threw his army to Butler, and attacked Petersburg. He was again defeated, and again he tried and was again driven. Genl. Lee made two attacks on him, and drove him to his works. Grant's cavalry raids came to grief. But concentrating his forces in the Valley, Hunter defeated the Confederates, and marched on Lynchburg, when he was driven out of Western Va., and Early advanced suddenly and entered Maryland, threatened Washington, routing the enemy at Monocacy. Early's cavalry raided through Maryland and Pennsylvania, and defeated all attempts to drive them from the lower Valley, till the middle of September, when he was driven back by a sudden accumulation of troops against him.

In Georgia.—In early spring, Genl. Thomas advanced against Dalton, and was repulsed. He fell back, and Sherman's reinforcing and accumulating troops assaulted and flanked Johnston, who gradually fell back, always fighting, to Atlanta, when Hood superseded him and made a most gallant defence of that place, till finally Sherman flanked him out of the city. Sherman lost heavily in his cavalry, but still is triumphant.

RAID ON LAKE ERIE.

Immediately on my arrival in Canada I went to Col. Thompson at Toronto, and made application to start a privateer on Lake Huron. He informed me of a plan to take the Michigan (14 guns), and release the Confederate officers confined at Johnson's Island. I immediately volunteered, and went to Sandusky, Ohio, to meet Capt. Cole, the leader. We arranged our plans, and separated. Cole staid at Sandusky. I came to Windsor to collect men, and carry them to the given point. On Monday morning we started, some from Detroit, some from Sandwich, some from Amherstburgh. When off Kelly's Island, I seized the " *Philo Parsons*," and mustering my men, found only some twenty there.

We went back to Middle Bass Island to procure wood and wait for the time when the steamer " *Island Queen*" came up, and we took her. I then started back to attack the Michigan, when seventeen of my twenty men mutinied, and refused to go forward, and this necessitated my turning back, thus abandoning Cole to be hung, a most cowardly and dishonourable affair.

Communication to a Canadian Journal.

MR. EDITOR,—You condemn the conduct of those who captured the two steamers on Lake Erie as infringing the laws of Canada. Cognisant of the facts, I wish to present them to you, hoping to win you to reserve your decision.

The United States is carrying on war on Lake Erie against the Confederate States (either by virtue of right or sufferance from you), by transportation of men and supplies on its waters ; by confining Confederate prisoners on its islands, and lastly, by the presence of a 14-gun steamer patrolling its waters. The Confederates clearly have the right to retaliate, provided they can do so without infringing your laws. They did *not* infringe those laws ; for, first, the plan for this attack was matured, and sought to be carried out in the United States, and not in Canada; there was not a Canadian, or any man enlisted in Canada. 2ndly, No act of hostility was committed on Canadian waters or soil. Any man may lawfully come into, or leave Canada as he may please, and no foreign government can complain of the exercise of this right here. These men embarked on an American vessel from Detroit, or sprang on to it while in motion, from Canadian wharfs. The boat did not properly *stop* at Sandwich, or Amherstburg at all, as the Customs will show. It touched at two American ports, and was not captured until within range of the 30-pounder Parrot guns of the 14-gun steamer. What act of hostility had been committed up to this time? Another boat containing thirty or forty United States soldiers was captured in an American port. After wooding up, the "*Philo Parsons*" proceeded to the mouth of Sandusky Bay for the purpose of attacking the "*Michigan*," when six-sevenths of the crew refused to do duty, and thus necessitated the abandonment of the enterprise.

3rdly. What is this *Michigan* that she can not be attacked? Is the fact that she carries thirteen more guns than the treaty stipulation between the United States and England allows, a sufficient reason why she is not to be subject to attack? England allows this boat to remain guarding Confederate prisoners, though she carries an armament in violation of the treaty.

Before these men are condemned, judge if they have broken your laws. No "murder" was committed, indeed not a life was lost. There was no searching of prisoners, no "robbing." It is true the boats were abused; but, Sir, they were captured by Confederates, enemies of the United States, and however questionable the taste, the right is clear. These men were not "burglars," or "pirates," enemies of mankind, unless hatred and hostility to the Yankees be taken as a sin against humanity, or a crime against civilization.